I0674327

TRACEFINDER: CONTACT

Tracefinder Book 1

KAJE HARPER

Dedication

For PJ who, with friendship and enthusiasm in all his incarnations, encourages me to try new things and not give up on old ones. I'm so glad you wrote that first email… Good luck with your newest goal!

Acknowledgements

I want to thank the friends who beta read this story— Tully, Kate, Lila, Kira, Jess, Gillian— and everyone who came up with titles or made helpful suggestions. You guys rock, from your comments and ideas to the sprints and encouragement. This wouldn't be half the book it is without you. A huge thanks to Ren for the proofreading and cover, and to Deb for formatting for me, *again*. after the heck I put you through with *Second Act*. My books also couldn't happen without the support of my ever-patient family, who give me time to write, and all of the community of M/M readers and authors, whose shared love of the genre keeps me publishing.

Contents

Chapter 1 1
Chapter 2 9
Chapter 3 23
Chapter 4 35
Chapter 5 47
Chapter 6 59
Chapter 7 79
Chapter 8 93
Chapter 9 109
Chapter 10 117
Chapter 11 131
Chapter 12 143
Chapter 13 155
Chapter 14 169
Chapter 15 185
Chapter 16 199
Chapter 17 217
Chapter 18 231
Chapter 19 247
Chapter 20 259
Chapter 21 279
Chapter 22 297
Chapter 23 309

Chapter 24 323
Chapter 25 341
Chapter 26 355
Chapter 27 369
About the Author 387
Other Books by Kaje Harper 388

Chapter 1

Nick ducked a chair that slammed past his head, and grinned even though it made his split lip bleed. A dozen men around him thrashed and grunted and wrestled each other to the floor of the bar, drowning out the TV with curses and the thudding of fists and feet. It was the best kind of chaos.

A big, bearded guy with whiskey breath crashed into him, snarled, and grabbed at his arm. Nick dodged and got in a low, fast punch. His hand sunk into his opponent's gut with a satisfying jolt. The man dropped to one knee, wheezing, and Nick leaped away from him, ready for the next source of trouble. There was one particular guy he wanted to get, but he wasn't fussy about who he took down along the way.

He laughed, feeling the adrenaline surge through him. Colors were brighter, sounds sharper, the rasp of his breath and the pounding of his heart and the pain in his lip melded in an excellent high. *This is so fucking good!*

The bar crowd heaved and shouted, a mass of struggling men— drunk, angry, punching, clawing. It was nothing like a choreographed movie fight. No fancy punches or across-the-room throws. The bottles that connected thunked solidly instead of smashing. This wasn't good guys against bad guys. This was bored, boozed-up, short-fused men set off by one stupid comment, some better men than others perhaps, but no saints. No white hats— not even Nick Rugo, for all that he was a cop. In another life.

Here, he was No-Knife Nick, known for starting fights as well as ending them. Also known for the time he took out a guy wielding a machete with one lucky punch. In this boonies dive bar, it was his claim to fame. Fists of steel, no knife needed.

1

A pair of men staggered toward him, pushing and shoving, their hands clenched in each other's shirts, heavy boots kicking and stomping. He dodged them and slid farther down the bar, trying to find his target. *There.*

He vaulted over the bar, ducked the bartender's reflex elbow jab, reached over, and dragged his quarry by the neck and arm across the bar and down to the floor behind it. The other man was big, and some of that was muscle, but he was also very drunk and caught by surprise. They fell together, and Nick got in two quick, short gut punches that drove the man's breath from his body. Nick pinned the guy's wheezing torso with his own weight, and growled in his ear, "When a woman says no, she fuckin' means *no.*" He leaned back enough to clock the guy hard across the jaw, half-hoping he'd break it. Do him good to have his filthy mouth wired shut for a month.

A flicker of movement from behind warned Nick in time to roll away, and the bartender's baseball bat hit his opponent's shoulder instead of Nick's head. He scrambled farther backward, empty hands held out, and found space at the end of the bar to clamber back to the customer side. The fight was still surging, spilling out into the street, and a far-off siren suggested someone had called the cops. It was time to be gone.

He edged to the wall, heading for the hallway into the back. A large male bulk blocked him, and he tensed to fight his way past, then relaxed as he recognized the man. Every bar had its top dog, and here, it was undisputedly Damon Kerr, but this was just Damon's younger brother. He was no threat— a big guy but quiet, slow, and stupid, and never one for any kind of fight. He usually stayed in the shadows and kept his mouth shut. It was pretty typical to find him with his back to the wall, simply watching.

As Nick ducked past, close enough that their shoulders and arms brushed, he said on impulse, "Come on, let's get outta here. Back door. I don't wanna get hauled in by the cops tonight. I bet you don't either."

He caught one glimpse of startled light-blue eyes, as big-little brother stared at him. Then the sound of fast-approaching sirens drove Nick on his way. Damon's brother could follow or not. Nick could *not* afford to get picked up, even if he was well outside his own precinct.

He dodged around three women who were yelling threats and encouragement at the men, hurried down the hall past the reeking bathrooms, and slammed the emergency bar to open the back door. The fire alarm went off, of course, but he could already hear at least three patrol cars coming, so who cared? He swung out into the alley and sprinted for the corner, hearing other footsteps behind him doing the same. As the first lit-up black-and-white

2

squealed into view around a corner, three blocks away, he made it to the sidewalk and slowed to a steady, innocent-looking walk.

He raised one hand to rub his nose, hiding his bleeding lip. The odds were the cops wouldn't give him more than a glance, as long as he moved casually and didn't draw their attention. He watched with deliberately open curiosity as they sped by, ignoring him.

The black-and-whites were safely past, pulling over in front of the bar, when someone behind him said, "You fight good."

He whirled, putting his back to the brick wall of the pawnshop beside him. Five feet away, Damon's brother stood eyeing him. The shop's awning cast a deep shadow, and Nick couldn't make out the guy's expression, but his body language was casual, not aggressive. "You're No-Knife Nick, right? Nok Nick? I'm Brian."

"I'm just Nick." He hated the short version of his nickname even worse than the long one.

"Oh." Brian nodded three or four times.

Nick wondered how simple the guy was. He'd never spoken to Brian before; in fact he didn't think he'd heard him say more than a yes or no to anyone, ever. Damon dragged the kid around like a big puppy, and the guys in Damon's circle treated him like some kind of mascot, although he was apparently old enough to be served beer with the rest of them. He didn't have the tilted features and short fingers of a Down syndrome kid, but his face was smooth and round, with those light eyes, a wide, full mouth, and fine-textured, flyaway white-blond hair. When Brian took a step out of the shadows, staring intently into Nick's eyes, the nearest streetlight backlit that hair in a pale halo.

"Are you able to get home all right by yourself?" Nick began edging down the sidewalk. He wanted to be gone— the pleasure of a good fight was outweighed by the risks now— but he didn't want to abandon some special-needs guy on a dark street in the bad part of town, no matter who his brother was. "Do you need help?"

"Good question." Brian took a step closer, then stopped and said more loudly and flatly. "No. I'm good. I know."

"Sure you do, Bry." The man who hurried up to them was one of Damon's friends, a heavyset guy called Booker. He was in his thirties with a full beard and dreadlocks, and wouldn't have looked out of place in a biker bar. Nick stood his ground, and kept his body language neutral.

Booker said to Brian, "C'mon. Let's get you the fuck out of here. And you, No-Knife, mind your own fucking business, you hear me?" He glared at Nick, grabbing Brian's arm in a meaty fist.

Nick shrugged, deliberately casual. "Back off, Booker. I'm gone."

He turned away, as if it didn't bother him at all to have Booker at his unprotected back, and walked steadily down the sidewalk. Two sets of footsteps followed him, but he didn't look back, and at the corner they hung a left while he went right. He waited until he couldn't hear them clearly anymore to pause and drop to one knee to adjust his shoe, glancing to his left as he did so. Booker had stopped at an SUV parked by the curb a block away. In the dome light, Nick could make out Brian's light hair as he got in on the passenger side. Then the doors shut, the light went out and headlights came on, and the SUV pulled away down the road.

Nick stood and resumed his casual pace for another five blocks to where his car was parked. A quick look around told him that no one seemed to be paying him or his car any attention. He clicked the door open and slid in, the dome light deliberately turned off. He pulled out from the curb and drove a hundred feet before switching on his headlights. Excess caution, maybe, but his plates were registered in his own name, and he was a careful man. Sometimes.

He ran his tongue across his teeth, tasting the blood from his lip. That seemed to be his only real damage. His knuckles ached a bit. Knowing where and how to hit people usually saved his hands. He'd have to explain away the lip tomorrow, but the guys on his shift already thought he was a bit accident-prone. He'd manage.

A few blocks farther down, he took time to pull over and dab at his face with a tissue. There was barely a smear of red on it. Good enough.

As he drove on, the adrenaline high of the fight faded to a comfortable buzz. He flexed his fingers on the wheel, oddly comforted by the soreness. The violent need inside him that had risen up, itching for blood and blows, was quiet again, settled for a while. And hopefully that bastard in the bar, with the grabby hands and entitled sneer, would think twice before mauling a waitress's tits again. *No means no, fat boy.* Between his punch to the guy's jaw, and whatever damage the bartender's baseball bat to the shoulder had done, it should be a pretty clear lesson.

He headed back down into the Cities. The closer he got, the busier the traffic. He eased his foot off the gas, dropping to a careful four miles over the limit. His brother cops would be out looking for speeders and drunks, making those dangerous traffic stops that could be anything from a priest with a lead foot to a felon with a gun. That would be him on the job tomorrow, and he wished them well, as long as they let him cruise on by right now.

When he finally turned in to his trailer park, he slowed way down, keeping an eye out for stray dogs, children, and drunks. Even this late, any of those were possible. In fact, as he pulled into the parking space beside his trailer he spotted two kids sitting on the step of the double-wide across the way. He could hear the parents inside fighting, drunken voices swearing at each other. He sighed, got out, and crossed toward them. "Hey, Tyrone, your folks fighting again?"

The older kid, a boy of ten, rolled his eyes. "Nah. I came out to see the moon eclipse, you feel me?"

"Smartass." Nick didn't put any force behind that, and the little girl managed a wavery grin as she looked up at him. He said, "You want me to bang on the door?"

Tyrone looked away. "Got no school tomorrow. I can stay up if I want to."

"Well, I have to work." Nick stepped up between them and pounded on the Carters' door.

The argument stopped and the door jerked open. "What?"

Nick said easily, "If you don't tone it down, old lady Cornish is gonna call the cops on you again. And I don't want the sirens waking me up, yanno?"

"That bitch," the kids' father said, swaying on his feet.

"Yeah, yeah, well, if she doesn't, Dreyfus will, or maybe I will myself. It's after midnight. Give it a rest, huh?" He gestured down. "Your kids and I need our sleep."

Bill Carter ran a hand over his face, and then looked at his two kids huddled on the step. "Damn. Okay. Yeah, we're done." He lowered his voice. "Ty, Keesha, come on in."

For a second the children stared at him. Then they stood up and filed past into the trailer. Their father slammed the door in Nick's face. Nick waited on the step, listening just in case, relieved when there were no more shouts or curses. The mother's voice rose plaintively for a moment, then quieted. After a couple more minutes, Nick headed back to his own place.

His good mood had turned bitter by the time he opened the door and let himself in. He remembered him and Ari once, at one of the foster homes, doing that same thing— sitting on the steps waiting for the couple to stop yelling, till it felt safe to creep back to bed. He was torn about Tyrone and

Keesha, wondering if he maybe should step in officially. But as far as he could tell, no matter how drunk the parents were, they didn't lay hands on the kids. And when they were sober, they were a decent family. There was love there alongside the fights. Nick knew firsthand how many worse homes could be found in the foster system. Best to let it go.

He kicked off his boots and tossed his nearly empty wallet into the dish, beside all the ID he'd pulled out of it before heading to the bar. The floor was cool under his feet and he suddenly missed his cat. Which was dumb, because she'd been gone a couple years, and she'd never really been his cat to begin with. At most, Jinx had been a freeloader, an aloof stray sometimes willing to come in out of the weather and allow him to make offerings of food. He'd never even petted her before she vanished as abruptly as she'd come. And yet, she'd been something to take care of. Someone who noticed if he made it home or not.

As he got ready for bed, he tried to get back some of the contentment he'd felt leaving the bar. He remembered the moment that dumb bastard had looked up from grabbing Shannon and popping the button on her blouse, and met Nick's glare. The moment the guy realized that "Get your fucking hands off the lady" was going to be followed through with a lesson in courtesy. The surprise in his stupid eyes when Nick, six inches shorter and forty pounds lighter, landed that first solid punch. Damn that'd felt good. And the rumble it started had been a bonus, topped off with the satisfaction of a second round with the tit-grabber. The guy'd never looked better than when he was laid out bleeding on the floor.

Nick slid in between the sheets and switched off the light. He licked his sore lip, the pinch of pain welcome, a reminder that he'd had his fun. Tomorrow he would put on the badge and the uniform, and follow the letter of the law. Tonight he'd let loose in the very best way, standing up for someone who needed it. But as he fell asleep, a vague worry nagged at him. He couldn't put his finger on it. His subconscious was telling him not to overlook… something important. Fucking subconscious wasn't saying what, though, and he was tired enough that he didn't puzzle at it for long before falling asleep.

****

Brian Kerr waited in his bedroom in the pool house he shared with his brother, pretending to sleep. The mattress was comfortable, but he turned restlessly between his silky sheets with their amazingly high thread count. His brother would've been surprised to find out he even knew what that meant. But then there were a lot of things about him that would surprise Damon. Brian hadn't shared his secrets with his big brother since he was… well, since ever, really.

It was getting late. Brian squinted at the glowing green numbers on the bedside clock radio. He often had a hard time with numbers and letters, and tonight the digital display swam before his eyes. He did better with his analog watch, and he pressed the stem to light it and check that instead. The shape of the hands told him it was after three in the morning.

He wondered if Damon had gotten arrested this time. Not that he'd stay in jail long for a drunken bar fight, unless someone had been hurt much worse than Brian thought. But he'd heard the guys bitching enough to know that getting arrested on a Friday might mean a jail cell till Monday. A weekend in lockup would not make Damon easy to deal with.

He rolled onto his side, rubbing his cheek against the pillow for comfort. The light *rasp, rasp, rasp* of his stubble against the Egyptian cotton was soothing, like ocean waves or wind in the trees. He slowed his breathing to match.

The urge to get up and leave, to just go, was strong. Walk out the door alone, leave Damon, leave Lori and Marston and this whole life, no matter what happened afterward. Tonight had been too much. Another fight, another evening of blood and battering and drunken craziness, while he sat like a lump and pretended he barely noticed.

He didn't know how much longer he could do this. He was twenty-one now. Once, he'd promised himself when he turned twenty-one he'd leave. Somehow. But the invisible shackles had clamped down so hard, he couldn't see a way out.

A door slammed, and he heard Damon yell, "Bry? You here, bro?"

He sat up and switched on his light. Cleared his throat, dulled and flattened his voice, becoming little dumb brother Bry. His stupid voice. His know-nothing voice. That was usually automatic, and he was surprised he even noticed tonight. One real moment, when he talked to that Nick guy as himself, had thrown him off-balance. He swallowed. "Yeah? Damon? 'S that you?"

His door swung open. "Of course it's me, moron." Damon stood in the doorway, looking him over. "You're okay? Not hurt?"

"I'm okay."

"Where the hell did you go? I told you, in a fight, get out of the way and stay put."

In a crazy moment, I followed this gorgeous man. "The door opened. The cops were coming. I went out."

"Jesus." Damon frowned. "It's a good thing Booker saw you. Next time follow orders, you hear me?"

"I hear you."

Damon came over and sat on his bed, reaching out to give his back a quick rub. "Well, no harm done. Don't want to lose you though." He patted Brian's head in the way Brian hated, like a guy with his dog. "At least you stayed with Booker, and didn't get hurt. Go to sleep now. Mr. Marston has work for you in the morning."

"Work." Brian's gut twisted sickeningly, but he thought he kept the bitterness out of his tone.

Even so, Damon held his gaze for a minute, his expression displeased. "Yeah, your kind of work. Important stuff. What only you can do."

"Find a man?"

"Of course. So rest up. You want to do your best for Mr. Marston."

No! "Yes."

Damon got up and headed for the door, saying over his shoulder, "Good night."

Brian waited until his door shut, then switched off his light and lay in the dark, rubbing his eyes. Very, very softly, he let himself say, "*No*. No, no, no." Of course, it was a futile gesture. Tomorrow, he'd say yes. Mr. Marston, his brother's boss, his sister's husband, would ask him to Find a man, and he would say yes. Maybe he'd be able to fail. Maybe there would be enough obstacles to make that believable. Or maybe the man he was asked to Find would turn out to be a bad guy, someone just as bad as Marston, and his conscience would let him follow through.

Or maybe he'd stand up and let it all out, every bit of anger and loathing, every secret he hid, everything. Use language like he wasn't some retard, use wit and insults and let all his hate out. Maybe tomorrow would be the day he'd make them kill him.

If only he could believe Marston would actually do that. He wouldn't, though. Marston was smart and knew how to control people. Marston would make some awful threat to hurt Damon, or Lori, and Brian would cave. And then he'd have revealed himself for nothing, and it would only get worse. He wished he had the nerve to kill himself, but he wasn't brave enough for that either. Instead, tomorrow he'd be asked to Find a man, and he'd say yes.

Chapter 2

Nick picked up the call from Dispatch as he cruised down East River Drive, along the water. "Rugo here."

"Be advised, Homicide wants you to stop by after your shift. Got a DB they want to talk to you about. See a Detective Anderson."

"Anderson. Copy." He felt a lurch of anxiety, but if the dead body in question had been someone he cared about, they'd have pulled him in right now. He still asked, "Someone I'm supposed to ID?"

"I have no other information."

"Okay. Got it."

Actually, there was no one these days close enough that he'd be their next of kin. There were other cops he hung out with sometimes, but a dead cop would have Dispatch going apeshit, not casually blowing him off. On the civilian side, he had a few friends, but since Charlie moved to Portland, there was not one person they'd pull him off shift for. *And how sad was that?*

He reminded himself it was his own decision. He kept his cop world and his off-duty world separated. He was friendly with neighbors who broke minor laws on a daily basis. He picked up guys for no-strings sex, liking to hang out and fight in rough bars— his off-duty self didn't fit with his squeaky-clean law-enforcement image. He was a loner by choice. It was better this way.

He continued his patrol automatically, curiosity simmering in the back of his mind. *Who died? Why me?*

By now, he knew some of the regulars on his beat. There were a few homeless guys he'd hauled in repeatedly to dry out in the tank. He could probably ID a couple of the battered women he'd made domestic calls on. He urgently hoped it wasn't one of them, or the guy whose abusive wife had been one sharper kitchen knife away from murder. *Been there, done that.* There were a couple of junkies who'd passed him information in exchange for a few bucks. In three years on the street, he'd met enough civilians that guessing was pointless.

At the end of his shift, he went back to the precinct, parked his squad car, turned in his log, and headed for the locker room. He hung up his uniform, since no one had puked on him or thrown anything at him today. Ignoring the friendly chatter of the other guys, he quickly pulled on jeans, a T-shirt, and topped it with his leather jacket. Time to satisfy his curiosity at last.

Homicide was inside a big old brick building in downtown Minneapolis. He IDed himself to the desk sergeant, who called upstairs. Anderson came down and met him in the lobby. "This way. We have some questions for you."

Nick shifted uncomfortably. "I thought you wanted me to ID a DB."

"First we need you to answer a few questions." Anderson led him upstairs and down a long hallway, pulling open the last door to reveal a small conference room. A lean, middle-aged blond woman looked up from her seat at the table but didn't stand. Anderson said, "Officer Nick Rugo," to the blonde and waved Nick in without completing the other half of the introduction. Nick walked past him, trying to seem at ease. Anderson stepped back and closed the door between them, leaving him standing there like a kid in front of the principal's desk.

The woman in the chair looked up at him for a while; then her eyes narrowed. "Nok Nick."

For a panicked instant, he was tempted to deny it, but he wasn't that dumb. He tamped down his reaction, trying to pretend it was just irritation, and said, "I really hate that nickname."

The woman waved at the seat opposite her. "Take a load off. It's been a long day. I'm Detective Olson." She tossed her ID folder across the table.

Nick sat, glanced at the folder, and tossed it back. *Detective Erika Olson.* "Narcotics?" He'd done six months with Narcotics working undercover his second year on the force, making minor drug buys. They liked fresh faces for that, before cop instincts started to show in the way you moved, the way you reacted. He didn't remember Olson.

"Yep." Olson didn't elaborate.

"Can I ask what this is about?"

"You can ask." Her smile was chilly. "But first you can answer a few questions. What takes you up to the Torchhouse a few times a month, Officer Rugo?"

Nick tried a wry smile. He'd been told he could be charming when he did that. "Would you believe it if I said the beer?"

"No." Olson folded her hands on the table. "Frankly, Officer Rugo, you have very little wiggle room here. Tell the truth, the whole truth, and we might get through this still on the same side."

Nick gritted his teeth. "I like it," he said, feeling his way. "I like rough bars. It's, um, how I grew up." In a manner of speaking, anyway. "I'm a good cop." He leaned forward, speaking with more emphasis now. "You can look at my record. Three years on patrol and not one citation for excessive force, not one upheld complaint." Not that there were no complaints, because every jailhouse lawyer who had to be wrestled into the patrol car was prone to claim brutality, but none of them had made it stick because none of them had cause. "I'm a damned good cop. And I love the job. But sometimes…" He didn't know how to explain it.

"Nok Nick has quite a reputation. So." Olson's expression was a little warmer. "Sometimes you want to punch someone?"

"Yeah."

"Have you ever thought about taking up boxing?"

It wasn't the same. Boxing was full of safeguards and rules, and the guy he'd be up against was likely to be an upstanding citizen. Not someone he wanted to hit. Not someone he wanted to hurt. He shook his head.

"Any objection to taking a drug test right now?"

"None. In fact, I want to." Any other time, he'd have resented the implication, but now he wanted to do anything that would place him firmly in the law-enforcement camp and not with the low-life crowd he hung out with at the bar.

11

"I'll have you do that at the end of this interview. When was the last time you were at the Torchhouse?"

"Friday night." If they had surveillance going on, they'd know that anyway.

"This Friday?"

"Yes."

"How long did you stay?"

"A couple of hours."

"What did you drink?"

"Three beers?" Going to bars wasn't about the drinking. He never wanted to get drunk enough to ruin the fighting, or to potentially blow over the limit if he got stopped on the way home. The beers were more camouflage than anything.

"Was this guy there?" Olson slid a picture across the table. A dead man, looking like he'd been in water somewhere. He'd clearly taken a couple of low-caliber rounds to the face. Still recognizable.

"I'm not sure. I've seen him, but I can't be certain about Friday night specifically."

"When did you see him last?"

"A couple of times, maybe a month ago? I don't remember exactly."

"Do you know his name?"

"I heard him called Stan."

"Last name?"

"Not that I heard."

"Who called him Stan?"

"A couple of his friends. Cory, Damon."

"Last names?"

"Damon Kerr. I don't know Cory's."

"Could you pick them out in pictures?"

"Sure. Probably."

Detective Olson bent down and pulled a tablet out of the bag at her feet. "All right, Officer Rugo. I want every bit of information you can give me." She touched the tablet, bringing it to life, and clicked on a picture of five men getting out of a car. Nick recognized the street outside the Torchhouse. "These guys. Do you recognize any of them?"

"That's Damon in front. That guy who was driving is called Roy. I've seen him at the wheel before…"

Two hours later he'd been wrung out of everything he could dredge from memory. He'd given it up as willingly as he could. They had pictures of the blond guy, Brian, too. Nick had wanted to defend the kid— to mention how unlikely it was that he was part of anything bad. But he didn't have those illusions anymore. He'd met plenty of innocent-seeming guys who'd turn around and kill someone for a buck.

So he just said, "Damon's younger brother, Brian. He's special needs of some sort, hangs out with his brother. Not likely to be a big player." Olson had nodded and moved on.

Several times Olson got up and went out for a minute, leaving him in the empty room, under the eye of the camera up in the corner. Nick figured she was checking on Stan's murder case as it unfolded, or verifying stuff Nick had told her. Hell, taking a leak, maybe. He shifted in his seat at the thought, wishing he'd done the same before coming in. Asking now felt like showing weakness. Olson came back for the fourth time, sat down, and leaned back in her chair, her arms folded across her chest. She eyed Nick. "Where'd you drink before the Torchhouse?"

"Huh?"

"You've been going there for six months, every couple weeks. You didn't suddenly decide to take up drinking in bars at the age of twenty-five?"

"No."

"So what was your previous bar?"

"Gruff's."

"Why switch?"

Nick sighed. "Gruff's is a biker bar. I got along okay there, mostly." He'd played pool there for about eight months, drunk, fought. He'd had a cooler nickname. "It's not a hangout for the hard-core clubs. No Hell's Angels, no One-Percenters, but lots of wannabes. Bikers are damned mobile, they cruise around town, show up anywhere. The third time I spotted guys I'd played pool with out on their bikes while I was in a patrol car, I decided I was pushing my luck. The guys at the Torchhouse are a mixed crowd, but it's mostly locals there. The bar's an hour out of town. The chance of meeting them down here is much lower."

"And yet there was Stan, shot dead right on your turf."

"He was *where*?"

"We pulled him out of the river, under the Central bridge."

"Oh." Nick considered that for a moment. He did make that loop over the river at Central more than once on a normal night, but even his healthy paranoia couldn't make it fit anything. "It's a coincidence. Has to be."

"Does it?"

"Yeah. It makes no sense otherwise. If they knew I was a cop they'd either kill me or toss me out. I barely met Stan, never talked to him."

Olson nodded slowly. "So you think they don't know you're a cop?"

Nick thought back to Friday night in the bar. He'd tossed darts, played pool, drunk a beer, punched a guy. All normal. Those clowns couldn't be that good at acting. "I'd swear not. No sign of anything. Not a sideways look, not a lowered voice."

"I'm inclined to think Stan showing up on your beat was coincidence too."

Nick took a slow breath, some of the tension seeping out of his shoulders. "Do you have a suspect?"

Olson raised an eyebrow at him. "Let's go back to drugs for a minute. Is there a lot of trafficking in the Torchhouse?"

"No. Minor sales in the back hallway by the bathrooms. More in the alley, I expect."

"Anything that strikes you as unusual? You did a tour undercover. Anything that makes you take notice?"

Nick thought hard, and eventually shook his head. "No. If there was, I probably wouldn't have kept going back. I can ignore the small stuff where I hang out, but…" He wasn't sure what his threshold would be. Hanging with the bikers, he'd ignored more than he was comfortable with in the end. That was actually the bigger reason he'd changed bars. The bikers were a nasty bunch, especially toward their women. He'd seen more than one girl take a vicious smackdown from her man at times when he didn't have enough weight on his side to object. A few more of those, and he'd either have killed someone or gotten himself killed trying.

"The last time you saw Stan, did you notice anyone hanging back watching him, not trusting him, angry with him?"

"No. He seemed to fit in just fine." Nick tried again to remember. "There's always a bit of tension, mostly between that crowd he hung with and the guys from the factory."

"So who would you put at the top of your suspect list?"

Nick frowned. He hadn't been paying proper attention. The bar had been his off-duty playtime, and he was coming to realize that he'd pretty much uncoupled his brain and his instincts. He'd let himself get comfortable, and get sloppy. It was embarrassing as hell.

They both looked around as the door opened. Detective Anderson stuck his head in and gave Nick a smile, before saying to Olson, "TOD estimate puts Rugo in the clear. At least personally."

Olson nodded. "Thanks."

"No rest for the weary." Anderson backed out and shut the door.

For a while Olson sat silently, staring at Nick. Nick wished he could tell what was going on in her head. He had no idea how much trouble he was in. If any. Really, he hadn't broken any major laws, and if he'd failed to stop others from selling a vial or two, well, he'd been on his own time and without backup. He was a street cop, not Superman.

Olson said, "Would it surprise you to know the DEA had a CI inside Vern Marston's operation?"

"Marston?" Nick tried to recall if he'd heard the name. Confidential informants were vital to narcotics investigations of course, but he was playing catch-up with whatever it was Olson knew, or thought Nick knew.

Olson prompted him. "Marston employs Booker Smith, Damon and Brian Kerr, Roy Delany, Cory Frank."

"Oh, them." He thought about the list. "Can't be Brian. He's obviously not smart enough to be more than a hanger-on. No way Damon or Booker is the informant..."

"Don't strain yourself. Stan was the CI, before he took a bullet to the gut and two to the head. He was due to meet a DEA agent a couple blocks from where he went into the river."

"Oh. Shit."

"Yep."

"Did we get much from him before that?"

"I'll let the DEA discuss that with you." Olson picked up her phone, dialed, and spoke into it. "I have Rugo. You want him?"

Nick couldn't hear the response, but Olson tapped the phone off. "They'll be here shortly."

After a long silence Olson didn't seem to feel the need to fill, Nick said, "Am I in trouble?"

"We'll find out."

It was another ten minutes before a tall thin Asian guy in a rumpled suit came in. He sat across from Nick, beside Olson, and flipped open his ID. "Takano, DEA. You're Nick Rugo?"

Nick nodded.

Takano eyed him, head slightly tilted. "You might do. You're a bit of an opportunity, if it pans out."

"If what pans out?"

"Would you consent to a drug test and a search of your home?"

Nick held back a flare of anger. "I said I'd test. Why would you search my house?"

"What do you know about Vern Marston?"

"Nothing. I heard the name for the first time in here."

"Well, you wouldn't be the only cop on Marston's payroll. We've been after him for a while. Stan was our best lead so far. He gave us a snippet here and there. We were turning the screws on him to get more, and now it's all wasted."

"Plus the guy's dead," Nick said dryly.

Takano made an impatient gesture. "He's no great loss. He was a street dealer first, before he got jumped up to Marston's bunch and then close to the inner circle. If Marston found out Stan was talking to the cops, though, he's going to be on high alert. Getting another undercover agent anywhere near Marston's operation just got a lot harder. Anyone new is going to be checked out six ways from Sunday before they even let him sweep floors."

"Right."

"But—" Takano paused, eyeing him intently. "—someone they already know, someone who'd been around for months before Stan died, might have a chance to get closer."

"Oh." Nick tried to hide his surge of excitement at the idea of going back undercover. He'd done it for six months, until his superiors decided he was becoming too recognizable to the street-level dealers. He'd returned to patrol without a protest, but he'd missed the adrenaline high, and the knowledge that he was taking bad guys and their drugs off the streets, even when it was just low-level buy and bust operations. And occasionally it'd been something more important. The times he'd spent a few days getting closer to some bigger target, gathering evidence for a large-scale bust, had been like catnip to him. "You're thinking you could use me?"

Olson said, "You did the training. I know your undercover status was revoked, but it wouldn't take much to reinstate it. You're already established as a regular in the bar where they hang out. You've been around them for six months. They're gonna be suspicious of any new face, but maybe not of you."

"What makes them worth the effort?" Nick had pegged the guys for mid-level thugs, mostly. He'd guessed they were running some kind of illegal operation, but if they'd been high-level, they'd have been drinking somewhere a hell of a lot nicer than the Torchhouse.

"Marston has his fingers in a lot of pies, including designer drugs. We were closing in on a supplier in San Diego two years ago. Then a bunch of his guys disappeared, and a couple showed up dead. The only one left who was willing to talk pointed us at Marston, said he didn't like the competition. We want Marston. And his home base is here."

"What do you want me to do? Can you spell it out?"

Takano leaned forward, hands flat on the table. "We're looking for someone to go deep undercover, likely for months. That might be you."

"Might?"

"Once we check you out— up, down and sideways— yeah."

"I'm clean."

"I hope so. Homicide says you're in the clear for the time of Stan's murder, and surveillance says you never hit their radar as connected to Marston's crew. Having you hanging out in that bar the last six months could be a fuckin' godsend. We want someone to get in close, to learn more than 'Drive here with this box.' Find out how Marston's operations are run. Where's the drug lab? How does he move the product around the country and out to the stores and streets? What else is he into?"

"Do you have any ideas?"

"He's officially listed as an importer. All kinds of things from around the world. Art, collectibles, high-end furnishings, and for the last four years, dietary supplements. He declares over two million a year from the legal imports."

"What's he bringing in along with it? The drugs?"

"Probably. Although some of the import items themselves may be stolen or counterfeits."

"You're after the drugs, though."

"We'll take anything that would put him away. So far, he's been careful. He moves a lot of different products here and on both coasts. The designer drugs are what've been killing people. The shit's sold out of vitamin and traditional medicine stores half the time, but either there's no records or the fake supplement invoices trace back to nonexistent companies."

"But you're sure Marston's involved."

"Positive. Busting delivery boys and trying to work our way up the chain hasn't got us anywhere, though. We did that for six months in San Diego, and the shit just showed up in new places."

"And he's big enough to be worth a full operation?"

"Designer stuff used to be small potatoes. Not anymore. The market's big, and expanding." Takano reached into his pocket and tossed a little ziplock onto the table. "What do you think those are?"

Nick eyed it. "Um. Minimarshmallows?" He touched one through the bag and it resisted, then crumbled, like something from a kid's cereal.

18

"Crunchberries."

Nick cocked his head to the side and squinted.

"Plug-and-play?" Takano waited. "Peeps?"

"Um." He was pretty sure real Peeps were bigger and squishy, with crystal sugar on the outside.

Olson reached out and pressed another of the little white shapes, crunching it flat. "Party drugs. The lab says it's actually a blend— a little Viagra, a psychedelic, and a dissociative. Supposedly makes you horny first, then high. Hence plug-and-play."

"Cute."

Takano said, "Not so much. It's one of a bunch of new compounds out there. We think this one's responsible for at least half a dozen deaths and many more hospitalizations. We want this shit off the street, and we want to put Marston away, yesterday."

"Deaths?"

"Hypoglycemia. That's low blood sugar. Blood pressure goes up and blood sugar drops so low that a few users have gone into a coma, even died. Their buddies thought they were asleep, until they couldn't wake them up. Three of the deaths were teenagers."

"Fuck. Can we test for it? Is it enough of an analogue to even bust anyone?" New designer drugs were sometimes out ahead of the law. If the particular drug wasn't yet listed as illegal, they might have no grounds to make an arrest.

"The psychedelic is, although we have to run it by a private lab for testing, so that can get expensive."

"Crap. Better than nothing, I guess."

"And now we're starting over with Marston's operation." Takano eyed him. "So how friendly are you with Damon Kerr and his men?"

Nick shrugged. "Not very. Enough for them to recognize me, sure. I've played pool or darts with some of that crowd. I fought his buddy Roy once, when he claimed I was cheating at pool."

"Did you win?"

"Hell, yeah." Nick couldn't hold back the grin tugging at his lips. "Big guys always think size is all it takes."

"Does Roy hold a grudge?"

"I don't think so." Guys like that usually respected someone who didn't take their shit and could beat them down. Nick tried to think back. "I played him again afterward. He seemed okay. I let him win. And I have a bit of a rep, so losing a fight to me isn't shameful."

"Speaking of your rep, I heard the story about how you got your nickname. It didn't happen while we were watching the place. Was that real, or a backstory you made up?"

Nick snorted. "Like I could walk into a bar and say, 'Hey, y'all, I just chased off a guy with a machete.' Right. Besides which, the name sucks."

"So what happened?"

"My second time at the bar, some guy was wandering outside with a blade a foot and a half long, looking for someone. He was hanging out in the shadows, drunk as hell, and when I walked up he must have decided I looked like the guy. He yelled at me, came at me with the blade. I got lucky and took him down, then kicked the machete away. He decided running was smart."

"You didn't call it in?"

Nick bit his lip. "No. The guy was gone, and I didn't ever see his face clearly."

"Prints on the knife?"

"Well, that would have been a bit of a problem." He remembered the gathered crowd, the buzz of excitement and approval. "One of Damon's guys, Joe, picked it up, thanked me for adding to his blade collection, slapped me on the back. I could hardly say, 'Wait, don't touch that till I get the cops to fingerprint it.' He probably still has it, but I'm not gonna ask." Joe had grinned at him, and slid a finger over the blade until a drop of blood welled up, running over the shiny surface. His friends had whooped and pounded Nick's shoulder. They'd pulled him into the bar and bought him drinks until he was hammered.

The mix of booze, relief, and adrenaline had made him high as a kite, so when someone asked his name, he'd said "Nick" without thinking, even though he usually went by Rick when he was out for fun. They'd asked why he took the guy on with bare hands, and he'd said, "Well, I didn't have a knife." He'd become No-Knife Nick, then Nok Nick, before the night was over.

"So they respect you?"

"They probably don't hate me." The last couple of guys he'd put his fists on had been local factory workers, the recent one for grabbing Shannon a time too many, another man three weeks before for breaking a bottle and threatening people with it. Since Marston's men and the locals mouthed off at each other and brawled over everything, they might figure Nick was more theirs than not.

"All right. We have a couple weeks before they'd expect to see you again. That'll give us time to get your undercover status reinstated and a good ID set up. We'll make you a long-haul trucker, since you have the background for it. That covers the irregular times you've been showing up, and with Stan gone they'll be looking for another driver."

"That's what Stan did?"

"Yeah. He worked the warehouse circuit, driving trucks, moving stuff around like a shell game. Unfortunately for Marston, Stan liked coke and decided to sell a bit on the side. We busted him for that, offered him the chance to flip on Marston instead of prison."

"He was dragging his feet, though?"

"Trying to play both sides. We offered him immunity and witness protection, but he said it would never work. Marston knew everything, could find him anywhere. I guess he was righter than he realized."

"Do you have anything solid on Marston?"

"Nothing that would stand up in court. Stan gave us bits and pieces, local addresses, but we know he held a lot back."

"Weird that an importer lives in Minnesota." You couldn't get much farther from the ocean if you tried.

"Not a bad location for drugs coming in from Canada. And his first wife was born here, so it could've been sentiment. He has an operation in Jersey, and one down near San Diego. He has a private jet and he flies out there. But this is home base."

Excitement fizzed in Nick's veins. No more drunk-and-disorderly busts and ticketing speeders. "Okay. So what's next?"

"If you check out, we'll set up your ID and background, and do some intensive briefing. You have to be perfect. This isn't like some street dealer, where you rub your eyes red, fake some track marks, and put on clothes that smell of piss. These guys are thorough."

"Like what?"

Olson said, "If they start looking at you, they won't fuck around. They're high tech, they'll go online, call your old school for records, check out any family, look for you tagged in photos on Facebook. Marston has a PI he uses for investigations, and the bastard's ex-FBI. Your background will have to be rock solid."

"Does the PI know what Marston does?"

Olson gave him a steady look. "He's too good at his job not to."

"Scumbag."

"Oh, yeah."

Takano said, "Detective Olson will be your handler, coordinating with us on the wider investigation. Are you in?"

A few objections came to mind, but none of them was half as strong as the pull that had him leaning forward on the table toward Takano and Olson. *Undercover. Adrenaline. Danger. Taking out the bad guys.* "I'm in."

Chapter 3

Stan is dead.

The certainty echoed in Brian's mind as he slowly came back to muzzy awareness, tucked into his own bed.

He wasn't surprised, or even sad, despite the nauseated churning of his desperately empty stomach. It'd be pretty stupid to be sorry now. He'd known— from the moment they handed him Stan's ball cap, the moment they asked "Where is this guy?" —what the ending would be. And he'd made it possible.

Marston thought Brian was some kind of tool, an object, like a GPS-thing he could put a name in one end and get a location out the other. GPS didn't care whether you were headed for a school or a bar or a whorehouse, it just spat out the directions. *Left here. Next right. You have reached your destination.* Damon had given Brian the ball cap like he didn't think Brian would recognize Stan's trace on it, or more likely thinking that Brian still believed this was only a game. "We need to Find this guy."

Marston had watched curiously, like always, because the man had a hard-on for the occult, and Brian was the best he'd ever found.

He'd held that cap, turning it in his hands, thinking. The yellow and purple Vikings logo on the front had weathered to mottled beige and lavender. The sweatband was stained. He'd sat and thought about Stan for a long time, before answering.

Stan wasn't a monster, but he wasn't a good guy either. Stan liked to hurt people smaller and weaker than him. Maybe not to destroy them, or set kittens on fire or anything. Not like Vince, who Brian hadn't minded one bit leading Damon to. But Stan did enjoy the power of having someone beg him for mercy, beg him to stop. He was at least a bully. Brian couldn't afford to track only monsters for Marston. There weren't enough of them. He needed to keep his desperate secret vetoes for the rare good guys.

"Yes. I can Find him." He'd used his flat, simple voice. Tried not to think how many times he'd said those words in the last five years.

"Do it." He could hear the eagerness of the hunt in Damon's tone. Damon was probably more of a monster than Stan, but Brian didn't get to pick and choose. Despite everything, Damon was his brother. Brian loved him and would never turn on him.

He'd held the cap, twisting it between his fingers, letting everything he knew of Stan— everything he could feel in this greasy, gritty piece of cloth— seep into that part of his mind where his Finding worked. He closed his eyes, focused on that feeling, on the colors and smells and touches that were Stan's trace, green and gray, sticky, clinging, stinging a bit like nettles, like fear, like the excitement of a boy with his hand in the cookie jar, sure he won't get caught. Smelling of greed and sour beer and something chemical-sharp, all dragged down by fatigue. *Stan*. Then he raised a hand, and pointed, off to the left. "That way."

It had taken over an hour. He'd kept his eyes closed. That wasn't necessary anymore, but he wasn't about to tell Damon so. Hiding everything was second nature now. He sat in the front seat of Damon's new SUV, with his hand on his own knee, index finger pointing left, right, a bit more left, a human Stan-dowsing rod. Until they circled the quarry, his finger showing them where Stan was hiding. Until they told him he could stop now.

Then he'd curled his finger in against his palm and passed out, like usual.

And now, when he woke, he was in his own bed, it was morning, and Stan was dead. That gray, sticky trace was gone from Brian's Finder brain, like it had never been there. Wiped away. Dying did that.

There weren't a lot of live threads in his Finder brain. Mostly these days, after he Found someone, they died. Damon's trace was still in there, of course, black and yellow like warning tape, sharp like broken glass, hot, smoky steel with the hiss of water on it. And Lori, two threads twisted together, one bright like tinsel, the other soft and fuzzy, tangled like the coat of a dog that hadn't been groomed in far too long, scented like roses underlaid with alcohol. Those two were bright and strong, and there were half a dozen others, fainter traces, some of them guys that Marston had sent him after, just to prove he could do it back at the beginning, or as a warning. But mostly now, they died.

Probably that was a good thing, really. Many of the traces had been hard to live with, choking him with the smell of rot and gunpowder, the hiss of an angry cat, the scream of sirens passing in the night. If his mind still held all the threads he'd followed, he'd be crazy indeed. Crazier. But there were a few threads he did miss.

For a moment he ached for Mom's peppermint and ashes, Zach's firecracker pops and cotton candy meltingness. But Mom had been dead for years and his childhood friend Zach almost as long. He couldn't remember their exact signatures anymore. And so he was free to go crazy if he wanted to. It didn't matter anymore.

He rolled over in bed and hid his face in the pillow. His mind was such a strange place. As far as he could tell, other people's memories didn't linger in those kinds of traces. He was crap at names, not great with faces. He remembered people by the feel of them, mostly. At least, the ones he'd cared to turn his Finder sense on and really learn.

He could taste-smell the faint lingering echoes of a couple of Damon's friends he'd hero-worshipped, and a few of the other kids from school, back before he dropped out. They'd be familiar if he met them again. Mrs. Harrison, who'd tried so patiently to teach him to read when he was six, until she transferred off somewhere. There was still a wisp in his mind of her whiteboard-marker-and-wet-dog thread, probably not strong enough to follow.

A few times he'd dreamed about running away to Find her. He couldn't run off, of course. Even if he'd been able to beef up the trace enough to follow it, he couldn't leave Lori with Marston, couldn't escape Damon. So now he just took comfort in knowing that she was still alive, somewhere out there. Maybe teaching some other lucky kids.

His attention was caught by a new thread, very faint. Bright like a blade, sparkling like polished amber. He wasn't sure who it was. Someone he'd touched, someone he'd made enough contact with to pull a bit of them to himself. Usually he had to focus and do that on purpose, but occasionally someone snagged his Finder attention for a moment. It would fade soon. Until then the puzzle of who lived... he swung his finger under the sheets... *that way*... was a good distraction from thinking about his part in Stan's murder.

His door creaked open, swinging wide without a knock, and he winced, immediately tucking his finger into his fist and controlling the motion enough not to show. Not that Damon ever really paid attention.

"You still sleeping?" Damon strode over to the bed and tugged the covers off his face.

Brian opened his eyes and blinked up at his brother. "No. Awake."

"Here." Damon handed him a quart bottle of orange juice.

He sat up immediately to open it, struggling with the cap because his hands shook so badly.

"You're such a spaz." Damon took it, broke the seal with a quick twist, and passed it back.

Brian drowned any impulse to reply in a long, life-giving guzzling swallow. Orangey, sugary goodness. His hands steadied as he drank it down. When it was gone, he wiped his mouth with the back of his hand and held out the empty bottle to Damon. "Gotta pee."

It was one of his few amusements, to make Damon do stuff by pretending not to notice he didn't want to. Damon took the bottle instead of making him trash it himself. Brian had peed the bed enough times after a Find that Damon immediately cleared his route to the bathroom without protest.

Brian shut the door behind him, fumbled his sweatpants down just in time, and leaned a hand on the wall. His head spun and his arm shook, but the OJ was kicking in so this probably wasn't going to be one of the times he collapsed into the toilet. He finished, and washed up without looking at himself in the mirror. Not like he was much to look at on his best days, but after a Find and a crash, he knew there would be dark circles under his eyes and a flat, pasty look to his already pale skin. He was a freak, and sometimes it was pretty clear to see.

He toyed with the idea of a shower, but he needed food more than he needed to be clean. Needed food even more than he needed not to see Damon for a while. He took a breath and tried to sink himself down into Bry, Damon's dumb little brother. Bry, who had no idea what he was being used for, who thought Finding for Marston was all a fun game. He pulled the door open.

"Hey, bro." Damon held out a granola bar. "On your feet?"

Brian looked down at his toes, acting simple, and said, "Yes." Bry should do that without thinking, check to see if he was on his feet, like a moron, but somehow today Brian was having a hard time letting go of all the stuff he wasn't supposed to know. This was going to be a Brian day, an acting day. The granola bar went down in two huge bites, life-saving goodness, and it kept him from having to talk.

"Get clean clothes on." Damon went to the closet, pulled it open, and tossed him a sweater and black sweatpants. "Lori wants us there for dinner."

Which meant Marston wanted to see his pet freak. "Okay." He turned away, pulling off his stale, slept-in clothes and tugging on fresh ones.

Damon barely let him get the sweater on straight before putting an arm across his shoulders. "Come on, kid. You look fucking washed out. One snack bar isn't enough. Let's feed you."

And that right there was what tied him up in worse knots than anything. Because Damon, who could stick a knife in a guy without blinking, really did care about him. And Damon and Lori were all he had.

He let Damon tug him out of his room, out of their pool house, and up the breezeway to the manor. His heart pounded from even that short effort, and his vision sparked, going dark around the edges. Damon's arm kept him upright. Damon let go once they were inside and Brian was steadier, but he kept following Damon down the hall, around the corner, into the smaller dining room. Where else would he go?

Lori and Marston were already seated. They both gave him a cool look, but he was beyond caring. His knees were trembly again, and he sat fast.

"The kid needs some calories," Damon said, dropping smoothly into the chair beside his.

Lori pushed a plate to Brian. "Eat this. Slowly."

He picked up a piece of pita bread, spread thickly with hummus, and stuffed it into his mouth. He added another piece almost before he could swallow the first. They'd found food like this got him back to speed, or what Damon laughingly called half-speed, the best. He needed the protein and energy, but meat and fat sometimes made him nauseous. He secretly treasured his memory of the time, after his first deadly Find, when Marston had tried to reward him with a big well-marbled steak. He'd puked it back up right on the white tablecloth. He wished he'd had the nerve to lean a bit farther and get it on Marston himself.

The hummus worked its magic, and his vision cleared, his heart slowed. After a dozen bites, he looked up.

Marston raised a half-full wine glass at him. "To success."

He copied the gesture with his water glass. "To success. What success?"

Lori's mouth twisted the way he was familiar with. How long ago had she forgotten he was anything but stupid Bry, her dumb twin? "Your success, Bry. You Found the man Vern was looking for."

"Oh. Yes, I Found the man." Repeating what someone had already said was one of his best defenses. It sounded appropriately odd, and it kept him from blurting out what he really wanted to say.

"You sure did." Marston leaned toward him, his expression eager. "What did this guy you Found remind you of?"

"Remind me of?" He really regretted explaining to Damon, years ago, how each person he searched for had a trace made of smells and flavors that was like no one else's. Damon had shared that tidbit with Marston, and now he always asked, afterward. There was no reason not to tell the truth, though. If Brian started lying about anything extra, he'd never keep it all straight. "Remind me. Reminding of something. He was greasy. Gritty. Beer."

Marston laughed. "Greasy. Perfect. A pity we can't tell him, eh?"

"I could tell him. If you want me to tell him." He kept his expression blank.

Lori reached across to pat his hand. "No, Bry, that's okay. We're done with him."

"Done." He wondered if Damon had done the killing himself. There was a hint of pleased excitement in his brother that made Brian think he probably had. Damon loved his guns and knives. "Can we eat? Can we eat more?"

"Of course." Marston touched a button by his place, and a minute later the cook came through the serving doors with covered platters. While Mrs. Jones served them, Lori chatted to Damon about hiring another driver, and whether the pool heater needed to be fixed. Brian waited until his plate was full, then shoveled a forkful of linguine into his mouth. It was really good, with lots of garlic and mushrooms and cheese in the sauce.

Even when he hadn't just Found someone, he had a hard time resisting Mrs. Jones's dinners. When he was this hungry, he could ignore the world and eat.

So he did that, plowing through a huge plate of pasta and chicken breast and zucchini, and pretending he didn't hear anything around him. When the plate was empty, he picked it up and licked it. Lori firmly took it away from him before he could do it again. "Gross, Bry! If you're still hungry we can get you more."

"I'm always hungry. It's good."

"He's had enough." Damon took his fork away too. "He's turning into a porker."

"He needs food after Finding."

"He's had a shitload already."

Brian put his dirty knife in the middle of Damon's plate. "I've had a shitload."

Damon's backhand smacked his chest, although not hard enough to hurt the way Brian kind of wished it would. "Don't swear, kid."

"You swear."

"Because I know how."

"I know how."

Marston laughed, a cool sound without much amusement in it. "Fight on your own time. Bry, tell me about the Finding."

"It worked."

"Was it hard?"

"It took a long time. A whole hour, I think. Maybe two whole hours." He kept his tone flat.

Marston lowered his voice. "Do you know who was hiding this time?"

He lowered his voice the same way. "I think it was Stan. Was it Stan?" He regretted a boatload of things about the last five years. Marston was well aware that he could recognize a trace if it was someone he already knew. He was never sure whether any of the questions afterward were meant to catch him lying, so he saved his lies, even when the truth hurt.

"Yes. You did well. You Found him. We'll play the game with someone else another day."

Bile rose in his throat, but he swallowed and didn't let it choke him. "We'll play the game."

Marston sat back and raised his glass, looking hugely self-satisfied. "And here's to Lori as well."

"Lori?" Damon turned to her.

"I'm pregnant," she said. "The baby's due in December."

29

"Congrats, little sister." Damon raised his own wine glass, and she clinked the rim with hers.

"Should you be drinking?" Brian blurted out. He quickly added, "Babies don't drink."

She laughed. "I'm the mom, not the baby." She took a long sip. "I'm not giving up a little wine for the kid. Mom was smashed out of her mind half the time she was pregnant with us."

Damon tipped his head toward Brian. "Maybe not a good example, Lor."

"Well, *I'm* fine anyway. And you are." She tossed her head, her fine blond hair falling neatly back into place. "And it's just one glass of wine."

Marston leaned over to lay a hand on her stomach, his eyes on Damon. "Don't worry. This baby is *very* important to me. I'm watching out for it." His eyes drifted to Brian, with an odd hunger in them.

"Watch the baby." Brian looked at Lori to break the stare. "You don't show a baby yet."

"No, thank God. Not yet." She gave Marston a sexy smile. "Will you still love me when I'm all fat and pregnant?"

"I promise, you'll be the most valuable treasure in my house. I only hope the baby is as special as you are." But as he said it, Marston's gaze stayed fixed on Brian.

Brian decided it wasn't his imagination. That was greed in his eyes.

He'd wondered, when Marston married Lori three years ago, whether there was more to it than a middle-aged man and a cute, sexy, and available young woman. Lori had definitely gotten all the looks in the family. Where Damon was hard and angular, and Brian was pale and pudgy and round featured, she was pretty, big busted, and wide hipped. Her eyes were sky-blue instead of ice; her hair was as fair and straight as his, but thicker; her mouth was wide, but fuller and proportionate. She'd had plenty of boyfriends, and plenty more who'd wanted her, growing up.

But she wasn't movie-star stunning, or talented, or brilliant enough to hook a man like Marston. And yet as soon as she'd turned eighteen, he'd dated her a few times and then married her. Maybe he'd hoped that as Brian's twin she had some shred of his talent. He'd no doubt found out better by now. Lori was all too normal.

Brian could imagine Marston turning his expectations toward wanting a child with some freak paranormal ability. For a moment, he wondered if Marston would make Lori duplicate their mother's drinking, trying to affect the baby the same way. Brian ached to grab up Lori and run. To get her and the baby safely away from here.

Except that she was studying the rings on her fingers, watching the lights of the chandelier making the diamonds sparkle. This life was what Lori always wanted for the three of them, growing up poor. She'd never leave just because Brian told her to. And Marston would never let them go.

He plastered a smile on his face. "Dessert? Do we get dessert?"

****

Three weeks later, Nick walked into the Torchhouse with new ID in his pocket, a beat-up Corolla hatchback parked half a block away, and a bit of extra drag in his step. He scowled, trying to look upset and pissed as he went up to the bar. "Jack. A double."

The only one of Marston's people he saw was Roy, hitting balls around the pool table by himself, trying to do jump shots. When Roy caught sight of Nick, he frowned and switched to running the table. Nick nursed his whiskey for a while, watching in the barback mirror while pretending not to. Some of the factory guys came in, and one of them challenged Roy to a game. Nick kept an eye on the play, while signaling the bartender for a refill.

He was very aware of the tiny recorder sewn into the fly of his jeans. With the advances in electronics, he no longer needed wires all over his chest like undercover guys used to. A casual pat-down wouldn't find anything. But those advances also meant the bad guys had bug detectors that would pick up any kind of transmitter, so he was just recording for now. Surveillance was being kept light, and no one would hear what went down around him till long after the fact. He was basically on his own.

He kind of liked it that way. He'd always been a lone wolf. He sipped his drink and waited.

The guy playing against Roy was good. After he won and money changed hands, Roy said, "Rematch?"

One of the other locals wandered over. "My turn. You sit out."

Nick spotted an opportunity. He shoved off his barstool, and went over to Roy. "If there's money on the table, I'll team with you, us against the two of them."

31

Roy stared at him. "What the fuck, Nok? You and me, on the same side?"

Nick shrugged. "My fuckin' truck died. I need the cash, and you're not half-stinking-bad. And I'm better. We could win this."

Roy opened his mouth, probably to tell Nick where he could go, when the factory guy put some bills on the table. "Money where your mouth is."

Nick strolled forward, his eyes on Roy, who was clearly torn between his dislike of Nick and beating the locals for cash. Nick slapped two twenties on the table next to the fifty from the winner. He pulled out the rest of his bills, made a bit of a show finding another ten amid battered ones, and cocked his head at Roy. "You in?"

While Roy stood glaring equally at everyone, the other factory guy got up and slapped his money down. "Fifty."

"Fuck." Roy dug in his pocket and added his. "Right. I tell you, Nok, you'd better play good."

"You watch your own balls, I'll handle mine," Nick said, deliberately not smiling at the double meaning. None of the others so much as noticed. Humor was clearly a lost cause here. "Toss for the break."

They flipped a coin and Roy won. He elected to break and made his first four shots, then missed one. Their opponents fielded the new guy first and he was good, but he got a bad bounce and ended up dropping the cue ball.

"Scratch," Roy said unnecessarily. "Go for it, Nok."

Nick chalked his cue slowly, drawing it out a bit, and then lined up his first shot. He played it safe rather than fancy, not rushing, double-checking each shot before taking it. The balls dropped neatly one after the other, until he could line up a single cushion shot for the eight ball, shooting soft, a little outside English, aiming to bank across the table and end up a hair beyond the pocket. As usual, he was a fraction short, which meant the ball dropped nicely, right where he wanted it. "And game."

"Fuck." The first factory guy kicked a chair. "Rematch?"

Nick shook his head. "I'm taking my winnings and getting smashed." He glanced at the guy holding the pot. The man peeled off his share of bills and passed it over. Nick tipped the bills in his hand toward his brow in a mock-salute. "Nice game." He went back to the bar, not looking over his shoulder. Not that he had to, since the mirror was so conveniently placed. He saw the other three glance at one another, then, as he'd hoped, Roy followed him across the floor.

"Jack again. Double." Nick put a bill down on the bar and slid onto a stool.

Roy sat beside him as the barback cleared a dirty glass and napkins from in front of them. "Hey, Nok. That wasn't half-bad pool."

Nick picked up his new glass and took a slow swallow. Either the whiskey was a better bottle or his taste buds were numb, because it was almost drinkable. He sipped again.

"You got a reason to get smashed?" Roy probed.

"Do I need one?" The last thing Nick wanted was to appear too eager to get to know his quarry.

"Hell, no." Roy flicked a finger at the bartender. "Bud Light. Bottle."

They drank side by side for a while. The bar got noisier as the evening wore on. Nick had picked Friday as his best bet for finding Marston's guys out on the town, but it looked like other than Roy it was going to be a bust. Roy got up, made a trip to the john, and stopped to talk to some guy Nick didn't know. Pretending to check the time, Nick snapped a pic of the guy, emailed it, and hit the delete-and-overwrite app to erase it. He tipped over his glass, pretending to be more drunk than he was, and ordered another.

Roy came back, got another beer, and kept drinking it in morose silence. Eventually he said, "What d'you do for work?"

"Drive," Nick said shortly. He took another sip, making Roy be the one to work for it.

"Truck? Cab?"

"Long haul."

"Like it?"

Nick shrugged. "It's not bad. *Wasn't* bad." He let his tone go bitter.

"What? You got fired?"

"Fuck you." He pushed his glass across the bar, stood, and turned to the door like he was leaving. It was a gamble, but it paid off when he heard Roy hurriedly get up behind him.

"Wait. What the hell?"

He swung around, rubbing his eyes as if stressed. "I didn't get canned. I'm my own boss, if I can ever get the damned busted truck on the road again."

"Oh." Roy wavered looking uncertain, then waved at a back table. "Hey, you won me fifty bucks. And there's no one else in this place I want to drink with tonight. Stick around awhile."

Nick let himself be persuaded. He bought a beer and carried it back to where Roy had settled at a small table.

Roy glanced at it. "Beer?"

"Cheaper. And I gotta drive home sometime."

"Yeah."

Nick dropped into the other chair and said, "So, Roy, what do you do when you're not playing pool?"

"This and that." He shrugged. "I run a warehouse, deliveries."

Instead of taking the tempting opening to ask about drivers, Nick grunted. "Boring."

"You'd think so."

Nick changed the topic to the Twins and the upcoming baseball season. Pretty soon he and Roy were having an amiable argument over how good Kirby Puckett had been and whether he lived up to his best-ever billing. From there they wandered into boxing, and mixed martial arts, and how fake TV wrestling was. Nick gave it a half hour, then got up and stretched. "Gotta go."

"I'll see you around?" Roy actually sounded hopeful.

"Only if I can't fix the fucking truck." Nick turned and left.

On the short walk back to his car, he was hyperaware of sounds behind him, his heart speeding up at each thump or footstep or car passing by. It was dumb— there was no reason anyone should think twice about him yet— but knowing every minute of audio from that little encounter was recorded took the evening from just another night out, to an undercover operation. The real shit was starting.

Chapter 4

Nick made it back to his car unfollowed, of course. He reminded himself it was *way* too early in the game for paranoia. Anyway, it would just reinforce his cover if Roy bothered to tail him the four miles back to his new apartment, and a bunch of glances in the rearview didn't show anyone behind him.

The apartment was small and stuffy, with a neglected feel, which was fine for the little-used home of someone who'd until now supposedly spent most of his time on the road. There were a few cheap but not awful furnishings, and a small TV. He'd been living here a week, learning the neighborhood.

One of the department's electronic data guys had changed the necessary records to show he'd been renting it under the name of "Nick Green" for the last four years. There were a ton of Nick Greens around, and the baseball player would help to spam searches. He had to trust that they'd covered his ass completely enough.

He hung up his leather jacket in the entry, tossed his keys and phone on the counter, and closed the blinds before unzipping his pants. The pocket inside the fly was hard to get at. He stripped and pried it open, then fished out the small recorder. A cable hooked it up to his phone, and a minute later his last two hours were on official record. He cleared the contact phone number from the memory, hid the recorder and cable in a baggie buried in a kitchen canister of dried beans, and stretched out on the bed in his shorts.

He'd thought he was calm, but his fingers twitched, and when his phone rang he jumped, so obviously there was some extra adrenaline floating around. At this point only Olson and the DEA should have his number. He still answered, "Yeah?" with a bit of attitude.

Olson's voice said, "Just letting you know we got the audio file. How urgent is it?"

"Not very." Since he was back up on his feet, Nick clamped the phone against his ear with his shoulder and fished in the fridge. There were some leftover Thai noodles, and he wanted food to sop up the bad whiskey. "I did meet up with Roy, helped him win some pool money. We're buddies now."

"That was fast."

"Luck, really. And I didn't push it. That's all there is on record, me bullshitting with Roy. He might've said something useful, but mostly he knows fuck-all about boxing."

Olson laughed. "Okay, we'll put it on file and get to it later. You're going back tomorrow?"

"Yep." Nick gave a fake sob. "My beloved truck, she's a goner. That engine's never gonna run again."

"Okay. The dead rig can sit in the repair shop for a while. You can run by there and cry over it anytime, if you think someone's watching you. We'll try to bust another of Marston's drivers, open up a job."

Nick set the food carton on the counter and pulled open the silverware drawer. "Right. Maybe someone else from Marston's crew will show at the Torchhouse tomorrow night."

"Good luck." Olson hung up.

Nick deleted the call record and set the phone aside. Narcotics had enough information to arrest one or two of the other drivers on small, unrelated charges, and make Marston shorthanded. Nick would hang around the Torchhouse, out of work, with long-haul experience and his commercial license up to date, ready to be hired. It was a plan.

He ate cold noodles out of the box, standing at the counter, as he debated heading down into the Cities. This might be his last chance to do it safely, unmonitored by his friends or his enemies. There were some decent gay bars in Minneapolis, and at midnight they'd barely be getting started. He could drive down, score some ass, and take care of his tension before the next stage of his undercover op began.

He couldn't quite get up the enthusiasm, though. Oh, he could get *up*. He rubbed himself through his boxers to prove it, but stopped after a minute. He was more restless than horny. Not in the mood to make the right conversation and the right moves. He'd probably hook up, no problem. Guys went for his combination of wiry muscle and angled features, and he'd been told his mouth was made for sucking dick. It just felt like too much hassle. He'd sometimes gone weeks, even months, with nothing but his hand. He could do it again.

Instead, he headed out at random, first walking around the block, then getting into his car. He drove into the city, down along the river, and cruised randomly. Old neighborhoods and newer ones, a few familiar from his foster days, none that were in his precinct. He glanced in the rearview now and then as he rolled down small streets made narrower by parked cars. Occasionally there was a car behind him, but none that got his Spidey senses tingling. In the end, he swung south and home as perhaps he'd always meant to. By now, he was sure he wasn't being tailed, and he'd done nothing yet to earn a tracking device from Marston. It should be safe.

He glanced over at the Carters' front door as he parked. Their trailer was dark, with no kids on the step. Of course it was one a.m., but still, that was good. He let himself inside his own place. His lights were on timers, and they were all off by now. He turned on the kitchen ceiling fixture and sat at his little table. The trailer was neater than it had ever been. Everything looked secure. He didn't know why he was there.

Maybe just making sure he *could* still go home. He'd spent years in foster homes, between age seven and eighteen, some good, some bad, mostly in between. The one thing they had in common was that when he left, he couldn't ever go back. The walls that'd sheltered him, the people who'd fed him, the sidewalks he'd chalked on and trees he'd climbed, all belonged to someone else now.

He'd moved into this trailer on rent-to-own as soon as he could swing it. This was the first "home" since his mom died— or maybe since his early, naïve days at foster number one— that he'd let himself actually get attached to. Hell, he'd probably die of old age in this little trailer. He looked around at the battered cabinets, the worn vinyl floor, the cream-colored curtains on the window, canisters shaped like roosters on the counter. There were lots of worse places.

He reached over and opened a drawer. His personal phone sat waiting. He turned it on and it chimed at him. In the four days since he'd last been home, he'd had some texts and emails, mostly spam, and one missed call. He hesitated, but it was two hours earlier in Portland. He tapped the number.

"Hey there." Charlie's voice was warm, rich, and amused. "Why are you still up? Having fun?"

"Kind of." Nick leaned back in his chair and crossed his ankles. "Starting a new assignment tomorrow. I might not be around much. I didn't want you to worry, if you don't hear." He realized it was a lie as he said it. Tonight, he wanted to know someone would care.

Charlie's tone got more serious. "Undercover? What kind of case?"

"You know I can't tell you that. Anyhow, I won't have my phone on me most of the time."

"Okay." Charlie took an audible breath. "Nothing bad, right?"

"Hell, no. Exciting." Nick tried to recapture some of the adrenaline he'd felt walking out of the bar. "It's good. Worth my time, not like ticketing drunks."

"They also serve who get drunks off the street," Charlie pointed out, very mildly for a guy whose law enforcement career had come to an end after being T-boned by a drunk driver.

"God, sorry." Nick rubbed his face. "It's late. I'm rambling."

"You sound a bit loopy," Charlie agreed. "You okay?"

"Yeah." Nick uncrossed his feet and sat up. He wasn't sure what he needed to say, just that there was something. "Drove around one of the old neighborhoods. Stupid memories, y'know?"

Charlie made an encouraging sound. It was one of his best traits. He actually listened more than he talked.

"Anyway, I wanted to make sure you wouldn't get worked up if I go darkside."

"All right."

"You're a good friend. I miss having you around." That was too much, too naked. He added quickly, "Tell me about your mom. Is she still trying to get you to join her knitting circle? What did she make for you this month?"

Charlie hesitated on the other end of the call, perhaps hearing more in Nick's voice than he wanted him to, but in the end he went with it, telling stories in his usual, cheerful way. Nick leaned back and relaxed, listening. Charlie's account of his mother's schemes to show off her "handsome son" to the daughters of all her friends made him snort with laughter.

Eventually, they said good night, simply and without fuss. Nick turned his phone off and slid it back into the drawer. He pushed the drawer shut with a little, final click, and shivered as if someone had walked across his grave. As if he'd closed a chapter of his life that couldn't be reopened. Nonsense, of course. His life as Nick Rugo would wait here safely for him to return.

He sat in his own kitchen for almost an hour, not thinking about anything much. Soaking in the quiet, the familiar. Then he let himself out, locked up carefully, and headed back to Nick Green's apartment.

****

Brian squeezed his chair farther into the corner at the Torchhouse and silently cursed himself for being a wimp. Another Saturday night at the bar, another night he hadn't been able to say no to Damon. It never changed. No matter how many pep talks he gave himself, no matter how often he practiced negative answers to Damon's routine "Come on, Bry. The beer's waiting," he still ended up meekly tagging along.

Five long years he'd done this. Back when he was sixteen, he'd been happy, flattered to be one of the guys. He'd laughed and taken sips of the beers they'd passed him, played the dumb puppy at their grown-up table. He wasn't sure when the fun had gone out of it. Maybe the first time he realized that they were talking about beating someone to a crippled pulp, and it wasn't a joke. Maybe when he saw Damon really fight— all silent, fierce intensity— punching the guy in the head long after he was down. He'd have killed the man if Booker hadn't pulled him off.

Maybe it'd been the time he'd gotten a little too drunk, and tried to explain evolution to the Christ-Saves guy at the next table, and done it too well. Damon had eyed him sideways. "Where the hell did you learn all that, Bry?"

He'd had to put on his dumbest slur, and say, "On TV. It's there, Damon. PBSes said it lots. I watched it a bunch of times."

For a second he'd been afraid that Damon wasn't buying the idea that he'd just memorized some TV program, but then Cory had got into a fight with some guy about darts, Damon leaped up to help, and by the time it blew over, Brian's lapse had faded from memory. Since then he'd never dared drink more than half a bottle. He'd told Damon too much beer made him sick, proved it with a finger down his throat in the dirty bathroom a few times, and now they all knew that dumb Bry didn't drink past the first round.

It made this whole going-to-bars thing even more stupid. He didn't care about the waitress's boobs, even if they all did. Damon, Booker, and Roy were ordering refills on beer, vodka, and cheese fries, and Damon probably wouldn't even let him eat more fries. Damon thought he was getting fat. Well, maybe he was, but who cared?

"Can I go home, Damon?" he asked. "I'm bo-o-o-ored."

"Shut up and stay put," Damon said, without even looking around at him.

Well, hell. He could get up and walk, of course, but Damon wasn't above sending Booker to haul him back to his seat. Booker was even bigger than him, and much tougher. Plus once or twice, Damon had threatened him with handcuffs. That hadn't sounded like a joke either. "All right," he said obediently.

Damon punched his arm lightly. "Tell the waitress to get you another Coke. Diet."

Diet pop tasted like ass. Or what he imagined ass might taste like, because he'd never had the chance to find out, although he kind of wanted to. By the time he unwrapped that thought, he'd hesitated long enough that the waitress was tapping her pencil on the pad, and looking at Damon, not him. "Diet Coke for the kid?"

"Yeah." Damon frowned at him as she hurried off. "What's with you? You can't even say two words?"

"I hate Diet Coke."

Damon poked his stomach. "Well, you're drinking it anyway."

"Why d'you care?"

"You're staying healthy." Damon's glare held something old and raw and dark in its depths. "You're staying here where I can keep an eye on you, you're not turning into a sickly tub of lard, and you're going to talk like a human. Fifty years from now, you're still gonna be okay."

The thought of fifty years of this made him want to puke, right there on the table. But he understood. He could feel the same dark waters where that came from, down inside, ready to drown him if he looked back too far.

"Where's Mom, Damon?"

"I don't know. Shut up and eat your hot dog."

"Why's Mom so sick?"

"Just shit she does to herself. Go to bed."

In the end, even Damon hadn't been able to keep Mom from self-destructing. So yeah, his determination to save Lori and Brian ended up as this friendly slavery, but it came out of the only good thing about Damon. He loved his brother and sister fiercely. He'd do anything to keep them safe. How could Brian want to fight that? He sat back in his chair, and when the Diet Coke arrived, he drank it.

Roy said, like he was continuing some conversation, "I've been checking him out for a week now. The truck is right where he said, the repairs would be almost seven grand, he lives in a crappy apartment. It all checks out on my end, so far."

Damon said, "Right. Let me talk to him. If he seems okay, I'll have security vet him properly for us."

Roy said, "There he is." He beckoned someone toward them.

Damon leaned over and snagged an empty chair, shoving it at the newcomer. Brian looked up and was stunned to meet No-Knife Nick's hazel eyes. He could almost feel the *click* as the thread in his Finder brain recognized a source. Here was the amber and shining steel he'd tasted weeks ago.

The trace had almost faded, but locking eyes with Nick reawakened it, twining the bright and the warm, the amber thickening to honey, with steel wound around it like a shield, the taste sweet and sharp on his tongue. He only realized they'd been staring when Damon whapped him on the chest and said, "Nick, sit. And Bry, quit staring at the guy, right?"

Brian dropped his gaze instantly, looking down at his hands wrapped around the Coke can. "Sorry. Not staring." His heart beat desperately fast, but he tried to look dull and bored. *When was the last time he'd pulled in a thread without even trying?* Not since he was little. Not since he'd learned how to turn that talent off and on. There was no reason a brush of arms and exchange of a dozen words should have given Brian this link to Nick, no reason except that he was an idiot, and yes, he'd already been watching Nick for months.

Watching him drink, watching him fight. Nok Nick had been Brian's secret little vice. He'd shown up now and then, unpredictably, in the mixed crowd of the Torchhouse. There were all kinds of guys who came through here, and most of them Brian either knew, or ignored, but Nick had been different. He was... *intense*, Brian decided was the right word. Like he was dialed up a notch more than the rest of the world. He drank like he needed it, fought with a wild anger that was almost joy, brooded like a loner staring into his glass, as deeply isolated as Brian. On the rare occasions he laughed, it was like the sun rising. He'd been Brian's obsession, and that one moment of touch and a kind word had been too much to resist.

Christ, he was stupid. And there was nothing he could do now. From here on, he'd know where Nok Nick was, or at least, he'd be able to Find him, forever. He didn't have to advertise that, of course. "I need to pee," he said thickly.

"Well go, then," Damon said with a rasp of irritation.

Brian headed to the bathroom and into one of the stalls, sitting down and putting his head in his hands. *What was Nick doing with Damon?* They hadn't known each other before, he was certain of it.

If you don't get back out there you won't find out. He could control himself. He'd just not even look at Nick. He stood and went to the sink, wondering why he was hiding in here. He should go back out, listen, see what was up. It was only when he was washing his hands for the third time that he realized the truth. He didn't want Nick to meet him as Bry, the stupid, slow brother of a vicious criminal. Bry, the guy who repeated half of what was said to him and forgot the other half. The guy who couldn't even read a menu to order his own food.

If Nick and Damon were hanging out together, that was the guy he'd have to be, though.

He'd made his choice very long ago.

Eventually he dried his hands and went back out. As he sat down, Damon said, "I almost sent someone after you to see if you'd drowned in the toilet."

He licked his lips, picked up the stupid red-and-silver can in both hands, and said slowly to the swirled logo, "I didn't drown."

Damon ruffled his hair carelessly. "No kidding." He turned back to Nick. "So you're looking for work?"

"I guess." Nick's voice was dense and smoky, deeper than Brian had remembered. "I need to fix my truck and I don't have near enough to cover it. Without the truck, I'm not earning. So yeah, a job would be fuckin' awesome."

"Any leads?"

"I put my name in with a couple of carriers, but no one's got back to me yet. Anyway, I'm not looking for long-term. Just enough so I can get my own truck back on the road."

Damon said, "My boss might be looking for a driver. Maybe. He does imports, has a bunch of drivers working."

"Yeah?"

"I can ask him. If you're interested."

Nick sounded suspicious as he asked, "What's in it for you?" Brian snuck another look at him. He had his arms folded across his chest, his head tilted like he was puzzling something out. The frown and the way he squinted his eyes shouldn't have been attractive, but somehow it was. Brian forced his gaze back firmly on his own hands. *Not looking at the hot guy.*

42

Damon said, "Roy says you play mean pool. I know you can fight, but don't usually throw the first punch. That's worth something in a guy that might end up workin' under me."

"You've been watching me?" Nick's tone suggested he was pissed.

"I watch everyone." Damon used the silky-smooth voice Brian hated. The one that said he was thinking about getting dangerous.

So Brian said, "He does. Damon watches everyone. He's a watching guy."

Sometimes that worked, defusing things by repeating the obvious. This was one of those times; they both looked at him, and when Damon said "Right, Bry, that's me," he sounded more his usual self.

Nick said, "Well, it's not like I care. And yeah, if your boss needs a good driver, I'm his man."

Damon pulled out a card from his pocket, wrote on it, and passed it over to Nick. "That's the online application link. Fill one out, and I'll tag it for extra attention when it comes through."

"Thanks." Nick tucked the card into the pocket of his jeans.

Brian ducked his head and didn't listen as the other men talked about sports and cars and traffic. He turned the can in his hands, around and around, watching the little nick in the rim slide under his thumbs with a tiny rasp. *It wasn't fair.* Guys he had *thoughts* about were supposed to stay over there on the other side of the room. Other side of the classroom, other side of the gym, other side of the bar. He was safe when they did that, and he could go home and think about them and beat off in the shower where Damon wouldn't hear him. It wasn't real, they weren't real, as long as they didn't cross the room.

Now Nick was sitting just a few feet away. He could probably see the way Brian's ears stuck out, the way his hair lay white and flat and limp as an old guy's. He'd likely noticed how Brian's shoulders were kind of round with chub, not muscle. Worst of all, he'd heard Brian be Bry, the dumb mascot brother. Bad guys wanted to make fun of that. Good guys wanted not to stick around to see bad guys make fun of it. No one wanted to get into the shower with it.

The fantasy's spoiled now.

Brian figured his sex drive was pretty low. He'd hear about people doing really stupid shit to get laid, and he couldn't understand that. But he did like to get off sometimes. Girls didn't do it for him, not really. Someone— he'd have thought Damon, but the way Damon acted maybe it was Marston— had sent him girls a couple times a month ever since he turned twenty-one. Some hooker with big boobs would show up at the door, say "I'm here for Brian?" And Damon would say "Have fun, bro," and leave.

He could get off, especially if they did it with their mouth. They always used condoms, so there was nothing icky about it. But coming with a girl felt like… like sneezing, a buildup of tightness and a release, a bit of relief. When they left, he was more glad than sorry to see them go.

He'd known for a long time he wanted guys. He'd also known that he had to keep it secret from Damon, which meant no real live guys, ever. But his shower guys had been important, and now Nick was off that list.

He rubbed the bottom of the can subtly against his dick, through his jeans. Despite his disappointment, thinking about a shower with the sound of Nick's voice and the feel of his Finder thread so close was making Brian restless and needy. He was half-hard. He was completely stupid.

Tonight he'd go online and cruise the sports sites Damon had linked for him, and find some guy with a hot, tight body and to-hell-with-you eyes, to imagine on his knees in the wet shower. It wouldn't be the same. Picture guys weren't as good as real guys, but he'd known since forever that you took what you could get.

After a while, Nick and Damon got up to play darts. Brian let himself watch them, his head tipped back against the wall and eyes half-closed. Damon was smooth and easy, no wind-up, just a toss that somehow went where it needed to go. Nick was hotter, sharp and fast, throwing with a snap that buried the tip deep. Damon won the first game, Nick the second, Damon the tie breaker. They came back to the table, Damon subtly pleased and Nick a good loser, not acting like he was unhappy.

To Brian's shock, Nick asked, "How about two on two? Roy and Bry look bored."

Damon barked a short laugh. "Neither of them can hit a barn. Play Booker."

For a moment Brian had the impulse to rebel. He wouldn't have to play well. He could say "I want to," and stand up next to Nick, and simply play the game. He wasn't even that bad, really. But he ducked his head and repeated dully, "Play Booker."

Nick shrugged and Booker heaved himself up out of his chair. Either Nick's luck was bad, or he let Booker win. Not long after, they were back at the table with another round of beers. Brian slid his thoughts further inside his head and let himself just *be* Bry. Slow, easy, no interest, no comment. The others were talking again, about food and girls and, for some reason, oak trees. Nick had some grudge about trees.

Bry didn't care, though. Bry lived in the moment and stole cheese fries from Booker. Then from Damon who smacked his hand. Time went by. Nick got up and made leaving noises. He shot a look at Bry that had a touch more interest than Bry thought he deserved, but he ducked his head and broke the eye contact. None of his business what Nok Nick thought, really. Not his problem.

Nick left, and Damon began some discussion with Booker about traffic and construction and driving routes that didn't matter since Bry couldn't drive. Well, he *could*, but not legally, because passing a written test for his license was never happening. When he wanted to go somewhere, someone else drove him. Like Stan. Who he'd killed, basically... He pushed that thought back down because Bry didn't know about that. Bry thought Finding was a game.

He stayed there, lazy, just Bry hanging with his bro and friends, through another hour of talk and Diet Coke and no more fries because Damon gave him *that* look. Then Booker picked up a girl, Roy was smashed, and Damon was ready to drive home. Like all those other nights. Brian didn't take a shower before bed. Despite his full bladder, he didn't even go to the can until he woke, hours later, with no choice. Half-asleep, pissing a river, he couldn't even try to think about anything.

****

Nick tipped his creaky chair back at the kitchen table, then thought better of it and let the front legs thump down. He was a bit buzzed, despite his efforts not to drink too much around Marston's crew. He plugged his audio recorder into the phone, sent the new file. Then he emailed a couple of pictures he'd taken of Booker and his girl. Odds were she was a one-night trick, but she wasn't on the known-associates list, and you never knew what might be useful. He deleted correctly, unplugged the phone, and set it aside. Done.

He was vibrating with a mix of whiskey and adrenaline. He wanted to hit something, or fuck something. He wanted to go out and drive really fast and yell out the window of his car, although the piece of shit Corolla they'd given him barely managed fifty miles an hour downhill.

He was on the inside with Marston's people.

Maybe.

Probably.

He'd tossed Damon's little business card on the table when he took off his damned jeans to get the recorder. Now he picked up the card and looked at the writing on it. He could get online and do the application right away, but that might seem too eager. He had a feeling that, with Damon Kerr, it would never hurt to hold back and pretend to be disinterested.

The guy was smooth and cold, always watching. Nick had planned to let him win at pool or darts, if necessary. But in fact, he'd had to work his ass off to win one game. Now Booker, he'd let win. He wasn't completely sure that had escaped Damon's notice either.

He slid the card aside. Tomorrow. Definitely.

He thought, briefly, about going cruising. But if ever, tonight might be the night that Damon put someone on surveillance. He'd made contact, and from here on he had to assume they were watching him. He could lose them, but dodging out from under a tail while driving a fuckin' Corolla wasn't suspicious or anything, right?

Nope, he was stuck at home tonight unless he wanted to pick up a girl, which he didn't. Coffee would also be a bad, bad idea with the way his nerves were strung tight, but he brewed some anyway, for something to do. The coffee pot was old, and there was a hint of burned taste to it. In a way, that was good, the nasty pucker of his mouth pulling him down off the high.

He stood at his small kitchen window, staring out at the street, sipping his bad coffee. A few cars went by, a few people on foot. One guy was weaving like he was drunk or stoned. He yelled at a passing car, shaking his fist, but the car went on, oblivious. Small town Saturday night.

By the time the coffee was gone, he'd relaxed enough to shower, put on sweatpants, and go to bed. He planned to rub one out when he got under the sheets— figured it would be easy, even if the hot water had blunted his tight-strung restlessness— but somehow he couldn't pick a favorite fantasy. He thought about guys and faces, mouths, hands, mouths sipping beer, hands holding darts. Moments from that evening kept intruding, his mind wandering into speculation about how many knives Damon Kerr had under his shirt; wondering whether Booker had been trying his hardest to win, or waiting to see if Nick would throw the game; trying to remember whether Brian Kerr's eyes were actually pale blue or gray. He reran bits of the conversations, wondering if some line he'd used had been out of character, or if some minor comment from Roy was worth remembering. It was unsettling and not sexy.

Eventually he did get himself off, without thinking about anything much, just friction and pressure in the right places. It took the edge off enough for him to sleep in this apartment that still didn't feel like home.

Chapter 5

Three weeks later, the apartment was all too familiar. As he closed his door, key out, ready to lock up and head to work, the handle grated stiffly through half a turn, then came off in his hand.

"Son of a bitch!" He kicked the door, barely holding back enough not to break it. To break it *more*. He had a theory, from the marks on the linoleum, that some past tenant had used the handle to tie up a large dog. It jammed half the time, rattled all the time, and had just come off in his motherfucking hand! For housing an undercover cop, choosing a place that barely locked was either negligence, or some kind of camouflage genius. He was leaning toward it being a fuckup, though.

He pulled out his phone and texted, *~Down in 5. door is busted.*

Of all the fucking wrong moments! For the first time, Roy was waiting outside for him.

Nick had been expecting his usual routine that morning— dress, eat a bagel, drink some coffee, and drive to the warehouse, same as every day since he'd started working for Marston. Instead, his phone on the counter had buzzed with an unexpected text from Roy.

~Picking you up. Be downstairs in 15 min

He'd texted back, *~???*

~Change of plans

Problem? Opportunity? Even though he was deeply curious, he'd taken the hint and hadn't asked again. He'd made sure Nick Green was a do-as-you're-told-and-ask-no-questions kind of guy, a guy who'd seem safe to expose to illegal shit. Nick Green wouldn't ask.

He'd pushed away an instinctive moment of panic. *They've made me!* That was dumb. If they had, they wouldn't have announced they were coming to get him in fifteen. They'd have grabbed him without warning. He drove deliveries from the big open warehouse to a small private one every day. They had plenty of chances to take him out if they wanted to.

So this might finally be something more interesting than loading and unloading trucks, and driving that small loop day after day. He texted Olson. *~Roy is picking me up for something new*

~Second GPS? Transmitter?

He thought about it. His phone was monitored 24/7 and it had GPS. That wasn't suspicious since most did, these days. He also had a panic button rigged to it, so he could call in the cavalry if need be. He'd been given a limited amount of high-tech gear, including a personal GPS beacon in a pair of boots, and a bigger recorder that would also transmit. Both might add a bit of safety, but they could be found if he got checked for bugs. *~Nope. Just watch the phone.*

~We'll cover you.

He'd erased the conversation and the number, and hurried through his caffeine. After some thought, he added his wristband camera, a leather studded cuff with a lens hidden among the metal grommets. It had no zoom or video, but he really hoped it would also be tough to recognize. He'd practiced aiming at stuff, although this was the first time he'd taken it out for real. At best, he'd get some useful new faces or locations recorded. At worst, he'd take pictures of the guys who were about to kill him.

Think positive, you wuss. They're not about to kill you.

He'd tugged the cuff into position, put his phone in his pocket, pulled on his Twins cap, and grabbed his keys...

And then the goddamn doorknob fell off.

Duct tape. It saved the astronauts in space, right? He dug it out of a drawer, stuck a big glob on the back of the handle, and forced it into the hole. It held the knob in place, didn't droop, much. He pulled the door shut behind him with his fingers under the gap at the bottom, and used a good bit more duct tape to hold it shut, down by the floor. Hopefully it would look like added paranoia, not necessity. He stuffed the roll in his jacket pocket and ran down the stairs.

Roy was parked at the curb in the same white, 270-horsepower GMC truck that Damon had assigned Nick on his first day. The engine was running. Nick went round and swung up beside him. It might've been natural enough to ask questions, but he kept his mouth shut. Luckily, Roy was the kind to fill a silence with his own voice.

"We're headed to the airport. Direct pickup this time. You'll help me load and unload, and whatever it is, don't jostle it. Some of this shit's fragile, and it's all worth money."

Nick glanced over, raised an eyebrow, said nothing.

After a few miles, Roy said, "Wherever we are, you stay with the truck. No wandering around. No questions."

"Didn't ask any," Nick muttered.

"True." Roy glanced at him. "You're not half-bad, for an arrogant bastard who thinks he can play pool."

Nick allowed himself a laugh.

"For real. You would not believe some of the morons we've had working for us. There was this one guy..."

Nick leaned back in his seat, made sure his hands weren't covering the recorder in his jeans, and let Roy talk. It sounded like the same complaining about bad drivers and ham-handed forklift operators that any warehouse manager might come up with, but maybe there'd be a useful name or reference.

When they hit 35-W the traffic got heavier, and Roy ran out of stories. They navigated the approach to the airport in silence and ended up in cargo pickup. The box that was brought out to them was medium sized, relative to what Nick had been handling for the last couple of weeks— maybe three by four feet and fifty pounds. Between him and Roy, they rolled the wooden crate carefully up the ramp, eased it off the dolly, and strapped it in securely. Roy added an extra layer of padding and yet another set of straps, tugging them a couple of times before nodding with satisfaction.

Nick paused, eyeing the arrangement. He'd found out that Roy would often explain stuff if Nick stared at something with disgust, like he thought it was done wrong.

Sure enough as they got into the cab, Roy said, "You might think that's overkill, but it ain't. This one time, a driver used an old rope to hold a crate in the back. He had to put on the brakes fast, and the tie gave way. The crate hit the wall and busted open. Ten thousand dollars of Chinese lacquer cabinet turned to kindling, like that." He slapped the wheel. "I don't take chances."

Nick nodded, didn't ask if that was what they were hauling this time. He'd bet it wasn't.

After a while, he could tell they weren't going to the small warehouse, which was the furthest into the operation he'd ever been. The more valuable ten percent of Marston's goods went there, but they'd turned too far north for that to be their destination. He tamped down his excitement as he realized they were probably heading for the Marston estate itself.

Half an hour later, they reached the estate driveway and turned off the road. Nick had studied a bunch of pictures of the place, both aerial and from drive-bys. None had done it justice.

The outer perimeter was a high brick wall, topped by an electrified wire. The gates were automatic, and double, with a keypad at the outer one, and an intercom, camera, and a retinal scanner between the two gates. Roy coded in the first one, stopped inside, identified himself and Nick, and faced out the side window to be scanned. He turned to Nick. "You gotta get out and stare into the lens. They need your eyeball print."

Nick shrugged, swung down out of the cab, and walked around the truck, trying to assess the defenses without looking curious. No machine gun turrets, anyway. He wasn't completely ruling out landmines, though.

The scanner was on a pole, and as he approached it, the camera part lowered and turned away from Roy's window to peer right at him. It was both cool and creepy. He walked up like he didn't care and looked into the lens. After a moment the red light on top went green. The voice over the intercom said, "He's recorded. Opening the gate."

Nick climbed back into his seat, and they drove through and onto the estate. The road wound through patchy forest for another quarter mile before turning into a circular drive at the house. Aerial pictures had shown a large mansion with a complex roof structure and three outbuildings surrounding a pool. From the drive, the main house resolved into something out of a BBC drama, with white marble stairs and columns, high graystone walls, and third-floor dormers.

Nick whistled slowly in appreciation.

Roy said, "Quit that," with surprising tension. He steered the van off the main drive and toward the side of the house. The other buildings came into view as they rounded the back corner. One looked like a guest house. The other two were more like garages or storage buildings, windowless brick blocks each about fifty feet long. Roy stopped down by the farther of the two, and maneuvered the truck around so he could back up toward the wider door. "Come on. Time to unload."

As they opened the back of the truck, the building door rolled up and a man stood there in the shadows. Nick recognized Marston immediately. He tried to ignore the way his pulse sped up as he turned to get the ramp into place. Roy approached Marston, ducked his head nervously in what was almost a bow, and went into the building past him. Marston didn't move, his gaze fixed eagerly on the interior of the truck as Roy came back out with a pallet jack.

It was kind of overkill— they could easily have carried the damned crate— but Nick helped Roy get it perfectly centered on the forks and kept a steadying hand on the side as it bumped slightly over the top of the ramp. Roy eased it down to the pavement as if the crate contained glass, then turned to Nick. "Close up the back, and stay with the truck."

Nick nodded and leaned against the ramp. For the first time, Marston looked away from the crate to run his gaze over Nick. It was a long, slow, cool appraisal. In a bar, it might have been followed up with some kind of challenge, but Marston blinked once, curled his lip, and then looked away, dismissing Nick.

Nick took a firm hold on his temper. *You want him to disregard you. You want to be underestimated.* He slouched a little more, turning away to raise and stow the ramp and roll down the door. When he turned back, the building door was shutting behind the other two men. He shrugged, in case anyone was watching, and hitched his hip on the bumper. It was a nice day. No one would wonder why he didn't sit inside the truck.

From where he was, he could see past the building to the pool. The June sun was warm, not hot, making this one of Minnesota's better days— something to enjoy before July's muggy heat and mosquitoes hit— but the woman lounging there sat in the deep shade under an awning. She raised a hand to her light-blond hair, her pose as studied as a magazine model's. He couldn't make out her face. Odds were it was Lori Marston.

He took a couple of pictures, rubbing his chin and hoping that the wristband lens was aimed right. To the woman's left, a smooth lawn studded with flowerbeds rolled a hundred yards toward what looked like a golf green, and then the surrounding woods. Behind her the guest house was big enough to have several bedrooms. An arched brick breezeway connected it to the main house.

"That's my house."

"Huh?" He jolted and turned, leaping to his feet. Then he felt embarrassed by the surge of adrenaline, because it was Brian Kerr who stood a few feet away, blinking at him in the sun.

"I live there." Brian pointed at the guest house.

"Oh. That's nice."

Brian nodded. For a long, awkward minute, neither of them spoke. Nick glanced Brian over. He looked younger than the twenty-one Nick knew him to be, maybe because he was so fair, his skin so pale and smooth. He was heavy-set and not really attractive, but there was a cool softness about him that seemed oddly remote, almost restful. If the guy'd been the practical-joking kind, Nick thought he could have pretended to be a ghost very convincingly. He seemed out of place in the bright daylight, even dressed in ordinary jeans and a blue T-shirt, with scuffed Converse sneakers in rainbow colors.

Nick was momentarily distracted by those sneakers. They were pretty damned gay. He couldn't imagine the conversation where Damon Kerr was persuaded to buy something like that for his brother, but he'd have liked to hear it. Out of habit, his gaze slid back up, noting that Brian had a helluva nice package in those jeans… He flushed, suddenly aware both that he'd dropped his guard and that he'd been cruising someone off-limits.

Brian tilted his head, almost like he'd noticed. "I won't tell."

"Won't tell what?" Nick glanced around. He was following orders, hanging out here.

Brian frowned, and for an instant he looked different, older. Then the door of the building opened, and his forehead smoothed out as he smiled his wide, happy grin. "Mr. Marston! Hi!"

Marston scowled at him, while gesturing Roy impatiently toward the truck. "What are you doing here, Brian?"

"Lori was sunning. I don't sun. I walk. Or I burn."

Marston sighed. "All right. Just don't get too much sun walking around, either. You should wear a hat. And remember this area's off limits. You know that."

Brian dropped his eyes to his feet and whispered, "Sorry, Mr. Marston."

Nick was caught by a sudden impulse to cheer the guy up. He took off his ball cap, and held it out. "Here, you can wear that. Keep your nose from being sunburned."

Brian glanced up, clearly surprised.

His eyes are a pale, pale blue.

Then Brian took the cap and put it on, tugging it down until his face was deeply shaded.

Marston glanced at Nick, then looked back at Brian. "Say thank you?"

Brian parroted, "Thank you."

"You're welcome."

"Come on," Roy called, hanging out the cab door to look back at Nick. "Get your ass in gear, Nok."

"Nok Nick," Brian said, with a sweet smile. "Ass in gear."

Nick laughed. "Right. See you 'round."

As they pulled away down the narrow track leading to the drive, Nick glanced into his side mirror. On its curved surface, Brian looked small and indistinct, the ball cap hiding his light hair. He stood alone, gazing after them. Marston had already turned to go inside.

"No questions," Roy said.

Nick turned his gaze firmly out the front, as if he had no other concerns. After they swung out onto the wide main drive and headed away from the house, Roy muttered under his breath, "Not that I know anything about the freaky shit Mr. Marston is into anyway."

Nick pretended not to have heard, but *freaky shit* went onto his list of Marston topics to investigate. They reached the gate and had to retina-scan again and open the truck for the boom camera to check the back, before driving out. Nick allowed himself a grunt of, "Thorough," as they turned out onto the road.

"Ain't no one gonna steal from Mr. Marston," Roy agreed. "And you didn't even meet the dogs."

That comment Nick definitely filed away to remember.

****

Brian watched the truck pull away, down the side and around to the drive. He'd felt Marston looking at him curiously, as if planning to say something else, but then the lure of the new thing he had in the experiment building pulled him back inside. Having that dark gaze move off him made Brian slump in relief.

He hoped whatever it was would keep Marston occupied for a long time. He hoped it was an *it* and not a him or her. Most of the magic stuff Marston played with was old, strange, and inert. But twice it had been a woman. He hadn't heard what had happened to either one. He'd never been asked to Find them, and he didn't want to know.

The ball cap on his head nagged him a little. It buzzed with the essence of Nick. It was clearly something he'd had for a while, long enough it had decided it belonged to him. Usually that didn't bother Brian. He had to open his Finder sense and Look at something to feel that connection and... *Oh, he was open.* He closed his outer eyes, and then closed down the inner one. *There. Better.*

The hat was just a hat, shading his eyes from the sun. It was odd how Nick made him screw up the habits of a lifetime. Well, of the last ten years, anyway. Or maybe it was his own need to get away that had him messed up lately. He'd stayed here, lived as Bry, so easily, so lazily. He'd almost forgotten he was more, until the approach of his twenty-first birthday had woken him up, like a hibernating bear... He looked down at himself and changed that to *hibernating groundhog.*

Either way, Nick had gotten tangled in his waking up. It wasn't Nick's fault, but it felt dangerous to think about him. Of course, running away would be dangerous, period. *Get out, now. Get out.* Just considering it made him antsy. Brian almost laughed at the thought that if he ran, at least Marston wouldn't be able to ask him to Find himself.

From the poolside, Lori called, "Hey, Bry? Would you bring me a pop? I'm too lazy to get up with this baby weighing me down."

She was wearing a bikini. She barely showed yet— less than a grapefruit. But he sighed and took his busted bubble of plans with him into the big house to fetch her a Coke.

When he brought it out, he sat down on the concrete in the shade, a few feet from her recliner. He'd always liked to sit on the floor. It was safe and solid and no one pulled it out from under him or tipped him over. People were less likely to talk to him or call on him for an answer when he was down there. He could watch and listen, and think.

He watched Lori as she drank, then set the can down, smoothed more lotion on her legs, and moved her lounger into the sun. She arched her back, pushing her chest out and shaking her silver-blond hair back off her face. It was a sexy move, and he assumed that Mr. Marston had come back out of the building. Lori's prime directive was hanging onto her rich husband and the good life that went with him.

He wondered if she knew Stan was dead. He thought so, which was a bad sign for how far she was willing to go to keep them all on easy street. It'd been a long time since he knew where her limits were. Sometimes he wondered if he really knew Lori at all.

Once, they'd been as close as two people could get, born within minutes of each other, growing up almost joined at the hip. Brian hadn't even talked until he was four, not because he was stupid, but because he and Lori had their own sign language, and if he needed to talk to anyone else, Lori would do it. He'd been shy, not dumb. Once upon a time, Lori had known that.

Then they'd started school, and she'd done well and he still couldn't read a three-letter word after a year of trying. He was put into the too-stupid-to-learn class the next year, and without Lori as a buffer, he was lost indeed. It had never been the same after that.

He remembered how hard she'd tried to fit in the next year. They hadn't been the only kids in school with secondhand clothes, but Lori'd hated it. She'd sat up late with Damon, planning out how to look like she belonged with the rich kids, their heads together as they whispered about shoes and book bags and how to score the good stuff. He hadn't seen the point, himself. He tried to help, though, by being extra nice to the kids she wanted to impress. That had been a total failure, and by the end of the year he could tell she was not only embarrassed by him, but forgetting who he actually was.

"Hey, Lor?"

"Yeah?" She leaned her head back and closed her eyes.

"D'you remember Mrs. Harrison?"

"Who?"

He'd wanted her to remember on her own, but it mattered too much. "First grade. I wanted her to be our mom. Remember?"

She shook her head without looking at him. "God, no. Grade school sucked. Middle school too. High school wasn't bad, though." Her tone turned satisfied. "I had high school *figured out*."

She had, too. How to talk like she came from money. Which kids to scorn, which to flatter, who to suck up to, who had actual influence, or actual bank. Which teachers would give her a pass for being a poor child whose mom had died. Which teacher would give her an A for letting him get a hand up her skirt. Lori had moved through high school like a shark through smooth waters. He'd listened to her schemes, and pretended not to understand. She'd been more Damon's sister than his by then.

She turned idly toward him. "What made you think of Old Lady Harrison now?"

"Dunno." He looked away, avoiding her gaze. "I thought you didn't remember her."

"I don't really. I remember you had a little-kid crush on her."

"She was nice."

"It was *first grade*, Bry."

He shrugged. Mrs. Harrison had been the only person, other than Lori herself back then, who took the time to actually *see* him. She'd sat him down in the reading area, on the little chair, and worked through recess after recess with him, patient as could be. After a while, she'd said he had some problem, and she was going to find out what to do to help him get around it.

That was exactly what she'd said. *Get around it*. Like it wasn't part of his stupid self. Like he could be smart and find another route. But then she left, and the new teacher was young, and she couldn't control the class. He went back to sitting in his corner and not making trouble and flunking every subject.

He wanted to say all that to Lori, but she was Mr. Marston's now, and Brian was very, very careful to stay Bry around Mr. Marston. "She thought I could be smart."

56

"Oh, Bry. You're not stupid." Lori got up and came over to him, lowering herself carefully to sit beside him. He leaned on her shoulder and she patted his head. "You have dyslexia, you know. We talked about it. It's not your fault. That damned school never did anything for you, but you have a job now, huh? A really nice place to live, and Vern likes you."

Mr. Marston is fascinated by me and uses me to hurt people, and it gives me the creeps. He didn't say that either. He'd never been sure how much Lori knew about Mr. Marston's business. He kind of hoped it was less than he did. "Yeah. It's a nice house."

"There. You see?" She patted him again. *Pat, pat.* "And soon you'll have a little niece or nephew. And then no one can take this house away from us ever again."

"The baby's more important than the house." He eased back enough to see how she reacted.

Lori curved her hand over her barely rounded stomach. "Yes. But I like the house, and I want it *for* the baby. I'll take care of my child like he deserves. This kid's never going to try to sleep in a room with a dozen strangers, in some stinking shelter. He's never going to eat cereal for dinner, or wear secondhand shoes. You remember that?"

Brian nodded, because he did remember the times in Goodwill, with Damon counting out a handful of coins he'd scammed, while they picked through the shoes for a pair that might fit.

"My kid's going to wear new Nikes, and laugh at the fee to go on every school field trip, *and* he'll bring a fancy, packed lunch. He'll have all this." She waved at the pool and the woods. "And maybe even more."

"What more?" He didn't like that calculating tone in her voice.

She looked at him, her blue eyes bright, flushed and pretty. She'd always been pretty. "Vern's richer than he told me. Even richer than all this. And we're going to get our share."

He frowned. Even if that was true, and he could believe that Mr. Marston didn't tell Lori everything about his business, still, how much more could anybody need? The house was a mansion, the car she used was a limo. Lori had more clothes than she could wear, and diamonds on both hands. A cool breeze blew down his back and he shivered. "Don't make Mr. Marston mad, Lor."

She smiled at him. "I can handle Vern."

No, you can't. She wouldn't thank him for saying so, though. Or listen.

She leaned over and kissed his head, gave his shoulders a squeeze. "Who'd have thought it, huh? Remember when we were in fifth grade? I used to steal kids' lunch money and buy us food on the way home from school, because half the time Mom forgot to shop. Remember the rat hole we were living in? And now look." She swept her gaze over the lush, landscaped garden. "I told you back then I'd get us out someday. Me and Damon, we said we'd make it. And here we are, and it'll get even better."

"Here we are," Brian repeated, because what else could he say? "This is good. This is plenty enough."

"Almost. I want to fix it so Damon never has to work again. Remember, how I promised when we were kids that I'd take care of him someday, like he did for us all those years? I'm almost there."

"I don't think Damon minds working. Not now."

"I promised. And he deserves it."

He remembered the first time, when they were eight. She'd said, *"Damon takes care of us, but no one takes care of Damon. So I'm gonna do that."*

He'd said eagerly, "Me too!" Because it was true. Mom sure didn't. Damon was fourteen, and he was the one they counted on for everything. He'd added, "I can give him backrubs, like I do for Mom. I can learn to cook better. If there's food."

Lori had given him a look tinged with pity. "That's nice, Bry. But someday I'm gonna make a bunch of money, or maybe marry a rich guy, and then we'll have it made forever. Damon can go to college like he wants to, and just have fun. I know I'll find a way to make us all rich one day."

Even at eight, something about that had made him shiver.

He said, "You should ask Damon what he thinks."

She hugged him again, then stood slowly. "Don't you worry, Bry. Trust me. I'll take care of everything."

She went into the house, closing the door behind her. Brian stayed where he was. He pulled his knees up to his chest and wrapped his arms around them. The sun on the water danced and sparkled, bright as gold. Traffic was a distant sound, in the world beyond the walls and the wire.

Chapter 6

Nick pushed open the door of the bar Friday night and glanced around, noting who was present and who wasn't. Damon and Booker were drinking whiskey and playing pool. Judging by the easy shots they were missing, those weren't their first drinks. Roy sat at a table with a couple of guys Nick had seen around the main warehouse but didn't know well. Brian was tucked in against the wall behind the same table, nursing a beer.

Most of the crowd were watching a baseball game on the big TV. Roy and his friends, for once, cheered along with the locals when the Twins scored a run. Nick stopped at the bar to collect a beer for himself, then made his way through the tables. He'd planned to sit alone and wait for Roy to call him over. Roy liked him enough to make that a pretty sure bet, and it looked less suspicious. But Brian shot him an odd look of appeal, a quick upward glance, immediately veiled behind lowered eyelids. Nick covered the extra ten feet and picked up a chair from the table next to Brian's, swinging it around.

Confidence is everything. He dropped down, tossed off a long swallow of beer, and said, "Hey, Roy."

"Hey, Nok. You wanna bet on the game?"

"Nope. I'm tapped out."

"You're a pussy."

"Well, if you're enough of a moron to bet on the Blue Jays, then maybe…"

They tossed insults back and forth for a bit. The Twins gave up a run. Got it back. Damon and Booker joined them, and the waitress brought another round. Nick drank his beer slowly, and listened more than he spoke. It was all bullshit though, about baseball and the weather and if fast food chains really put pink slime in their burgers. Nothing useful.

Damon and Booker made their way up to the bar and brought back fresh drinks and three women. Nick wasn't sure if the girls were pros, or just dressed that way. The crowd got drunker. Two of the women sat on Damon's left and right, hands on his thighs, while the third lounged in Booker's lap, sliding her fingers around under his shirt. After a while, Booker said, "I'm outta here." He got to his feet unsteadily, slung his arm across the woman's shoulders, and turned toward the door. The way the woman balanced his lurching weight suggested she was very familiar with handling drunks. Probably a pro.

Damon ran his hand through the hair of the woman on his right, closing his fingers and tugging. From the wince on her face, he was being rougher than she liked. Nick tensed, battling the instinct to start something if Damon didn't ease up. He clenched his teeth, and found Damon watching him, his gaze cool and expressionless. Damon pulled the girl around a bit farther, then opened his hand and let her go, just as Nick was thinking he'd have to comment to stay in character. Nok Nick didn't let anyone rough up a girl.

The woman pouted extravagantly. "You messed my hair."

"Sorry, baby." Damon handed her a folded bill. "Go tidy up and get yourself a drink." He immediately put his arm around the other girl.

As the Twins racked up two runs in the seventh, drawing cheers from the bar crowd, one of the new guys leaned forward, glanced around, and murmured, "Hey, d'you hear what they're saying about Stan?"

Nick could feel everyone at the table tense up. There was even a little gasp of breath from Brian's direction, and Nick's heart sank. Clearly Brian wasn't completely innocent and ignorant. Damon rocked back in his chair, and his voice was lazy on top, but cold underneath. "No, Coop, what do they say?"

The new guy, Coop, shrugged and dropped his gaze. "Don't matter."

As a cheer erupted for another Twins' homer, Damon dropped the front legs of his chair to the floor with a thump and reached out to grab Coop's shirt front, pulling him a few inches closer. "Tell us."

"Well, um, he was shot, right? Word is, he was trying to run from Mr. Marston and didn't make it." Coop glanced into Damon's eyes, then looked down. "I heard that Mr. Marston has his ways, you know, if you try to get away from him."

"Ways?" Damon didn't let go of the guy's shirt, but his grip must have eased because Coop was able to lean back slightly.

"Yeah." Coop managed an unconvincing smile. "It's crazy talk. Like, Mr. Marston has a pet werewolf, and if you try to run it'll track you down. Smell you out." He gave an exaggerated sniff.

"Werewolf." Roy laughed loudly. "Right. Don't bullshit me."

The other guy at the table leaned forward, with drunken bravado. "It's true! I heard it too. He has this, this monster that he keeps locked on his estate, and if you try to run away, he'll set it loose. It tracks you and finds you, no matter where you go. Sniffs you out." He snorted loudly. "Digs its claws into your face." He raised a clawed hand.

"Maybe not a werewolf," Coop said. "But something. Weird. Like, magic. An ugly, vicious magical thing that you can never escape. You sign on with Marston, and his demon makes sure he owns you."

Damon was clearly about to speak when Brian beat him to it. "I want to go home." Brian's voice was loud, although his attention was fixed on the pop can in his hands.

Roy grinned sloppily. "Don't worry, Bry. Damon won't let Marston's demon get you."

Damon smacked Roy hard enough to knock his chair back. "Shut the fuck up. Bry, you have to wait. We're busy, and anyway, no one could pass a breath test."

"I want to go." Brian repeated, flat and hard. "Now!"

"These guys are idiots. Watch the ball game."

"Yeah," Coop said. "Sorry, Bry. We won't freak you out any more. Who cares what kind of ugly were-dog Marston has, right? You're his brother-in-law. He ain't never gonna sic it on you."

Brian shoved his chair back and stood.

Damon leaned past the girl beside him to grab Brian's belt loop. "Whoa, whoa. Stop, right now!"

"Damon!"

61

The brothers' eyes met and something unspoken passed between them. Into the momentary lull, Nick said, "I only had two beers in two hours. I can drive him."

They both turned to stare at him, Brian startled and wide-eyed, Damon with a narrowed consideration.

Brian suddenly smiled. "Okay. Yeah. That'd be good, right, Damon?"

Damon shook his head slowly, rubbing at his lips with one hand. "No, Bry, you don't go off with strangers."

"He's not a stranger. He's Nok Nick."

"He's not in the security system."

Roy said, "But yeah. He was there yesht... yesterday. No, couple days. He's in it."

Damon gave him a cold look. "Then you can go along, make sure everything goes okay."

"Aw, Damon. Come on, I'm halfway through my drink. Bry doesn't need the both of us."

Brian said, "I don't need babysitters."

Damon reached over and took the glass out of Roy's hand. "I'll take care of this for you." He put it to his lips and tossed off the remaining half. "Now go. In fact, use your truck, not Nick's."

Brian frowned. "Nick's okay. I can go with Nick."

"Don't argue, bro." Damon paused to pull the girl beside him into a kiss, then pushed her away. "You can hang out here, or go home with Nick and Roy. Make up your mind."

Brian stared at the woman, who winked at him and licked her lips. Brian flushed. "Nick and Roy."

"Right." Damon pointed at Nick. "You drive. No speeding. If you get busted, the cops will be the least of your worries."

"Got it."

"Roy, you make sure Bry gets home, then bring both your asses back here."

"Aw, fuck you." But he was getting up obediently.

"Give Nick your keys."

Roy dug in his pocket, and held them out. "You wreck it and I'll cut your balls off."

Nick said, "You do that." He tossed the keys in his hand, his mind racing through the possibilities. Not as good with Roy along, even if he was drunk and careless tonight. "So where is the wonder Roymobile?"

Brian laughed. "He has a truck. No wonder."

Roy turned and headed for the door, and Brian followed him, leaving Nick to bring up the rear. The night outside the bar was warm and breezy enough to keep the bugs down. Roy pointed out his pickup, and when Nick popped the locks, he crawled in the back of the extended cab and stretched out on the bench seat. "I'm gonna catch some Zs. Lemme know when we get to the gates."

Nick and Brian climbed into the front, and Nick pulled out of the lot. For the first few minutes, no one spoke. Then there was a loud snort from the back seat, followed by a snore. Brian laughed and looked back over his shoulder. Roy snored again. Nick flicked his gaze to the rearview. Roy's mouth hung open, and if he was faking that little thread of drool, then he deserved an Oscar.

"He's sleeping," Brian whispered.

"Yeah."

"Good."

Nick wasn't sure why it was good, but he nodded.

Brian went on in a low voice, "Thank you for driving me."

"You're welcome."

"You gave me a hat too. That was kind."

Nick shifted uncomfortably in his seat. *Kind* wasn't what he should be aiming for on this assignment. "It was just an old hat."

"I guess."

Out of the corner of his eye, he could see Brian studying him, eyeing him up and down as if looking for something. Finally he grumbled, "Quit staring at me."

"Sorry. You're not like them."

"Like who?"

"Any of them." In the dark cab, that barely detectable voice sounded almost normal. Until Brian added, "You taste good."

"I *what?*" He barely remembered to keep it quiet. He couldn't help a quick glance at Brian's lap, and then up to his mouth.

Brian actually chuckled. "Not like that. But I won't tell."

"You can tell any fucking body any fucking thing you like," Nick muttered.

"You're clean. Sharp, maybe, and some hard bits, but none of you is dirty or nasty."

Nick wondered what Brian's psych diagnosis was. He'd figured the guy was just slow, but that comment was distinctly weird. "You haven't seen me after a couple days on the road. Dirty and nasty's about right."

Brian shook his head. "That washes off." Roy's snores from the back paused, and Brian turned to check on him. A moment later the sound started up again, though, and Brian turned back to Nick. "Roy would steal your last dime. Damon would cut you to the bone, and not care."

Nick figured that was about right. "What about you?"

Brian gave a bitter little chuckle. "Me? You heard them. I'm a werewolf."

The tone set up an odd ache in Nick's chest. Damon really shouldn't drag his brother around with him. The bar crowd was clearly not good for him. "Come on, Brian, they didn't mean you. Anyway, there's no such thing as werewolves, right? You know that? They're just make-believe."

"Are you sure?" Brian's eyes glittered in the passing streetlights.

"Of course I'm sure."

"Marston has some weird stuff in his experiment place. You never know."

"His experiment place?" Nick felt a twinge of guilt asking questions of Brian, but it was too good an opportunity to miss. Not that he expected Brian to know anything important, but every detail helped.

"You saw it. You brought the box."

"You mean where we dropped off the crate the other day? That concrete building?"

"Yeah."

Nick waited, but Brian didn't add anything more. Finally he asked, "Why do you call it that?"

"That's what it is."

Nick checked Roy again in the mirror, then lowered his voice still more. "What kind of experiments?"

Brian leaned toward him, slowly, until his shoulder touched Nick's and his breath came warm against Nick's cheek. For a moment he just stayed there. Nick was suddenly aware that it had been far too long since a man had breathed in his ear with real intentions, and that he shouldn't be thinking about that stuff with this child-man leaning into him.

Brian whispered in his ear, "Magic experiments."

The disappointment made him frown. "Okay."

Brian glanced back at Roy, and repeated, "Really. Magic. He likes magic."

"Magic can be fun."

"Not this. Not his kind. You should stay far away from him."

"I will."

Brian gripped Nick's arm suddenly, his fingers strong and urgent around Nick's wrist. "Don't laugh. You shouldn't be here. You don't belong here. Damon does. Booker, Roy, Cory, Joe, Coop. They belong. And me, I guess." He let go of Nick and slumped in his seat. "And me. Not you."

"Why not?"

Brian was silent for a long time. They were getting close to the estate, and Nick slowed as much as he dared. Roy snored on in the backseat. Nick had pretty much decided Brian wasn't going to answer him when Brian's hand landed on his thigh. "A lot of reasons." Brian's low voice had a soft note. "Mostly because they'll pull you down. Right now you haven't hurt and killed people for no reason. Stick with Damon long enough and you will."

"He's your brother."

"Doesn't mean I don't know what he is."

Nick turned to stare at Brian, unable to make words and tone and man fit together. Then Brian said loudly, "Turn in here."

Roy woke with a snort and sat up. "Don't miss the fucking driveway."

Brian said, "Home. Home, home, home." He pointed. "Turn here, Nick Nak."

"Ah, hell," Nick grumbled, steering for the gate. "Don't give me another nickname."

"Nick Nak." Brian grinned at him, blank and guileless in the light from the floods above the gate. "I like it. I like you. Nick Nak."

"Pull up more," Roy muttered. "Punch in the damn code. Four shix one sheven. An' eyeball the camera."

Nick followed directions. The outer gate swung open and let them in. Nick let the camera ID him, but the guy on the other end of the speaker made Roy sit up and give him the okay before opening the inner gate to let them through. As the gate shut behind them, dark shapes rose from the grass across the lane, and two pairs of eyes glowed in the headlights. For a stupid second, Nick thought, *werewolves*.

Roy said, "Damn dogs'r out. Pull right up to the house before you shtop."

Dogs. Of course. "Got it," Nick agreed.

The drive wound through the trees, a row of lights creating a bright path through the darkness. Nick couldn't see the dogs, and wondered if they were following or had stayed by the fence. Roy was slumped low in his seat again but not snoring, and Nick thought he was probably awake.

Nick pulled up right in front of the house. "Is this good, Brian? Or should I pull farther around?"

"This is okay." Brian unbuckled his belt, and met Nick's eyes. "You should think about what I said."

Nick wasn't sure which part he meant— *werewolves? Marston's magic? Damon pulling him down?*— but said, "Sure. I'll do that," to placate him.

Brian shook his head sadly. "You won't."

Nick blinked, unable to respond. It was so frustrating. There was this odd connection between Brian and him, moments when Nick thought he'd really like to get to know this guy better. And then he'd be reminded of Brian's limitations, and his weirdnesses.

Really, he should be buddying up to the guy as much as possible to pump him for information, but Nick hesitated to do that too. For all Brian's time spent tagging along with Damon, there was something separate and untouched about him. Nick didn't want to mark that with betrayal, even if Brian might never know what he'd done.

Roy said loudly, "Quit talking stupid and get out, Bry. I wanna go back to the girls."

Nick could almost see shutters going down over Brian's eyes as he reached for the door handle. A sudden thought made Nick grab Brian's wrist. "Wait. Are the dogs out there?"

Brian froze for an instant, the skin of his arm warm in Nick's grasp. Then he turned his wrist to break the restraint, and opened the door. "Doesn't matter. They know me." He climbed out and stood at the bottom of the steps with his back to the car.

Roy said, "Delivered. Let's get back to the damn bar."

Nick put the car in gear, but didn't take his foot off the brake. "You think he's okay? He's not going inside."

"Not our problem. Anyway, he lives here and the dogs are for his protection, remember?"

"I guess." Reluctantly Nick let up on the pedal, and the truck rolled forward. As they circled and headed down the drive, Brian didn't move, either to climb the steps or to look back at them. Nothing moved in the shadows. No werewolves, no magicians, no guard dogs. As they pulled out of sight, Nick flicked a look in the mirror. Brian was still standing there at the foot of the stairs, his shoulders slumped, his blond hair lit white by the floodlights.

"So what's his problem?" Nick asked. Roy was nicely drunk and he had absolutely no hesitation about asking *him* questions. "Brian, I mean."

"Besides being dumb?"

Nick wanted to protest the word, but only managed to say, "Is he?"

"Hell, yeah." Roy leaned back into the corner of the seat and tipped his hat forward. "You're pretty stupid too if you can't tell."

"Yeah, well, I was—" He wasn't sure what. "Just wondering if Damon dropped him on his head as a baby, if that's why he drags him around everywhere."

"Damon says he was born that way. Stupid and slow. He basically raised Bry and his sister, 'cause their mom was a junkie."

"So is the sister, Lori, like, slow too?"

"Hell, no." Roy shifted in the back seat uncomfortably. "Sharp as a knife, that one. And she's Mrs. Marston to you, or else Damon and Marston will eat your guts for breakfast."

"Ew." He made a gagging sound to lighten things up. "That's disgusting. Eating guts."

Roy laughed. "Hell, you think tha's disgusting? There wash— was this one time…"

The story was long and drunkenly confusing, but ended with someone's head coming off with spurting blood. Nick laughed and topped it with an invention of his own. Any squeamishness he'd ever had'd been pretty much taken care of by life in foster care, followed by three years on the force. Roy's stomach was clearly cast-iron too, and they spent the ride back to the bar trying to gross each other out.

When they got back, Coop was gone, Damon had two girls hanging on him, and everyone was drunker. Roy dragged Nick up to the bar and ordered them each a beer. As they turned away with their bottles, Roy tripped over some local guy's feet and fell against him, grabbing the man's arm to keep from falling. The man shouldered Roy away roughly. "Keep your hands off me, you stinking faggot."

Nick steadied Roy and handed over his beer. "Hold this."

Then he turned and plowed a fist into the man's gut. The man grunted and swung back, slow enough to be easy to dodge. Nick landed an off-center punch. "Get him, Nok!" Roy slurred. The local guy's roundhouse blow skimmed Nick's neck as he ducked away, and he grabbed the man's arm, tugging him into a rapidly clearing space.

This was good. He could fight homophobia, and bond with his homies at the same time. It was all good. He landed another body blow. The man gasped, "You're all cocksuckers."

Nick shoved him contemptuously, hard enough to slam him back against the bar. The man roared and came after him. Nick thought about Brian, sitting in this bar, night after night, maybe gay, listening quietly. Thought about all the gay-bashing that went on, every foul word and story. As the man came

68

at him, he ducked sideways and landed a punch into that soft midsection so hard that the man doubled up and crumpled to the floor like a used tissue, coughing, vomiting his beer.

There. Got your ass beat by a faggot. It felt good, even if the guy would never know. The man's buddy glared at Nick, at Roy behind him, and Damon, suddenly standing a few feet away. The buddy reached down and hauled his friend up off the floor. "C'mon. Forget them." He maneuvered the stumbling, retching man toward the door.

Roy held out Nick's beer. "Thanks, man."

Nick took it, drank a long pull. "No sweat."

"Good work," Damon said. "Come on, Nick, have a seat. Enjoy the beer and the girls."

"Thanks." Nick followed them to the table in the back. He could hang out, drink, joke, and dodge having to go home with a girl. He'd done it often enough. And if he kind of wished he could have hung out with Brian instead, and tried to find out what made that guy tick, it was a fleeting thought. Not even worth considering, really.

****

Brian stood at the bottom of the front steps, listening to Nick and Roy pull away down the drive. He didn't look back or move until the sound of the truck faded. Then he turned aside to the path that led around the house toward the breezeway.

Mr. Marston was out of town, flown off somewhere to check on his other businesses. He did that pretty often, and sometimes Lori would ask Bry to come over for dinner, so she didn't have to eat alone. But it was well past dinnertime now— she was probably watching TV, or taking a bath. He wished he could go in and talk to her, for real. He needed someone to tell his confusion to, and his fears. Someone who might say it was okay to be two people in one body. Or not, because probably it wasn't.

He tried to pretend he was like an actor, or a spy. Like, Brian was who he was, and Bry was a part he played. But sometimes he *was* Bry without meaning to be, even alone in his room, talking to himself in stupid repeats and baby words. Plus there was no denying that he was a fuckup, and could be stupider than he ever realized. The worst lately was when Brian came out when it wasn't safe.

Like in the truck, talking to Nick. Bad, bad idea, with Roy in the back and Nick on the edge of being sucked into Damon's kind of trouble. If he'd been smart, he'd never have shown Nick anyone except Bry. Which made it hard to believe he was really in control of his mixed up self.

He'd asked once. His special ed class got a tour of the town library, and there was a librarian. She was old with white hair, and she seemed nice, like she loved the books. She'd acted like none of the questions his classmates asked were any different from what a regular person might want to know. And he figured she'd never see him again, most likely. So when the others had moved on, he'd lingered and asked, "Is there a word, like, for someone who has two people inside them? Like, a good guy and a bad guy, or a smart one and a dumb one? In one person?"

She'd looked at him kindly and said, "Well, if it's really two separate identities, two completely different people, we say 'multiple personality' or—" she'd said 'schizo-something,' which he much later found out was schizophrenic "—but it could be just a person who has a range of behaviors." She'd smiled at him. "Do you know someone like that?"

He'd wanted to tell, but then his teacher turned and did that loud-whisper-library-yelling thing. "Bry! Keep up with us, please."

So he'd smiled back and said, "No. Just wondered."

He'd dreamed of going back and finding her and getting more answers. But he hadn't paid enough attention to where the library was, and he had trouble getting anywhere when he couldn't read the street signs and the bus numbers. Lori would've probably helped, if he'd let her, but he didn't want to ask those kinds of questions in front of Lori.

So he'd just imagined, sometimes at night, that he sat down in that red fabric chair in front of her desk and asked her about finding out stuff, and how he could get smarter. In his dreams, she'd smiled that same way and said, *"Why yes, Brian, we can teach you to read all of this."* And she'd waved around the library at all the books. But when he opened his eyes, he was in that same tiny crowded apartment room they'd lived in, with Lori sharing the bed because it was cold. There was an inspirational poster of Lori's on the wall, and he only understood what it meant because she'd told him. That was his life. He was at least smart enough to know the difference.

Still, he sometimes wondered if he was schizo, and if so whether there was a cure. Even now, he still didn't know much more about it than the word, really. Randomly cruising YouTube, listening to stuff that looked like science in the hope of answers, wasn't useful. Damon's response to that word was a growl of *"Forget it."* Maybe Nick would know, but he was never going to say that word around Nick.

He paused on the front path as two dogs broke out of the trees and loped across the lawn toward him. There were four dogs who patrolled the grounds at night. They ran in pairs. He didn't know if they'd been trained that way, or just liked each other. The bigger pair, Witch and Brute, stayed over by the gate, and they were okay— they wouldn't bite him or anything— but he thought Witch didn't like him much. Of course, she didn't like many people.

This pair was Luger and Glock, and they did like him, almost as much as they liked each other. Sometimes he pretended they were gay dogs, and loved each other, and knew he was like them. Sometimes he worried that he was really messed up, and told himself they were simply dog-buddies, like Booker and Damon but with thick fur and fangs.

As they approached he dug in his pocket for the corn chips he'd stashed there. He held the broken pieces out in his palm. "Here, guys. Slim pickings tonight. They dumped a ton of salsa on the nachos."

The dogs slowed as they reached him, plumed tails wagging. They were some special breed, like dark, long-haired Shepherds. They had amber-brown eyes that glowed when the walkway lights hit them right. They licked the chip crumbs off his palm, and he giggled. Luger rose on his hind legs to sweep his tongue over Brian's face.

Brian pushed him away, laughing. "What? Did I get salsa on me? Or beans? You shouldn't eat too many beans. You'll get dog farts and the bad guys will hear you coming."

Then he remembered he was one of the bad guys. These dogs would die to protect him and Damon and Mr. Marston, and that was just wrong. He knelt and wrapped his arms around Glock, burying his face in the dog's thick ruff. "If you see real bad guys, worse than Mr. Marston, you run away, right? Don't get hurt?"

The dog rumbled a small sound in its throat, and leaned into him. They wouldn't run, though. If trouble ever came, they'd fight. Maybe it never would happen. Maybe Mr. Marston would go on forever, safe here on his estate.

Brian hugged the dogs and ruffled their fur, and turned his pocket inside out so they could lick the last crumbs off the lining. When every bit was gone, he stood and told them, "That's it, guys. Go to work." There were cameras around the place, and if whoever was in the security room saw the dogs spend too much time with him, they might get mad.

As he rounded the corner of the big house, Brian was surprised to see a light on in Mr. Marston's study. No one should be in there with him out of town. The blinds were shut, but the line of yellow around them shone steadily. Not just someone opening the door for a moment, then.

The breezeway had an eyeball camera too, and Brian waved at it as he let himself in. You were supposed to ignore the security team, but he sometimes liked not doing what he was supposed to. Instead of going to his own room, he turned and unlocked the door of the house. Maybe it was Lori who was still up. He headed down the hall, past the dark kitchen, to the door of Mr. Marston's study. Putting an ear to it, he listened, but heard nothing loud enough to carry through the wood.

He'd never opened this door without knocking first, but for some reason, tonight he reached out and turned the knob. It swung silently ajar.

Lori sat at the desk, a file folder in her lap. Brian huffed a little sigh of relief and she looked up, saw him and yelped. Then she slammed the folder shut. "Dammit, Brian!"

"I thought there was a burglar."

"Right. Who got past the dogs, and the cameras and the retina locks, and then came in here with the lights blazing."

"Sorry, Lori." It kind of rhymed, so he said it again. "Lori, sorry."

"Don't be a dork." But she looked less mad. She liked him better dumb than smart.

"Whatcha doing?"

"Looking up things. Family information." She put a hand on her stomach.

"For the baby?"

"Kind of."

"Mr. Marston might not like that." He felt uneasy, imagining the scene if Mr. Marston walked in on them here in his private space.

Lori tossed her head. "He's in San Diego. I talked to him an hour ago. Anyway, it's his baby and we have a right to stuff."

"What stuff?"

"Never mind." Lori stood, crumpled a sheet of paper into her pocket, and slid the file folder back into an open desk drawer, which she shut and locked. "All done, anyway. Did you have fun at the bar?"

He gave her a disbelieving look.

"Sorry. Was it okay, at least?"

He remembered the ride home, and Nick's quiet voice in the dark. "I guess."

"Damon's not back yet, is he?"

"No. There was a girl."

She laughed. "There's always a girl. Who gave you a ride?"

"Roy. And Nok Nick. Roy was drunk."

"Roy's always drunk, too."

He waited, worried that she might ask about Nick. But she just came and linked her arm through his. "Since you're up, you can come watch a movie with me, all right?"

Well it wasn't like he had anything better to do. "Which one? No horror."

"Okay. How about *21 Jump Street*?"

"Again? You like Channing lots."

"So? He's hot."

He was. Not that Brian would say so. "Popcorn?"

"Sure." She patted her stomach. "I'm eating for two."

The movie was simple, familiar, and he didn't have to talk. Sometimes, he could pretend it was like when they were small, and Lori was still the better twin. Before she changed. He ate popcorn and didn't let himself think about anything but the story.

Afterward, he went home to his room and undressed to his shorts and got into bed. He lay back, staring at his ceiling. It was almost one in the morning. The pool house was quiet and dark. Damon was still out, somewhere.

Brian fought the impulse to Find him. He could do it; it wouldn't take much. He'd open his Finding eye and Look for that familiar trace, make sure Damon was still alive and out there. If he didn't follow that trace for long, if he just sampled a hint of Damon's smoke and steel, he wouldn't suffer too much for it. A headache tomorrow would be the worst he'd feel. But there was no reason to do it at all. Damon was fine. He'd be home eventually. He always came home.

Brian slid a hand down himself from the softness of his belly over the fabric of his shorts. He could distract himself this way. It was a good time to jerk off, with Damon away, and no one to listen to him. With Nick now off-limits, he felt let down and a little sad, but he stroked himself through his shorts anyhow.

It wasn't the first time he'd crushed on someone and had to make himself walk away. From the time he was twelve, there'd been one after another of Damon's friends he'd watched and wanted, silently and from a distance. When he was fourteen Lonnie'd said, "Why's your brother hanging out with us so much, Damon? He's creepy. He's always watching me." Damon had smacked some manners into Bry without ever knowing it was more than stupidity, and he'd learned to be more careful.

So, really, this was just one more time, one more guy he'd have to wean himself off. With Lonnie and the others, he'd made a point of looking for bad stuff. Lonnie was short-tempered and mean to girls. He talked trash about teachers and cops and parents and everyone. Once Brian got past obsessing over the width of his shoulders and the smooth way he moved, there was plenty to dislike about Lonnie.

With Nick... he was kind of stuck. Yeah, Nick had a temper too. But Brian had never seen him smack down someone who hadn't needed it. He said *fuck* and *shit* a lot, but he never, ever said *faggot*. He dressed kind of sloppy, but he didn't smell bad or have greasy hair or shirts with sweat-stained pits like some guys at the bar. And he talked to Brian like they were equals, almost. Like Brian might talk back the same way.

He was scared that one day he might.

Determined, he shimmied out of his boxers and took himself in hand. Sex was good. Jerking off, which was all the sex he'd get for a while, was just fine. He tugged and stroked himself, and his body got in on the act. He didn't need to think. He could do this, rub and touch and feel good. He came pretty quickly, and lay panting in the aftermath for several minutes. When his breathing was normal again, he grabbed some tissues and wiped up. All done.

After perhaps an hour of dozing off and on, he heard the door opening downstairs. He sat up in bed. The sounds were totally familiar— Damon locking up again, getting a water from the fridge, coming upstairs. Brian called, "Hey, Damon. Say good night?"

Damon appeared in the doorway. "Hey. Why aren't you asleep?"

Brian shrugged. He had a hard time sleeping in an empty house; Damon knew that.

"You know, when I'm out, working or having fun, you don't need to wonder if I'm coming back. I'll always come back, bro."

Unless you can't. "I know."

"I promised, right? I take care of you and Lori. Guaran-damn-teed."

"Right."

"So Nick got you back okay. Sorry about the guys at the bar. They didn't mean nothin' by it."

He'd almost forgotten them, thinking so hard about Nick, but now their words came back to him. "I'm nasty."

"The hell you are. You're no more nasty than you are a werewolf."

"I'm tired of being a freak."

"You're not a freak. Well, not like they think. You're never gonna be normal, but you're a valuable not-normal."

"Great."

"It is." Damon took a step into the room and waved at the wide-screen TV, the solid furniture. "All this? That's 'cause you're weird. If you weren't, I'd never have caught Marston's attention telling him about you. I'd still be shuffling papers in the warehouse. He'd never have met Lori. We'd still be poor and fighting for every fucking crumb."

"I guess."

"You bet your ass. So you're a useful kind of weird."

He didn't want to be useful. He really didn't want to be this tool that Marston pulled out, like a knife or a gun. "I want to stop."

"Stop what?"

"Finding. For him." He knew he'd never really stop Finding. It was part of him. But maybe he could use it for good stuff, like lost kids and puppies.

"You can't." Damon came into the room, getting up close in his face. "You know that. Don't even say it. If he thinks you won't do it when he asks, he'll find ways to make you. Horrible ways, Bry."

Brian swallowed at the images that flashed through his mind. He wasn't brave, especially if Marston threatened Lori.

"It's okay, bro." Damon sat on the foot of the bed, looking at him. His breath smelled like stale beer, but he didn't seem drunk.

Brian bit his lip, holding back words. Because it really wasn't.

"Come on. It's not that bad, right, working for Marston? Jesus, think about when we were little." Damon's mouth twisted bitterly. "Remember the trailer where there was no fucking heat except the antique plug-in portable? I was never sure if we'd freeze to death or burn down. Remember when Lori got pneumonia, and Mom wouldn't take her to the doctor 'cause she'd put all our money up her arm? Remember when you were ten and they were going to kick us out of the apartment again and I went out and got the rent money in one night? Do you want to know what I did for it? Do you?"

Bryan stared into the dark depths of Damon's eyes and shook his head hard. He really didn't. Mom had somehow found an apartment that had decent heat and hot water and a door that really locked. The building was solid brick, and if the stairwells smelled like piss, and there were junkies shooting up in the alley, it still was better than the two years they'd just been through. Damon had been sixteen, and he'd dropped out of school because Mom couldn't keep a job. Brian remembered that year.

Damon's trace had slowly gotten smokier and colder all that year. He'd seen the changes in Damon's eyes, heard them in his voice, tasted them in his thread. And said nothing, because Damon was making sure they never were down to half a bowl of cold cereal for dinner, or got tossed out the door for missing rent. "I can do it," Brian said reluctantly. "I remember."

Damon ruffled his hair, then punched his shoulder. "Good boy. As soon as I found out Marston was hot for the kind of freaky shit you do, I knew we were on our way. And here we are. I'm *never* going to have to come up with rent in one night again."

Brian ducked his head. He'd wondered for so long, he had to ask, "Did you ever hate taking care of us? Did you get creeped out by my freaky shit?"

"What? Nah. Your talent was fuckin' useful, right? Even when you were a kid, tracking Mom down before she spent her whole paycheck? It was good. Weird as hell, but good."

Brian opened his mouth, but saying anything more would open a whole can of worms. He'd never be able to ask what he needed to know without sounding different, smarter, without letting Brian out for Damon to see. So Bry said, "Okay, yes, okay."

"Right." Damon gave him another friendly smack to the shoulder and stood. "Get some sleep. Tomorrow's a Mario day, and he'll want you to help mow the lawn and shit. You have a real job there too, bro. The yard wouldn't look half as good without you working for Mario. And you get to work three days a week, instead of two damn minimum wage jobs, fourteen hours a day, just to make rent."

"I know."

"If Lori gets sick, we don't worry about paying a doctor. If I want new shoes, I go out and buy fucking new shoes. Two pairs if I want. We have it made."

"We have it made."

"Now sleep."

"I'll sleep."

Damon laughed, a softer sound. "Yeah, lucky bastard. Mario doesn't start work till nine. I have to be out at seven-thirty."

"I'm lucky."

"Good night, Bry." Damon headed for the door.

"Good night, Damon brother."

When the door shut behind Damon, Brian curled up on his side. Damon was right, in a way. When he'd been nine, freezing in that winter trailer, melting circles in the ice on the inside of the walls with his finger and wondering if his whole arm might freeze and fall off, he'd thought he'd kill for a nice, warm room. And now he did that: he killed for these comforts. His punishment was to know what a bad man he was. If he had to admit the whole truth, it'd probably be hard to stop Finding for Marston, if it really meant going back to being that cold and hungry and scared all the time. He was selfish. And bad. He had no right to judge Damon for the things he did.

For a moment he had a stupid impulse to get out of bed and sleep on the floor with no covers, as if being willing to be a bit cold and uncomfortable could change what he was doing. He knew better, though. Nothing would ever fix this. But it kept Damon happy, and Lori safe too, and that was worth the stain on his soul.

Chapter 7

Around four the next Friday, Nick sat in a conference room at headquarters, watching Olson, in the seat to his right, flip through the papers on the table. Across from them, Captain Freemantle had insisted on sitting in, and Takano was hanging back, letting Olson handle the briefing. Agency pissing contest— you had to love it. After seven weeks the local brass was clearly getting impatient with the operation and the resources being used to support him.

"We've made some progress." Olson slid the papers aside, pulled her laptop over, and projected a map of the area. She clicked to mark the map with nine locations around the Twin Cities, indicated with red and blue stars. "These are the warehouses Marston uses. Stan only gave us the blue locations. The four red ones were located by Officer Rugo's efforts. Two of the red ones shipped supplements to the stores we've had under surveillance." She turned the two orange. "We then arrested two additional local drivers, which removed them from Marston's roster."

Nick hid a smile, remembering Roy's drunken rant after that happened.

"As a result, Officer Rugo has recently begun making trips here." Olson added a yellow star. "We believe this is the warehouse which receives the shipments of peeps, combines them with other supplements, and dispatches them to the retail locations. We've identified the following health stores and head shops where Marston Enterprises delivers supplements." Dozens of green spots appeared. "Not all of these sell peeps, but we made successful buys in several." Several of the greens turned orange.

"Any real arrests yet? Any success in getting this shit off the street?" Freemantle asked.

"We're still gathering information," Olson said. "There's no point in closing down one shop, or stopping one truck, and making Marston suspicious."

"Don't teach your grandmother to suck eggs." Freemantle leaned forward, letting his considerable bulk slide the table an inch toward Olson and Nick. "Sometimes you can nibble around the edges. If not, then do you have an end game by now? Where are you going with this one, Lieutenant? Give me something I can take to the bean counters to justify the expenses on my monthly report."

Takano said, "Right now you could close down a bunch of sales points. We can even get a warrant for the warehouse, thanks to Officer Rugo's ingenuity in getting us a sample from that location."

Nick grinned. He'd managed to engineer a natural-looking accident with a forklift, spilling cases across the floor. A couple had broken open, and one he'd helped along a little. Walking around with a sample hidden in his sock had been an odd kind of high. Roy had decided they needed to search all the guys, because stuff was missing after the cleanup. Nick had held his breath until Roy told him to help with the pat-downs, rather than being searched.

They'd found one guy with four bottles in his jacket, all dumb herbal nothings. Roy fired him on the spot and sent him off. When they were done, and still two short, Nick suggested maybe the packer miscounted. Roy had been antsy and angry, yet never looked at Nick with suspicion. It'd been a real adrenaline rush.

Freemantle said, "Can we tie anything to Marston?"

"Maybe. Officer Rugo can testify that the people who work at the warehouse are employees of Marston's, but the ownership is buried deep in shell corporations. Legitimate shipments from that location have 'Combined Distributing' packing slips, and the registered owner is a Chinese national."

Nick had to say, "We still don't know where the lab is. Maybe there's enough information in the files at the warehouse. But it'd be a hell of a gamble to count on that and make our move now."

Fremantle turned to him. "Can you get into the office and check the files?"

"Not yet. Maybe one day." Roy was starting to think of Nick as his buddy, someone who'd help with security, not a risk. But he still kept the files locked away.

"So what's the plan?"

Takano said, "Give Officer Rugo some more time." He looked at Nick. "He's trying to get closer to Damon Kerr."

Olson said, "Officer Rugo's been to Marston's home more than once. Damon's starting to trust him. And if anyone has access to Marston's paperwork, it's going to be the Kerrs."

Nick wasn't sure Damon ever trusted anyone, but otherwise that was right. He nodded.

Freemantle said, "Maybe you can use the other brother. The younger one. From your reports, he's not half as smart as Damon, and he lives on the estate too. He's a loner, no friends. You said he hangs out at that bar. There's an opportunity there. Get close to Brian Kerr."

Nick swallowed the unpleasant taste of that, and reminded himself Marston's drugs resulted in dead kids. "Yes, sir."

"All right." Freemantle closed the file in front of him and pushed it across the table to Takano. "Two more weeks and we'll review again. If we're not making substantial progress, we'll have to reassess our participation level. At least we can take down the head shops. Those same places carry artificial marijuana like the K2 that kid killed himself with last month. We want them out of business."

"They just pop up elsewhere if we don't get the supplier," Olson pointed out.

Freemantle heaved himself up. "Then go get me the fucking supplier, before we have to shut this down."

"Yes, sir."

Takano rose as well and followed Freemantle out.

Nick uncrossed his arms and huffed a breath. "So that went well." He fought back a flood of irritation. They were doing their best. He'd get Marston, if they'd only give him time to work.

"Actually, that wasn't bad." Olson smiled at him. "Between the local drug buys, and surveillance, and your cover expenses, the operation is running up a bill with no results so far. That always makes the brass antsy. Plus letting the DEA run the big picture chafes his ass."

"Can't have cost that much yet," he muttered.

"Not enough for them to scream, anyway. You're doing good, Nick." Olson stood and stretched. "Want to go out and get a beer?"

"Nah. I do too damned much of that with Damon's crew." He'd never been a big drinker, but Roy was out almost every night, which meant Nick's best tactic was to be there almost as often, buddying up. The fact that he'd been among the searchers and not the *searchees* at the warehouse showed it was working.

Olson eyed him as she shoved her chair back. "How do you feel about your cover? Still solid?"

"Sure. No problems." He had a moment's memory of Brian saying *"I won't tell"* but he was pretty sure Brian meant his suspicion that Nick was gay. Not that it couldn't also be an issue...

"The phone numbers we set up for your supposed cousin and uncle got calls Friday that had to be Marston's people. Someone asking about you, like they were looking for an out-of-touch friend. They said a couple of things that contradicted your cover, like they were testing."

Nick felt a chill. "Problem?"

"No. The officers said all the right things back, corrected the errors. We have recordings, if you want to hear, but they did good. You didn't get any backlash, right?"

"Not that I saw." That was before the warehouse incident. If Roy had been suspicious, he'd have treated Nick differently.

"All right then."

"I wonder why they're checking further now?"

Olson shrugged. "Maybe they're thinking of offering you a move up?"

"We can hope."

"Yup." Olson slapped his back. "So. No booze? Want to get a chili dog from next door?"

Nick hesitated. The long-term op wore him down sometimes, with the constant, nagging worry about blowing his cover. The hole-in-the-wall food joint next door was always full of cops. It would take a pretty damned brazen crook to spot him in there. "Sure, sounds good."

The place was getting busy, close to the change of shifts. They got chili dogs and pop and took them to a table in the back. With people walking past, they didn't talk about the case at all. Instead Olson told a funny story about her brother-in-law and a loose dog, and Nick bitched about the people in his trailer park. He relaxed and laughed and watched the guys coming off shift stopping in for takeout. It was good to remember this was his real life, this here, once the investigation was over. He'd be one of those guys in uniform, walking in, stretching out the kinks from driving all day. Badge and gun belt and simple good guys and bad guys, no in-between puzzles with unreadable ice-blue eyes.

After half an hour, Olson headed back to her office to do more paper shuffling. Nick decided to take a run by his trailer to check up on things, maybe change the timers on the lights. He could even spend the night, if he wanted to. Roy was out of town at his sister's, so Nick Green could skip a night hanging with him... although Fridays were Damon's most common night out. He was supposed to be getting close to Damon, and Brian. Maybe he'd make it a quick run home.

When he pulled up to his place, Tyrone and Keesha were playing ball in their dusty yard. They waved, and when he got out, Tyrone came over. "Hey, Nick. Where you been?"

"Around. I'm gone a lot right now." He wasn't surprised Tyrone had noticed the change in his schedule. The kid was observant.

"You off arresting some bad guys?"

"Something like that. What have you two been up to? School going okay?"

"You forget somethin', Mr. Policeman? It's summer. Ain't got school."

Nick shook his head. "I haven't got school."

Tyrone laughed. "You ain't never got school."

"Smartass." Nick caught him in an affectionate headlock.

Tyrone giggled, then pulled free and sobered. "Seriously, man, I wish you'd be around more. The other night, Mom and Dad got into it bad. You're good at cooling them down, y'know?"

Nick felt a lurch of guilt, even though he couldn't ever be there 24/7 for these kids. He might just as easily have been away on a regular night shift. "It worked out okay?"

"Yeah. No damage. But Keesha was scared."

"Was not." Keesha kicked her brother's shins with her bare toes. "You were."

"A bit." Tyrone looked down at his feet in the dirt.

Keesha said, "We come over and looked for you, but you ain't here. Ty said we could stay with you maybe, but the door was locked."

"Sorry." He sat down on his front step and the kids joined him. He looked at Tyrone. "You know if it gets real bad you can call 911."

"Me and what cell phone?"

"Um." It was easy to forget not everyone could whip a phone out of their pocket. Ty was tall and smart and seemed older than eleven. "Any neighbor's."

"Hah. I can't call the cops. Dad would be soooo fuckin' mad."

"Don't say fuckin'." It was an automatic response.

Tyrone laughed bitterly. "Yeah. That's my problem right there. I swear too fuckin' much."

"Sorry. You know if I *am* home, you can come over."

"If."

"Don't you have anyone, an aunt, grandma, somebody you could call?"

"Not here. When we lived in Chicago we was just a block from Aunt Marcia, but not here."

"Damn."

He sat for a while. Keesha leaned in against him and he put an arm around her. Tyrone set his elbows on his knees and rested his chin in his hands, staring out at the trailer park in silence. Eventually, Keesha said, "Mommy was sorry she yelled, and I got me some new shoes."

Nick looked down at her dusty bare feet and pretended a gasp of admiration. "Ooooh, yeah, those are the fanciest shoes I've seen in years."

Her little fist smacked his thigh. "Stupid. They're for school and church. I like the dirt between my toes."

"I always did too," he agreed.

She smiled at him and he grinned back.

They both jumped as the kids' mother appeared in the doorway across the street. "Ty! Keesha! Dinner! Get your butts in here."

Ty jumped up. "Gotta go. You gonna be around more, Mr. Cop?"

Nick hesitated. He'd decided he'd go hang out with Damon after all, but maybe he could go back to the original plan. As he debated, Ty frowned and shook his head. "Never mind. We gotta go. See you, Nick."

The kids dashed across the narrow road without looking for traffic, and Nick winced. "Stay safe," he muttered. They ducked inside past their mother. She waved at Nick and closed the door.

Not my problem. Not my circus. Not my monkeys. Except he did feel responsible. But he had other important things to do too, and usually after a night of heavy boozing, their parents had a couple of good days, so they should be fine. Unlike other kids who might be buying peeps to get high, and ending up dead.

He unlocked his door and went in. For a couple of hours he puttered, doing a little cleaning, changing light timers to a later setting. He had a shower, and then lounged around stark naked, letting the air dry and cool him. He called Charlie and shot the breeze for a bit, picked up a book and read a chapter, got online and checked some favorite porn sites. He let himself be Nick Rugo, who had a real friend and read books and was gay, if not out. But when eight o'clock rolled around, he pulled on some baggy jeans and a T-shirt, making sure he'd never written his name on the tags. Clean socks came next, and he tugged his biker boots over them. Time for fun, booze, and crime. Time for Nok Nick to come out to play.

He ran by the apartment for his damned crotch-recorder, then headed for the Torchhouse. When he arrived, the bar was filling up fast. Damon was there already, at a back table with Booker, Joe, and Coop, and Brian was tucked in against the wall. Three women shared the table, cuddling up to Booker and Coop. Booker waved him over. "Hey, Nick, grab a chair."

He reached for one, spun it around and straddled it. He'd made that a trademark. It was a bit theatrical badass, but it kept the girls from sitting in his lap. Brian pushed a beer toward him. "Here Nick. I didn't drink it."

"Hey. Thanks, man." He smiled at Brian, hating himself for the way Brian's eyes got brighter. He was pretty damned sure by now that Brian was gay, and what kind of hell would that be, with Damon and his women always around? Plus the only guys who would hit on someone with Brian's limitations would be douchebags. Like him. He'd been ordered to get closer to Brian, and he hadn't said no. He picked up the bottle and drank it, deliberately tipping his head back as he swallowed. If he was going to be a douche in the name of the investigation, let it begin. It wasn't like he'd take it past flirting.

The server came by, and they ordered a round. Coop bitched about Roy taking off for the weekend without, well, something he was already too drunk to articulate. Nick nodded and pretended to agree with him. Coop wasn't worth his time. He did what Roy told him and didn't have the brains to look beyond the end of his beer.

Another woman who Nick had seen a few times came and knelt beside Damon's chair, winding her arm around his neck. She whispered in his ear, and he laughed and kissed her. One of the other three got up off Booker's knee to drape herself over Brian. "Hey, baby," she said. "Why don't you let me give you a good time?"

"No, thank you," he said primly.

"Aw, come on. I'll take good care of you. Mama can treat you right."

Nick saw Brian flash a look of urgent appeal at Damon as he said, "I really, really don't want to."

Damon didn't seem to notice. Nick turned to the woman. "Hey, we could go for a romantic walk outside. There's a full moon. We could go down to the river."

She laughed at him, holding up one foot to show a three-inch spiked heel. "Do these look like I want to take a walk?"

"I want to walk," Brian said. He reached out to touch Damon's sleeve. "I don't want any Mama. I want to walk."

Damon frowned and turned to the woman. "Leave my brother be." He pointed at Joe. "Go try it out on him instead."

"I want to walk, Damon." Brian's voice rose, and he pushed his chair back. "I want to see the river."

"Oh hell, Bry."

Nick said, "We could go out to the river. I don't mind."

Damon looked at him, eyes narrowed. "Why would you do that?"

Nick shrugged. "I was in a mood to walk anyway. It's nice out, and I spent the whole damned day driving. Brian may not be a hot chick, but at least he didn't wear stupid spike heels. He can tag along."

"You sure?"

"Why not?"

"All right." Damon turned to Brian. "You got your cell phone?"

"Yeah, Damon, I got the cell."

"You stay with Nick." Damon said to Nick. "You're responsible for him."

For some reason, that irked Nick. "He's not a baby."

"You don't know what the fuck he is or what could happen. You're gonna walk around the damned streets at night? You watch him."

"Sure. No problem."

"Good, good, good. Let's go, Nick." Brian bounced to his feet and rushed toward the door so fast that Nick had to hustle to keep up.

Outside, the air was soft and warm. The sky was mostly clear, with the occasional wisp of cloud drifting across the full moon. Brian didn't stop to look, but set a brisk pace toward the river five blocks away. Nick strode beside him, willing to let him take the lead.

After two blocks Brian slowed and blew out a breath. "Okay. I thought Damon might stop us."

Nick took a quick look back. "I don't see anyone."

"Nope. Free at last." Brian turned his face up to stare at the bright moon. "Thank God Almighty, we are free at last."

Nick blinked, then recognized the quote. "That's a speech."

"Yes. I heard it." Brian shrugged and continued toward the bridge at a slower pace. "It's not right, of course."

"What isn't?"

"The speech. For me, now."

"Oh."

"I'm not a slave."

Nick was about to say "Of course not" when Brian added, "Not really."

"What?"

Brian didn't say anything more, just wandered on along. The first two blocks had been busy, but now the bars and restaurants were giving way to stores, mostly closed. They passed a couple of men headed back toward the bars, and then the sidewalk was empty. The sound of their feet became audible, in soft counterpoint. Brian crossed the next intersection and turned toward the Ninth Street bridge.

The bridge was a short arch over the water, perhaps two hundred feet of stonework and railing, twenty feet above the dark surface. Brian walked along and paused at the top of the span, looking down at the reflected moonlight, gleaming crescents broken across the rippling surface. "Pretty."

Nick stepped up to the rail beside him and leaned on his elbows. "Yeah, it is."

Brian said just as casually, "Are you gay?"

"Huh?" It was a jolt right down to his toes. "What the hell? I don't ask you if you're gay."

"No. I am though."

"Shit! Don't just say that." Nick glanced around quickly. They were alone. There wasn't even much traffic on this side street. No one had heard. "I don't think gay is a safe thing to be around your brother and his friends."

Brian lifted one shoulder. "Doesn't change it."

"Still." Nick hesitated, off-balance.

"So, are you?"

"It's not a safe thing to be," Nick repeated firmly. He didn't want to lie, but he couldn't afford to tell the truth. He was totally unprepared when Brian turned and kissed him, a quick fumble of lips against the corner of his mouth. He reacted instinctively, shoving Brian away hard.

Brian stumbled and went to one knee. He flung up a hand as if to ward off a blow. "I'm sorry, Nick! Please."

"No, it's okay." Shame burned in him, looking down at Brian's pale, scared face. He reached down to help him up. After a frozen moment, Brian took his extended hand and let Nick haul him to his feet. Nick tried to keep his tone irritated, and in character. "Sorry, Brian. But you fucking surprised me."

"It was dumb."

"Yeah, a bit. You can't just kiss someone, especially someone who hasn't given you any signals they might like it."

"What about the way you drank that beer?"

"Huh?"

"Wasn't that a signal?"

Nick flushed, remembering he'd thought of it as flirting. He couldn't admit that, though. "It wasn't meant to be. But I guess if you took it as an invitation that explains the kiss."

Brian's sigh was long and deep. He turned to the water again, leaning his hips into the stonework. "No. The kiss was because I'm tired."

"It's pretty late."

"I'm tired of acting. Tired of faking it. I'm tired of Damon and girls and pretending I don't know what my brother does."

"With girls?" Nick wasn't keeping up with this conversation.

"No, dummy. I know what he does with girls. I've done some of it." Brian turned to him, and there was a spark in his eyes— different from anything Nick had seen there before. "I've had girls suck me. I've sucked guys off. I'm not a child."

"You… well, I know that, but… really? Guys where?" He had a momentary flash of Brian on his knees, light-blue eyes wide with anticipation. Or would it have been fear? "Did someone make you do that?"

Brian's response was almost a growl. "Aargh. No. At school in the locker room. A guy said, 'How 'bout you suck my dick?' So I did."

"That's not right." Nick wanted to go back and pound that bastard into the wall. "He shouldn't have made you."

"He *didn't*." Brian pushed Nick's shoulder. "I chose it. Can't you understand? I was sixteen and I wanted to. I'd always wanted to. When he let me touch him it was like the best thing ever. We did it again a few more times, before Damon pulled me out of school. And there was another guy, although we never did more than hands. I'm gay."

"Oh. Well, okay." Nick rubbed his lips. "But still, you shouldn't just *tell* someone about it."

"You're not 'someone.' You're the only other gay man I know. And if I don't tell somebody soon, I think I'll drown."

Nick remembered being in the police academy, wondering every day if he'd look at someone wrong, say something wrong. Officially, it was okay to be gay on the force. Unofficially, not so much. Sometimes he'd thought he would crack. He'd gone out to a bar and picked up a trick and reminded himself who he was. Brian didn't have that option.

He was jeopardizing his cover by calmly standing here. Nick Green would punch the hell out of anyone who even suggested he was a fag. He really should throw a punch, or at least get mad and yell and walk away. He'd be dead if his cover was blown. But as Brian stood there, the mingled pleading and resignation in his expression gutted Nick. Brian looked like a man in a killing flood, clinging to a thread of hope.

No one was drowning on Nick's watch.

He lowered his voice. "Okay. You can talk to me, but if you tell Damon or anyone, we'll both be in a shitload of trouble."

"I won't."

God, Nick hoped that was true. He tried to fit gay and Brian Kerr into one picture. "Do you ever, um, date?"

"Girls. Damon sends me girls sometimes. It's not too bad."

Nick winced. "Do you like the girls as well as guys?"

"No. But I can pretend. I'm really good at pretending."

"You live with Damon?"

"I have my own room."

"In Mr. Marston's house?"

"In the pool house, remember?" Brian's stance relaxed, and he turned to lean back on the stone railing. "Damon and I live in the pool house. Lori and Mr. Marston live in the big house. It's a comfortable place to live. I've been in much worse, lots of times."

Nick remembered his briefing had said the Kerrs' mother was an addict who ODed when Brian was a teenager. No doubt he had lived in worse. "I'm glad you have a nice home."

"It's not home. It's a place to stay. But when Lori has the baby then it will have to be home, I guess."

"Lori's having a baby?"

"Yeah. Not for a while yet. Once she does I guess we'll never leave."

"Do you want to?"

"Oh, yes. Since forever, but Damon's right— I like the soft bed and the good food. I get what I need from Mr. Marston. I should be grateful."

"Do you work for Marston too?" Nick hadn't figured out what Brian did. He'd never seen him in a warehouse, and he clearly didn't drive.

"You don't want to know." Brian bit his lip, then blurted out, "Do you think I'm stupid? Or crazy?"

Nick hesitated. *How do I answer that one?* "I think we're all a bit weird in this life. So how can I judge?"

"So you *do* think so." Brian blew out a breath and turned back to the water. "It's okay. Everyone does."

"Maybe you have some other gift."

Brian's laughter was harsh and went on far too long. Eventually, he muttered, "Maybe."

"It seems like your brother takes care of you pretty well." *Please tell me that's true.*

"Damon does his best. He always has. It's a bad best sometimes."

"Bry, listen—"

"Don't call me Bry!" Brian suddenly pushed up close to him, pale eyes stormy. "Not now. I'm Brian."

"Damon says Bry."

"Yeah. He does. I don't like it when *you* do."

"Okay… I guess… It's a nickname and I don't know you that well."

"Or he doesn't."

91

"What?" Nick rubbed his forehead, and muttered, "I think this whole conversation is above my pay grade."

Brian laughed shortly. "I could make a shrink crazy, huh?"

"Do you have one?"

"A shrink? Nah. I'm just stupid."

"So you're not, like, off your meds or anything?"

This time Brian's laugh was oddly light and joyful. "It feels like it." He stepped away from the rail and turned in a circle, arms outstretched. "It feels like for once the fog is lifted and I'm out. Free. I can say things and the sky doesn't fall." He tipped his head back and turned again, staring at the moon. "Hey, Man in the Moon, look at me. Do you see me? For real?"

The next time he spun faster, then staggered against Nick. Nick caught him to keep them both upright. Brian's head came against his shoulder, face upturned. Brian's hands clutched his arms, and their eyes met. Then Brian said, "Bad idea. Bad, bad." He pushed free and turned back toward the town center. "Come on."

Chapter 8

Nick followed Brian away from the river, back toward the bar, content to stay a step behind. He didn't want more of their crazy conversation right now. He'd thought Brian was slow and shy and simple, but that was obviously not the whole story. Whether Brian was really crazy or just scared, he couldn't tell. But he clearly wasn't simple.

When they walked back into the bar, Booker and Damon were playing pool, while the girls and the other two guys hung out at the table. As Damon was taking his shot, Brian marched up and said, "I want to go home!" Damon groaned as the ball bounced off the cushion an inch to the left of the pocket. "Bry. We've talked about pool and staying quiet. How many times have I said it?"

"Too many. Can I go home now?"

"Did you have a good walk?" Damon glanced over at Nick.

Nick nodded, not sure what he was conveying. *Yes, we survived. I didn't let him drown. No, I'm not going to tell everyone the crazy things he said.*

Brian said, "It was good. There was a moon. Can I go home now?"

Damon sighed. "I need to finish this game you just fucked up for me. We have a bet."

Nick said, "I could drive him again."

Damon frowned at him, considering.

Nick spread his hands. "Hey, man, it's not that far. I can't drink much tonight anyway. I've got that headache aura thing going." They'd put a history of migraines in his cover profile, as a convenient all-purpose excuse.

93

He'd told the guys too much booze would set them off, as a reason to back off the alcohol.

"Okay." Damon glanced around the table, as if planning to ask someone to go with them again. Joe was clearly well on his way to smashed. Coop was lip-locked with one of the women. Damon said, "Bry, you call me when you're in your room, right? Nick, you need the gate code?"

"Yeah. Or I could have Brian code me in."

"He can't remember it. Here." Damon dug a scrap of paper out of his pocket and picked up a pencil from the ledge by the dart board. "Four numbers. Punch in, drive through, eyeball and voice in the inner gate. Right?"

"Got it." Nick took the slip.

"Get your ass back here after. I want to see you back right away."

"Sure. Whatever you say."

Brian grabbed his sleeve, jerking at it. "Home. Right now."

Damon said, "Sorry. He gets like that."

Nick shrugged his best nonchalant shrug. "No sweat."

Brian tugged him toward the door. Nick went along, acting as if he was embarrassed and reluctant, although frankly it beat another night watching the guys get smashed. A couple of the locals muttered something at Brian as he pushed past— one sounded like "Dumb freak" —but they glanced over toward Damon's pool table and didn't go any further.

Brian laughed as the door closed behind them. "Great night. Super night. Where's your car, Nick Nak?"

"That way." He waved. "And if I can't call you Bry, you can't call me Nick Nak."

"Okay. That's fair." Brian danced along the sidewalk. He was a bit heavy, a bit clumsy, and he should have looked ridiculous, but he didn't.

Nick opened the passenger door. "Seatbelt."

"Yes, boss." Brian got in, and Nick rounded the hood to his side.

He expected Brian to start babbling again as soon as they left the lot. For someone who'd spent so many nights sitting silently drinking pop, Brian had caught him by surprise tonight. But instead he sat looking out at the dark streets. Nick was tempted to let him be, except he was supposed to be taking advantage of the opportunity to make friends.

"That's quite a place Mr. Marston has. With a pool and all? Not that Minnesota's a great place for a pool."

"Lori likes it."

"Do you swim?"

"Not really. A bit. Damon made me."

"Made you?"

"In the pool. When we moved there. He said, 'Stupid not to know how. This way, if you fall in one of the ten thousand lakes you won't sink.'"

"Makes sense."

"Yeah. Damon doesn't want me to drown."

Nick remembered the sense he'd had of Brian, almost under water. "There's more than one kind of drowning."

"No, there's not. Water fills your lungs and you die."

"Maybe there's more than one kind of water, then."

He expected Brian to say something literal about rivers and seas, but instead, after a pause he said, "That's kind of like poetry."

"What is?"

"Drowning in different water."

Nick tried to shrug it off. "I'm no poet."

"Me neither."

There was another pause. Nick turned onto the highway and picked up speed.

"I don't know what I'd do without Damon," Brian said reflectively.

"Have you ever had a job?"

"Like, for money? I bagged groceries after I dropped out. Then I moved boxes. Now I mow the lawn. Damon got me the jobs, though."

Nick shifted in his seat. There was always some innocent who got caught in the crossfire when they made arrests. Criminals had children and wives, and you couldn't let that affect you. "Have you ever lived on your own?"

"No. Not ever." After a bit, Brian added, "I could. I think. Some stuff would be hard."

"There are people who could help you, if it ever came to that."

"I thought about it, you know. About running away. I'm twenty-one, and I could go to some city and find a job, I think. But it's hard, and everyone would be so angry."

The thought of Brian out there on his own, being preyed on by every lowlife, made Nick wince. "I could help you, maybe. If you really wanted to leave." Witness protection might actually work for Brian, shielding him while getting him away from the coming crash of Marston Enterprises. The *hopefully* coming crash.

Brian shook his head silently. Nick debated whether to push, but he wasn't sure what Brian could understand, or what he knew and might offer as testimony. A defense attorney would rip Brian to shreds in a courtroom. This was something to approach slowly, after getting to know this strange guy a lot better.

"So, what do you like to do? Watch TV? Sports?" Luckily, Brian wasn't sharp enough to wonder about the abrupt change of topics.

****

Brian answered Nick's now-ordinary questions with half his brain. Which meant the answers barely made sense, but he was thinking hard. Leaving Marston, Damon, and everything, all on his own, was something he'd decided was impossible. How could he travel far enough to be safe, with no money, unable to read a bus schedule, unable to even punch in a damned phone number to get information without messing it up? Not to mention, Damon had put GPS tracking on his phone, so if he ever did leave, the phone would have to stay behind. He'd resigned himself to the impossibleness of it.

But if Nick would help…

The question was, why would Nick help? He worked for Marston now. He didn't have a lot of money, if his car and clothes were anything to go by. Why would he risk a good job to help Brian? Not that he'd offered, really. He'd said, "maybe." Did he want sex? If so, would Brian pay that price to get away? Was it even a price, to have sex with a hot guy like Nick?

Brian realized he'd just said the Bears were his favorite baseball team. *See, I can manage to sound dumb without even trying.* But the way Nick said "Oh. Okay," with that let's-humor-him voice, stung. "I'm not really a sports guy."

"I gathered." Nick sounded amused. "So, movies?"

"Oh yes." Brian racked his brains. Surely you could tell a lot by how someone reacted to movies, and which ones they liked. If they thought *Black Hawk Down* was better than *The Princess Bride* that told you something, right? He could start there. "I like *Princess Bride*." He waited for Nick to look blank, or call it baby stuff, like Damon did.

Instead Nick grinned. "Hello. My name is Inigo Montoya. You killed my father. Prepare to die."

Brian laughed out loud in delight. "You know it!"

"I used to check under my bed for Rodents of Unusual Size."

"I wanted a sword."

"You know what else was cool?" Nick said, "*Robin Hood*. Have you ever seen it?"

"There's an old one with no colors and a music one and a new one that—" He caught himself in time to avoid too much enthusiasm. "The new one is good."

"What about *Pirates of the Caribbean*?"

"I want to ride the big wheel."

"Without someone trying to stab you through it, though."

"Yeah." His chest felt warm and full. "Good movies." He wanted to talk about the way the *Pirates* movies used music to make you feel the emotions. Maybe with Nick he could even say that the men in the movie were hot. He wanted to ask if Nick thought a person really could do some of those stunts, if they were good enough, or were they all completely faked. He didn't, though. He said, "I like movies."

"Me, too."

"There was a theater we used to sneak into, near one place we lived. Damon fixed a door with chewing gum in the lock and he'd sneak me and Lori in the back." It had been warm and comfortable and for a glorious month they'd stayed there for hours each evening, hiding down among the seats if anyone came past, while Damon went off to his job, and Mom shot up somewhere. One time Damon got in trouble and couldn't come back for them, and they saw *X-Men* three times, until Lori fell asleep right there, hiding under a broken seat on the sticky, popcorn-crunchy floor. Brian stayed awake, keeping watch, and Damon came for them at last, in the middle of the night. "I wanted to be Wolverine."

"The healing would be good," Nick agreed.

"Now I have Netflix." Brian sighed deeply, realizing that would be another thing he'd have to give up if he ran. It might not seem like much, but movies saved his soul. "Damon pays for it. Or maybe Mr. Marston."

"It's not that expensive. I have it."

"Oh." Brian realized he had no idea what things like that cost. "Damon does the bills."

"Sure. But you could learn, if you needed to."

"Maybe." He'd sunk at school without much hope, foundered on the rocks of Mrs. Harrison believing in him, trying so hard, and still failing. He'd tried later with no better luck. He and math were enemies, at least on paper. Almost as bad as him and words.

He realized they were less than five minutes from the house. His breath came short. He wasn't ready to be done with tonight. Definitely not ready to be finished talking to Nick and thinking about escape. Thinking about why Nick might help him. He said, "Turn here," and pointed at a dark driveway.

Nick pulled off the road instead and stopped. "What's here?"

"A place. I want to show you."

Nick let the car sit on the shoulder, idling. "Damon might get worried."

"It's not far. Trust me." He always hated when Damon said that to him, but Nick just nodded, pulled back out onto the road and made the turn. That was a good moment.

The drive was gravel, and rough. Nick's car bounced over the ruts. A couple hundred yards in, they came to the old boarded-up house. In the moonlight it looked spookier than in the day, but Brian knew it well. He jumped out of the car, ignoring Nick's "Hey! Wait!" behind him.

He leaped up the sagging front steps and shouldered the door the right way. The top gave, opening a wedge of dark space, and he squeezed inside.

"Wait up." Nick followed him in and stopped, looking around. "What is this?"

It was a room, dusty and empty. The floor above had mostly fallen, and the upstairs windows let in the moonlight. It was much dimmer than sunshine, but enough. Brian pivoted in a circle, seeing nothing but familiar bare walls.

Nick lowered his voice. "Brian, why are we here?"

"This is my place."

"You, um, own it?"

"No. No one does. Well, someone does. But no one comes here. Every footprint on the floor is mine. Except yours now." He'd never brought anyone else to his place. He was both high and terrified at having Nick here.

"You come here a lot?"

"Not a lot. I don't want Damon to know. But sometimes." When the walls closed in at home and he needed to feel like there was a part of him that wasn't Damon's or Mr. Marston's, a part they couldn't touch, he'd sneak out and come here. "I like it."

"It's kind of cool. Falling apart, though." The floorboards creaked as Nick took a couple of steps. "I'm not sure it's safe."

"I don't care." He really didn't. If he died here, that would solve his problems.

Nick moved closer, his tone soft and low. "I want to help, Brian. I want to be your friend."

Hope was dangerous, but Brian had never had a night like this. The thought that he might have found an ally, someone with a better use for him that wasn't his Finding, made him fly. If he didn't ask tonight, he never would. He said, "Can I suck you?"

"Jesus, Brian, no!" Nick looked horrified. He took a step back.

Of course not. He was so, so stupid. The awful look in Nick's eyes made his gut churn nauseously. He backed up too. "Sorry. That was bad. Can we go?"

"It wasn't bad." Nick reached out as if to touch his arm but he backed another step toward the door.

"Let's go!"

"Listen, Bry, I just—"

"Brian! And I'm leaving." He thought he might be sick, actually. He didn't want to puke in here, in his space, even though this place was now stained with the memory of Nick's horror at the thought of his mouth down there. He got his fingers around the edge of the door. It was trickier than getting in, but it was so urgent he slammed his fingers into the gap, not worrying about the pinching. He yanked and made it through, letting the space snap shut behind him. Nick could figure it out himself.

He strode to the car. For a moment he wanted to jump in and drive it away. Leave Nick standing there on the steps with a long walk home. Hah. Except he had no keys, and hadn't ever had a license. If a cop stopped him, Damon really would kill him. He turned to head out through the woods toward the mansion and ran right into Nick. Nick grabbed his upper arms with strong fingers.

"Let go of me." He struggled hard.

Nick opened his hands immediately. "Yeah, I'm not holding you. Just listen for a second."

"No!" He didn't want to hear how he was too ugly or too stupid or too inexperienced to be worth having, even one time in an abandoned house. Sure, Nick might say it was too risky or he was too tired, but Brian knew better, and he'd heard a lifetime of lies already. "I want to go home. Now!" He let Bry come out. The good thing about Bry was that he could be petty and loud and childish and get away with it. It was better than crying. "Now! Now! Now! Now!"

"All right." Nick backed up a step. "Okay. We can do that."

"I can walk." He pointed. "It's there."

"Not in the dark, you don't. Damon would kill me."

Brian hesitated. He really might, and however sad Brian was that Nick wasn't going to be his salvation, he didn't want him hurt. Not for real. "Okay. Drive. No words."

Nick opened his mouth, then closed it again and gestured at the car. Brian got in and buckled his belt, looking resolutely out the window. In the reflection from the dome light against the dark window he could see his freakish face, skin like bread dough, mouth pressed flat, eyes like dirty ice. No wonder Nick hadn't wanted him. Who would?

He heard Nick get in, and the car started. The light went out, letting him see the night outside as they did a three-point turn and headed back down the gravel drive. The view hadn't changed— still pretty, with that big moon shining down to frost the trees in silver— but that just made him ache. Pretty was never for him. Somehow he'd forgotten that.

As they neared the gate, he managed to squeeze words past his tight throat. "You won't tell Damon?" Any of it. The house. His clumsy attempt at seduction. He would die if Damon heard one word of this.

"Of course not." Nick's tone was subdued. "But Brian—"

"Don't."

As they passed through the first gate, another car turned in off the road and came up to the gates behind them. Brian turned to look at it. It was a limo, long and black and sleek and expensive looking. Nick flicked a glance back too. "Do you know who that is?"

He shook his head. Occasionally Marston had visitors, but not at this hour. "No idea."

As Nick looked into the camera, the speaker voice said, "Nick? Wait there."

"I'm bringing Brian home."

"Wait there. We're coming out." The second gate didn't open.

Brian fidgeted in his seat. He didn't like the security guys anyway, and tonight of all nights he just wanted to go to his room and curl up on his bed. He knew he should've walked home.

After about five minutes, the inner gate rolled open enough to let one guard through. Brian could see the second waiting inside the gate, and shadowy shapes suggested all four dogs were ranged across the lawn. The nearer guard came toward them and up to Nick's window. "Hey, Brian," he said across Nick.

"Hey, Leo." Leo wasn't too bad. He mostly ignored Brian, and he didn't sneer.

Leo said, "You're Nick Green. Mind if I check the car?"

Nick said, "No. Although isn't this overkill? You know Brian, right?"

"Just procedure. Can you pop the trunk?"

Nick did so, and Leo walked around, shone his light under and into the car and in the trunk. Then he slammed down the lid. "Okay. Drive on through." He hit a control on his belt and the inner gate slid open for them. As soon as they were through, it shut again. Nick drove fifty feet down the drive and slowed. Brian turned to look out the back. In the arc lights at the gate, he saw Leo bent over, talking to the driver of the limo. After a minute he straightened and moved to the rear window.

"You have no idea who that might be?" Nick murmured, driving at a snail's pace.

"No." Brian wasn't sure he wanted to know, either. Anyone visiting Mr. Marston in the dark in a limo was likely to be trouble. "If you turn here, you can drive closer to my house."

"Okay." Nick turned off the circle drive and headed along the side toward the pool house.

"Stop here."

Nick braked to a stop. "Are you going to be okay?"

From what? Brian wasn't sure, but he said, "Yeah. You should go right back to Damon."

"And you'll call him?"

"Oh. Yeah." He'd forgotten. He really was that dumb. He got out, pulled out his phone, and hit the right symbols. As he held it to his ear, he watched Nick slowly turn the car and head back to the driveway. The strange limo passed by the beat-up little car, heading for the front of the house.

Damon said in Brian's ear, "You're home?"

"Yeah. Damon, there's a car here."

"A car?"

"A limo. A big one. Leo let it through the gate."

There was a moment of silence. "Do you know who it is?"

"No."

"Look, I'll come on home now. You go to bed, right? Stay out of the way and don't worry."

Perversely, that made him want to go look. "I want to know."

"When I find out, I'll tell you. Go to bed. Now!"

If he didn't say yes, he didn't have to obey. "Don't drive drunk."

"I'm not drunk, moron. I'll be there soon. Go to bed."

Brian clicked his phone off and stuck it in his pocket. He wasn't a moron and he was twenty-one and he was done obeying every single order Damon gave him. He let himself into the breezeway and turned for the big house.

He could hear voices from the foyer, and made his way quietly toward them. As he reached the end of the hall, he could see Mr. Marston standing in the vaulted entryway. Two formally dressed strangers stood just inside the door— a dark-haired woman in her twenties, and a man with gray hair and ruler-straight posture.

The man said, "Vern. Aren't you pleased to see us?" He had a posh English accent.

"Henry." Mr. Marston's tone was flat and controlled. "This is a surprise. And is that Veronica? It's been a while."

The woman said, in the same BBC tones, "Since I was ten, yes. Hello, Uncle Vern."

Brian swallowed silently. *Uncle?* He hadn't realized Mr. Marston had other family. He wondered if Lori knew.

Mr. Marston said, "Come on in. I'd have the housekeeper make up rooms for you but she's gone for the day."

"Perhaps your wife can assist us. Lori, isn't it?"

"That's right." Mr. Marston pulled out his cell phone and touched it, his eyes still fixed on the two strangers. "My dear, we have unexpected guests. Would you come down to the foyer and greet them with me?" Whatever she said wasn't audible, but he murmured, "Thank you," and put the phone away.

The Henry guy looked around and said, "This is nice, Vern. Very attractive. You've done well."

"Thank you."

"Father would've sent his regards, if he'd realized we were coming."

"Father would have sent his disapproval, more likely. How is Father?"

"Getting older. Sadly so."

"To be expected." Mr. Marston turned at the sound of footsteps on the stairs. "Ah, Lori. Come on down."

Lori appeared at the bottom of the stairs. She was wearing a fancy silver dress and had her light-blond hair tucked up in a sleek bun. Brian thought she looked like a modern version of Galadriel from *The Lord of the Rings*. He saw her hesitate a second, and a flash of fear came and went in her posture, almost too fast to see. He knew it, from years of watching her, and also saw the moment she set her nervousness aside and put on her most superior expression. She came forward much more slowly and deliberately than usual, gliding across the floor to tuck her hand into the crook of Marston's arm. He seemed unmoved, but Brian thought there was a hint of puzzlement in his expression before he said, "Henry? This is my wife, Lori Marston. Lori, my older brother Henry Granton, and his daughter, Veronica Granton."

Lori held out her hand, and drawled, "So pleased to meet you."

Henry hesitated, then took it briefly. "Indeed." He glanced at Mr. Marston. "She's as pretty as I'd heard. And as young."

Brian recognize the tightening of Lori's jaw that meant she was pissed, but she just said, "Were we expecting you, Mr. Granton?"

He raised his eyebrows. "Weren't you?"

"No."

"You announced on your Facebook page that you were expecting a baby. Of course we were interested. We're here to bring good wishes from your child's British relatives."

"Oh." For once Lori sounded unsure of herself. "I didn't realize."

Granton said, "Even though Vern didn't invite us to his wedding."

"That's right, I didn't." Mr. Marston patted Lori's hand where it rested on his arm. "I didn't go to the trouble of changing my name and crossing an ocean for fun. You know how Father felt about it."

"Well, Father's not in charge anymore. So when my secretary came across Lori's posts, I decided to visit you and see for myself." Granton held out a hand. "I missed you, Vern. No hard feelings?"

Slowly, Mr. Marston reached out and shook hands. "It's good to see you, Henry."

"And you." After a moment, staring into each other's eyes, Marston let go of Lori, and the two men exchanged a stiff hug.

Veronica said, "Maybe we can have some coffee and catch up? It was a long trip."

"Sure." Mr. Marston gestured. "The family room's that way." He turned toward the hall, and spotted Brian before he could duck out of sight. Since everyone else had followed the gesture, they were all staring at him.

Brian lowered his eyes, wrapped Bry tightly around himself and stepped forward. "I heard voices. New voices."

Mr. Marston said calmly, "Come and meet some relatives." Brian stopped far enough away not to shake hands as they were introduced. Both Granton and his daughter eyed him with curiosity that shaded into a familiar judgment. *Not worth my time.*

Brian said, "I can make coffee. I know how."

"You do that." Lori smiled at him, a social smirk that went oddly with the caution in her eyes. "Bring it to the family room."

"I can do that. Family room."

Veronica snickered audibly. Brian turned for the kitchen, ignoring it. Better than her being interested in him. The front door opened and the security guard looked in. "All clear. Any orders, Mr. Marston? Is the limo staying?"

"It's a hire car," Granton said.

"Then no." Marston waved at the door. "Bring in their bags and tell the driver he can go. Escort him off, and go back to standard patrols."

"Yes, sir."

Granton said, "You have twenty-four-hour security, Vern?"

"This house is remote, and I have valuables to protect, not least my lovely wife." Marston smiled at Lori. "Shall we sit down, dear? You shouldn't stand too long in your condition."

Brian hurried out, glad to be free of the strangers and the odd posturing. Making coffee was really easy, with the fancy drip machine. He set it for ten cups, put the larger carafe under it. And waited. He'd skip having any himself. His stomach was churning with the effects of the day. He decided to deliver the coffee and leave. Curiosity wasn't enough to make him sit there feeling like a barely tolerated pet while they talked past and around him.

When he brought the tray to the family room, they were seated on the leather armchairs, conversing in low voices. They stopped as he approached, and Lori pointed at the low table. "Good. You remembered the milk and sugar. Set it there. Carefully."

Like he was some kind of servant. He put it down, suppressed a sudden urge to tip it over "accidentally," and straightened. "I'm going to bed. Good night, Lori. Good night, Mr. Marston. Good night, new people."

"Get some sleep," Mr. Marston said.

As he headed out, he heard Veronica say, "He's your brother, Lori? That must be difficult."

He didn't wait to hear what Lori might reply.

It was a couple hours later when Damon came into the pool house. Brian was awake, watching a movie on his iPad, and he paused it to go downstairs. Damon looked up as he reached the ground floor. "Hey. I thought you were asleep."

"Nope. There were new people."

"Yeah. Marston's brother and niece." He ran a hand over his head. "I hope Lori knows what the hell she's doing, inviting them here."

"I don't think she invited the new people."

"Whatever she did. The niece is older than she is, and neither of them look happy about the baby, whatever they pretend."

Before he could go on, Lori burst in the door. "Well, shit! *Shit!*"

Damon immediately seemed taller and straighter. "What's wrong?"

"I didn't think they'd come here. I thought… fuck, I don't know what I thought."

"What did you *do*?"

"Nothing much. I was going through Marston's stuff, some old papers from way back, and I found out he'd changed his name."

"You just found that, laying around?"

"So maybe I was digging in the safe. But you know, he used to be The Honourable Vernon Granton, second son of the Baron Tomesmuir. Seriously, he's like a British noble guy. And his father is rich. All I did was ask a few questions online about what if Vern had a kid and how noble titles work, and next thing you know they're on our doorstep."

Damon growled wordlessly. "Lori, I told you a hundred times to stay off the fucking social sites! Nothing is private there."

"My profile is friends-only. And I just asked questions."

"And posted that you were pregnant?"

"Yeah, but, you know, only on my own page. As Lori Marston, not linked to anything Granton."

"Well, clearly Granton or his people were already watching you or had a search running. You never know who someone is online. Their secretary's probably a buddy kissing up to you on Facebook. I told you, don't put your private shit out there."

"Hey!" Lori took a step toward Damon, up in his face. "It's okay for you! You hang out with real friends like Booker all day. I'm here in this empty house with only the cook and the maids and the guards, and Vern hates if I talk to them. Online friends are my only friends! And if I want to chat with them, I will!"

Damon didn't back down, just glowered harder. "Right? Look where it got you! How dumb can you get?"

Brian hated when they fought. "Are the Grantons our friends and relations? Relations and friends? Enemies and friends?" He hummed a couple of notes of a random tune.

Damon threw him an annoyed glance, but his anger cooled. "The real question is, what do they want? How long will they stay, and how law-abiding are they? Will they make trouble for Vern's business if they see too much?"

Lori tucked a strand of hair back into her bun-twist-thing. "Maybe not? Vern once said he learned smuggling at his father's knee. That it was the family business."

"Really?" Damon stared at her. "Now that's interesting."

"Yeah." For a moment, as Lori and Damon smiled at each other, Brian could see the resemblance. Damon had a different dad, and darker hair and skin, but there was something the same in the curve of their mouths and eyes.

Damon said, "For now we hunker down. Lori, you play the airhead pregnant wife, thinking only of her baby, and keep your ears open. Brian, you stay out of sight. Better they go on thinking you're nothing special. Anyhow, that way you won't say the wrong thing."

"I wouldn't."

"Shush now. Lori, keep me posted on what they do, what Vern says. You're right— if Vern stands to inherit anything when their old man pops off, it could be a windfall for us, but we need to be cool until we know more about the stakes."

"Got it. Will do."

"Good girl."

"Vern's not happy with me."

"No doubt. You were an idiot. Dumber than Bry. But he won't do anything bad when you're carrying his baby, right?"

"He'll say stuff."

"Come on, girl." Damon put a hand under her chin. "You're tougher than that. You've been called names before, and you let it slide off."

Lori pushed his hand away. "I know. I just prefer when Vern's being my sugar daddy."

"Don't we all? Go get some sleep. Be ready to keep your ears open tomorrow."

"Okay." Lori suddenly hugged Damon, who wrapped an arm around her. "Thanks, big brother."

"Remember— when something gets in your way, you make it your bitch."

Lori blinked hard and then grinned. "Oh, yeah. I can do this."

When Lori was gone, Damon turned to Brian. "You should go to bed too."

"I will." He hesitated. "Do you think Granton and Veronica are bad peeps?"

"Bad *what?*" There was an odd expression on Damon's face.

"Bad people. Like, dangerous?"

"Oh." Damon leaned back against the counter. "I don't know. Odds are they're not, what with the toffee accents and the high-end clothes."

"Mr. Marston dresses fancy sometimes." He'd once thought you could judge a man by his clothes, but he'd learned different early on. "But Mr. Marston doesn't have a toffee voice. I wonder why?"

"Whatever. You're weird, Bry. Go to bed and stay far away from those two. The less they see you, the better."

"Okay." He went to his room and closed the door. It didn't lock from the inside. Damon said he had no need of locks, and what if he had a nightmare or got sick or something. Usually he didn't care, but tonight he wanted to lock himself away, with all the little barbs of words sticking out of his skin. He felt like that art picture he'd seen one time of some saint, with arrows stuck in him all over. *"You're weird. You're dumber than Bry. He's your brother?"* Maybe a big old spear for the one of Nick's voice saying, *"Jesus, Brian, no."* There were days he convinced himself that he was just acting a part when he was Bry. Then there were days like this, when he knew to his core that he was something less than normal.

Chapter 9

Nick woke with a pounding headache and a mouth that tasted like old socks. The sun coming in the window told him it was late morning. He needed to get up and go clean up, if he could make it without puking.

He sat up in bed, holding his head. Jesus Christ, he needed to not do that again. He'd left Brian and gone back to the bar as ordered, only Damon was gone and Booker insisted he join a drinking game. He'd wondered from the glitter in Booker's eyes if it was some kind of test, and he hadn't dared refuse. He couldn't remember who won, but he had a vague recollection of wanting to hit people, and drinking until he was too drunk to actually connect. He hoped to hell that he'd taken a cab home.

He made it to the bathroom, and met his own bloodshot eyes in the mirror. Unfortunately, getting drunk hadn't erased all his memories of the previous evening. The look on Brian's face in that old house was still vivid. He'd seen guys look less gut-punched when he'd laid them out on the floor with his fists.

Well, what had Brian expected? That Nick would suddenly be interested in a blow job there in that dusty, abandoned space, with no lead up, no warning? That Nick was that desperate for sex? What kind of idiot took a simple conversation for a green light like that?

The kind of innocent that Brian is, maybe?

He felt queasy about the whole thing, and knew part of it was because, for just an instant, he'd been tempted. Not by the blow job, but by the moment leading up to that. He'd felt a connection, some kind of resonance between Brian's confusing, sparkling elation and his own loneliness. Heat flushed his face. If Brian had offered a hug, a kiss, instead of sex, Nick might actually have stepped up close…

He managed to deflect his fist enough to punch the wall instead of the mirror. The drywall dented under the bruising impact. *Fuck!* He winced, shaking out his knuckles. *I'm the idiot!* Maybe he *had* given off some kind of signal. He clenched his teeth, closed his eyes.

A red mist rose up behind his eyelids. *Serve and protect.* It was his mantra, his reason to get up in the morning. But this *fucking* assignment was mixing things together, mixing the violence and the job, making him serve innocents and hurt them all at once. It *sucked!* His other hand snapped out without intention, sweeping the cup holding his toothbrush off the sink. Ceramic shattered on the tile with a satisfying smash. *Good! More!* Things ripped and thumped and squished.

By the time the red veil receded, the floor was littered with every vial and tube from the medicine cabinet, there were two more dents in the wall, and his only small towel had been torn into four ragged squares. His hands hurt.

Fuck.

He stood, breathing hard, looking at the wreck of his bathroom. *Damn it.* The pain in his throat from hangover dehydration made him gag. He took a controlled breath. And another. Damn.

He was better than this. He'd worked for years to be better than this! *This* was his father, coming home drunk and swinging randomly. This was his teen years, angry at the world and letting it ruin his life. He was an adult, a cop. He hadn't broken his own things in anger for a long time now.

Slowly, he bent and picked up the squashed tube of toothpaste. He brushed off a trail of blue gel with his finger, capped it, and set it down neatly on the edge of the sink. A trickle of cold water seeped from the tap and he washed his hand off.

Okay, one setback. It won't happen again. He just needed to reassess. Plan better. Be smarter.

So he couldn't completely separate the job and the violence? That was nothing new. He'd just have to find his control again.

So he had to hurt someone innocent to do his work? Nothing new there either. How often had he shrugged off a desperate mother or wife or kid tugging at his arm, begging him not to arrest the guy who stood between them and complete poverty? The job was never simple; it never came without pain to someone.

The only difference was his control. He'd lost it for a moment there, but he'd be fine. He was fine. He could do what it took, even use Brian Kerr, if that's what was needed to shut down the drugs and the deaths and the deeper pain.

For a moment he closed his eyes again, but for the right reason. He took slow, meditative breaths and sorted through his hangover-fogged worries. Some things were part of Nick Green's life, some were Officer Rugo's, nothing belonged in both worlds. He firmly set his concerns for Brian Kerr where they belonged, as part of the larger case. He wouldn't hurt the guy on purpose, he'd try to be smarter, but in the big picture he and Brian were both small pieces. Dead teenagers and dangerous drugs trumped both of them. He took a last, counted breath and opened his eyes.

Time to clean up the mess and move on.

He picked up the debris, sacrificing the smallest scrap of towel to wipe the ceramic shards off the tiles. Then he showered long enough to feel half-human, dressed, and sat at his table, sipping coffee and browsing online. When the cotton in his brain cleared, he called Olson and asked about the limo license plate he'd sent in. Unfortunately it had turned out to be a rental, and they didn't have enough probable cause to get a warrant.

Nick didn't let himself feel any regret as he said, "I wonder if Brian Kerr might know who it was. I drove him home yesterday and he was willing to talk a bit. If I had his phone number, I could call, see if he wanted to meet up. Maybe see the ball game this afternoon."

"Won't it look suspicious to Damon? You wanting to spend time with Brian?"

"Maybe. I think I can make it work." Even his mistake might turn out for the best. "I kind of insulted Bry last night. I'll bet he complained to Damon about it, but even if not, I can explain. I'll tell Damon I want to make it up to the kid."

"Would Nick Green care?"

Good question. "Nick Green knows Damon's a freak about protecting his brother. He wants to stay on Damon's good side. I just have to play it right."

"You wouldn't call Damon first?"

"Odds are he'd tell me to forget it. If I call Brian first, I'm more likely to get something in play." If he had to use Brian to make progress in the case, he would.

"Would Nick Green have his phone number though?"

"I don't think Brian's sharp enough to question that. If he is, I'll tell him Roy gave it to me when I was designated driver."

"All right." She took a few minutes, then read off a number. "Do you want additional coverage if you meet Kerr?"

"Nah." It was the last thing he wanted. "Not unless it gets complicated. I'll tag you if need be." The right cell phone code could send the *"Find me and follow us"* message, or the *"I need help right the fuck now!"* message. He was covered without costing the case money to tail him and Brian around.

"Okay. Good luck. If you find out anything, call me and I'll get the research team on it."

"Right." He hung up, punched in Brian's number, and hesitated. He suddenly had a flash of Brian's fumbling kiss and the sweetness of his face staring up at the moon in wonder. Deliberately, he flexed his hand, feeling the sting of his scraped knuckles. *You already made this choice.* He hit the call button.

"Yeah?" Brian's voice sounded thick.

"It's Nick. Did I wake you?"

"Nick?" His tone cleared immediately. "No. I've been up a couple of hours." Then the eagerness turned cool. "What do you want? How'd you get my number?"

So much for *not sharp enough*. "Roy gave it to me. Don't get mad. He was pretty smashed."

"Okay. Back to question one. What?"

"Um. Well, I felt bad about last night."

"Don't!" Brian said before Nick could get more words out. "Don't even think about it, all right?"

"Not all right. Brian, I was kind of a douche, but you also didn't let me explain."

"It's over. Done."

"Well, sure, fine. I'd still like to spend a bit of time with you, talk some more."

"You're kidding, right?"

"No." He didn't mention the ball game. That was smoke for Olson, or Damon if need be. He thought he knew better bait for Brian. *"Spiderman 2* is out. Have you seen it?"

"No."

"You want to?"

"Like, go to a movie? Together?"

"Yeah." He realized he'd better qualify that. "Not as a date. Just, you know, it'd be fun. I haven't gone to a movie in ages."

There was such a long silence, he wondered if Brian had set the phone down. "Brian? Still there? We don't have to."

"Hush. Thinking."

"Okay."

After another long pause, Brian said, "*The Muppets Most Wanted* would be better."

"You like it better? I thought you might enjoy seeing Andrew Garfield." *In spandex.*

"I would but... If I say I want to see Spidey then Damon might take me. Or Lori. But they hate the Muppets."

"And?"

"I can do this. I can say I really, really want to see Miss Piggy. Like, tantrum-y."

"Sure." He was beginning to wonder what he'd gotten himself into.

"Bry does that for me. I can be awful and nag and whine. And then this time I'll say 'Nick would take me.' And I'll call you."

Nick got up and paced. "Maybe this is a bad idea."

"No. It's genius! Perfect. Listen. I'll whine at Damon until he's ready to pop. Then I'll call you and you can be all, 'No, no, I don't mind. I'll take the hit for you, Damon. I even kind of like the Muppets. Kermit is badass.'"

"No way Kermit is badass. Miss Piggy, now. She will take you down." Brian's gurgle of laughter warmed Nick, until he remembered this was all a fake.

"Okay. When?"

Nick grabbed his tablet and checked. "There's a matinee at one."

"It'll be all little kids. How about later."

"Three-forty?"

"Sure. Okay. If I start whining around one, that gives Damon time to get pissed."

Nick said, "Is he even home?"

"Yeah. We have a gym. He's working out. I'll go bug him soon. This will be good. I'll call you."

"All right."

Brian hesitated. "You will say yes, won't you? If Damon calls? You won't say 'It's too dumb and little kid for me?' You won't change your mind?"

"Nope. I'll wait for a call."

"Okay." Brian's voice got soft, like he was shy. "I'll talk to you soon, Nick."

He set the phone on the table and eyed it like it was a bomb. *What have I just done?* He'd told Brian this wasn't a date, but what if he hadn't understood that? What if he was setting the guy up for another sucker-punch? He almost called back to cancel, except he remembered the anxiety as Brian said, *"You won't change your mind?"* How often had someone promised something to Brian and not come through?

Instead he called Olson.

"What? Problem?"

"Not really. If it works out, I'm going to catch a movie with Brian Kerr later. But I wondered." He needed to know, and fuck invasion of privacy. He reminded himself this was an investigation, not a date. "What's Brian's background? Does he have a medical diagnosis? How, um—" What was the "good" term these days? "—how challenged is he?" *Did I kiss a child?* Although, really, Brian had kissed him.

"Let me pull up his file."

There was a pause. "Okay. Brian Michael Kerr. Born December twenty-third, 1993, so he's twenty-one. Left school soon after he turned sixteen. His school record suggests he was in special-ed classes from second grade on up, although there are gaps. He moved around a hell of a lot. There's an IQ test from 2001 that says "Uncooperative" in the notes and gives him an IQ of sixty, which is obviously too low for how he functions. No arrests. No work record. There's not much there."

"No counseling, or medications or anything?"

"Not that we found. You think he's crazy?"

"No! Not crazy. Maybe, um, something. Bipolar. I don't know." Brian had said *"Bry does that,"* like Bry wasn't him. "Split personality? He's hard to pin down."

"If he is, we have no record of his being treated for it. But then we have no medical records for him at all."

Nick rubbed his lips with the backs of his fingers. "All right. I guess I'll find out."

"Do you think he might be dangerous? Do you want backup after all?"

"Oh, hell no. He's not dangerous. I'm actually worried he might be fragile, and get hurt."

"Well, sometimes you have to break eggs, right?"

Brian is not an egg.

Olson's voice hardened. "We need those drugs off the streets. We need to know where they're made. If Brian Kerr gets hurt doing it, that's a fair price to pay."

Except to Brian. "Of course. I know that."

He set the phone aside and went to his closet. Nick Green dressed for shit. Although this wasn't a date, so who cared, right? He grabbed a pair of clean jeans and a blue T-shirt. Done. His jeans all came with clever little pockets, and he dug the voice recorder out of hiding. It'd fit in the usual spot, into the placket of the fly. He hesitated.

What if he didn't bring the recorder along? This was only a fishing expedition, after all. Making connections. Did he really need to record their day?

Am I really out of my mind?

He slammed his hand on the back of the kitchen chair, hard enough to tip it over with a bang. Dammit! He hated being so caught up in his own head that he'd start making mistakes. He had a job to do. He was going to do it. He turned the recorder on, slid it into the placket, and pulled on the jeans. There.

For an hour he puttered around the kitchen, the phone silent on the counter. He'd begun to wonder if Brian had changed his mind, when it finally rang.

Brian's voice warbled, "Kermit and Piggy, Kermit and Piggy. Say yes. Say yes."

"Say what?"

Brian's voice was replaced by Damon's. "Hey, Nok Nick, sorry about that. Brian has it in his head you're gonna take him to see the Muppets."

"What the hell? The movie? Brian?"

"Yeah. He called you before I could stop him. How come he has your number?"

"I, um, called him this morning. I got his from Roy one time, when he was wasted and insisted I should have it. Bry seemed really freaked out last night when I dropped him off. Something spooked him bad. I wanted to be sure he was okay."

"Next time you call me, not the kid, right?"

"Sure, Damon."

"And whatever spooks him is none of your business."

"Got it."

"In fact, you don't fucking call *anyone* else in the company but Roy, without asking me first!"

"I got it!"

"But anyhow, you're gonna pay for messing that up by taking the kid to a Muppet movie."

"I what?"

"You got earplugs in? You owe me a favor and I'm calling it."

"I owe what? I don't owe you shit. And he wants Muppets? Really?" He let it hang for a moment, as if reluctant. "That's fucked."

"Hey, watch your mouth. You owe me your job. And you don't have to like it, just do it. We got shit going on here, and I can't spare another driver today. Take him there, keep an eye on him, bring him back." Damon's voice was gruff.

"Seriously?" He could hear Brian in the background chanting "*Muppet movie, yeah, yeah, yeah. Muppet movie, yeah. With Nick, Nick, Nick, yeah.*" No wonder Damon sounded frustrated.

"Yes!" Damon snapped. "I don't know what the *fuck's* got into the kid, but if you want to be useful, you can start now."

"Um. Sure. I don't really mind that animated crap too bad. Didn't get much of it as a kid." They'd given Nick Green a deprived childhood background.

"Right. So get the fuck over here. You'll take him to the theater, watch out for him, and bring him back."

"I could do that. Any chance he might want to see the new *Spiderman* instead?" He heard Brian in the background chant, "*Kermit and Piggy. Kermit and Piggy!*"

"Don't sound like it."

"Well, it's only a couple of hours."

Damon grunted. "Okay. You come get him. I'll tell the gate to expect you."

"See you in thirty."

Chapter 10

Getting through Marston's gate was fast and easy this time— the code, an eyeball, Nick's name, and he was in. The limo was nowhere in sight. He pulled round to the pool house and Brian was waiting outside with Damon. He rolled down the window. "Hop in, Bry." Brian frowned, but hurried to the passenger side and got in.

Damon came over to Nick's window. "He's being an idiot today. Don't let him eat any sugar crap, all right? No pop, no candy."

"Okay."

"Here's some cash." He handed a couple folded bills through the window. "Take him out to eat too. Real food, with protein, not greasy crap. Maybe do two movies. It'll be a lot quieter here without him."

Nick took the money. "Sure thing."

"I'll count you all the way off the hook, if you keep him out till ten."

"Got it."

Damon glanced in at Brian. "You, meathead! Whatever ant got into your pants, that has you bouncing off the walls, you lose it before you come back, right? Or I'm gonna bust your ass till you learn to be quiet."

Brian lowered his eyes. "Yes, Damon."

"And you, Nok." Damon narrowed his eyes at Nick. "Anything happens to him, anything at all, and I'll have your guts and Mr. Marston will cut your heart out."

Nick figured his character would say, "Fuck you." But he added, "I'll watch out for him."

Damon slapped a hand on the car roof and stepped back.

As they wound around the drive, Brian stayed stiff in his seat. It wasn't until they were out on the road, and picking up speed, that he slumped back and smiled. "Okay. Miss Piggy, here we come."

"What did you do to Damon?"

"I was annoying. I can be."

"I bet." Nick decided he wanted to know. "Why does he want you to stay away till ten?"

"I don't know. Probably for Granton and Veronica. They don't like me."

Nick was glad he had the recorder on after all. "Who are they?"

"Mr. Marston's relatives from England. They think I'm embarrassing."

"Is that who was in the limo?"

"Yeah. They're all snobby. Lori says he's a lord something-or-other."

"Granton is?"

"Their father. Mr. Marston's father. I don't know why they came."

"For a visit?"

"I guess. You probably shouldn't ask questions."

"Sorry." Nick wondered about another approach. "Hey, we're going to be way early for the movie. It's not even two yet. You want to get some lunch? Or walk in the park or something?"

"I ate. I like to walk."

Nick drove them to the river park and found a place to leave the car a block away. It was a nice Saturday, although the air was humid and warm. The park was full of families, parents pushing strollers, kids playing tag and feeding the hordes of greedy ducks that came up out of the water at the first hint of breadcrumbs. Nick led the way across the grass with Brian a step behind him, down toward where the lawn changed to rougher weeds. He stopped. "Hey, tuck your jeans into your socks. There's bound to be ticks here."

118

"How nice." But Brian did as he was told. Nick bent and shoved his own hems into his boots.

"Come on." Nick headed out first, down the root-ridged dirt pathway. The sound of the kids faded behind them. After five minutes of scrambling, and a couple of muddy spots, they came to a little grassy clearing. A huge old tree leaned out over the river, half its root structure exposed. Someday it would give way and fall into the water, but for now it made a long seat, almost as wide as a table, out over the water. Nick went first, climbing up and walking out ten feet, before sitting with his feet on a side branch. Brian came and sat beside him.

Below them, the water flowed in swirls of brown and green. Overhead and all around, the branches of the big tree arched in a canopy creating a private space. A woodpecker drummed somewhere behind them, crickets chirped, and the occasional mosquito was just a familiar part of summer. Brian looked around carefully. "This is nice. Is it your special place?"

Nick didn't want to lie. "One of them. I've been here a few times. I thought you might like it."

"I do."

"It's not special like the house is for you." He hesitated. "I really am sorry."

Brian shook his head.

Nick swallowed hard. The recorder was on. He shouldn't say anything he didn't want his fellow cops to hear. For three years on the force, "I'm gay," had been one of those things.

There was no absolute need to go there. Just because Brian had looked eviscerated last night, just because Nick felt guilty, there was no reason to open himself up further. Despite whatever was on last night's record, he hadn't gone too far yet.

Or he could remember that Nick Green wasn't really him. He could always say this was part of his cover, getting Brian to trust him, pretending to be gay. Though even that might open a door he could never fully shut.

He cleared his throat. "I didn't turn you down last night because I don't like you or, um, because you did anything bad."

"Yeah, right. You looked like I might bite your dick off."

"You surprised me."

"It was a simple question."

"Brian, I know that's what you did before. A guy said, 'Suck me,' and you did. But it's not that easy."

"Why not? I wanted to. You're a guy. Why couldn't it be just sex?"

"Well…"

"Because I'm ugly? Because I'm stupid? Because I don't know how to do it right? Pick one."

"None of those!"

Brian turned to look at him, eyes bright, blinking fast. "*Don't* you try to tell me it's because you're not gay. I'm not *that* stupid."

"I never said you were. And, um." The words froze on his tongue. *It's just a cover. You can take it back, later.*

And yet, he'd always sworn he wouldn't lie about this. If someone actually asked, he'd tell the truth. He'd just made damned sure the topic never came up. Now Brian was asking, and the look on his face, the way he held his breath, showed how much this *mattered*. "Um, I *am* gay." There. He'd said it aloud. He took a breath, then another. "But I don't know you very well."

Brian let his breath out in a rush, then frowned. "So you never had sex with someone you didn't know?"

"Well, um, sure. But this is different. You're not some stranger I'll never see again, either."

"A stranger would be *better*?"

"It would be easier." He couldn't add that as a cop, having sex with a suspect could screw up his career. Especially gay sex. It helped to remind himself of that, though. "Listen, you confuse me. One minute you're chanting about Miss Piggy like a five-year-old, the next you're, well, like a normal guy."

Brian looked away. "I hate the word normal. There is no universe in which I'm normal."

"I'm sorry." He put a hand on Brian's arm. Brian shrugged it off roughly, and moved a few inches farther away. Nick searched for words. "Normal is way overrated. I'm not normal either. I'm not sure anyone is. But you're, um, more different. At times. Sometimes you're differently different."

At least Brian laughed. "Uh huh."

Nick lowered his voice and tried to speak gently. "What's going on with you? Can you tell me?"

For a long time Brian sat silently, watching the water flow past. His pale fingers rubbed up and down the seam of his jeans, up and down, until Nick really wanted to reach out and stop him, but he made himself wait patiently. Eventually Brian said, "Have you heard about people who are really two people? Two personalities. Like, in their heads?"

"I guess."

"Like, I saw Conchita Wurst on TV, right? She's a singer, with a dress and a beard, and she's a man sometimes and, um, not sometimes. She even uses two different names, and she's a star, so maybe it's not so bad that I'm the same way."

"I suppose." Nick decided to hang in there, despite his instinct to bail on this conversation right the hell now. "Do you feel like a woman sometimes?"

Brian turned to stare at him. "No!"

"I'm not getting it."

"I'm Brian, but Bry is the stupid me."

"Oh? Oh." Nick was struck by the simplicity of that, the way it explained things. Brian was smart, or at least, not really stupid. Bry was much more limited. Although, split personality might explain things, but it was far from simple. He felt a little sick. This was so out of his experience. "So there are two people in you and one is smarter?"

"Maybe?" Brian looked back at the river. "I used to think I only pretended to be Bry. When it was safer. When it was useful. But now, sometimes I think I don't get to choose who to be. It just happens."

"Mm. How long have you been two people?"

"God." Brian rubbed at his eyes. "Forever. Maybe since I was six? Or maybe eight? When Lori and Damon started playing games I didn't want to play, and it was easier to become too stupid to join in."

"What kind of games?" Nick tensed. He'd done a lot of domestic calls as a patrolman, and some of what the adults had called *games* had been sick as hell.

"For money. Like, Lori would take lunch money from kids at school. She'd tell the little kids I'd beat them up if they didn't pay me, 'cause I was the biggest kid, but I didn't want to. And sometimes she and Damon would go out and tell people they lost their bus pass, and needed money to get home. People would give them a couple dollars to ride the bus, but they didn't get on it. They'd just ask the next people too."

"Con games."

Brian snorted a humorless laugh. "They said it was games. I hated it. Especially when the littler kids were scared of me. A couple times I gave the money back, and told Lori I did it because it was just a game, right? Like I was too dumb to know different? She stopped asking me to play."

"Oh, Brian."

"They thought I couldn't tell what it was. It was stealing."

"Yes."

Brian's voice got higher and faster. "But it was for us, for buying food and stuff. Because Mom used drugs, and she never had grocery money. Half the time it was Damon who brought home enough so we could eat. So I was bad if I was stealing, but I was also bad for taking Damon's food and not helping him steal. It was easier to be too stupid to understand."

Nick nodded silently.

"Lori's real smart about people, about how they think. She helped Damon come up with schemes, even better than the bus pass one. They got good at the cons, and they stopped asking me. So I tried to take care of Mom instead. Like, that could be my thing to help our family. I Found her when she was lost, and I made her come home, and I cleaned her bed and made her drink and eat. I did help."

"I'm sure you did."

"Yeah. But she died. When I was sixteen, she ODed. I couldn't wake her up. Damon called 911 but the ambulance took forever. We lived in a bad neighborhood, and it always took forever for help to show up. They were too slow, and she died."

Nick's chest hurt. "You said she took drugs. If someone's an addict, you can't fix them. They have to want to stop themselves, and if they won't, they usually do end up dead."

Brian scrubbed his face with his palms. Fine tremors shuddered across his body, like all the hurt in his voice was crawling over his skin. Nick almost reached out to touch him, for comfort, but Brian hadn't wanted that. Nick scooted a bit nearer anyway, until his knee was against Brian's thigh.

Brian said, "Sometimes I thought if I was smarter and better in school, Mom would've wanted to stay with us. But I know that's not true. Damon's really smart, and he got As and had jobs and earned money, and she kept doing drugs anyway. Lori's smart, and really pretty, and it didn't help. Nothing mattered more to Mom than the drugs."

Nick said softly, "I'm starting to think you're pretty smart too."

"Maybe. Bry is dumb, but I'm not so bad. But I never came close to graduating."

"Einstein flunked some classes. School's not the only way to know if you're smart."

"I have bad dyslexia." Brian met his startled glance. "What? Enough teachers said it. But none of them could fix it. I can say the word, but I couldn't begin to spell it. I can't read it. When I look at letters and words and numbers, they dance on the page like they're drunk."

"Okay." Nick felt a rush of optimism. "That's not the same as stupid at all! There's got to be answers."

"Maybe. But they won't help with Bry. And I need to be Bry to live with Damon." Brian suddenly got to his feet, balancing on the wide trunk. "Let's go see a movie."

"Wait." Nick stood too. "Do you *have* to stay with Damon?"

"You know Damon." Brian dusted off his jeans, not looking at Nick. "Do you think he'd let me walk away?"

"You're his brother. He seems to want you to be safe. Maybe if you showed him you're smarter than Bry he'd let you live on your own?"

Brian shook his head. "Do you know what Damon does? Do you know what's in those trucks you drive?"

"No," Nick lied. "Not my business."

"Well, I don't want to know. But I do, some of it. I know a lot of things. And I'm useful to Mr. Marston. They won't let me go."

"Useful how?"

Brian shrugged. "Even more important, if I'm Bry, if I'm stupid and I don't understand, then sometimes I can say no without saying no."

"Useful *how?*" Nick grabbed Brian's arm. "Are they...?" What? He couldn't even come up with a scenario that went with Brian being of use to Marston. Drug mule? Con games again? Brian was too old for the sex trade, surely, no matter how sweet his face might be. Or maybe not. "What do they make you do?"

Brian freed his arm and reached out to put a finger on Nick's lips. "Shhh. It's a secret."

"I can keep a secret."

"Not that one." Brian tugged at Nick's shirt gently. "Come on. I want to get off this log."

Nick did as he was told, his thoughts racing. If Brian really had information, if he was willing to testify and could make himself believed, the whole case might break open. "I might find a safe place for you, away from Damon."

"But he's my brother. He's all I have, him and Lori and now the baby."

"And Marston? You want to stay around him?"

Brian kicked at the moss on the bank. "He's Lori's husband. She's having his baby. We're all linked together now." He took Nick's arm. "You won't tell anyone, about me and Bry? Promise you won't tell."

"I might be able to get help for you."

"No! Promise! I trusted you."

"All right," Nick said reluctantly. "I won't say anything." He wouldn't have to, after all. The recording would say it for him. He mimed zipping his lips shut.

"So now we'll see movies." Brian hurried toward the trail back to the park. "Were you telling the truth about liking Muppets? I have to see it to talk about it to Damon. He sometimes knows if I'm lying. But you could go into *Spiderman 2* instead. I wouldn't tell."

"I love Muppets." Nick caught up to Brian. "I want to see you snort popcorn up your nose at the jokes."

"*You'll* be snorting popcorn." Brian's voice was light and easy. "Just wait."

It was a surprisingly good afternoon. Brian was different when he wasn't guarding himself. He was anything but dumb, although his speech patterns were uneven, and there were odd gaps in his knowledge. They talked movies all the way to the theater. When Nick tried to slide in questions about how Brian lived now, whether he worked on the estate, *what the fucking hell Marston used him for*, Brian dodged them. Nick did pick up hints of his past here and there.

"I never saw the end of that one. We got chased out of the theater."

"This one shelter we stayed at, all we watched was the Sci-Fi Channel."

"Damon made us swords out of these bits from a packing crate and we played pirates all over the room, until Mom couldn't stand it and took them away."

When they were in the lobby buying popcorn, Nick laughed at something Brian had said and bumped his shoulder. He turned to find the counter guy looking at them with a little curl of his lip that screamed *disgusting fags*. "You two want just one? To *share*?"

Nick was about to get in the guy's face, when Brian said loudly, "Popcorn! Pop! Pop! Pop! Popcorn! I want salt and butter and salt and caramel and cheese. Can I have cheeeeeese? Pleeeeease?"

He saw it happen, the moment when the guy behind the counter decided they weren't two fags, but a mentally challenged guy and his keeper. Which for some reason was more socially acceptable. The man looked straight at Nick, ignoring Brian, and asked, "What do you really want?"

Nick was very tempted to make him ask Brian, but he could feel a little tremor in Brian's shoulder against his, so he said, "A large. Cheese."

When they were settled in the theater with the tub of popcorn between them, he murmured, "Was that on purpose?"

"I don't know." Brian sounded miserable. "I ruined it, didn't I?"

"Ruined what?" It had creeped him out a little, but he said, "That was cool. This place is a little too close to your brother's hangouts to be out and proud."

"Oh." Brian slowly drew the sound out. "Ohhhh. Yeah. I don't want Damon to know."

"So that was good." Nick dared a quick pat to Brian's leg. "Fast thinking."

"But weird, huh? Of course, in *Rain Man*, Dustin Hoffman is pretty weird, and it's not such a bad thing. Although I guess he goes back to the asylum in the end, so it's not a good thing."

Nick tipped the cardboard tub toward Brian. "Have some popcorn and stop thinking so hard."

They saw *Spiderman 2* as well, afterward, because neither of them wanted to leave. For dinner, Nick picked a quiet café almost twenty minutes away. It was well out of the local circle of bars and diners that Damon and his friends seemed to stick to. Even at the little table in the back, Brian was subdued, but he ate everything put in front of him and answered direct questions. Nick ordered a second beer and lingered. It was long past dark when Brian looked at his watch and said, "It's after ten. We have to go."

"You can tell time?" Nick wished he could grab the words back, but Brian just tipped his wrist toward Nick.

"With this watch. It has big hand, little hand. I used to get mixed up but I'm okay with it now."

"That's great. Useful."

"Yeah. We should go."

Nick tossed a couple of bills on the table and stood. Brian led the way out to the street. A wind had picked up, and a stray piece of paper scudded down the sidewalk. Brian stomped on it, picked it up, and scrunched it into his pocket. "Rain's coming."

"Yeah. Feels like."

"I don't want to go home."

Nick paused, his door half-open. "Seriously?"

"No. I mean, I don't *want* to, but I have to."

"Your call."

"Home." Brian got in and fastened his belt. "I just don't want today to be over. I never, ever told anyone about Bry and Brian before."

Nick backed up, then pulled out into traffic. "You know, you *should* be careful. That was smart. Even with me, you should probably be *more* careful." He imagined Brian with some random guy, all open and laughing, sharing a dozen details that could be used to knife him in the gut. "You don't know me any more than I know you. I work for your brother and Mr. Marston. I could be as bad as anyone."

"You're not."

"I hit people. I hurt them. You've seen me fight." He might have exaggerated his temper as Nick Green, but that didn't mean it wasn't real.

"You never hit people who don't deserve it."

"The hell I don't!" He braked for a stoplight and stared at Brian. "Where'd you get that crap from?" His heart sped up. All he needed was for Brian to say something like that to Damon.

"I pay attention." Brian's tone was serene. "You hit that fat guy when he grabbed Shannon's—" He made a curved-hands gesture at his chest. "—after she said stop. You hit the guy who said 'faggot,' and the other guy who called the blond kid a cocksucker. You punched the guy who tried to drag his wife out by her hair, and the one who threw his glass at the bartender, and..." It was a fairly long list. Nick couldn't have come close to repeating it. What's more, it went back to his second night in the bar, and the knife incident.

"You remember all that? You were watching me?"

"From the first night. You came in. You had a black leather jacket and faded jeans. You drank beer. There was a guy at the pool table, and he was drunk. He tried to hit that other guy with his cue, and you took it away from him and tossed him out of the bar. Then you came back, and you laughed and said, 'Anyone up for a game?' You beat Little Joe and then bought him a beer with the money you won."

"Um. Wow."

"After that, I always noticed you."

Nick wasn't sure if that was flattering or not. He was fighting damned hard not to let Brian get under his guard. He went with *not*. "God, Bry! That's, um, that's creepy. I never had a stalker before."

"Oh!" Brian went rigid. Nick glanced over. Brian's eyes were closed, his lips pressed into a thin line. Another glance a moment later showed a tear sliding down his cheek, although he made no sound.

"Shit!" Nick pulled over suddenly onto the shoulder, and got out. He raised his fist and slammed it down on the roof of the car. Inside, he saw Brian flinch and was darkly pleased even as it nauseated him. Deluded idiot!

Brian had no fucking idea what he was really like. He was no white knight, no hero to be watched from afar. He was a lying, violent, undercover cop, and there were very few things *more* likely to fuck up Brian's life than for him to fixate on Nick.

He breathed through clenched teeth, until he had control back. Then he dropped heavily into his seat.

Without opening his eyes, Brian said, "I'm sorry. That was bad, right?" His voice got higher and younger. "I shouldn't have watched you. You were different from the others, and I wanted wrong things, bad things. I'm so sorry."

"Jesus. Brian, no."

"I'm ready to go home now."

"Brian, stop. Listen to me." He reached out and touched Brian's arm. Brian flinched violently, then froze again. "Can you open your eyes and look at me?"

Brian shook his head.

"All right. I'm flattered, really, that I caught your attention. I guess I can understand."

"Damon will kill me."

"What?"

"Well, not kill me. He wouldn't. He might hit me though. He'll be so mad."

Nick shook his head, lost. "About what?"

"When you tell him I stalked you."

"Aargh." Nick pounded the steering wheel, making Brian flinch again. "Why the hell would I tell Damon?

"I… don't know."

"Brian, listen up. Yeah, okay, that was a bit creepy, but understandable, I guess. Just, don't keep doing that. I can't be your boyfriend, or fuck buddy, or whatever. But the last thing I want to do is tell anyone you're gay, or I'm gay, or you're weird, or whatever. All right?"

"I guess?"

Nick scrubbed his hand over his hair and put the car in gear. "You keep quiet, I'll keep quiet, no harm done. I'll take you home, and—" He stopped dead there, because he wasn't sure what came after the "and." He should be angling to see Brian again. Even the tidbits of information Brian dropped might be useful, and he'd bet if he played along, he could get Brian to open up a lot more. The thought of using him that way was making him feel sick, though. Brian might not be the bewildered child Nick had imagined he was, but he didn't deserve to be played and betrayed.

"You're better off keeping your head down, all right? Stay quiet, stay safe. If you want to leave Damon just say the word and I'll help you."

"No thank you." Brian's eyes stayed closed and his voice was thin.

"We'll be home in fifteen minutes."

Brian nodded.

The rest of the drive was silent. Nick could feel the tension in Brian beside him. In his head, he rehearsed things he might say, ways to break this new ice. But all of them were just the beginning of a new betrayal, really. He'd forgotten for an hour or six that he was a cop and Brian was a suspect and a bit strange. He'd acted like they were becoming friends, and of course Brian had been thinking about being more. The guy was so lonely he'd probably think the girl who smiled when she took his order at McDonald's was a friend.

At least Nick's new fuckup had fixed that problem. They were far from friends now.

He pulled around the pool house, and into a darker space between the lampposts, to let Brian out.

Brian parroted in a high voice without opening his eyes, "Thank you for the lovely evening, Mr. Green."

"Fuck that." Nick reached for his arm, but aborted the gesture without touching him. "Can I talk to Brian, not Bry?" *God, this was weird.*

"I don't know. Can you?"

He'd take that as a yes. "I'm sorry this got screwed up. I know that was my fault. Don't be mad, okay? I had fun, talking movies with you. You're a pretty interesting guy, and a lot smarter than you give yourself credit for. Someday, some man will realize that too, I swear."

"And someday pigs will fly." Brian opened his eyes and looked straight at him. His pupils were so wide they looked black in the dimness of the car. "Well, that was the best day ever. Until it wasn't. Have a nice life, Nick." He slid out of the car and strode off toward his door.

"Son of a *bitch*!" Nick almost broke a finger on the steering wheel that time. But there was nothing to do but watch the door swing shut behind Brian, and turn the car around, and go home.

Chapter 11

On Monday morning, Brian stood at the kitchen counter, having breakfast with Damon, when Lori came flying in the breezeway door. The red of her cheeks and flash of her eyes signaled her flaring temper. Brian eased back into the corner by the fridge, holding his mug in front of his face as a fragile shield. Lori ignored him, reaching for Damon's mug. "Give me that."

"Get your own, bitch." But Damon let go of it and turned to the cabinets to get down another cup.

Lori took a long swallow and sighed. "God, yes."

"What? That big, fancy kitchen can't manage to make coffee in the morning?"

Lori took another swallow. "That British witch has convinced Vern that coffee is bad for unborn babies."

"Seriously?" A smile twitched Damon's lips. "Sucks to be you."

"Screw that. When are they going home already?"

"Don't you know, girl? You're living with them."

"Don't remind me." She wrapped both hands around her cup. "I don't know. I don't know anything, apparently. They're making me crazy. Henry has a stick up his ass and thinks Vern should divorce me, and his daughter is a cast-iron bitch."

"You call that dude Henry?"

Lori managed one of her cooler smiles. "Oh yeah. I said 'Mr. Granton,' being all polite. And Veronica said, 'Oh, don't be so formal. You should call him Uncle Henry.' And she smiled like she was so clever, the way it made me sound too young for Vern. So I said, 'Sorry, Henry, I thought you guys liked a bit of formality. But sure, I can do first names. It seems like my niece Ronnie is a bit confused, though.' And I turned to her and said, 'You can call me Aunt Lori, of course, Ronnie.' She said, 'Ver-on-i-ca,' like she wanted to spit. I said, nice as pie, 'Oh, of course, so sorry. Nicknames are our American way, Veronica. But I'll try to remember.'"

Damon snorted. "You want to be careful. Don't get Vern angry."

"Yeah, he wasn't too pleased. But he didn't like her treating me like we weren't married either, so that was okay. I don't think he likes Veronica much, but he does seem to like Henry. Unfortunately."

"What did they do yesterday? I had to make that run to Mankato."

Brian had stayed in his room and watched *Frozen* and *Beauty and the Beast* on his iPad. A few times over. He hadn't been hungry.

"They went to church first. Can you believe it?" Lori flicked her hair back off her shoulders. "Vern said I could stay in bed, so I did. Then we went out and did the tourist thing. Ver-on-i-ca kept talking about how 'new' and 'raw' the architecture was, and how hot and bright everything was."

"Maybe she'll get sunstroke."

"I wish. Vern finally said something about not missing the English rain one bit, and she shut up. Then he took them out to a show and a bar. He made me come home and rest. I hope they have awful hangovers." She turned to Brian. "Hey Bry, Mario comes to do the lawn this morning, right? Any chance you could accidentally start mowing right under the yellow guest room window?"

Brian bit his lip, which allowed time for Damon to say, "That's just down from Vern's study window, isn't it?"

"No," Brian said immediately. "Can't."

"Good boy." Damon frowned at Lori. "Don't get carried away. They'll have to leave soon, and you want Vern glad to see them go, not mad at you."

"I know."

"So stay sweet as sugar and let it slide on off."

"I'll try. But if she keeps going on about how young I am, I'm going to find a way to show how dumb she is."

"Hey, young is good. I bet Henry wishes he had a wife your age."

"Maybe. He watches me, but if I catch him, then he presses his lips together like a preacher watching two fags kiss."

Brian winced, and set his cup on the counter to cover it.

Damon said, "Keep your eyes on the prize."

"I am. I'm cool. That's why I came here to blow off steam. It's weird, you know, to see Vern acting like he cares what Henry thinks."

"He might be faking it. Don't forget, Marston can smile and shake someone's right hand as he slides in the knife with his left."

"That's my husband you're talking about." Lori pouted her lips theatrically, then glanced at Brian. "You're not listening, right Bry-baby?"

"Not listening," he repeated automatically.

Lori looked back at Damon. "Well, I'm going to finish this coffee and then go back and hang on Vern's arm. Maybe I can make Henry feel old."

"It's a plan."

Brian put his mug in the sink. "I'll go. I'll wait for Mario by the gate. We always start near the gate."

"Sure. Put on your hat and sunscreen though." Lori gave him a quick one-armed hug. "You have to take care of yourself."

"Yes, Lori." He went up to his room, and grabbed a hat off his shelf. It wasn't until he was halfway to the front gate that he realized he'd grabbed Nick's cap. He touched the brim and let his Finder eye open for an instant, searching for the familiar thread. *That way.* The flash of headache as he closed it again made him rub his eyes. That had been stupid. Really stupid, because it reminded him of things he'd been trying to forget, of how Nick's hand felt on his arm, how Nick's voice sounded above the soft rush of flowing water. For a minute, an hour, he'd been like everyone else, with a friend who liked the same stuff he did, and who talked about it normally, and told jokes.

It hurt, remembering he'd joked to Nick that the only early matinée he'd ever liked was the *Star Wars* one, where all the noisy kids read the opening out loud, and he finally found out what the words rolling back on the screen said. Nick had laughed, then. Only it hadn't been just something funny to say; it was true. That was how his life went. His truth was a joke to most people. No doubt it'd ended up as one more brick in the not-good-enough-to-fuck wall that Nick put up between them. He said that word again, aloud. "Fuck."

He wanted that. Someday, with some man he chose. Some man who chose him. He had to believe it could happen or he might as well have jumped off that tree into the river. If Bry was all he could be, if this life was all he'd ever have, then why bother? He trudged down the drive, eyes on the ground.

Mario startled him, stopping the truck a few feet away. "Hey, Bry. Lost in thought? I almost ran into you."

"No. Sorry."

"That's okay. You want to get the riding mower out right here? I'll pull over."

"Sure."

Mario pulled to the side of the drive and got out to let the trailer ramp down. Brian hopped up on the mower and backed it carefully down to the ground. He loved the mower. He'd never pass a written license test, but he knew how to drive it, and this one had plenty of power. He liked looping in tight around trees, and rumbling across Mr. Marston's acres of lawn.

What did it say about him, that something so simple was entertaining? Would a normal twenty-one-year-old guy get a kick out of a riding mower?

As Mario closed the ramp, a car swept down the drive toward the road, passing close enough to make Brian wince. He recognized one of Mr. Marston's cars, driven by Veronica.

"Who's that?" Mario asked.

Brian shrugged rather than explaining.

Mario watched as the gate opened to let the car through. "Well, let's hope she doesn't hit anything with Mr. Marston's BMW. All right, you get to work. I'll meet you by the house when you're done."

There was almost a meditation to driving. Brian had tried meditation once. The libraries in the schools he'd gone to never had a lot of books on tape, and he was embarrassed to ask which was what, so once he'd ended up with a tape on how to visualize your center and chant. He'd tried it, enough to see where it might work for someone, but then he'd returned the tape and stopped. Some kinds of activity were almost the same though, almost like chanting, when you did it over and over and over until the pieces all felt the same and didn't mean anything. It was soothing. He swept back and forth and back and forth across the wide front lawn, keeping the rows neat and even.

He let himself fall into a dream where this was a real job. Every day, he'd go out and cut people's lawns, or shovel their snow. Every night he'd come home to a little house of his own, with two dogs. He'd feed the dogs and walk them, and go inside, and there would be a guy, maybe. A dark-haired guy with bright eyes, who'd smile when he saw Brian, and pet the dogs, and say... His imagination ran out of steam. The guy looked too much like Nick, and when he deliberately made him more like Ricky Martin, then the whole thing became a puppet show.

He sped up, making a reckless turn on a sloped section that had the tractor tipping under him. *Who cares? Why not live it up, and no loss if I fail?* He turned again, playing with the limits, feeling the heavy bulk of metal under him lift and slide. He tugged the steering, correcting it, and heard a wheel thump back to the earth.

A voice yelled, "Bry! What the hell?"

He slowed, glancing at Mario who was running toward him. Brian let the lawn tractor slow and stop. Mario dashed over and clamped a hand on the wheel. "Whadda you think you were doing?"

"Huh?"

"This isn't a toy! Stupid boy! If you get crazy, I'll tell Mr. Marston you shouldn't drive it anymore."

Brian felt heat rush over his face. "Sorry."

"You know what he'd do to me if you got hurt? Do you? Idiot!"

"I'm sorry." He squeezed his eyes shut, aware of tears prickling behind the lids. It was nothing new, getting yelled at for being dumb. He should be used to it. He couldn't understand why this time hurt more.

"Get off."

Brian clutched the wheel with both hands. "No. Please! I'll be good. I'll be careful. Please!" *Don't take this job away from me!*

Mario's tone softened. "Well… I'll give you one more chance. But right now, Mr. Marston wants to see you. So jump down and go on. He's at the storage building. He said come straightaway."

"Oh." Slowly, he unwrapped his fingers from the warm plastic. *Mr. Marston wants you.* He knew what that meant. And yet, obediently, he slid down off the seat and turned for the house, wiping his sweaty palms on his thighs. *Mr. Marston wants you at the storage building.*

It might not be too bad. Mr. Marston imported weird stuff from all over, and sometimes he wanted Brian to come look at it, or touch it, or let him wave it over Brian's body like a weirdness-detector. Pretty much nothing happened. That was better than Finding.

When he rounded the house and reached the experiment place, Mr. Marston and Mr. Granton were standing in front of the closed door. Mr. Granton was saying, "Insanity! You still spend your money on that *trash*?" He waved at the concrete building. "It's all a hoax. After forty years, how can you not admit it?"

Mr. Marston's eyes found Brian, his look hungry and calculating. "All a hoax, huh? Care to bet on that?"

"All a hoax. Like the woman who swore she could curse your enemies and make them die? Remember that knife that was supposed to only cut someone if they told a lie, or the chalice with the power to heal wounds on the full moon. You should have got a two-for-one special there, because neither of them *worked. Nothing works.*" Mr. Granton's British accent thickened. "You've spent a fortune— my fortune and now your fortune— looking for magic, and none of it ever changed one molecule of water into wine."

"So make a bet. What will you give me if I show you something you can't explain?"

"Bet?" Mr. Granton stepped closer to Mr. Marston, ignoring Brian's approach. "I have a bet for you. If you prove it to me, I'll pay you a million dollars. But when you fail, you'll declare that common little tramp's baby an impostor, illegitimate. You keep it out of the line of inheritance."

Mr. Marston's smile was sharp. "So confident. Well, I am too. Agreed. Will you add to the bet? If I win, you publicly declare that baby Father's legitimate heir, after you, to the fortune as well as the title."

"Never."

"Not so confident now?"

Mr. Granton glared at him. "You made life a circus for Father and me, chasing after bogeymen. You stole family funds for your little games. Why should I offer anything?"

"Well, the title will pass from you to me to my son. That's out of your hands, as long as I have a son and you don't." Mr. Marston's voice was as calm as ever, but crisp and dry. "The only way you can do anything about it is to make this bet."

"All right then." Mr. Granton gave a sharp nod. "Prove it. Convince me." When Mr. Marston held out his hand, they shook on it for a second.

Mr. Marston said, "Come here, Bry."

Brian stepped forward. "Where's Damon?"

"We don't need Damon for this."

"For what?" Mr. Granton said.

"For your demonstration." Mr. Marston gestured down toward the garage. "Let's go choose a car, shall we? Come along."

He turned and walked toward the side door, and Brian followed silently. Mr. Granton walked beside him, throwing curious glances his way. Brian stared at Mr. Marston's back and didn't look aside in return.

Inside the garage, the row of cars sat ready and gleaming. Brian thought with an ache that he would've been washing the Hummer and the Porsche today, if his job had gone uninterrupted. It was one of the Monday chores, to polish all the cars in turn, even the ones that hadn't left the garage for weeks. Mr. Marston gestured at the Hummer. "Bry, get in front. Henry, take the seat behind me."

"Why?"

"You'll see." Mr. Marston opened his door. "Get in, Bry."

Teeth clenched and eyes downcast, Brian did as he was told. His mind was racing. Who would he be set to Find? Would this be just a game, or was Mr. Marston combining business with pleasure? There was no doubt he was expecting pleasure, from the dark gleam in his eyes.

When they were buckled up, Mr. Marston reached into his pocket and held something out toward Brian. "Take that."

"Wait!" Mr. Granton reached forward to snatch away the braided silver chain. "That's Veronica's!"

"Yes. I promise, she'll get it back."

"How did you get it?"

"The clasp broke. I told her I'd get it fixed. She said she was very attached to it."

"She wears it often." Mr. Granton closed his fist over it. "What are you planning?"

Mr. Marston laughed. "If you really think it's all a hoax, why should it matter?" He let that hang for a second, then said, "But if it reassures you, we're just going to find her. You've heard of dowsing for water? Well, Brian here dowses for people."

"Explain. Now."

"Don't freak out, as we say in America." Mr. Marston's smile showed he was enjoying the moment. "He won't hurt Veronica. He'll just find her. Wherever she is, no matter how far away, right, Bry?"

What could he say? "Yes, Mr. Marston."

"So, Henry, do you know where your daughter is?"

Mr. Granton leaned forward fast. "She went shopping. Why? Did you do something to her?"

"Hell, no. She's out there, somewhere, shopping. Or lunching." Mr. Marston waved a casual hand south. "Minneapolis is a big city, with lots of choices. If you needed to find her, what would you do?"

"I'd call her. Or get GPS records."

"I have a different way. Give that chain to Brian."

"You're kidding." Mr. Granton's fingers unclenched, but he didn't hold the chain out.

"No. Hand it to the boy. You're about to see that there are more things in heaven and earth than your narrow world admits."

Reluctantly, Mr. Granton reached out and tipped the warm metal links into Brian's hand. Mr. Marston said, "Find her."

For a moment the possibilities danced in Brian's brain. *He could refuse, say there was no link, pretend to try, and fail...* He could screw Mr. Marston over and there was no way for him to know it was on purpose. Except that Mr. Marston didn't take excuses when the stakes were high, and these were awfully high. And as Mr. Granton's frown began to ease, Brian knew he'd rather win this game than lose it. After all, Lori's baby was the stake. He shut his eyes, slid the chain between his palms, then closed his hand over it.

Veronica's trace began to filter in. The chain was hers, all right. There were hints of other people, a woman, a man, like wisps of mist blowing by, but her trace was strong and dense, perfume like the counter at the department store, mingled scents of flowers and musk, and dampness with a hint of salt. "That way." He pointed to his left.

He held on to her trace as they drove out of the garage, and turned left. His finger swung to point straight ahead, moving automatically, locked on. He paid no attention to the sounds of the Hummer, of the gate. Mr. Granton muttered about fakery, and Brian just stayed fixed on the trace. Like so many nights, when he was younger.

As a kid, he'd known people had a taste, a smell, something that leaped from their bare skin to his if he touched them just right. He could have recognized Damon in a crowd of other boys in the dark, from that steel-taste in the back of his mind. But it hadn't been until he was ten that he'd tracked down and Found Mom.

His hand swung right and the car swayed as they drove. Back then he'd walked, feet aching in too-small sneakers, on that dark wet night. Damon had gone out earlier, worried and mad, and Lori was sad, and Mom hadn't been home in three days. There was no food, and a notice on the door, and they needed Mom, now! So he'd started walking, looking for her, following her. And he'd realized that her trace was there, like a trail of candy-sweet and sweat-sour, like dust and a window that didn't quite shut, with the wind blowing in cold through the gap.

If Damon had been home, he'd never have managed to get away, but Lori eventually quit tugging at his arm and followed along as he crossed streets and walked down dirty sidewalks. He'd turned in at a flight of broken cement stairs. The old man sitting on the steps had said, "You don't want to go in there, kids." But Mom had been in there, he knew it, and he'd pushed on past.

The floor was dirty, and the rancid smell almost drowned Mom's candy-sweet out of his head, but there she was. She lay on a mattress, staring out the smeary window. When she saw them, she smiled and said, "Hey, kids. Is it dinnertime?" Like nothing was wrong. The man in the corner laughed and laughed, as Lori helped Mom get up and come with them. "She'll be back," he'd called after them. "Sweet crack whore. She'll be back."

She had gone back.

After that, Brian had always been able to Find her, though. For a while it was better. He showed Damon where to go get Mom when they needed her, and she didn't do the drugs quite as much. But then she started getting worse again. Then she died.

He pressed his eyes tighter shut, pushing the past away, focusing on perfume and salt. He hadn't Found many women besides Mom. That was why she was on his mind. And this was just a test, like when he was small, when Finding someone was a hug and a laugh. This would be like Finding Mom or Lori where they were okay afterward, not like man after man he'd Found, only to feel the trace suddenly cut off and gone, leaving an empty place like it was gouged out of the world with a knife. This was better. He could do this one, easy.

As they drove, he became aware of the conversation going on, like a TV in the background.

Mr. Granton. "I'm still not buying this."

Mr. Marston. "You will."

After a pause, Mr. Granton. "How did you find this, um, psychic? If he is what you say."

"My first wife. I met her in New Orleans. I'd been almost ready to give up on the paranormal. I'd had high hopes for the practitioners there, but I was never convinced. Then I met Stephanie."

"And she was psychic." Disbelief was clear in Mr. Granton's voice.

"If you like. She ran a game for money in the pubs and bars. She'd bet with a group of people, pass around a covered bowl and tell them to each drop in a small item they'd owned for at least a week. Then she'd pull each item out and tell them whose it was. Boom. Boom. Boom. No mumbo jumbo, no messing around. And she was never wrong. I watched her. One guy dropped in his brother's watch and she told him the person who owned it wasn't there. I hired people to test her. They dropped in each other's items. She was never wrong."

"Some trick. Mirrors in the bowl. A confederate."

"That's what I thought. So I started dating her, and watched. I tested every variation. She won every bet. After I married her, she said talents ran in her family. She could always match a person to their trace on objects. She'd done it since she was a girl."

Brian tried to focus and listen at the same time. It wasn't easy to keep Veronica's trace in his mind and still understand what was being said. He missed a few words.

"...heard that she had passed away?"

"Yes." Mr. Marston's voice held no emotion, no sorrow. "She went into liver failure. The docs gave her weeks to live, and then she told me that her grandmother in Minnesota was a faith healer. We relocated here. Her grandmother visited every week for a month, doing the laying on of hands, and she started looking much better. But her grandmother had a stroke and died, and within three months Stephanie was dead too."

"My condolences. Still not proof of anything."

"I went looking further. It wasn't a big family. Stephanie's parents were dead, but she'd lied about having no siblings. She had one sister, and the sister had three children. By the time I found the paper trail, the sister had also died. But her three children survived, and the oldest was just twenty-one, the younger two fifteen. Two boys, one girl. I approached them slowly and carefully." There was heavy meaning in his tone, and it wasn't hard to put it together.

Brian shuddered, and managed not to open his eyes. Veronica's trace almost slid out of his grasp, thinning like smoke, shreds of damp perfume tattered in his surprise. He clenched his fists, struggling to hold on. His pointing hand wavered, firmed up, wavered. He locked on better, breathing through clenched teeth, and kept pointing. *His aunt. Mr. Marston's first wife. And she'd had this talent too*. He ached to ask how, why, what it meant. They'd had a grandmother, an aunt they'd never known, family.

Years of pretending not to understand anything let him keep his face expressionless.

Mr. Granton said, "You married the girl? Lori is your first wife's niece? What's her skill, then?"

Mr. Marston lowered his voice. "I hired the oldest boy, investigated all three. I found at least one genuine talent. At least one. That's all you need to know, Henry."

Mr. Granton's voice got softer too. "Can he hear us?"

"No. Anyway, he wouldn't understand. His brother says he's like a homing missile, locked on, barely even knows we're here. He'll either point his way to the target, or lose the trace and pass out. I've seen it dozens of times now."

Thanks, Damon. Brian tried to think of that description as a gift from his brother, a chance to hear and learn more than he should.

The first few times he'd Found someone, Brian really had been locked on his search. He'd only survived Finding his mom because Lori had been there to pull him out of traffic and keep him from walking into walls. And since then, yeah, he'd faked that same oblivion, not wanting to know where they went, what they did, how the hunts ended. He hadn't wanted to hear the plans or the excitement. Closing his eyes, acting deaf and dumb, and passing out, had been easier.

They were getting close; he adjusted his aim a fraction to the left. Then suddenly they were past and going the wrong way. He swung around, eyes still closed, acting the robot, being the robot. He jammed his finger on the back of the seat and didn't let himself make a sound.

"He's Found her." Mr. Marston slowed the Hummer, turned right. Brian adjusted his aim, and again, as they made another right turn, and another.

"That proves nothing. This could be a random location."

"You could call her. Ask if she's in the Galleria. Or we can park and get out, and he can walk right up to her."

"She might have mentioned the Galleria. I want to see him go all the way."

"All right."

There were turns and bumping, presumably as they parked. Brian kept his eyes squeezed shut and his aim locked on. When the motor shut off, he sat there, still and stupid, pointing back and to the left, until Mr. Marston opened his door, unlatched his seatbelt, and pulled him out.

"Walk now," Mr. Marston said loudly in his ear. "Find her." He tucked Brian's hand in his arm, like a blind man's, and then draped something over Brian's pointing forearm. "Go."

Brian shuffled forward blindly, making it as difficult for Mr. Marston as he dared. He tripped over a step and swayed against Mr. Marston, who grabbed him tighter and muttered, "Get his other side."

Mr. Granton's hand under his elbow was cold and hard, like a skeleton's grasp. Brian walked a little better, not wanting to lean against him. He still pointed, adjusting.

"People are staring," Mr. Granton muttered.

"You wanted proof." Mr. Marston sounded amused. "We're two men taking our handicapped nephew out for a trip. Minnesotans are polite. They'll look and then glance away. No one cares."

Brian knew they were close. He picked up speed, tugging against restraining hands. Then he heard Veronica say, "Father? Is something wrong?"

Brian let go of her trace. Like a cut string, the ends whipped around him, flipping back to her. He fought to stay upright and conscious. Passing out here would be embarrassing, no matter how Mr. Marston might spin it.

It wasn't bad. It really wasn't bad. He'd let go on purpose this time, rather than being cut loose as the trace vanished. No one died. He could do this. He breathed hard, his knees shaking, leaning on the supporting hands under his elbows more than he wanted to. Then he couldn't control it anymore. He decided to hell with embarrassed. "Gonna puke, Mr. Marston."

He opened his eyes because he wanted to see the reaction, but he only got a quick glimpse of amusement before he was spun and expertly aimed at a tall trash container. He lost what was left of his breakfast in an acid stream that clogged his throat. He heard Veronica say, "Oh, God. He's *disgusting*," in that posh accent. He wished he'd managed to hit her shoes.

He heard the faraway sound of Mr. Granton saying, "Vern. This is going to be a problem."

And Mr. Marston's reply. "You wanted the full show. Don't worry. His ID says he's narcoleptic. We're covered."

Things went black with sparkles, and he swayed, falling limply, something hard under his hip and back and he thought it might be a bench, but he didn't care. Then it all went away.

Chapter 12

Nick dropped casually into his chair at the now-familiar conference table in headquarters. He'd taken care to shake off any possible tail before arriving. Once in the building, he'd ducked into the bathroom to tidy up a bit and gather his nerve. And now here he was. Freemantle had been waiting, with Olson and Takano.

By now Olson, at least, had to know about that recording with Brian Kerr. Maybe they all knew. Maybe they'd all heard him out himself.

He'd thought about erasing it. He'd figured he could summarize the interesting bits, and lose the actual recording. There was no real need for them to hear him saying "*I'm gay*," or talking about blow jobs. He could go on like he had been, not telling. But who knew whether something in all of Brian's chatter might turn out to be useful to the case? And hadn't he sworn that if someone asked, he'd tell? There was a difference between silence and a cover-up, and he was not that sort of guy. He'd sent in the full recording.

He tried to see if they were looking at him differently. Takano gave him a casual nod, same as ever, Olson was turned away, and Freemantle wore his usual pissed off expression. So far so good.

Takano said, "We're getting the impression that the lab may be in this country after all. Perhaps in the Southeast, maybe the one of the Virginias, North Carolina, or Tennessee. Tracking records for suspicious vehicles regularly point us that direction."

"That would be good, right?" Nick said. "A better chance to shut them down?"

"Oh yeah. Any time I don't have to coordinate with international law enforcement I'm practically doing cartwheels."

Olson said, "We checked up on Marston's limo visitors. They entered the country at MSP direct from London Heathrow. The Honorable Henry Granton and his daughter Veronica. It took some digging, but Interpol says the old lord, Baron Tomesmuir, was a smuggler in the seventies, eighties, and nineties. Alcohol and tobacco, in and out of Britain, France, and the Netherlands, they think, mostly tariff evasion. He was never arrested, made some good money, then was badly brain injured in 1998. Some tougher, more vicious types moved in on the game."

Freemantle said, "So Marston's the son of a smuggler?"

Takano said, "Seems that way. Vern Granton traveled down to New Orleans in 1996, married Stephanie Conroy in 1998, got a green card, and disappeared. A year later there's a DMV record for Vern Marston. A few years later Stephanie and Vern Marston moved up here to Minnesota."

"He's not an illegal, then."

"No. The name change might be shady, but that's a paperwork mess, since New Orleans was hit by the Katrina flooding. He could claim it was among the records lost to water damage. It might even be true."

"Is the brother, this Henry, being watched by Interpol?"

Takano shook his head. "Scotland Yard says they had their eye on him, but decided he wasn't a big player. Mostly it's the old man's money he's spending."

Nick's stomach unclenched as the meeting's focus stayed on the case. "I wonder what Marston thinks about his brother showing up."

Olson turned to him. "Brian Kerr might know. The way you played him along, acting like his buddy, worked great. I bet there's more he could tell you." There was a hint of caution in her eyes and voice. Nick thought he should be grateful for the hint that he could claim it had all been an act. The temptation was so strong he tasted blood from biting his cheek. No. Just no. He had to say it now, or he never would.

"I'll try to get more. But I didn't lie to him about being gay." He was going to continue calmly and found he couldn't. The breath left his chest in a rush and he was empty, waiting.

The silence stretched. He could feel his heart racing, pumping blood in a frantic search for oxygen he didn't have. It was Takano who said finally, "Well, it sounds like that'll come in handy with Kerr."

"Right." Olson's comment was more grunt than words.

Nick breathed in painfully, trying not to make a sound.

Freemantle looked away and said to the air in general, "I don't see why everyone feels they need to throw that out on the table. I don't care, personally, but why not just keep it to yourself? You hear me?"

Nick said, "Yes, sir. I could have lied and said it was just to get closer to Brian. But if you believed me, then I'm still waiting to come out someday, and if you didn't believe, would you trust me again?"

"Ever heard of Don't Ask, Don't Tell? Just keep the private stuff out of the workplace."

"They repealed that because it made people crazy," Nick said dryly.

"Okay." Freemantle held up a hand. "I know we have other gays on the force. I guess it's a fact of life now. Let's move on. What's the plan?"

Takano said, "Rugo'll keep collecting license plates and pictures of the drivers, maybe put a couple more trackers on outgoing trucks. We have guys doing the same on the loading docks at Marston's New Jersey and San Diego warehouses. We're getting more transponder info and weigh station data. It's coming together to find the lab."

"Does Marston check his fleet for tracking devices?" Olson asked. "Could that be why we're not seeing a pattern with them yet?"

"I don't think so. We're careful, and if he'd spotted our transponders, I think we'd have noticed him really upping security. That's one thing Rugo's watching for— any change in alert level."

"So what else are we paying Rugo for?" Freemantle asked. "Other than buddying up to Brian Kerr."

"Becoming Brian's buddy *is* part of the plan, if it lets Nick hang around Marston's estate."

"Any chance he might convince Kerr to turn on Marston, maybe even testify?"

Takano looked at Nick, an eyebrow raised. "Rugo?"

Nick said carefully, "He might be willing to help. Maybe. He doesn't seem happy with his life. But I'm not sure what kind of witness he'd be. I'd hate to go for a conviction based on his testimony."

"I'll second that," Olson said. "The kid is one fry short of a Happy Meal. He actually calls himself by two different names and his voice changes and everything. He's either a great actor, or he has serious mental issues. Put him on the stand and he's going to look totally nuts. Completely unreliable."

Before he could stop himself, Nick protested, "He's not that bad!" Although, yeah, Brian on the witness stand for a hostile cross-examination wasn't a pretty thought. "He is a bit... challenged."

Takano said, "Then we'll use any info Rugo can get from him, but not plan to put him on the stand other than as a defendant."

"You can't charge him!" Nick knew it was a mistake the moment he said it. He backpedaled. "I mean, at best, he'd cop an insanity plea, easily. It's a waste of time."

"Right." Takano gave him one more long, narrow-eyed look and then moved on to logistics.

When the meeting was over and Freemantle and Takano had hurried out, Nick sat and waited. Olson took a moment closing her laptop, slipping the papers into a file. Then she got up and said over her shoulder, "Chili dog?"

"Sure thing." Nick was pleased with how casual he sounded.

The diner wasn't crowded this time, in the middle of the afternoon. Olson snagged a table in the far corner, and Nick sat with his back to the room, accepting the twitchiness of having people behind him for the benefit of not being as visible. They ate the first few bites in silence, then Olson said, "You doing okay? Long-term deep cover can be a bitch."

"I'm fine." He took another mouthful, then decided to just ask. "Did it bother you? That recording?"

She clearly had a sadistic streak, because she made Nick wait till she'd finished her hot dog before wiping the corner of her mouth and saying, "You know what bothers me? You're not seeing Brian Kerr as a suspect or a tool anymore."

Nick swallowed back a protest he couldn't make believable. "I'm trying."

"Okay, I'll give you that. Try harder."

"Yes, ma'am. And the… rest?" He didn't say it aloud in the open room.

Olson shrugged, and kept her voice low. "My kids have gay friends. I really don't care."

"And Freemantle?"

"What does that country song say? He's a product of his raising. He's not aware of being a bigot. But if he gets on the Green Line train at midnight, and a stranger gets on, he'll look twice at a white man and four times at a black man. If you walk into the john while he's pissing, odds are now he'll hurry out."

"Like I have any interest in his shriveled dick," Nick muttered.

"Stupid reflexes die hard. He won't deliberately step on your career. You're not the only gay cop he's got."

"I know." He did. He'd seen a couple in the Pride parade. He hadn't joined them.

"There's several in uniform, men and women, and a couple more detectives. Hell, gay marriage is legal now. Some of those guys have their spouse right on the benefits form and everything."

"Three cheers for progress."

"Well?" She raised her eyebrow at Nick's bitter tone.

He could feel himself flush. "That was stupid. Yeah, it's progress. It's good. I just wish it wasn't a *thing*."

"Well, I wish I hadn't screwed up my knee too much for basketball. You'll deal."

He wanted to say that no one threatened to beat your face in when you quit basketball, but he liked the way Olson was blowing it off. He should stop there, shouldn't ask, but he did. "You think everyone will find out?"

"Realistically? Yeah, eventually. Maybe not while you're undercover, but later, yeah. At some point someone will say, 'He's not bad for a homo,' or something stupid, and there you'll be. If not Freemantle, then someone else. The audio evidence will be heard, transcribed. I'd say it's a done deal."

"Well, I was never meant to be more than a street cop anyway."

"It shouldn't matter, but you're right, it may. Luckily, I'd bet high rank and politics were never gonna be your destiny, no matter how many girls you might fuck."

"True that." He sighed, and realized that, for all his nerves about the fallout, it was a weight off his back being out. He felt lighter, looser. He grinned. "I think I want another chili dog, how 'bout you?"

"I could eat another one," Olson agreed.

****

Brian blinked his itchy, sticky eyes, squinting through half-closed lids. His mouth was worse, gluey and odd tasting.

"You moron," Damon growled from somewhere near his head.

He worked his mouth, trying to get his dry tongue to move. "I need to pee."

Damon had to take half his weight to get him up off the bed, and almost carried him to the john. He peed a river, glad he was at least awake enough to hold his own dick. When he was done, Damon steered him back to bed on shaking legs and eased him down. He closed his eyes. Then a straw tapped his lips, and he opened his mouth like a starving baby bird. The liquid was something thin and sweet and flat, and he drank it like he was dying, so fast he whined when the straw was tugged out of his mouth.

"Slow down or you'll puke," Damon said.

"Sorry."

The straw returned for another wonderful minute. He sucked until there was an empty slurping, then opened his eyes. Damon held a plastic bottle, and glared down at him with stormy eyes.

"Sorry?" he repeated, because he wasn't quite sure what had happened.

"You are so fucking stupid."

Brian winced but didn't close his eyes. Damon didn't mean it like that, this time. He meant it like even smart people could be stupid, maybe, probably. "What did I do?"

"You don't remember?"

Brian had a vague memory of sitting with his eyes closed, Finding, Finding, while something cold rode beside him. "Not exactly. I Found someone. Were they dead?" He bit his lip, because he wasn't supposed to know about the ones who got dead.

"We had a rule. You never, ever go Finding without me. Right?"

"I think it worked."

"Did you drink a bunch of fluids and take your glucose tablets first?"

"Um."

"Did you do *anything* to prepare except get in the car and start?"

He took refuge in, "I don't remember."

"Well I'm pretty fucking sure you didn't. When I got here, you were out cold on the bed, and I do mean cold. Not doing much more than breathing. I had hot water bottles on you and corn syrup in your mouth for half an hour before you began looking human."

"Sorry?"

"Fuck sorry. What happened?"

Brian tried to remember. "It was Mr. Marston. He said, 'Find Veronica.' He had her chain. They had a bet."

"A bet?"

The money was the easy part. "A million dollars."

Damon bounced up off the bed and paced around the room. Brian watched his jerky strides, not moving even his head when Damon disappeared out of his side view. Lying still was wonderful. The usual headache was descending on him, and he closed his eyes again.

Fingers touched his lips. "Take your pain meds."

He opened his mouth for the tablets, which were followed by a straw again. Water this time, cool relief for his awful mouth. "Thanks, Damon."

"Well, you scared me. Remember the first bad one?"

He shivered. He sure did. He'd been sixteen, and by then the family had been used to him being able to Find Mom when they needed her. It'd wiped him out to do it, but not much worse than a day with the flu. There was even the night Lori didn't come home from her date, and Damon asked if he could

Find her too. And he had, and that wasn't too awful either. But when Damon asked him to see if he could Find a guy he worked with at the warehouse, someone he didn't really know, it hadn't gone so well.

It turned out that Finding a near-stranger was a lot harder than Finding Mom or Lori. A whole lot harder. He'd collapsed, passed out completely, and Damon had ended up taking him to the ER. He'd been unconscious in the hospital for two days, before waking up hooked to IVs. The next day, Damon had unhooked him and sneaked him out, and they'd all moved, again, to where the hospital couldn't find them to send the bill.

After that, Damon had tested and experimented a lot more with Brian's talent, before offering it to Mr. Marston on a platter. Weird to think Mr. Marston had already known about them, and been waiting.

Sometimes he wondered what might've happened if he hadn't snuck out of the hospital. What if he'd talked to the nicest nurse? She might have said, "You're sixteen. Your mom's a junkie, one bad shot away from being dead. Your brother's a crook, your school didn't teach you anything, and you need help." What would he be now? Except, he wouldn't have wanted to leave Damon and Lori, and for all he knew, he might be worse off. Really, his life was cushy now, if he didn't look at it too hard.

Damon said, "Are you going to be able to go down and eat some dinner?"

"Down? Like, at the table?" He didn't want to. He wanted to hide here until he was sure his head wouldn't fall off. Being Bry let him whine, "Damon! Don't wanna. My head hurts!"

"I know. But now that Marston was…" Even Damon lowered his voice. "Was dumb enough to show what you can do to an outsider, we need to act like it doesn't half-kill you."

"It doesn't." He tried to sit up, and had to let himself fall back. *Nice soft pillows.* "Not much."

"Not when you fucking do it right. We have an hour. We'll get more liquids and calories in you, you can have a hot shower, and if you can sit at the table and eat, and act like everything is fine, then that should be good enough. You don't need to talk. Probably better if you don't."

"Is it today?"

"Is what?"

"When did I Find?" *How long was I out?*

150

"Oh. No, that was yesterday. It was okay for you to rest, afterward. Granton knew you'd passed out. But we don't want anyone to find out you can't just turn around and do it again."

"I can eat." *Hopefully.* Finding made him ravenous, like he'd run a marathon, but the headaches sometimes made him nauseous and the pain meds made him loopy. "Shower?"

"Give the meds time to work."

"Sure." He closed his eyes and drifted off for a while, because the next thing he knew, Damon was shaking him.

"Come on, bro. Ten minutes for a candy bar and a shower."

By the time he'd cleaned up and followed Damon into the dining room, he felt a bit more human. The tablets had turned his headache into a dull throb, and he was still so hungry he thought his spine might be sticking into his belly. He ducked his head at Mr. Marston, ignored everyone else and said, "Food?"

"Of course." Mr. Marston's voice was satisfied. "Glad you could join us. Have a seat."

"I can always eat." He sat next to Damon, across from the Grantons, keeping his eyes on the tablecloth. There was a plate with hummus toast ready, and he shoved a piece in his mouth.

Mr. Granton said, "That was an interesting performance, Brian. Where did you put the tracking device?"

Brian blinked, but didn't answer. Any discussion would be something he'd far rather leave to other people.

Mr. Marston said coldly, "Are you implying he cheated?"

"Well, I'm not convinced. There are explanations other than mumbo jumbo."

Mr. Marston's voice dropped another notch. "Are you implying I lied?"

"He might be fooling you too."

Mr. Marston made a disgusted sound. "You watched. He had no idea what we were asking until that very moment, and no time to prepare. And he still Found her."

Mr. Granton raised his voice and spoke more slowly. "Brian? How did you find Veronica at the mall?"

He kept his eyes down and his tone flat. "I Found her."

"I know. But how? What did you do?"

"I looked and Found her."

"Did someone help you?"

"Mr. Marston gave me her chain. He helps me Find." A little bile rose in his throat at the reminder, and he took a big swig of his water.

At that moment, the cook came in with loaded plates, and they were all quiet as she passed them around. Brian's plate was extra loaded, and he dug into a big forkful of scalloped potatoes, stuffing his mouth full.

Mr. Granton said, "There's no such thing as magic."

Mr. Marston raised a cool eyebrow. "You had the evidence. Are you going to welsh on our bet?"

"What bet, Father?" Veronica asked.

"He bet me a million dollars." There was dark satisfaction in Mr. Marston's voice. "If I could prove that the *mumbo jumbo* I've wasted so much time on was real. I proved it."

"I disagree," Mr. Granton said. "Yes, that was interesting, but I bet there's a cheat in it somewhere. Perhaps the brother helped him."

"I tell you what, *brother*." Mr. Marston was using the snake-voice that Brian hated, the one that slid smooth and low, and hid the knife until he struck. "One more challenge. Double or nothing. You write out an IOU for two million dollars, all witnessed and legal, and then you take it with you and you go hide. Anywhere."

Brian heard Damon shift restlessly in his chair, but no one interrupted Mr. Marston.

"You find a place no one could know about, anywhere within a hundred miles. And then I'll have Brian Find you. If he hasn't in twenty-four hours, you can rip up the paper. If he does, I'll take the money. And…" Mr. Marston paused. The room was silent— so silent Brian could hear a car on the road, half a mile away. He didn't look up from the smooth white linen beside his plate. "And maybe, for calling me a liar, I'll take some interest out of your skin. Or I might let his brother do it. So. Henry. You want to take that bet?"

Mr. Granton cleared his throat. "No need to be unpleasant about it."

"No need at all."

"Perhaps we can agree to differ."

"For a million dollars, I might agree to that."

"A million *more*?"

"I'd settle for the original bet. Exactly as it stood."

"Well." There was another long silence, although not as tense. Then Mr. Granton said, "I suppose, until I can prove otherwise, it was pretty convincing."

Veronica said, "Father. A *million* dollars?"

"We'll talk later, darling."

"We certainly will," she muttered.

Brian dared to glance around the table, before stuffing his mouth full again. Lori took a dainty bite of the prime rib. "When do you need to be back in England, Henry?"

"Oh, no rush at all. Much of my business can be done remotely."

"Not as well as in person, I'm sure." Her smile looked warm and admiring, but Brian could see the glitter in her eyes.

"Well, naturally. But meeting new, um, relations…" His gaze dipped to her midsection and back up. "It's much more important for me to do this personally."

"How lovely." Lori's voice held a flick of annoyance.

Veronica turned to Damon. "So perhaps you can tell us more about what your brother does than just, 'I Find her.'" She made her voice thicker in her mimicry, but looked at Damon under lowered lashes, and murmured, "I'm sure you're the genius behind it."

"It's a natural talent." Damon also lowered his tones to something more friendly. "I'd be happy to tell you what I know."

The clamp of Damon's fingers on Brian's knee under the table kept him from turning to stare. He reminded himself that Damon was far more careful than he was. If Damon gave her any information, it was a good bet it would be lies.

The conversation moved to Veronica's shopping expedition, and attractions in the area, while Brian shoveled in as many calories as he could hold. He ate until his stomach told him it couldn't take one more bite. When he glanced up, Veronica was looking at him with that little curl of her lip. Deliberately, he swiped the back of his hand across his mouth and grinned at her, letting his jaw drop open on that last half-chewed mouthful. He'd have burped if he could.

She glanced away toward Damon. "I'd love to check out that marina you mentioned. Oh, but I suppose you have to take care of your brother again after his ordeal?"

"Nah," Damon said casually. "He'll go for a walk or watch TV or whatever. He's good."

"I ate too much," Brian said loudly and flatly. "I'm gonna hammock."

"Hammock?" Veronica wrinkled her nose at the word.

"Lie out in a hammock," Damon explained, although it should've been obvious. "We have one strung up in the garden. So if you do want to go sailing, I'm at your service."

Veronica smiled warmly at him. "Sounds great."

Brian could tell that Damon had somehow gotten into Veronica's pants already, whether for leverage or information or simply to prove he could, Brian didn't know and wasn't sure he cared. The whole thing left him exhausted. He cut into their chat to say, "I'm done. Can I go?"

"No dessert, Brian?" Mr. Marston asked.

He shook his head. "I'd puke. Right on the table."

All five of them winced. That was satisfying. He pretended not to notice the reactions as he stood and wandered out.

Chapter 13

Brian's head throbbed at the brightness of the sunshine as he left the mansion, but he didn't care. Better than being inside. The hammock was in back, down by the pool. He didn't stop, just grabbed the throw blanket from it as he walked past and kept on going. Its lovely, swaying, upholstered softness called to him, but he wanted to be farther from that house and those people.

He made it out to the putting green behind the end of the garage before running out of steam. There, he lay on the smooth grass and rolled the blanket under his neck for a pillow. The sky overhead was a clear summer blue, with lacy clouds drifting past. The sun was warm on his skin, easing some of his aches. No doubt the ground would feel hard later, but for now he felt cradled in the summer day, on the solid earth that was always what it seemed to be. The way people seldom were.

He dozed for a while, waking up stiff but not as bad as he'd figured. Maybe that was the pain-killer. Not much time had passed, judging by the sun, but his stomach felt empty again. He thought about going to scrounge a snack from Mrs. Jones in the kitchen, then decided not to when trying to sit up made the world tilt. His vision had an odd, fuzzy quality to it. His thoughts seemed a bit fuzzy as well, and went around for a few minutes. *Can you be too fuzzy to know you're fuzzy?* The solid earth was still solid, but it wasn't the comfort it had been.

On an impulse, he dug his phone out of his pocket and hit the most recent number, because some people could be trusted with your secrets. "Nick?" Nick hadn't told Damon about any of his secrets. Brian was grateful enough, and fuzzy enough, that the rest didn't matter. However screwed up things had become between them, all he remembered now was the solid feel of Nick's knee against his own.

"Brian? Is something wrong?"

"I wasn't sure you'd answer."

There was a pause. "I'll always answer if I can, I promise. Are you okay?"

Brian stared up at the sky. A small flock of birds flew by against the blue—dark shapes that he couldn't have named even if he knew about birds, which he didn't. "I'd like to know about birds. More than what's a sparrow and what's a hawk."

"Um, I'm not that good with birds. Is there a reason you need to know?"

"No. Just saying." He felt lighter, the pain in his head easing as the drug did its work. This was good, lying here warm, with Nick's voice in his ear. "I like this. It's like you're right here next to me."

"Brian, are you okay? Did you take something, a medication?"

"Just the usual. My head hurts. But not so much now."

"Should I come over?"

"Oh, no. No way. But I wanted to talk to you, because I can. I can say I miss you and you're probably really hot when you take off those baggy jeans and stuff. I can say it and it's okay."

"Yeah, it is, but be safe, right? Is there anyone else around?"

"Nope. Just me. Just lying out in the sun by myself."

"Well, don't get burned, right?"

Brian laughed. "That's such a Damon thing to say."

"I am not Damon." Nick's tone was fierce and hard.

"No, you're not. You're not a liar and a thief and a killer." He swallowed hard, hearing that come out of his mouth. "Nick? Maybe I'm not okay?"

"Where are you?"

"On the grass. Golf grass." He rolled over and got up. The world was a bit spinny, but that happened sometimes when he got up too fast. Probably all his blood had gone to his stomach digesting lunch, and left too little in his brain. A walk would fix that. "I'm going to the house."

"What house? Brian, stay put, all right. I'll get in the car right now. I'll come to you."

"I think Mr. Granton hates me. I think I'm too full of lunch and I should walk it off, and then my head won't spin."

"Brian?"

"Meet me at the house. The one where." He couldn't say it. "Where. The old one."

"Are you sure?"

"Please?" He let Bry come out for a moment, because he suddenly needed this so bad, to see Nick. "Pretty pretty please with sugar?"

"If you're sick you shouldn't wander in the woods."

"I'm going anyway." He said it firmly enough to make it stick. "You can come or not come." He turned off the ringer on his phone and put it back into his pocket.

Now to make it true.

It was easy to say he was going to walk a mile and a half. Harder to do it with lunch sitting like a lump in his stomach, and his head trying to float up off his neck. He straightened his shoulders and wrapped the throw around him like a cape, knotting it at his throat. *Super Brian, magical Finder, heads out into the unknown in search of true love.* Well, that was pretty stupid, but in search of true lust maybe. Marston hadn't sent any girls to him in a couple of months, and as much as he didn't want the girls, he missed the simple touch of hands on his skin.

Maybe this time would be different. Maybe Nick wouldn't look at him like he was crazy or ugly this time.

Or maybe he was tripping on whatever the hell Damon had given him, because there was no-chance-in-hell. He headed into the woods anyway. It was probably a good thing he couldn't quite picture himself with Nick. Hiking a mile and a half with a hard-on would've been difficult.

Partway along the path, he met Luger and Glock on patrol. He petted them, rubbing their soft ears and running his hands through their ruffs. He was tempted to stay there, because they were alive and warm and they liked him. They licked his wrists with warm tongues, and bumped against his knees. But they weren't people. He wanted Nick.

"Okay, guys, go on back to work. I'll see you later."

They stood behind him on the path, watching him go, before trotting off on their rounds.

He left the path and angled into the rougher scrub. The boundary fence wasn't much farther on. Sooner than his fuzzy brain expected, he spotted the glint of wire and stopped, looking at it. The first time he'd explored this far, he'd wondered if it was electric, or had cameras, and turned back. By now he knew he wouldn't get zapped, but there were spying eyes.

Spy eye, up high, blind eye... He shook his head and smacked himself lightly. He needed to focus now. One good thing about poplar trees, blackberry, and buckthorn— they grew fast. Once he'd figured out where the cameras were, he'd made places to get through the fence. Marston's occasional clearing crews couldn't keep up with the rampant growth of the Minnesota brush. Brian untied the throw blanket from around his neck, wadding it up. He didn't want to leave it here.

Man, you're not thinking today. Well, that was hardly anything new.

He bundled the cotton under one arm, dropped down and crept awkwardly through the weeds, ignoring the tug of brambles in his hair and the scratch of twigs against his arms. He reached his half-buried log against the base of the chain link, and slid it back enough to open the low escapeway under the wire. The cotton throw was easy enough to push through.

He lay flat, rolled onto his back, and stared up. The fence stood out above him, cold and silver amid the fast-growing greenery. The space he'd made underneath the wire was waiting, just big enough, barely enough. He wriggled under the edge, careful to keep flat, wincing as the points of wire scraped across his chest.

He'd always gone through the other way up until the horrible, awful time the wire snagged on his belt loop. Half an hour of panic, crying, shoulders not able to flex enough, scrapes, and crawling out of his pants, had taught him face up was safer. *Safer, slower, sliding, escaping...* The wire points dragged down his belly and he sucked in a stomach-breath and pushed with his heels. Then he was through and under the brambles on the other side. He crawled along under the bushes, around a tree and then another, to where he felt safe standing up.

His clothes were a mess. Of course they often were. But soon he'd see Nick, so he brushed and tugged and dusted at them, thumping his jeans with the throw and scrubbing at his hands and hair until he was as clean as he could get. He felt dizzy, like he'd just got off a playground spinner. He wrapped the blanket around his shoulders, blinking to clear his eyes.

Too late to go back, even if he wanted to. Which he didn't. He leaned one palm on the solid tree trunk behind him, gathering strength, and then glanced around the smooth bark, back at the fence. It still stood there, serene, unaware of its defeat. He smiled at the thought that he'd broken out of prison again.

His house, his special place, was only a bit farther on through the trees and scrub. There was even a trail of sorts.

When he reached the front steps, he ran out of steam. The sagging porch was shaded, and he sat down, wadded the blanket up under him, and tilted his head back against the wall. Insects hummed in the overgrown yard, and somewhere a frog croaked. A tickle on his arm was probably a mosquito, but he couldn't be bothered to check. Traffic was no more than a distant hum.

He didn't want to go inside yet. He was scared it would seem different now. He'd been with Nick in there, and that might have changed it. But the bulk of the house, the way it stood solid between him and all he'd walked away from, was still good. He let his eyes droop shut, and didn't pull out his phone. Nick would come, or he wouldn't come, but Brian could live inside this moment. And the next. And the next.

The sound of a car on the gravel woke him out of a doze. It couldn't have been long, because his neck wasn't even stiff. He blinked his eyes open and didn't stand up. Nick's old beater skidded to a halt on the gravel, and Nick threw the door open and hurried toward him.

Brian smiled, lazily, his heart soaring at how good Nick looked, even in that scruffy T-shirt and the jeans that were an awful, baggy waste on a man like that. "Hiya!"

Nick slowed abruptly, and climbed the steps to his side. "You okay?" He squatted and reached out as if to touch Brian's face, then pulled his hand back.

"I'm good, real good. I'm extra fine now." He realized he was doing Bry's voice, the singsong flat tone, and deliberately stopped. "For a gay man, you dress like crap."

Nick blinked. "That's rich, coming from you."

"Lori buys my clothes." He felt his face heat.

"Why?"

"Because she likes to shop?" Why did he still let her do that? He wasn't sure. "Come on, sit down. I'm glad you're here."

Nick slowly lowered himself to the worn boards, and Brian tugged some of the blanket out from beneath himself. "You can lean on that. Less splinters."

"Thanks." But Nick sat forward, eyes fixed on him. "What's going on?"

Brian waved his hand. "It's a sunny day. I'm enjoying it. More now that you're here." He wondered idly if those pain meds had some kind of truth serum in them. Even if they didn't, it was a reasonable excuse for letting go of his control.

Nick touched him then, steadying his chin to look into his eyes. "Are you on drugs?"

"Pain-killers, for my headache."

"Prescription?"

He shrugged. "Whatever Damon gave me. I didn't ask."

"You just swallow whatever pills he hands you?"

"Pretty much." Brian smiled, thinking of *The Princess Bride*, and changed his voice. "I do not think it was what he thought it was."

"Jesus, Brian, should I take you to a doctor?"

"God, no." Brian stared at him. "I'm just a bit high. It's kind of nice, actually. Usually Damon goes real low dose on my meds, to where it barely touches the pain. He's a freak about overdosing."

"So am I." Nick's hand was still on Brian's jaw, a gentle grip, but he must have realized it in the same moment, because he let go.

Brian missed the warmth. He sighed. "I trust Damon. I have to. I know he has a cruel streak, and he breaks laws, but the one thing I could always count on was that we came first."

"We?"

"Me and Lori. No matter what Damon did or why, it was part of keeping us safe and fed and alive. That was rock solid. Still is." He turned enough to meet Nick's worried gaze. Worried, or maybe sad. He didn't want Nick to be sad. "I think everyone needs that, you know? Someone who puts them first, no matter what."

"I guess they do." Nick's voice was low.

"So I have to trust him. It's the only thing he asks back from me." Brian closed his eyes again, leaning his head against the wood. He fumbled sideways with his fingers, enough to touch the loose denim over Nick's thigh. Without asking, feeling daring in his floaty goodness, he wove the fabric between his fingers and held on.

****

Nick looked over at Brian's closed eyes, and then down at his pale hand, fisted in Nick's dumb jeans. He wanted to yell at Brian, and demand to know what Damon had given him. He wanted to haul him off for blood tests and antidotes and then lock him in a safe house somewhere. He knew he was overreacting— Brian was awake, mostly coherent, breathing fine— but he didn't care. *I'm taking you to see a doctor, now!*

The words were stopped in his throat by a dozen considerations. He's high, not sick. You could blow your cover. He might get in trouble for a positive test— you know Olson would use it to put pressure on him to turn informant.

He also was shamefully aware that some of his anger, even after seeing that Brian didn't look that bad, was tinged with jealousy. What had Brian said? *"I think everyone needs that, you know? Someone who puts them first."* Nick hadn't had that for a long, long time. And he hadn't been able to be that for anyone else. Not since he'd looked out the back window of the social worker's car and saw Ariana waving goodbye to him from the Taylors' front steps. He'd been nine that day.

Nine and stupid and angry, and willing to use his fists too freely. The Taylors had told him they were sick of his fighting. No matter that one kid had pulled a girl's hair, or that another was stealing a little kid's lunch money, or that the two guys had called him names first. By the time he'd unleashed all his pain on them, *he'd* become the bad guy.

After the third fight that ended in bruises and blood, the social worker had come and told him to pack his things. He'd done it, stoically. He kind of liked the Taylors, but this was their fourth move in two years and he knew nothing lasted. It wasn't until he said, "Ariana's not packed yet," and the social worker gave him that look, that fear had slid its icy way down his spine. "She has more stuff than me. We'll have to wait."

"Ariana's staying here."

"She can't. She's my sister."

"The Taylors are thinking of adopting her. You want her to have a good home, don't you?"

"She's my *sister*." He'd said it again, like somehow that would matter. Like a nine-year-old had any say in what adults did with a five-year-old.

"Then you should be happy for her. I'm sure the Taylors will let you visit."

"*Visit!*" He'd realized then that it was really happening, they were taking him away from Ari. He'd begged and pleaded, promised to be good as gold forever, if only, if *only*. All in vain. The social worker, probably familiar with angry kids, said, "If I have to drag you out kicking and screaming, do you think the Taylors will let you see her at all? Well, do you?"

He'd held on for just a moment to the fantasy of unleashing all his darkness and overwhelming this stupid, skinny, uncaring woman, and grabbing Ari and running for it. But Ari would never be able to outrun grown-ups, and even Nick wasn't dumb enough to think he could take care of her by himself. So he let himself be coerced downstairs, managed a last hug with Ari, who'd been bewildered and sad, and a handshake from Mr. Taylor that burned like poison on his skin. He'd had one last look, driving away.

When he asked and begged to go see his sister, after two weeks of being so good in the new place that he might have given a saint lessons, he was told the Taylors had gone on vacation. Two weeks later, they were still traveling. A month after that, he was told they'd moved a hundred miles away. That was part of why they'd ditched him. No sense making a move like that with a kid you weren't going to keep.

He'd promised Ari he would write, and he did, but he didn't know if she ever saw his letters. She was five, and she didn't write back.

Two months later, he snapped when one of the other kids was mean to the newest little girl. The bruises he left on her tormentor's face lasted longer than his own stay in that house. He moved again, and again, and the next time he found someone to ask about Ari, no one would give him her address. He never found her again.

As a cop, he'd thought he might track her down at last. He'd accessed some records, but the trail went cold after her adoption in Mankato. The Taylors merged into a sea of similar names. And Ari was gone.

So, no, as he watched Brian breathe slow and easy in the bright summer sunshine, he realized he hadn't been anyone's person to rely on in a long, long time.

"I could do that for you too," he said without thinking, because Brian shouldn't have to depend on some vicious, criminal brother who gave him street drugs. "Be someone to count on. If you really needed me."

"You did come when I called you," Brian said without looking. "That was real good."

"Of course." Nick frowned at him, ignoring the little spark of warmth that gave him. "Although, what the hell have you been doing that makes you look like shit?" Brian had dark circles under his eyes, and his skin was pasty and pale. He looked thinner, even if there was no way he could have changed that much in just a couple of days.

"Like shit. What every man wants to hear. Nice."

"Sorry. I'm a blunt kind of guy."

Brian's lips curved upward. "I don't mind blunt."

"I'm also real observant, and right now I'm observing that you didn't answer my question."

"I have a headache."

"Migraines?" He'd had one foster mom with those, and the whole house tiptoed around for days when they hit. "Or, is it something new? Are they getting worse?" There was no reason for brain tumors to suddenly scare him, but they did.

"Like migraines. Don't worry. I've had them for years. It'll go away."

"All right." Nick turned to lean back on the wall. That way, he could press his shoulder against Brian's and trap Brian's hand between their thighs without being too obvious. The contact soothed something in him. "I worry about you."

"That's nice." Brian leaned against him more, head tilted so his hair brushed Nick's temple. "What if…?"

The silence went on so long that Nick finally said, "If what?"

Brian's voice had a faraway quality. "What if there was a way to go, to get away from here, from Marston and all the bad stuff, and just you and me go somewhere? As friends I mean. I'm not coming on to you this time."

"Go away how?"

"Pick a city. Start over. I want… well, the dyslexia's like a trap because I can't even read the destinations on the damned buses, or the schedule for the train. It's hard to go."

Brian paused. Nick made an encouraging sound.

"I can't fill out a lease, or read a help-wanted ad, so living on my own is likely to go bad fast. Even if I got hold of some starter money. But with you, maybe I could."

Nick told himself the lift of his heart meant that he was excited about reeling Brian in as an informant, out from under Marston's reach. Brian as a witness. Just that. "Maybe I could. Help you get out, I mean. Find a place for you to stay, some help with the paperwork, even a job, maybe." He wasn't sure if Brian knew enough or could seem stable enough to be offered actual witness protection. But he could try, if it got Brian out.

"What about you? Would you quit working for Marston?"

"I, well, I don't know. I need a job." When Brian was silent he added, "My truck's dead. Repairs would cost more than she's worth. I can't afford to walk off with no money and no job."

"What if I got money?"

"How?"

Brian cracked open one eye, his fuzzy pale-blue gaze an inch from Nick's face. "Steal something of Lori's? She has diamonds."

"God, no." Nick wanted to offer his own money before Brian got caught by Marston, stealing from his own sister, except he couldn't, because Nick Green didn't have money. "I'm working. I can save some."

"Marston's not a good person. If you work for him, you have to become a not-good person too, or at least you have to teach yourself not to care."

"Is that what you did?" Nick asked softly.

Brian's sigh could have blown out candles a hundred miles away. "I tried. I think I failed. I don't want to go back, but I know I have to."

Nick tried to lighten the mood. "Oh, yeah, he'll have his werewolf track you down."

Brian jerked sideways, putting space between them. "No, he won't."

"Of course not." Nick turned, gripping Brian's arms. "That was a joke. I'm not making fun of you."

There was something infinitely sad, inexpressibly lonely, in the depths of Brian's eyes. "Okay."

Nick hadn't come here for this. He'd specifically *not* come here for this. And he wasn't going to take it any further, but that look pulled him forward, like a black hole in space drawing him in, until their mouths touched. Brian kissed like he did everything, slowly, a little off-center, with an innocence that a twenty-one year old guy should have lost long ago. He opened to the tip of Nick's tongue, just enough so they could taste each other. Nick rubbed his lower lip under Brian's, where the rasp of near-invisible blond stubble showed this was a man he was kissing.

They separated eventually, slowly, stopping just a few inches apart.

"I shouldn't have done that," Nick said.

"Probably not. Why not?" Brian blinked, looking dazed but happy, thank God, and not like he was drowning in dark water anymore.

Nick grasped for the easiest answer. "Damon would kill me."

Brian drew back farther. "You're right. I'm sorry." He looked down and hunched, becoming smaller and more lumpy. "My fault. I'm dumb."

"Not dumb." Nick hated it when Brian pulled back into that flat nothingness, all his light hidden behind Bry's dull gaze. Nick reached out and ran his thumb over Brian's lower lip. "You deserve a man who'll make you happy. I wouldn't mind finding out if I'm that man, except I'm not sure there's a way to do it and stay safe."

Brian reached out too, touching Nick's jaw, and sliding his fingertip up the hollow of Nick's cheek. "What do you deserve?"

To be shot, probably. "It's complicated."

"*Life* is complicated."

"Thanks, Yoda, like I didn't know that."

"Yoda would say, 'Complicated, life is.'"

Nick was surprised into a laugh. "So he would."

"What if I could get a lot of money?" Brian asked. "Enough to not have to work for a long, long time. Would you help me get away then, if you didn't have to work for Marston? If Damon was a thousand miles away?"

"You wouldn't want to be that far. You said it. He's the one person who puts you first."

"Mm. But one day he's going to get himself caught, or killed. Or do something I can't pretend I don't know. If I leave now, I can say I never stopped trusting him."

The cop in Nick was clamoring to come out. His recorder was on, hopefully not making little rasping noises when his dick half-responded to Brian's touch. "What does Damon do that's so bad?"

Brian's smile was bitter. "He kills people. But never in front of me. So far."

"Jesus." Nick stared at him. "You shouldn't just say that."

"Why not?" Brian's voice was getting floaty again, and his head lolled back. "Not like anyone can prove it. And after all this time working for Mr. Marston, you have to know what he is. What we all are. Dirty. One way or another. You won't stay clean for long."

"I'm not clean now."

Brian took Nick's hand and pressed it to his cheek, nuzzling into it, his sparse growth of beard rough on Nick's palm. "You're still okay. The amber's not smoky yet."

"You're not making sense."

"Head hurts."

Worry rolled in Nick's gut. "Should I find a doctor after all?"

"No. I think I need to eat. Low blood sugar."

"Are you diabetic?"

"Just get low sometimes."

"Do you carry anything? Candy?"

"Forgot." Brian looked at him. "Don't worry. I'll head home and find something."

"You're not walking all that way." Nick could feel how Brian's body sagged against him. "Come on. My car. I might have a candy bar or something in there, and I'll drive you home."

"I'm not supposed to be out."

"You can blame it on the low blood sugar." Nick got an arm under Brian and levered him up. Brian smiled sweetly, and made it to his feet mostly under his own steam. The steps weren't as hard to navigate under Brian's weight as he'd been afraid of, and he got him into the passenger side of the car easily enough. He dug in the glove compartment without success, then into the pocket on the driver door where he found a pack of mint gum. "Will this help? It's not sugar free, anyhow."

"Can't hurt." Brian took the pack and shook out a couple of sticks.

Nick turned the car and headed down the drive. Brian chewed vigorously, adding a third stick. "Mm," he mumbled. "A bit better."

"Spit it out when the sugar's off, and chew some fresh ones."

"Duh." Brian stuffed the rest of the gum in his pocket, then got out his cell phone and tapped the icon for Damon.

The car was quiet enough to hear Damon say, "Bry? Where the hell are you?"

"Not sure," Brian said thickly around the gum in his mouth. "I got wibbly-wobbly. I called a car."

"You called a *what*?"

"A Nick. With a car. He has me."

"Where are you? Let me talk to Nick."

"He's driving."

"Going where?"

"Home, Damon. Where would I go?"

Nick thought he could hear Damon grinding his teeth. "Okay. You're with Nick in his car coming home from whatever-the-fuck dumb thing you did?"

"I went walking. I needed sugar. Nick has gum."

"Next time you fucking call *me*, Bry. Right?"

167

"I pushed the wrong one. Wrong button one. Nick's."

"Okay. All right. How the fuck did you get to a road?"

"I walked. I think I walked."

"You what? Shit. Never mind. Just stay with Nick until I see you. Okay? No wandering. I'll let the gate guy know you're coming." There was a click as Damon hung up.

Brian spit his wad of gum into one of the wrappers and took a fresh piece. "That kinda worked."

"Kind of? It sounded good to me."

"It should be, except he'll wonder how I got past the fence and the dogs too."

"Well, how did you?"

Brian's smile was wide and sweet. "They like me."

Chapter 14

Nick drove toward Marston's place in silence. He tried to be pleased that he was making connections with the drug dealer's inner circle, that he had another good excuse to go onto the property, but he felt queasy about that kiss and the lines he was crossing. Brian ought to be just another informant, a hook into Marston's lethal operations, but he wasn't. Nick wasn't sure what Brian was now.

He coded in through the outer gate, and stared into the camera as usual. The inner gate began opening, but before they were through it, the sound of a shot rang out from the direction of the house.

Nick swore. "Brian, call 911." *Small caliber. Handgun probably, single shot.*

He accelerated down the drive. Brian didn't reach for his phone. "Nick." His voice went singsong. "No calling 911 on Mr. Marston's place unless the main house is on fire. It's a rule."

Nick cursed again, realizing how far he'd fallen out of character. For all his care in talking about his job and truck, he'd begun thinking like Nick Rugo, not Nick Green. Green would never call the cops for a gunshot. He had a history of violence, and several arrests. Nick Green hated cops.

They reached the circle in front of the main steps and he braked to a stop, unbuckling and slamming the door open with a bark of "Stay put!" at Brian. At the front walk, he paused, listening. Raised voices could be dimly heard somewhere behind the house.

From close behind him, Brian said, "Come on!" He took off running across the lawn toward the corner of the house, and Nick had no alternative but to follow.

"Dammit, Brian, wait up! Don't just run in there."

"I hear Lori!" Brian didn't slow down as he rounded the side of the mansion and sprinted toward the back.

They came to a stop a few feet from a cluster of people. A man in a dark suit lay huddled facedown on the ground. Damon was kneeling, his hand on the victim's neck. As they reached the group, Nick pushed ahead of Brian, an arm across his chest keeping him back. Nick flicked a glance at each person, assessing threats. He couldn't spot any firearms, but he moved farther in front of Brian anyway.

Damon stood and said, "Dead. No hope."

"You son of a *bitch*!" A dark-haired young woman who he recognized from pictures as Veronica Granton whirled around, shouting at Marston who stood watching a few feet back. "You *bastard*. You did this."

"Hardly." Marston didn't look up from contemplating the body on the ground. "He was my brother. Plus he owed me a million dollars and he hadn't paid up yet."

"So what?" She took a step toward him, then another, raising her fist. "Now you'll inherit the barony when Grandfather dies. That's worth more than a million."

As she opened her fists into clawed fingers, Damon moved behind her and caught her wrist, locking his other arm around her waist. "I wouldn't, Brit-girl."

"Go to hell!" She struggled in his hold. "He killed my father!"

"I doubt it. But either way, you don't get to hit him."

"Either way?" Her voice went shrill. "He's a murderer!"

Damon gave a shove that spun her away from him. "Prove it."

"I'll call the cops."

"You do that." Damon dusted his hand off on his thigh. "I'll tell them you knew he'd made a bet with Mr. Marston for a cool mil, and you killed him so you wouldn't lose all that money."

"You wouldn't. You liar!"

"Try me. I'll say I heard you threaten him, and saw you run out here a few minutes ago. We all knew about the bet."

Behind Nick, Brian said loudly, "Is Mr. Granton dead? He bet a million. I know."

The look Veronica flashed over Nick's shoulder was pure venom. "You don't know anything, you barmy twit."

Nick couldn't see much of Granton, who was crumpled on the ground in a heap of dark, expensive fabric. He took as step back, to where he could feel Brian's shoulder against his back, and kept his attention on Damon and Marston.

Lori Kerr stood behind Marston, wringing her hands silently. A heavily muscled guy with the build and stance of a bodyguard stood next to her. He was familiar from surveillance pictures of Marston's staff, but Nick blanked on his name. Another bodyguard arrived from the other direction, breathing heavily, and pulled up short at a hand signal from Marston.

Marston said, "Veronica, I'm sorry about Henry. I promise, we'll figure out who did this, but it will only make things worse if you go off half-cocked."

"Half-cocked?"

Damon's voice never lost its cool menace. "That's right. You really want the cops going through your father's things? And yours?"

"I don't care." She tossed her dark hair, but Nick could tell something in that threat had hit home. "What else can we do? He's dead. We have to call them."

Marston said, "Damon, do you see the gun?"

"Yes, sir." Damon pointed toward the body. "Under his elbow."

Marston looked up and over Nick's shoulder. "Bry. Come here. I want you to touch this."

"Oh, no you don't." Damon got between Marston and Nick, further shielding Brian. "Not yet. No."

Nick couldn't see his face, but after a moment Marston nodded reluctantly. "Later, then, if we can't find out who did it."

Veronica squatted close to her father's body. "That looks like Father's gun. It was locked in his suitcase. He always brings it when he travels abroad."

"Well. How useless." Damon stepped away from Brian and Nick, and went to Lori. "Hey, girl, you all right?"

"I'm fine." She shivered. "He's really dead?"

"Yeah." Damon looked at the bodyguard. "Nathan, Mr. Marston will review the surveillance tapes from the last hour."

The bodyguard nodded. "I'll get them set up, but you know this is a dead zone." He pointed to a camera above the nearby door. "That sweeps the approach, but you can't see right here along the wall."

"Really?" Marston had seemed detached until now, but that tone was anything but. "Explain!"

"Well, we sacrificed actually seeing the door to have a good wide angle of the approaches."

"So whoever did this came from inside the house?"

"Probably. I'd have to recheck the tape. No one can watch all the screens simultaneously, and, um—" He ducked his head and glanced at the other bodyguard standing across the path. "—Chuck had stepped out of the room for a minute. I sure didn't spot an approach."

"Do we know *anything*? Did that fucking expensive system put anyone in the clear?"

"Well, just a couple, sir." Nathan didn't meet his employer's eyes. "I saw Green and Brian arrive, coming onto the property, and the retina camera registered Green just about when I heard the shot. We'd have to check the tapes to see if anyone else was outside within a field of view. I'm not aware of any."

"Damn." Marston's fierce gaze swept around the group. Nathan ducked his head, Lori flushed, and Veronica chewed on her lip, her arms hugged across her stomach, still breathing fast. Damon focused on the body and didn't even look up. Nick felt the force of Marston's stare in his turn, and tried to channel Nick Green. Green would glare back. Green didn't take shit from anyone.

Brian laughed, then said, "Sorry. No laughing. Someone's dead."

"Yes, Bry, someone is dead." Damon looked up at last. He glanced coolly at Marston. "What do you want to do, sir?"

"Well, we're *not* inviting the police in here." Marston glared at Veronica until she nodded.

Nick filed away her reaction. Either she was up to her own pretty neck in something illegal, or she knew her father had been. Otherwise she'd still be screaming for the cops.

"I'll investigate—" Marston began.

"Right," Veronica drawled. "Because there's no problem with having the murderer investigate the crime."

"You're the one who knew he had a gun, Veronica. You're the one losing a million in family cash. And," Marston added, "you're clearly not heartbroken."

"You have no idea how I feel," Veronica said through clenched teeth. "None!"

"Well, who do you want to have investigate? Who's in the clear? Lori, where were you when he was shot?"

"In my room. Alone." She pressed her fingers to her mouth. "I think I'm going to be sick."

"Not a good moment for it, dear." The words were whimsical but the tone was steel. Lori nodded and looked away. "Who else? Damon?"

"I was waiting in the pool house to meet Brian and Nick."

"Nathan?"

"In the security room, sir."

"Watching useless monitors."

"Yes, sir, it would seem so. I didn't see Mr. Damon on-camera, since all we have are exterior views."

"Who else is on the grounds?"

"Mrs. Jones is in the kitchen. I ran past her, and told her to stay put, sir. Jack is on patrol with the dogs, down along the south fence last I saw them. I radioed him to keep the perimeter. I hope that was all right, sir?"

"Yes. Fine. So not one of us can prove we weren't here shooting Henry."

"No, sir. Well, except Brian and Green, of course. They were together in the car, at the retina cam, when it happened."

Brian said, "There was a shot. Nok Nick said it was a shot. I wasn't sure. It might not be."

Damon said, "It was a shot, Bry."

"And he's dead. So he was shot."

"Yes."

"I was safe with Nok Nick."

Veronica began laughing, a tinge of hysteria sharpening her voice. "Oh. God. Let's have Brian investigate Father's murder. Perfect!"

Marston turned to Nathan. "Any chance it was an outside job?"

He shrugged. "Not without inside help, I don't think. The camera system is a good one, for what it was designed to do. To approach this location, they'd have to get past the fence and the dogs, then loop a recording, or get smuggled into the house somehow."

Damon said, "Henry may have been a greedy bastard, and he probably had enemies, but I don't really see anyone putting that kind of work into killing him. He's not a big player, and he's been off the property more than once. There'd be easier times and places."

"Unless he wasn't the real target? Maybe he spotted someone suspicious, pulled his gun, and they took it and killed him instead."

"Could be. Sounds like him. Clumsy."

"Father was a good shot," Veronica protested. "You're covering for each other."

"Well, maybe he didn't want to shoot his own daughter," Damon suggested. "Maybe you turned the tables."

"Fuck you!"

"You did, sweetheart." Damon's smile was more shark than lover. "And you were pretty boring doin' it."

Marston's "Stop!" was like a whipcrack. "Fight on your own time. You're right, the only people in the clear are Brian and Nick."

"Maybe Brian's the liar," Veronica suggested.

"Brian's the one truthful person on this whole estate," Marston said. "Nick can investigate."

"Um. Wait." Nick took a step forward and glanced around. Brian stared down at his feet, cheeks pale. The rest were staring right at Nick. *I can't do this. Investigate an unreported murder, without authority, for Marston's benefit.* Except, what an excuse to pry around! Before he could say more he saw Brian sway and close his eyes. "Damn." He jumped to get a hand under Brian's elbow. "Damon, he needs some food or sugar or something."

Damon fumbled in his pocket and came out with a roll of tablets. "Here, glucose." He tossed them, and Nick made the one-handed catch and unwrapped one.

"Brian, open up. Eat this."

Brian opened his mouth obediently, and Nick popped the tablet in.

"Now sit down." There was no handy chair, but he steered Brian over to the wall and eased him down. "Stay."

"Woof," Brian said around his candy.

Nick dropped the rest of the roll in his lap. "And eat more of them."

He turned back to the group, avoiding Damon's curious gaze. "So, Mr. Marston, sir. Are you, um, serious? I mean, I know nothing about detecting except, like, watching CSI on TV."

"Damon can help you. You watch Damon and keep him honest."

Damon said, "Oh, right. Sir, if that's Nok Nick's job, you might as well shoot him now."

Marston turned his glare on Damon. "You think this is funny?"

"No, sir."

"It's not funny. Yeah, Henry was a jerk, but he was my brother. No one gets away with killing my brother! Whether he was the original target or not, I want to know who shot him and I'll return the favor, slowly, a dozen shots from the ankle to the heart. And if he wasn't the target, then we need to figure out who, or what, was. Or still is." He stared at each of them in turn." *Is. That. Clear?*"

Even Damon froze at the venom in Marston's voice. "Yes, sir."

"I'm calling in the rest of the security team to patrol, plus that guy Winchester to check the computers and cameras."

Nick cleared his throat. "Wouldn't they be better choices to investigate?"

Marston said, "I can't trust anyone who has security-system access and no alibi." He strode over to stare down at his brother's body. "You think this a challenge? This is a fucking insult to me? They screwed up, big time." He paused, his hands clenching and unclenching. "In fact, Damon? Who was that dog trainer? Call him up and get four new dogs. And shoot the useless ones we have."

"You can't!" Brian scrambled to his feet. "No!"

"No what? Are you talking to me?"

"You can't kill them." For a moment Nick clearly saw Brian, not Bry, glaring out of those pale eyes, alert and aware, then the shutters came down. Bry started chanting loudly, "No dead dogs. No dead dogs!"

"Bry, stop it," Damon muttered, grabbing for him. "Shut up!"

Brian dodged his grasp. "No dead dogs! No, no, no, no." For a moment Nick saw Marston weighing the impulse to smack Brian down for his insolence. Maybe Brian saw it too, because he dropped to his knees, hard enough Nick winced at the crack as his kneecaps hit the tiles. Brian didn't even pause. "Please, Mr. Marston. Please, please, no dead dogs? Please, sir?"

Brian's begging changed the stormy expression on Marston's face to distaste. "Oh, all right. If it matters that much. Damon, tell the trainer to pick up the old ones and take them away. Far away. Better, Bry?"

Nick saw Brian's hands were trembling but his voice was bland and happy. "Oh, yes, sir. So much better, sir. Thank you, sir."

Nick went and reached down to haul him to his feet. "Come on, Brian. You can help Damon and me. Um." He glanced around for some task that a supposed idiot could do.

Damon said, "Stand here, Bry." He led him to the corner of the house, twenty feet away. "Stand here, watch the drive and yell if you see anyone coming."

"Okay."

Lori said, "I need to lie down. I'll have Mrs. Jones bring you a sandwich, Bry."

Damon said, "Everybody use the front door, not this one. Better keep the area closed off."

Marston said, "I'll send Leo to you when the security team gets here. Then I'll be checking my personal collections. Henry might have interrupted a burglary."

"Yes, sir. You have a weapon?"

Marston gave Damon a dark look. "Of course."

Veronica said, "What about Father? Do we just... leave him there?" Nick heard the tremor of a sob in her voice.

"For now." Marston looked down, his jaw tight. "You can stay nearby while Damon and Nick investigate, if you really want to, but don't touch anything. We'll decide how to deal with his, er, body later."

"You've no heart, and no sodding soul, do you?"

"I traded them for wealth and power." Marston paused. "Of course, so did your father, and my father. It's the family way. I haven't decided if you've finalized your trade yet, but I think so."

Veronica made a sound like an angry cat, but knelt by her father's body without more words. Marston said, "Nathan, with me. Chuck, you too. We'll wait in the security room till the team arrives. Give me your guns."

Nathan glanced at Chuck, then dared to say, "Sir, I can't protect you without my gun."

Marston held out his hand. "You also can't shoot me. I'll take my chances. Come on."

Reluctantly, the guards pulled the weapons from their holsters and handed them to Marston, who tucked one into his jacket pocket, and passed the other to Lori. She hesitated, but took it with a familiarity that told Nick she'd handled one before. Marston nodded to Damon. "Let me know what you find out. Lori, my dear, if you're going to rest, we'll check your room on our way. Come along."

Marston strode off, past where Brian stood, the guards walking at his side. Lori trailed after them, throwing a couple of glances back toward Damon. Damon made a shooing motion with his hand, and she hurried to catch up to Marston. Once they were out of sight, Nick turned to Damon, trying to sound casual despite the fact that his heart was going a mile a minute. *This was so fucking big. If Marston and Damon hid the body, he'd have a provable crime, recorded and witnessed. Probable cause for a warrant. This could break the case open.*

At the very least it was evidence tampering. At best, accessory after the fact. Nick was acutely aware of the audio recorder that was capturing these vital moments, as he said, "All right, Damon. Where do we start?"

****

Brian stood against the rough stone of the house and sucked on his candy. He didn't have to stay there. He wasn't actually doing anything useful. But he took comfort from being within sight of Damon and Nick. He was shaky and sick to his stomach, and he didn't think it was low blood sugar. Until now, he'd known that violent death walked through his life, striking down men he'd met and sometimes men he'd tracked. He'd felt the blank spaces in his head, but he'd never seen it.

His mom's body, withered and filthy in her bed, had been bad enough. But they'd all known it was coming, no matter how much he'd fought the awareness. This— the bloody end to a healthy man— made him shudder. That could have been Damon. That could have been Lori! Who knew who the killer might have targeted? He took a careful breath, reminding himself that the two men speaking in low voices behind him were safe together, and the best protection he could hope for.

Other than the dogs. Oh, God! For an instant his legs shook, and he felt the ache of bruises on his knees. That had been close. *Witch, Brute, Luger, Glock, stay safe*. They were good guard dogs, but not supernatural. How could they know that someone they'd trusted was a threat? He made a vow not to get close to the new dogs. Not if they were disposable like that. He hoped Luger and Glock would get a nice new home.

"Here. For you."

He jumped, and realized that Mrs. Jones was a few feet away, holding out a napkin-wrapped sandwich. "Oh. Thanks."

She glanced past him. "That's Mr. Granton that died, right?"

Brian realized that even after three years, he still didn't trust her. But it was common knowledge. "Yes. Dead, dead, shot dead."

She sniffed and glanced at him. "Well, he won't be much missed." She turned and headed back toward the door.

Brian stared after her, trying to figure out that comment. Mrs. Jones was usually silent and unnoticed, cooking and serving and supervising the cleaning staff in perfect style. She ran a tight ship. Brian had once made a cleaning girl cry when he walked into a room that should have been finished for the day and wasn't. She'd said, "Don't tell Mrs. Jones!" and he'd played the fool and said, "Tell what? It's sunny today," to make her look less scared.

So Mrs. Jones was always there and seldom seen, and for all he knew, maybe she'd decided Mr. Granton was better off dead. He looked at his sandwich. It could be poisoned. Maybe she was going to kill them all.

Hunger and common sense made him finally take a bite. If she wanted to poison him, there were easier ways and times to do it. The sandwich was good— thick-sliced beef on homemade bread with mustard. He made himself eat slowly. These after-Finding days were odd, making him ravenous one minute and sick to his stomach the next. But this time the food went down tasty and comforting.

"You think she'd make me one?"

He jumped again, knocking his elbow against the wall, and turned. Veronica stood eyeing him, her head tilted, expression distant, like Brian was some kind of rare bug she was deciding whether to watch or squish.

"She cooks. She's a good cook." Stating the obvious was always an easy opening. There was mustard on his fingers and he sucked one and then another, loudly.

Veronica pressed her lips tighter, looking wonderfully grossed out. "I suppose she is. Although her puddings are rather sweet."

"We don't have pudding."

"Never mind." Veronica came a step nearer. "So who's this guy Nick? Why is he allowed to touch my father and I'm not?"

"Nick is Nick. Nok Nick. He fights good and drives."

"Does he work for your brother or for Uncle Vern?"

"He works hard."

She made a disgusted sound in her throat. "I'm expecting sense from the village idiot." She brushed past him toward the front door.

As she passed, he said, "You're not crying for your daddy."

She whirled to look at him, eyes stormy. "No, I'm not. Should I?"

Brian shrugged, uncomfortable with the intensity of her stare. After a second, she turned and walked off, her steps precise and her back stiff as a rod. Brian let out his breath.

Nick came toward him. "What did she say?"

Brian lowered his voice to a murmur, fighting his instincts. "She… she…" For a moment, Brian and Bry battled for control, and he had to clear his throat and start again. "Nothing interesting. She doesn't seem to be grieving much. She asked about you."

"What about me?"

"Who you were. Who you worked for. Why Mr. Marston would let you investigate."

"What did you say?"

"I said you were Nok Nick and worked hard."

Nick's gentle slap on his shoulder felt like a medal. "Well done. Let me know if anyone else says anything odd."

"Mrs. Jones said he wouldn't be missed."

"Mrs. *Jones* did? That's interesting." After a moment Nick shook his head. "Well, we have no real clues yet. Damon says you should go rest."

"I'm always tired the day after."

"Day after what?"

It was a casual question. Nick wasn't even looking his way, his attention on the sound of a car approaching down the drive.

Brian flushed, his heart fluttering in panic. He'd forgotten Finding was still something he hadn't shared, and *couldn't* share, with Nick. "After a headache!"

"Right." The car appeared, one of the black SUVs the security firm used, with the logo on the door. Nick stepped in front of Brian as it pulled around to the front. When the guys got out, Nick said, "Anyone you don't recognize?"

"The thin guy in the back."

Nick called, "Hey, Damon, your backup team is here."

Damon grunted, and came over to them. Brian was confused, double minded, caught between Damon and Nick, Bry and Brian. He pressed his fingers to his mouth to stay silent.

Nick asked, "Who's the skinny geek?"

Damon snorted. "That's Winchester. He's the tech guy. If anyone can tell us if the cameras got looped or the system failed, he can."

"Got it." Nick moved away from Brian. "Hey, go lie down. You still look like crap."

Damon said, "Maybe stay with Lori until we can check this out a bit more. Keep an eye on each other."

Brian licked his lips, and said slowly, "I can do that."

"Good boy. I'll come talk to you later."

Nick said, "You have my number, too," but he was already turning back toward the body on the ground.

Brian went around and in the front door. His least favorite guard was standing off to the side, watching as he came in, a hand on his weapon. Brian ducked his head, not meeting his eyes as he scurried past. Lori's room was up the stairs and to the left. Her door was shut, but when he knocked, and called her name, she told him to come in.

He'd wondered if she might be crying or at least curled up on the bed. He'd had a small fantasy of for once being her protector, watching over her. He should have known better, of course. She had an open backpack out on the bed, with clothes scattered across the covers.

"Are you, um, packing? Leaving?"

"Come in and shut the door. No, I'm not leaving. Vern makes me keep an emergency grab-and-go bag ready, like Damon does with you, and I realized none of the slacks in it will fit me anymore. I'm swapping in some fat-lady clothes."

"You're not fat."

"Not much. But I will be." She folded and rolled black sweatpants into a small wad, stuffed them in a pocket, and glanced at him. "How are you, Bry? You look like crap."

If one more person said that, he was going to crap on the rug and show them what it really looked like. "Headache."

"Well, sit. Or here." She swept the clothes to one side. "Lie down and keep me company."

Lori's bed was high and soft, and lying down sounded too good to pass up. Brian gingerly lowered himself onto it. He wondered if maybe he could help Nick investigate. Maybe he could ask Lori questions. She certainly wasn't a killer, but she often knew surprising stuff, and she'd refuse to answer for Nick. It was hard, though. He had so many years of going with the flow. He started tentatively. "Mr. Granton is dead."

"Yeah. Cry me a river."

"You didn't like him?"

"No. Did you?"

"No," he admitted.

"I didn't kill him, though," Lori said. "I don't know who did."

"Mr. Marston?" Brian decided to toss that out there.

"No way." Lori stared at him. "Jesus, Bry, he was pissed as hell about it. Not that he liked Henry much, but he was his brother. That counts for him."

"Oh."

Lori had always liked to talk. When he was small, he'd used that to buffer him from everyone else by letting her be their voice. He'd grown up listening to her talk at will, until she might've been surprised at the things she'd said to his uncritical silence. Later he'd learned that if he wanted to know something Lori wasn't telling him, keeping quiet was better than direct questions. So he closed his eyes, tried to relax into the cushy mattress, and waited.

Sure enough, after a few minutes of rustling about, she said, "It doesn't make sense, though. I don't know who'd have bothered. I mean, I probably hated him more than anyone, for the way he wanted to cheat this baby out of the inheritance, and I still wouldn't have killed him. And if it was one of the maids mad at him for grabbing their ass, it seems like overreacting."

"He grabbed maids' asses?"

Lori laughed humorlessly. "He grabbed my ass too. I told him Vern would cut his arm off at the elbow, and he never did it again. But he was just a slimy, small-time jerk. So I'm kinda scared that the killer was gunning for Vern instead."

Brian wanted to say that someone coming for Vern would have brought their own gun, but he couldn't figure out how to put it, and couldn't really be bothered. The room was warm and the bed soft. He said, "Maybe Veronica did it."

"I wish. I don't think so. With Henry dead, most of the Baron's money and property goes to Vern as soon as the old man dies. Vern told me. She's all about the cash, and I'm sure she'd rather her father got it for a long lifetime first."

Brian nodded, enjoying the way the room tilted and spun when he did that. He nodded again, for the swooping feeling. This was *good* stuff Damon had given him this time. "Maybe he grabbed her ass."

"Bry! Although, who knows? Maybe he did. But how would she know about the cameras? Why kill him here, and not a thousand other better places? They went sightseeing, hiking. Hell, I don't know."

"Nick will find out. And Damon."

Lori sat down on the bed. "You like that guy Nick, don't you?"

Even through the buzz of the drug, he felt a lurch of worry. *Not her business.* "He's nice. He likes Muppets. He hits people—" He barely cut off the words *who say faggot.* Maybe it was a truth drug.

"You like that he hits people?"

Brian shrugged, rather than try to rescue that comment.

"You're weird. Just remember, there's you, me, and Damon. We trust each other. No one else."

Brian was going to remind her that they knew Nick wasn't the killer, but it was safer to say, "Not even Mr. Marston?"

"Vern? Hell, no." She laughed. "He likes having a young wife in his bed, so he's good to me. Plus you and Damon are useful to him, but he'd sell us out in a minute if he had to. I don't think he shot Henry, but we can't trust him."

"You married him." He'd worried at the time that she didn't know what she was getting into. They'd been just eighteen. Damon had worked for Mr. Marston for a few years by then, and Brian for two. The way Mr. Marston suddenly dated Lori the minute she turned eighteen was creepy, but Lori and Damon had both been pleased.

"Bry, I told you then and I'll tell you now. I knew exactly what I was doing. It was for Damon and you and me."

"Okay."

"And there's no place in our plans for anyone getting shot, so Damon and Nick had better figure out what the hell is going on, and fast."

"I'll stay," Brian muttered. "I'll protect you." He topped off that ridiculous idea by falling asleep.

Chapter 15

Nick had never expected to be sitting down for dinner in Mr. Marston's house, almost like one of the family. A dysfunctional family, of course. Veronica was missing and the computer geek Winchester was there instead, but still, it was surreal. He pushed his chair back slightly, to have more room in case he needed to get up fast, and draped the white linen napkin across his knees. Somehow he'd ended up next to Brian, who looked rumpled and sweaty like he just woke up, but less pale and washed-out than he had been. Nick spread his legs enough to accidentally tap Brian's knee with his own, and Brian nudged back without looking at him.

The silent housekeeper set salads and plates in front of all of them, and refilled water glasses. The table was set with wine glasses but Marston had turned his over, and no wine was in evidence. Marston took out his phone and tapped a button. "Leo, please escort Mrs. Jones safely off the property."

The housekeeper looked at him, visibly startled. "But the dessert? And the dishes?"

"Put the dessert on the sideboard, and dishes can wait until morning."

She lowered her gaze. "Yes, sir."

"I don't need to remind you not to gossip about today?"

"Of course not."

"Good." He smiled thinly. "I know this has been very, um, upsetting to you. There will of course be a large bonus in your check this week for all the difficulty."

"Thank you."

"Now go get ready to leave. I'll have someone text and let you know what time we want you and the rest of the day staff to come in tomorrow. No one is to show up until I say so."

"Yes, sir."

When she had left the room, Marston looked around the table. "Winchester. You start. Security status?" He took a forkful of braised pork and turned his gaze on the computer guy.

Nick tried to eat and listen. Basically, the geek didn't think security had been tampered with. If it was an outsider, then the guy had to have made it on and off the property while evading all the cameras. The guards had searched the house, grounds, and buildings in pairs, and found no one. Damon reported their own results which found nada and nothing. Henry Granton's bag held an accounts ledger and his tablet, which was still password locked, but they found no obvious reason for anyone to want him dead. No threatening notes, to or from Granton, no kiddie porn or stolen diamonds, and the little vial of prescription pills was surely just personal use.

Marston sat back from his empty plate, and glared at Nick. "Anything to add?"

"No, sir." He'd taken a few pictures of the ledger and Granton's phone log with his wristband cam, without Damon seeing him do it. They might give the DEA something useful. He wanted to seem reliable and just a bit dumb, not put himself forward. "What else can I do to help?"

"Besides the sweet fuck-all help you've been so far?" Marston frowned at him. "You ever use a gun, Nok Nick?"

"Yes, sir." They'd made one of his supposed foster dads an avid shooter, and given Nick Green a juvenile history of gun misdemeanors, so Nick wouldn't have to fake-fumble with weapons. Marston probably knew that. "Not today though, sir."

Marston sighed loudly. "I know that. I'll give you a gun, and I want you to stay in the pool house with Brian and Lori tonight."

Nick's own *"What?"* was lost in Lori's exclamation. "What the hell? Vern?"

"I want you both safe, my dear." Marston turned to her. "We know the killer was probably inside this house, stepping out that back door to kill

186

Henry. We don't know what he really wanted. The pool house is small, only two doors, easily protected."

"So who gives me their room? I'm not sleeping on the damn couch."

"I will," Damon said. "I'll stay downstairs."

"And we'll put Nick upstairs," Marston said.

Fuck, fuck, fuck. Nick had counted on going home and downloading all his recordings. "I'm not trained as a guard."

"The ones who are, I don't trust. Anyone new I might bring in locally, could be working for my enemies. You're not the shooter and didn't have enough clearance to be the security leak. You're it. You want to work for me? This is the work. You in or out?"

He'd seen them cover up the murder. He'd helped Damon load the body in a car trunk for disposal, somewhere. All through it he'd felt Damon's eyes on him, watching for a flinch. Watching for any sign he wasn't as hard-core as the rest of them. If he said *out*, it was a good bet he'd join Granton. "I'm in, sir."

"Right. Finish your meal. You'll need the energy."

It was an hour before they'd moved Lori's things to the pool house, checked it out thoroughly, and settled her and Brian in the TV room with blinds drawn, watching some movie. Finally, he could slip upstairs into the bathroom. He had to trust that the lack of indoor cameras extended here, as he pulled out his phone and dialed.

"Listen up," he said, fast and low. "I'm at Marston's for the night. Lots happening. A car left the estate around six-fifty."

"We tracked it," Olson's voice said. "It dumped a load into Sugar Lake. We're going after it now."

"Body. Henry Granton."

"Should we ID him right away?"

"Can you wait? I'm guarding the Kerrs. Things are moving. Gotta go."

"We'll keep it under wraps for now. Stay sharp."

Nick clicked off and erased his log, tucked the phone away, and flushed the john. Damon was at the base of the stairs as he came down, and he was careful to look a little irritated and not at all nervous. "This sucks, you know? I had things to do."

"He'll pay you."

"I guess. I could use the money."

"It'll be easy duty."

"You think?" He glanced at Damon. "You're not worried the killer could come back? Who do you think did it?"

Damon shrugged. "I know it wasn't these two, and I doubt they were the targets either, so this should be a slow night for us."

"Well, Brian obviously isn't a target. No reason to kill him."

Damon gave him a strangely long stare, then nodded.

"But Mrs. Marston? With Marston's own kid? She could be a prize for a killer, or a snatch."

Damon nodded. "Yeah, but... you want to know what I think?" He dropped his voice low. "I think Marston did it himself. Granton might have been his brother, but the first time he started threatening to drag Lori and the baby through shit? No one threatens what's Vern's." His eyes glittered narrowly.

Nick nodded, his mind racing. Was this some kind of test? A loyalty ploy? If so who was he supposed to side with? Damon or Marston? He wasn't convinced by Damon's story, but Nick Green might be. He couldn't deny it made a neat picture. "So all that snarling and shifting guards around is cover?"

"Shaking up your security is never a bad thing."

Nick said casually, "But would he risk murder?"

Damon laughed. "Nick, Nick, you're not in the little leagues now. If you knew the men Marston's had killed, you'd know this is nothing. He probably enjoyed the satisfaction of doing it himself."

"So you're not worried tonight?"

Damon lifted one shoulder. "We put two guards in the big house watching each other, outside Veronica's room and outside Mr. Marston's. And Mr. Marston can take care of himself. I'm gonna spend the night awake patrolling down here. Tomorrow, we'll see. I think he's swapping the security crew with some of his guys from San Diego, just in case. But I'm not really expecting trouble."

Nick wanted to keep Damon talking. He was usually more closemouthed than this, even when drunk. "He can just shuffle people around like that, one city to another?"

"Sure. He pays well, and he has a squeeze on most of them. They have no choice."

"He doesn't have a handle on me." Nick tried to sound angry and cocky.

"Ya think?" Damon raised an eyebrow. "We just covered up a murder. You helped."

"Shit." Nick needed to act like that was a shock. He took a hard breath, bit his lip, let his hands curl into fists. "*Fuck!*"

"Right. He owns you. And me. But he's not that bad, if you keep your mouth shut and do the work."

"What work do you do?"

Damon stopped short and looked at him. "Remember the part about mouth shut?"

"Yeah."

"That." Damon strode on to recheck the front door, then made his way to the breezeway door beside the kitchen.

Threat? Confession? Or just advice? It was nothing that would stand up in court anyway.

Nick looked into the den. Lori sat on the couch, staring at the screen. Brian sprawled in a recliner, his eyes half-shut. When Nick stepped into the room he looked up, gaze bright and aware. "Problem?"

"Nope. You guys just hang out. All's quiet."

"The movie's nice and noisy. Wanna watch?"

Lori said without turning, "We're fine, Bry. Nick doesn't want to watch the dumb movie."

"Not a dumb movie!"

Nick realized he could hear the shifts in tone, the way becoming Bry made Brian's voice go thicker and flatter. Was that on purpose, or was it really not under Brian's control? No matter how this went down, he had a feeling Brian would need a load of therapy, if he managed to stay out of jail. If not… God, Nick wanted to grab him and haul him away from his cold sister and violent brother and psychotic boss. Instead he said, "I've seen it. It's a good one. But I should probably keep watch."

Brian gave him a slow, grateful smile and turned back to the screen. Nick stepped back a couple of paces from the open door. It had been so long since Ariana, since the last time he'd wanted this badly to make someone safe and happy. And he was so fucking confused, because his perception of Brian kept shifting, from little brother to definitely not brother-like.

Of course, he couldn't afford to feel either one, not in this situation. Nick Green was too tough a loner to fall for anyone, and Nick Rugo had a job to do. The fact that Brian's smile lit his eyes with a warmth Nick wanted to shelter and share was no excuse.

Brian was a nice guy, a kid, almost, caught in a bad situation that he'd have to survive on his own.

Kid. Caught. *Remember that, Nicky-boy.*

He kept his distance for the next few hours, through the end of the movie and Lori's munchies, and another movie, and getting brother and sister upstairs and into bedrooms. Damon slipped out the door to make a sweep around the building, and Nick settled in at the end of the upstairs hall on a folded blanket. He had a wall at his back, a borrowed gun in a shoulder holster, and a clear view of the stairs. He was good to go. A dim light from downstairs filtered up enough to make things visible, without destroying his night vision completely if trouble arose outside. Although Damon had told him firmly that those two bedroom doors were his only concern.

Soft, light snores started to filter though one of the doors. The other one opened silently. Nick sat where he was and watched Brian come toward him, barefoot, fingers a bit clumsy as he buttoned a Star Wars pajama top across his chest.

Brian slid down the wall and sat beside him. "Hi, Nick." His voice was more breath than sound.

"You're supposed to be asleep." Nick knew a whisper carried. He went for soft low tones too. "Is there a problem?"

Brian jerked his head in a quick negative. "I can't sleep. And here you are."

"On guard, remember. With Lori there." He pointed to her door. "And Damon downstairs."

"Lori can sleep through anything. We both can, because Damon doesn't."

"Huh?"

"We had to." Brian bowed his head to look at his hands. His hair was tousled like dandelion fluff, and shadows hid his eyes. "We lived in crap housing, full of noise. Mom sometimes got loud at night, too. But Lori and me could sleep, because if the guy she was with tried to make trouble, Damon would know. Damon always slept with a knife in his hand, and one eye open."

"Did he ever use the knife?" Nick felt like a traitor, with that recorder in his jeans, but it wasn't like they could use hearsay anyway.

"Threatened a bunch of times. Cut one guy. Lori and I were hiding under the bed. She was a lot prettier than Mom by then."

And didn't that just paint the picture? "I'm glad he was there."

"Me too. Mom was, well, she tried to be a good mom, but at the end... it was like she didn't even see us anymore. We were these lumps, these things, between her and her smack. But I guess, you know, at least she never sold us out. And she could have. Guys would have paid for Lori. Mom didn't ever do that."

How sad was it that the best thing about your mom was that she didn't pimp you out? Nick slid his left hand over enough to pat Brian's knee through his pj pants. "I'm glad you all made it out okay."

"Well, depends what you mean by okay."

They both froze when Lori's snoring suddenly stopped, followed by a snuffle and a cough. They sat silently, unmoving, the warmth of Brian's leg burning against Nick's palm. Then her soft snores resumed. Nick snatched his hand back.

Brian chuckled softly. "Told you. She's a bear to wake before ten in the morning."

Nick knew he should send Brian to bed, but he hadn't heard Damon come back in yet. He told himself he might pick up something useful if they kept talking. "How'd you end up working for Mr. Marston?"

"Damon did first. He always had jobs, supporting us because Mom shot all her money up her arm. Some of those jobs hurt him. I could see it, and feel it, like he got smokier and darker and sharper."

"You should be a poet."

"Sorry. That was dumb."

Without thinking, he gripped Brian's knee and shook him gently. "Stop calling yourself dumb. I meant it. That sounded kind of cool."

"Oh!" Brian paused, looking into his eyes. His pupils were wide, and Nick could see the little dark silhouettes of his own head against the pale blue. "Wow."

The moment stretched, and Nick shifted restlessly on the blanket. "You said he had jobs?"

"Mm. Yeah. He started working for Mr. Marston, and as soon as I was sixteen he said I should quit school. They weren't teaching me anything anyway. I worked in Mr. Marston's warehouse first, moving boxes. Then, um, other things I could do. Then Mr. Marston saw Lori and decided to marry her and we came here."

"Weird." Nick spoke without thinking. "Sorry. I mean, she's pretty but still, he must know a lot of pretty women."

"Yeah, they don't feel like they go together. But I guess they do." Brian leaned closer, so their shoulders touched. "It's hard to know why people do things. Why does Damon hurt a stranger, when he'd cut off his own arm for me? Why does Lori not get scared that she can't trust her husband?"

"She can't?"

Brian threw him a look. "She says no, and she says it doesn't matter. It would matter to me."

"I guess she's getting other things out of it."

"Sex? Money? Security? Yeah, I suppose. And now the baby." Brian was silent for a minute. "Damon and Lori want us to be safe and to have enough not to ever get evicted onto the street. And Lori wants even more, I guess."

"What do you want?" Nick knew it was the wrong question before it left his mouth.

Brian said nothing through several heartbeats, through a rasp of Nick's breath and the prickle of sweat down his back. Then, as Nick hunted desperately for a way to defuse this, Brian rose to his knees, surprisingly smoothly, swung around and across Nick to straddle his outstretched legs, and leaned in to kiss him. Nick opened his mouth to protest, and his voice was stopped in his throat by the awareness that Damon might be somewhere nearby. Before he could do anything else, Brian's hands gripped his biceps with surprising strength and his tongue swept between Nick's parted lips.

Nick was stunned to immobility as Brian's weight came down against his chest and thighs. Brian kissed oddly, the pressure of his lips and thrusts of his tongue mistimed, unpracticed. Nick raised his hands, gripping Brian's hair to steady him and tilted his head to make more room. He gentled the kiss. As he rubbed their lips together, licked, sucked gently, Brian followed suit, mimicking, learning. When Nick took his lower lip in gentle teeth and tugged, the sound Brian made was needy. And a bit too loud.

They froze at the same moment, listening. Nothing stirred downstairs. Nick took his first coherent breath in a while. He let go of that silky hair. "Shh. We can't—"

Brian kissed the rest of the words out of his mouth. He rocked against Nick, grinding into his lap, their groins pressed together. Between kisses he murmured, "Please, please." Nick thought of the recorder, thought of his superiors, looked at the blown delight in Brian's eyes, and said nothing. He could have said he was on guard. He could have invoked the threat of Damon. But looking at Brian, he could almost see the bleeding wound that pushing him away again would cause. He cupped Brian's soft, round ass, pulling him in harder, kneading firm flesh with his fingers, and kissed him back.

Brian adjusted his position, arching, flexing, then threw his head back and rode against Nick's lap, his hands clamped on Nick's arms. His weight pressed them together. Nick's cock was painfully hard in his jeans. As much as he wanted this to be just for Brian, he was more turned on every moment. He couldn't help responding to that frotting motion, although he tried to be silent. Surely the driving friction would be all that the recording picked up.

They breathed faster, lips pressed shut against any sound. Brian's eyelids drooped closed, and the cords of his arched neck stood out. The faint light shone off the damp skin of his neck, the angle of his clenched jaw, and the haze of blond stubble there. His cock was bigger than Nick's, rock hard under the thin pants. All male, and not a child at all. He hesitated for an instant, chest heaving, staring at Nick with need and something close to fear. Nick breathed, "Yes. 'S okay, Brian."

Brian whined— high and almost inaudible— and shuddered. He thrust against Nick frantically, rising up enough to have room to move. When he came, he made no sound, but Nick could feel the clenching of his ass cheeks. Nick squeezed his eyes shut against the sight of Brian, head bowed back in pleasure, and fought not to come in his jeans.

Brian collapsed against him, and Nick's arms rose automatically to wrap him tight. Brian burrowed his face in against Nick's neck. He breathed, "Oh. Wow."

"Sh." Nick freed a hand to stroke his back in slow circles, then eased him over enough to get his holster clear and within reach. He was supposed to be on guard here, and he was screwing everything up. He was so hard it hurt, and he was not— *not*— getting off tonight. And that was final. This had been for Brian, because he had needed it. Nick hadn't yet crossed his own line in the sand. He slid his hand up to cup the damp back of Brian's neck.

Brian sighed, shuddered, and then pulled back and broke his hold. "Thanks."

Nick managed a smile, like he wasn't wound tighter than a drum. "That was all you."

Brian looked down and murmured, "You didn't come."

"It's okay."

Quicker than Nick could dodge, Brian snaked a hand between them and grabbed the taut ridge of Nick's erection through his jeans. Nick closed his eyes, seeing stars, and whispered urgently, "Stop. No clean clothes."

"Oh." But Brian didn't let go. Instead he fumbled with button and zipper.

Nick started to panic, between the risk that Brian would feel the recorder and the risk his superiors would hear him get off, and... "Stop!" he gasped.

Brian paused, his hand gripping Nick's now-naked cock. The purpling, damp head stuck out beyond his fingers, a pearly drop seeping free. Brian looked straight at Nick and waited, not moving, not stroking, not letting go.

Tell him to let go.

Nick stared into Brian's eyes. There was something strong and unexpected there. Brian wasn't asking permission, he was daring Nick to say no. It was a challenge, a demand. Slowly, an inch at a time, Brian slid backward and leaned down, his gaze fixed on Nick's.

Say stop.

The soft lips, that had gasped and begged under Nick's, opened undeniably, wide and round and ready. Nick reached down, but he didn't push Brian away, or touch his face. He pressed his palm over that damned spying bulge in the denim, spreading the fabric. He prayed that his hand would at least muffle the sound and said nothing as Brian's mouth closed over him.

Brian blew him without art and without hurry, slow up-and-down suction that was silent and hot and seemed to pull Nick's breath out his cock. Down, and back up, cheeks hollow, lips furled. Each slow dip, each retreat, wet and long and tight, took Nick further out of himself. This was no one he recognized, sitting here on the floor in a criminal's pool house, yards from a man downstairs who would probably cut his throat if he knew, letting a guy he couldn't understand give him the most simple, crazy, intense blow job he'd ever had.

Brian pulled all the way off and leaned in to kiss him. Nick opened his lips, helplessly, tasting sweet-salt precum on Brian's tongue. Then Brian slid back a bit more, hunched over Nick's shins, and sucked him down right to the root, his throat closing, tongue pressing. Nick barely kept himself from shouting as he grabbed Brian's hair and came in dark, slow, body-shaking waves until his vision blurred.

For a moment they were still and silent. Nick's body vibrated with little tremors that ran up and down his thighs and shivered through his belly. Brian eased up off him and swallowed, before bending to lick him in one long slow stroke from base to tip. Nick bit back a gasp and eased his hand out of Brian's hair. He kept the other pressed over his jeans. He couldn't think yet, didn't dare think what that might have sounded like.

Brian's smile crept wide, and then wider, satisfaction with a touch of what looked like glee. He murmured, "I've been dreaming about that."

"I've had nightmares," Nick growled, still completely off-balance.

The way Brian's face shut down to stillness was unreal. Bright eyes gone flat and cool met Nick's angry look. "I'll go to bed now." It was Bry's voice, Bry's look, and Nick almost threw up, right there on that hallway floor. This time it was his fault.

"No. God, Brian, I'm sorry. You were…" The recorder was taking down every word. He tried to make a touch of his hand be his praise. "I just… we can't do this. I work for Marston. Your brother would kill me. You're so much younger." There were so many other reasons, and he couldn't say any of them.

"And dumber."

"I'm beginning to think you're smarter than me."

"Weirder, then. Crazy. Loony."

Nick winced. "I don't know. Brian, sometimes you're this guy I'd love to have met in a club or a bar somewhere. And sometimes…"

"Sometimes I'm the guy who should hold someone's hand to cross the street."

They heard the downstairs door open and then close, and Nick had to bite back his response. They held still, listening, tensed for action, until Damon called up from somewhere out of sight, "It's me. All clear outside. Nick, you good?"

Nick swallowed and called back softly, "No problems."

"I'll camp out down here. Stay alert."

"Right, Damon."

He and Brian sat, barely breathing, as they listened to the faint noises of Damon walking around downstairs. The footsteps receded toward the kitchen at back of the house.

When he thought it was safe, Nick went on as quietly as he could, "Look, I know about hiding. I grew up in foster homes where gay was *not* a safe thing to be. I hid myself real well. You've seen more of me than most anyone I can think of in real life."

"Really?"

The thread of hope in that word was something he should have crushed. It would be a kindness. Instead he touched Brian's jaw, and brushed a fingertip over to his lower lip, still damp and a little sticky. "Really. But Brian, I never hid the way you do. It scares me, a little."

"It scares me too, now," Brian said. "I used to think everyone did that, had an inside person and an outside one."

"Well, I guess we do." *Have I ever let anyone see the real me?* This dangerous hallway was the wrong place to even have that thought. "But… maybe not everybody's are as different as yours."

"Yeah. I know that. I'm not sure how much longer I can be both and not end up split in two. So I guess I am pretty loony."

"You need help. Maybe once this is over."

"Once what is over? This is my life, Nick."

Man, he needed to get back in character. Nick shifted position and took his hand off his fly. He said in as offhand a whisper as he could manage, "You never know. Things change. Maybe once we catch the shooter and Marston and Damon go off high alert, things will get better."

Brian looked at him and then shrugged, looking somber but not full shutters-drawn Bry. "I should clean up." He slid off Nick's legs and stood. A little smile flashed across his face, and he murmured, "I got spunk on Chewbacca."

"Go clean up and sleep," Nick muttered back, zipping himself up. "Tomorrow's another day."

Brian nodded, and then slowly his features went slack. He said, loud enough to be heard downstairs if Damon cared, "I woke up. I gotta pee."

"Bathroom's right there," Nick said the same way. "I'll keep watch."

Brian went in and shut the door, running water and flushing. Nick pulled his clothes straight, tugging his shirt down flat, as if that would erase what happened. His breath rasped in his chest, still uneven. That had been a crazy risk to take.

When Brian came out, he was half-naked, his pj pants in his hand. His legs were pale and dusted with blond hair, his ass and tummy were rounded, his cock a good size, even when soft. He looked over at Nick, and touched his tongue to his lip hesitantly. He said clearly, in singsong belied by the brightness of his eyes, "Good night, Nok Nick."

"Fuck you," Nick replied, shaping the words without sound. He smiled to show he didn't mean it.

Brian ducked his head and didn't smile back, but his back was straight and his stride easy as he went back into his room. Nick felt the dumb smile melt off his own face. He stood, stretched, and leaned on the wall, touching his holster to make sure it rode where it should. The only thing breaking the silence was the low rasp of Lori's snores in the room right across from where Brian had gone to bed. Without pants. Brian, who was somehow tangled up in Nick's mind in ways he didn't want to think about.

He straightened his shoulders and tried to find Nick Green's fuck-it-all frame of mind. His hamster-wheel brain failed to settle down and shut up. That moral line that he'd been so proud of respecting? Well, that was blown out of the water now. Sapped, mined, machine-gunned and… blown. Shit. *Shit!* What had he done?

And yet, part of him wanted to open that bedroom door and do it some more, to see what Brian looked like with no clothes on at all and that lazy sex-smile on his lips. Nick held back a growl of frustration. He wanted to hit something, or smack himself unconscious.

The recording would show everything, no matter how he tried to delude himself about static and muffling. Sex sounded like sex. Sure, he'd got some hearsay evidence against Damon and Marston. Sure, he could claim he now had Brian safely hooked to become an informant. But he'd let a guy suck him off on the job, and there was a recording of it. He couldn't imagine any way that would sound good to Olson and Takano. He almost wanted something big to happen now, a fight, an attack, something to override the sick feeling of having fucked up royally.

Chapter 16

The morning light had brightened outside when Nick jumped back against the wall at the sound of heavy footsteps on the stairs. His hand leaped to his holster, even though he'd had all night to take the edge off his anticipation.

"Yo! Me!" Damon grinned as he came the rest of the way up. "Gonna shoot me? I like to see a guy taking his job seriously."

"Fuck off."

"You're all done here, Nok. Off duty."

Nick lowered his hand, trying to look sheepish. "About fucking time. I'm no bodyguard."

"Then it's a good thing you didn't have to do anything except look tough."

"Fuck you." Nick relished the way Damon was bantering with him, as if they were friends, when he had Damon *nailed* for messing with a murder. He was bone-tired and still vibrating with adrenaline. He'd managed to silently text Olson with some of the details of what'd gone down with Granton. Each text had to be short, and immediately deleted. He didn't give the code that it was safe to text him back, with the three Kerrs so close by, but all night he'd expected to get the "go" signal. Olson now had probable cause to move in. He'd waited, listening, for the cops to arrive, and it never happened.

Now it was eight in the morning, full daylight outside, and all was still quiet. *What the hell were they waiting on?* He wanted to stick around the mansion and get more info, but he also wanted to get somewhere safe and call his fucking superior officers. "What now?"

Damon raised one eyebrow.

"Are we investigating any more? Do I just go show up at the warehouse? What?"

"Marston's security from San Diego is here. You go back to being a driver."

"Now?"

"You were up all night. Take the day off. I'll let Roy know."

"Okay…" Nick stretched, while he tried to think like Nick Green. Green followed rules and wasn't curious. He'd say, "I'm gonna get paid for last night, right?"

"I'll even throw in a bonus."

"I'd do it again, if the money's good."

Damon's smile shaded into something superior. "I think we'll leave it to the pros now."

Nick muttered, "Like your pros did Granton any good."

"That's none of your business."

"Right. Got it. I'm gone." Nick pushed past Damon on his way down the stairs, although not too roughly. "If anyone else gets dead, don't call me." He didn't glance back at Brian's closed and silent door, even once.

An unfamiliar bodyguard stood outside the pool house, clearly waiting for him. The man fell into step beside him. "Mr. Marston wants to see you."

Nick nodded as if it was no big deal. He followed the guard into the main house and to a paneled study on the ground floor. Marston sat behind a large wooden desk, and he looked up at the guard as they entered. "That'll be all. Wait outside."

"Yes, sir." The guard stepped back out, closing the door behind him.

There were chairs in front of the desk, but Marston didn't gesture at them, so Nick stood there, pose casual, jaw thrust out with a hint of irritation. *Nick Green is tired and annoyed and wants to get the hell home to bed.*

Marston said, "I don't need to tell you to keep your mouth shut, do I?"

"Nope." Nick waited a beat, and added, "Sir."

"I won't forget that you pitched in to help, but don't get a swelled head."

Nick shrugged.

"I may have more work for you, coming up. But if you start to get chicken, if you even think about going to the cops—"

"Fuck the cops."

"*If* you do," Marston continued, "I can find you and deal with you, anywhere, anytime. And I'll know. I have cops on the payroll, and if they so much as see your toe in the door they will tell me. You're either an asset or a liability."

Nick dropped his gaze. "I just wanna earn some money. I ain't seen nothing."

"Good man. Get out of here. Go home."

Nick waved a mock salute, keeping it more respectful than sarcastic. As he opened the study door, he could hear a woman's voice complaining loudly upstairs, her words lost in the shrill tone. He glanced up. "Sounds like Veronica's not happy. Will she make trouble? I don't want to go to jail for moving a fucking body."

Marston said, "That's *Miss Granton* to you. And she's finding out my limits. No one's going to jail."

That's what you think. Nick pressed his lips together, hoping he looked worried rather than gleeful, and nodded. When he left the room, the new guard fell in at his side again. "This way. I'll show you out."

"I think I can find my fucking car."

The guy grunted and kept walking. When Nick got into the Corolla, the guard got in a black Jeep parked on the verge, and turned down the drive behind him. All the way through the gate, and down the road, into town and right to his apartment, the Jeep was barely a car length back. It was a very unsubtle reminder. With the guard's eyes on him, Nick didn't even reach for his phone on the drive.

Inside his apartment, he let himself sigh heavily, although his mind was racing. The place was thoroughly bugged. The day after he'd first driven Brian onto the estate, he'd come back to find a few tiny marks in the chalk dust across his doorway. A subtle sweep with a sensor had showed more than one device in place. Pretending to hunt for a cockroach in the dark with a flashlight sparked a shine off at least one camera lens, aimed at the front door.

He'd left it all in place, avoiding any visible search. Nick Green wouldn't suspect bugs in his house and car, not yet, when all he supposedly knew was that Marston was rich and shady. Green didn't know squat about the level of crime, or the real money involved. At least not till today. So he'd had to keep his characterization going 24/7 lately.

What would Green do after a night like that? Irish coffee. He brewed a cup, poured in a splash of whiskey, made to look more generous than it was by his thumb half-over the top of the bottle. He inhaled the steam, then took a sip. Nick Rugo was fond of good Irish too.

After a bit he wandered into the bathroom and washed up, still not going for his phone. The bathroom was the second most likely place for a camera. A lot of people felt safe behind a locked door in the john— if they were doing something hidden, that would be the top spot for it. He thought about jerking off for the camera, relieving some of the tension, but he wasn't in a mood to play around. It wasn't until he reached his bedroom, pulled off his shirt, and stretched out on the bed that he got out his phone.

Nick Green was known to play a lot of games and surf the net on his phone. He propped some pillows behind his back, sitting where the only thing looking over his shoulder was the unblemished plaster wall. He pulled the top blanket over his jean-clad legs, and went online. After a few minutes he shifted to texting. *~Data download soon*

He added the code for being willing to receive as well as send. A message popped right back silently. *~Waiting.*

He reached casually under the blanket, unzipping his jeans, scratching his balls. He didn't know for sure there was a camera in the bedroom. It would've been overkill, for a low-level guy like Green. On the other hand, today Marston might well have added one. Under the cover of the blanket, he slid a now-practiced finger into the little pocket and eased the recording device out a couple of inches.

A few minutes later he got ear buds out of his bedside drawer and plugged them into his phone with the data cable piggybacked in. He put one bud in his ear, let other droop down across his chest to the blanket. Slowly, carefully casual, he got the recorder connected up and sent the vital data on its way. It was a long, slow upload. He pretended to play around on Facebook while it ran. Eventually the *Completed* symbol flashed.

He texted, *~Got it?*

~Done.

He casually tugged the blanket higher, put the other ear bud in, scratched himself, sealing the recorder back in his jeans. *~Why didn't we take action? You found the body?*

There was a wait. Nick figured his contact was passing him over to Olson. He took the time to erase the existing text thread. A few minutes later an answer came back. ~*Found. T wants to wait. SD has a lead on the lab. We don't want to spook M.*

That made some sense. If a search of Marston's home didn't lead to the lab location, the rest of his operation would be alerted and shut down. Nick knew Takano had someone on the inside in San Diego as well.

He typed, ~*What now?*

~*No change. Keep going.*

~*M says he owns local cops.*

~*We figured. But they haven't made you yet, so nothing changes. No hint who he has?*

~*Nope. Plural cops.*

~*We'll keep looking. Stay safe.*

He hesitated, wondering whether to add anything. He'd crossed another line with Brian. Not that undercover cops had never had inappropriate sex when their cover demanded it. Sometimes you bent rules or even broke laws if there was no other way to avoid suspicion. But maybe he should confess it first, before Olson heard the audio?

In the end, he couldn't decide how to even open the topic. Maybe it would slide on by, with all the other great stuff on there. ~*Wilco. Out.*

He deleted the whole thread again, and played online for another fifteen minutes before yawning widely, setting the phone to charge, and getting out of bed. He stripped to his boxers, tossed the jeans in a drawer, and went back to bed. But despite his exhaustion and the comfort of the sheets, he couldn't drop off.

****

Brian sat in his familiar corner in the Torchhouse, five days after the murder, five days after sex with Nick, holding his Diet Coke. He pretended to take a sip from the near-empty can, and watched Nick playing pool with Booker out of the corner of his eye. Since that night in the hallway, they hadn't spoken. They'd helped cover up a murder together. They'd jizzed on each other, even if that was all it was to Nick. Every day, Brian expected something to happen— for Nick to say something about the sex, for cops to suddenly appear, for Damon to find out he was gay and go ballistic— and day after day, nothing did.

Across the barroom, Nick made a fancy shot, dropping a ball into a distant pocket. "Game."

Booker slapped him on the arm. "Fuckin' lucky shot. Give me a chance to win it back?"

Nick's gaze slid to Brian's face and shied away fast. "Beer first." He turned his back and headed for the bar.

Brian bit his lip. *Even two seconds of eye contact too much for you, Nick?*

Although, it was kind of both of their decisions not to talk about it. He'd stayed in bed late the next morning, not coming out of his room, and told Damon he had a headache, when actually he didn't want to look at Nick in the daylight. He couldn't believe he'd done that, been bold and strong and made Nick hold still for a blow job. And then Nick had said *"Nightmares."*

He might've just meant the craziness of having sex with Damon downstairs. He might've meant needing sex so bad he was willing to risk lowering his guard and getting shot for it. *Nightmares* didn't *have* to be an insult.

In the light of day, Brian had been appalled at the risk they'd taken. The risk *he'd* taken, because Nick had sat back and let him drive and it had been amazing. But Damon could move like a cat. If he'd come upstairs at the wrong moment... Brian's headache in the morning hadn't been all fakery. That would've been a scary, awful thing.

But then Nick left, and since then, it was as if that moment in the hall had never happened.

His attention was caught by the restless movement of a big man standing against the wall, a couple feet to his left. The San Diego bodyguards were a tough-looking crew. They were not amused at being assigned to watch him drink pop and be dumb. Bry clearly creeped them out, so he was Bry around them as hard as he dared.

Mr. Marston had decided that if Bry or Lori went anywhere they had to have extra protection. Lori got two bodyguards instead of the usual one, and Brian got his own personal guard where before Damon had been it. He hated it.

But since there was nothing he could do, he'd sat back with a stupid expression on his face and listened as Mr. Marston rearranged the whole protection plan for everybody and everything. When the new dog handler came in with four black-and-tan Shepherds, to introduce them to the people they were guarding, he'd put his fingers in his ears so he wouldn't know their names. They'd sniffed him when told to, but not one of the four had given him so much as one wag of its tail. Their amber eyes watched him like he was lunch. He knew he wouldn't be wandering off to see his safe house anytime soon.

Otherwise, life went on. He'd mowed the grass yesterday. He'd swum in the pool. He hadn't called Nick, and his own phone had been silent. Veronica was in and out, suddenly turning up around corners like a harpy on a castle wall, all glowers and sneers. He was jumpy and on edge, waiting for something else bad to happen.

The new, unfriendly guards, and the way everyone was tense and snappy, made it worse. They still didn't know who shot Mr. Granton, and he couldn't tell if anyone was really trying to find out. He was beginning to wonder if Damon was right about it being Mr. Marston. Although it wasn't like anyone was bothering to tell anything important to the mansion's village idiot.

And then tonight, Damon had said, "It's been a hell of a week. We deserve a beer." And here they were, extra bodyguard and all, and here was Nick. Not looking at him. Ever. *Wonderful.*

He finished the last sip of his flat pop, and stared at the TV screen behind the bar. There was some kind of girls' mud wrestling happening. The men in the place had half their attention on their drinks, and half on bouncing boobs smeared with pudding or whatever was in that pit. Even his bodyguard looked over there again and again.

Unwillingly, Brian's eyes went back to Nick, just to make sure there was one other guy in the place who thought it was the dumbest thing they'd seen in years. So he caught Nick's expression when an Amber Alert flashed up on the screen.

The missing child was a girl, dark curly hair caught into two pigtails, a tooth missing in her wide grin. Brian saw Nick go pale, saw his mouth open in shock. A moment later the expression was gone, but Nick's attention stayed glued to the screen. Brian strained to hear the TV over the chatter, which hadn't dropped much despite the emergency announcement.

"...since ten PM last night. So far law enforcement and volunteer searchers have not found any trace of the missing girl. Keesha was last seen wearing a white T-shirt and green pajama pants. Anyone with any information..."

Brian stopped listening, because he saw Nick turn away abruptly and come toward their table. Without even a glance at Brian, Nick told Damon, "I'm feeling like shit. Something I ate, probably. I'm heading home. See you tomorrow."

Damon waved a hand. "Sure. I'll beat Booker at pool again for you."

Nick laughed, although Brian could see the effort in it. "Yeah. Thanks." He pressed a hand to his stomach as he turned away, but his pace toward the front door was quick and determined.

Brian stood abruptly and yelled in the general direction of his bodyguard, "I need a crap. A big, smelly crap!" He didn't pause to look, just took off running toward the bathroom. He'd bet the new guy would walk, not run, to guard him from danger while he took that crap.

He ducked into the hallway at full speed and slammed the bathroom door open with a smack of his hand as he passed, letting it swing shut behind him for his bodyguard to see. The door at the end of the hall had an alarm, but he'd hung out in the kitchen now and then, and he knew those guys propped their door open to duck out for a smoke. He swung into the kitchen. There were two people working the griddle and fryer, and they stared at him, but he was a regular and they were super busy. He waved at them and slipped out the door and heard no outcry behind him.

Sure enough, there was Nick striding toward his car, cell phone to his ear. As he started to get in, Brian put on a burst of speed and yanked open the passenger door, tumbling inside. He squeaked as he met the muzzle of a gun, inches from his nose.

An instant later, Nick grunted and the gun disappeared. "Get out, Brian. I'm sick. I need to go."

"I can help you find her."

"You *what*?"

He'd left the bar on instinct, and now he knew why. He could help. He could be the good guy for once in his sorry life. "I can Find her. It's what I do."

"What are you talking about?"

Brian glanced toward the bar. "Look, there's no time. They'll miss me, and then they'll come looking, and they'll want to know what you're doing and you won't be in time to help—" *What had her name been?* "—Keesha. Just drive."

"Get out."

"No!"

"Fuck!" Nick slammed the car in gear. "Get down then. Below the windows."

That made sense. Brian squeezed down toward the floor, in the dark cramped space that smelled of stale fast food and feet. The car accelerated, braked sharply, turned, accelerated. He was queasy, clutching at the seat, but he said nothing until several minutes had gone by. Then he asked in a small voice, "Can I sit up now?"

"Fuck. Yeah. Wait, do you see my cellphone down there? I dropped it when you freaked me the hell out. What were you thinking?"

"That I could help." Brian felt around and located the phone under the seat. He wriggled up, and handed it over. "Here."

Nick stuffed it into the cup holder. "Start talking."

"I saw you. You know that little girl." He was sure of it.

For a moment he thought Nick would lie, but then he said, "I knew her older brother for a bit, yeah."

"It's not good, a little girl like that missing so long."

Nick actually shuddered. "No, it's not."

"I've Found a lot of bad people, for wrong reasons. I want, just once, to Find someone good." *For you.* He didn't say that part.

"I don't get it."

Brian felt the bitter twist of his lips. "Why do you think Mr. Marston went to the expense of putting a bodyguard on me? It's not because he loves me."

"For your sister's sake?"

"Hah. No. I'm useful to him. You remember?" He didn't want Nick to think of him that way, but he needed to talk fast, before Nick decided to dump him out on the side of the road. "Remember those guys who said you couldn't run from Mr. Marston because his nasty werewolf would track you down wherever you went? That's me."

"You're saying you're a *werewolf?*"

"No! There's no such thing as werewolves. I don't think." He hesitated, distracted by the thought that there wasn't supposed to be talents like his, either. "That I know of. What I am is a Finder. Like, um, Mr. Marston once said I was a human dowsing rod. Those fork-thingies people hold in their hands to find water." He'd made Damon look up dowsing for him, afterward, so he'd know.

"So you what? Hold a forked stick in your hand and it points to missing children?"

"I hold something of theirs in my hand. A shirt, a key, a battered baseball cap." He knew his voice had become thinner, darker, but he had to go on. "I see a trail, like a ribbon, mud and crushed peppermint and gun oil, tangled, ribbon, pointing. I point. We follow the trail to the end. And the person is there."

Nick's voice was quieter too. "Then what happens?"

Brian wanted to dodge, but he couldn't go on doing this; he needed to tell someone. "Maybe they just get scared enough never to cross Mr. Marston, ever. If it's Veronica, she laughs. If it's guys like Juan, or Trevon, or Stan, they die."

"You *kill* them?" Nick glanced at him, wide-eyed.

"Not *me*!" He rubbed his face. "I pass out, mostly. But when I wake up, well, it's not really my fault if sometimes they're dead, right? If they were bad men." It *was* his fault. He was a killer, pretty much. It was a lie to deny it. But maybe he didn't have to be today. Not this time.

"You find… bad men."

"It's what he keeps me around for. To Find people so they can't hide from him. After that, what Damon does, or Mr. Marston does? I can't stop them. For me, it's just a Find. And then I pass out."

There was a long silence, then Nick pulled over to the curb. "You have your phone?"

"Oh! Wait, yeah!" Damon could trace him by his phone! He'd almost forgotten. He rolled down the window and tossed it out into the night.

"Fuck! What did you do that for?"

"So he can't find us."

"There is no *us*. Listen, you're right, I'm going to go help look for Keesha. You're going to stay here until your brother picks you up."

"No! You need to believe me. I can help."

"I know you want to."

208

"*NICK*!" He'd never yelled so loud in his life, and Nick's face went blank with shock. "I can do this. I swear, on anything you like. I can Find her if I just touch something of hers. Please." He put his hands together, begging. "Please, please, I've been Finding bad men for so long and it's like slime on my brain, in my head, I can't get it out. Please, let me use this talent for something good. Just once! Oh God, oh God, please." His voice was shaking and he had no words, nothing left.

Nick said, "This talent. How long have you had it?"

"Since I was little. I Found my mom when she hadn't come home for too long. We brought her back home. I did it a few times, until Damon believed I wasn't just remembering stuff she'd said, about where she was going." He bit his lip.

"So you've found other people, like, psychically? Lots of them?"

He didn't want to think about them. "At first, we didn't know how hard it was to Find a stranger. I ended up in the hospital asleep for two days. But Mr. Marston was so pleased… now I can do it easier."

"And *that's* what you do for Marston? Track people down?"

"And mow lawns." He didn't say that he'd rather cut grass. He just waited.

"You said you found a guy named Stan? Where'd you find him?"

He wondered why Nick cared, but tried to remember. "In the city somewhere. Lots of traffic, downtown? Near a river bridge, I think. I keep my eyes closed and don't look. I'm sorry."

"Hm."

They sat on the side of the road in silence. Cars passed. Finally Nick said, "You really think you can find Keesha?"

"If she's alive. If I have something of hers to hold. I can't Find dead people."

"And your… 'Finding' doesn't hurt them somehow? You said they died."

"I Found Veronica. You saw her, after. They only die if Mr. Marston wants them dead."

"Ah. Why Veronica?"

"He had a bet with Mr. Granton."

"For the million dollars they all talked about when he died?" Nick sounded startled.

"Yeah. Against something to do with the baby inheriting. I'm not sure. It was also about showing me off, somehow. What I can do." The dark pleasure Mr. Marston had taken in the process was about much more than money, he was certain.

Nick stared ahead blankly.

"What can it hurt?" Brian reached out to touch him, but the stone stillness of Nick's face made him pull back before making contact. "If I fail, she's no worse off. If I Find her, what else matters compared to that?"

"Why haven't you done something like this before? Found a missing kid?"

Why hadn't he? He'd asked Damon, once or twice or three times, but Bry had forgotten all the reasons he couldn't ever help people. In the end, he sighed. "Damon's rules. And Mr. Marston's."

Nick pressed his lips together, and nodded. "All right. But we need to do something to keep your brother from going ballistic when he finds out you're gone. Shit. *Shit!* What a mess." He slammed his hand on the wheel, but pulled out onto the road anyway.

"Give me your phone," Brian said.

"Huh?"

"I'll call Damon. Okay?"

"And tell him what?"

Brian laughed, and was surprised to realize it was with real amusement. "I'm a nut case, right? I'll tell him I'm dragging you along on my nuttery."

That must have sounded as dumb to Nick as it did to him, yet Nick passed him the phone.

The screen didn't have the familiar icons. He realized once again, with a lurch in his stomach, how dependent he was. Without that phone he'd tossed, with Damon's face and Lori's on it, he couldn't even call for help. "Can you dial?"

Nick took it, dividing his attention between phone and road, then held it to his ear. "Damon? I have your nutcase brother here." He handed it back to Brian.

Brian pushed his worries away and said brightly, "Hi. Damon? I'm with Nick!"

"What the fuck are you doing? You're supposed to be in the bathroom."

"It was yucky, smelly, stinky, and my bodyguard hates me. I went for a walk."

"You what?"

"I left. It's okay. I'm on an adventure. Nick found me."

"Well, Nick had better bring you right the fuck back."

He caroled, "No. No, no, no to the no. Adventure!"

"Brian, you shithead!"

"It's fun. It's not bedtime. I hate beer. I hate mud-women."

"Look, you don't have to come back to the bar." Damon's tone softened. "I thought it would do you good to get out, is all. He can take you home instead."

"Adventure! Then home."

"Brian!"

Nick reached over and took the phone, steering easily with one hand. "Hey, Damon. How about I take the kid somewhere, maybe for a walk or a movie. I'll bring him home in a couple of hours. That way he gets his adventure."

"I thought you were sick."

"I'm a bit better. If I start to feel like crap, he can come catch a movie on my TV instead."

"All right. You'll watch out for him?"

"Sure."

"I can send his guard to meet up with you."

Brian leaned over to say close to the phone. "No way, no way. He hates me, Damon! No guard! He's mean."

Damon sighed. "Fuck. Nick? If you get sick, call and I'll send someone to get him. And text me where you are, where you go, right? Stupid dumb-ass brother. Thanks."

"No problem. Oh, hey, when I told him I was going to call you to come get him, he tossed his phone out the car window."

"He did what?"

"Yeah. Somewhere on the south side of 81. But you know, he doesn't need it tonight and it'll be hard to locate in the dark. I can take him there tomorrow and keep dialing it until he finds it."

"Fuck. Okay. I should take it out of his skin. Son of a bitch."

Nick clicked his phone off.

Brian said thoughtfully, "We might get the phone on the way back. It'll light up in the night. Except, no, I'll be passed out."

"And I'll have to explain that to your brother. He'll kill me."

"He won't. He knows how I get. Just tell him you don't know what I was doing, before I keeled over. That's really, really important. You don't know about Finding. Not at all." He bit his lip. Maybe this was too dangerous for Nick. Marston was really possessive about his talent...

"You're sure you can do it, though?"

He let out a long breath, and made his choice. "I have to try. 'Cause if we Find Keesha...?"

After a moment, Nick said, "Yeah. Worth it."

"How long till we get there?"

"Forty-five minutes or so."

"I'm gonna nap. And if you have any food in the car, I should eat it." He should drink something too, but he'd manage without.

"Should we go to a drive-through? Get you more?"

"Nah. I ate dinner, don't need a meal. Just a top-up."

"There's candy in the glove compartment," Nick said. "I bought some sugary kinds."

After my last episode. Brian hugged the idea that Nick'd wanted to be ready, in case he needed it, in case he rode in this car again. Maybe Nick hadn't been ready to cut him out all the way. "Thanks."

They drove in silence. Brian sucked on the honey-lemon and citrus drops, one after the other. It kept him from saying anything dumb. *Do you believe me? Do you hate me for working for Mr. Marston? Do you hate me for sucking you off in the hallway? Do you?* Too many questions, and he wasn't sure he wanted the answers. Anyway, that wasn't what mattered now. He closed his eyes and gathered his strength.

****

The trailer park was lit by the flashing light bar of just one black-and-white. Nick imagined that last night it'd have been like a fireworks display. A missing seven-year-old? That would've had everyone out in force. But twenty-four hours later, the search would be spreading and thinning out. He wondered what the details were. A stranger? Just missing? He assumed Tyrone was fine, or the news would've said something. He'd have called in to his precinct to ask for details, except he couldn't do that with Brian Kerr in the passenger seat.

This was a bad idea. This belonged, in fact, in the Hall of Fame of Spectacularly Bad Ideas. Not just coming here while undercover, which he could maybe get away with, as long as his face didn't end up on-camera anywhere. But bringing Brian was crazy. He'd had second thoughts, and third thoughts, as they drove. Actually, he wasn't sure they made numbers high enough for the thoughts he'd had.

But it kept coming back to two things. Marston did treat Brian like he had real value, and Brian claimed he could do this. And little girls missing for over twenty-four hours rarely came home unhurt, and some never came home at all.

So he had to give it a shot. At least he'd had the car "accidentally" debugged in a carwash after the Granton murder. Marston wouldn't easily know where they were. If there was any chance of success at all, he'd sacrifice the investigation and his safety and anything else, to bring Keesha home.

He parked in the shadow of his own trailer, reaching into the back for a sweatshirt with a hood. "Brian, you stay here, okay? There's cops in there, and the less they see you the better."

"Okay."

"What should I bring out for you?"

Brian opened his eyes. Their ice-blue color was always startling, no matter how often Nick saw it. "I need something of hers— something she loved and held lots is best. Something she wore is okay too. But not new stuff. It has to know it belongs to her."

"Clothes have feelings?"

"No, not, oh, well I can't explain it. Something of hers. And, if you could, if they don't mind, like, a glass of water? I should fluid-load. The time I went to the hospital I was dehydrated."

Brian said it very casually. Nick wasn't sure if that was hopeful, or the opposite. "All right. Something of hers, and water. And then?"

"I'll let you know." Brian leaned back and closed his eyes again.

Nick looked at him. He looked older with his head tilted back, tightening the skin over his jaw and cheekbones until they showed through his round face. His mouth was still full, his hair near white and baby fine, his eyes wide set. Not a handsome face, but when he wasn't dull-eyed and slack-jawed, he was easy to look at. *God, please let him be telling the truth.*

Nick tugged the hood up to hide his face, got out, and approached the Carters' trailer. It was lit up, every window bright, but silent. He rapped on the door. A uniformed officer opened it. "Can I help you?"

"I'm a friend, from across the road. I've been away."

He didn't get more than that out before there was a commotion behind the cop and Tyrone yelled, "Nick!"

The cop held the boy back, while pulling the door open. "Come on in, sir. Let's not give the reporters a show."

Nick almost turned to look as he stepped past. "I didn't see any."

"I'd bet they're lurking somewhere. I'll take a quick look around." The cop went out and closed the door firmly.

Tyrone glommed onto Nick's side, damp face pressed tight against his chest. "She's gone! She's missing!"

"I know." Nick detached Ty enough to take a couple of steps farther in.

Suddenly he was being pummeled by hard small fists. "You promised! You said if we needed you, to call! She was gone and I called and called! You lied!"

He caught Tyrone's wrists. "Hey, easy. I'm so sorry. I came as soon as I could."

"You lied." But Tyrone slumped and lowered his arms.

Nick pulled him in for a hug. "I'm here now. I want to help."

A hard female voice behind him said, "What kind of help you gonna give us, Nick? You got some miracle up your sleeve?"

He turned and stood straighter. The last twenty-four hours had aged Sue Carter, and booze and life hadn't been kind to her before that. There were deep circles under her eyes and her hands clenched and unclenched on the hem of her sweatshirt.

"Sue. I'm so sorry this happened."

"Yeah. So. What're you gonna do?"

He couldn't say he had a psychic in his car, or a werewolf, or whatever Brian was claiming to be. It would be cruel. He said, "I guess I'm just going to look, like everyone else. But at least I had to be here."

She sighed painfully. William appeared in the doorway and she turned to him. He wrapped an arm around her, and Nick remembered that for all the yelling, and the loud fights over money, and the booze, he'd never called the cops on these two because they loved each other, and they loved their kids. He said, "I'm sure we'll find her."

William's eyes met his, over his wife's head, and they were bleak and cold as if he already was picturing his little girl's funeral. "Thanks, Nick." His voice was hoarse, barely a thread. He bent to say to Sue, "Hon, I'm going to go out again and just walk around."

"I'll be here." She tugged his shirt straight. "Be careful, now. It's—" She caught back a sob and patted his arm. "It's da-ark out there. Go on. I have faith you'll find her."

William ducked his head, not looking at Nick as he went out. Sue sniffed hard, then said, "Nick? Can I get you, I don't know, coffee?"

He was going to say no, then remembered. "You have bottled water, or pop? Something I might take along?"

"Sure. Someone dropped off a case of Coke for the volunteers. I'll get you one."

When she'd gone out, Nick dropped to one knee beside the boy. Tyrone was taller than him that way, and he had to look up. He said softly, "Listen, Ty. I've been working on this estate where they have dogs." That was true enough. "I kind of borrowed a tracker without telling them." Also true. "Can you find me something of Keesha's? Something a dozen people haven't handled?"

"Sure." Tyrone rubbed his face. "You think you can find her? Really? There's been people and dogs and all, and she's still gone."

"I don't know. I want to try."

"It's all my fault."

"I bet it wasn't."

"No, really." Tyrone looked at him with damp, red-rimmed eyes. "She wanted to get in my bed, 'cause it was noisy." He bit his lip. "And I said no, 'cause it was too hot. And after I went to sleep, I guess she went out."

"You can't blame yourself if you were sleeping."

"If I'da said yes, I'd know when she got up."

"It's not your fault." Nick pulled the boy into a hug. He came stiffly, then melted with a soft cry. Nick cupped the back of his head. "Not. Not your fault. If she didn't wake you, it was because she wanted to sneak out. I bet she'll know better from now on, right? Once we get her back, she won't leave you behind again."

"You think? You'll find her?"

"Go get me something and I'll try."

Tyrone broke free, blinked hard, and then ran out down the hall. He was back with a grubby little stuffed rabbit before Sue came back with the Coke. Nick thought she might be having a cry in the kitchen, but if so, she was doing it silently. Tyrone held out the rabbit. "Here. That's Flop. She got new toys now, but sometimes she still sleep with Flop."

"Perfect."

"Can I see the tracking dog?"

"Um, not now." He lowered his voice. "I could get in really big trouble for borrowing him, so you have to promise not to tell anyone. Not a word, ever. Can you do that?"

"I promise!" Tyrone mimed zipping his lips shut.

Nick took the toy and tucked it into his pocket, then, as Sue came back into the room, turned to accept the Coke she held out. "Thanks. I'll keep in touch. Call me if they find her first. When they find her."

"Yeah." Sue's eyes were redder than her son's. "When."

The cop came back in the door as Nick was heading out. "All quiet." His eyes met Nick's with a carefully cool gaze. Nick could almost feel the guy struggling to keep a distance for all his heart was worth. A boatload of pain was probably on its way for this family, despite their optimistic words. None of them were really fooling themselves.

Chapter 17

The air outside the Carters' trailer was calm and cool. Nick took a breath, raising a hand to shield his face from view just in case. No lights flashed, no one jumped out of a car for an interview. If Keesha'd been a child from a wealthy suburb, instead of a trailer park, he'd bet they'd still be hip deep. Well, this worked better for his purposes.

He pulled out his cell and texted his handler. *~Taking personal time tonight. Went home. I'll be back on in the morning. I'll check in then.* He added the response-allowed code.

A moment later the answer popped up. *~OK. Enjoy your night off.*

He hesitated for a moment in the middle of the front yard, wondering if he should leave Nick Green's tracked cellphone here, and get his personal one. Except this one had Damon's number in it. And going into his trailer meant letting Brian see where he lived. Crap! No good choices. He pulled the battery, stuck the phone in his pocket and hurried across to his car.

Brian's face looked pale in the wash of the dome light.

"Did that cop see you?"

"I ducked down low."

"Are you okay?"

Brian swallowed visibly but he gave Nick a firm nod. "Ready."

Nick reached in his pocket, suddenly reluctant to pull out the toy. What if this was some elaborate game, or some insanity of Brian's? What if this was some kind of creepy, voyeuristic… He couldn't hold that thought, seeing the tremble of Brian's hands. Whatever was happening, it wasn't easy for Brian. "I got a favorite toy."

Brian cleared his throat. "Should work."

Nick took the rabbit out of his pocket and held it out. The dome light shut off, leaving them shadowed. Brian didn't reach for the toy. "Problem?" Nick asked.

"I, um, when I touch it and handle it, I'll know if she's dead."

"Oh!" He hadn't realized. He looked at the dim, fuzzy shape on his palm. Right now, Keesha was alive, somewhere, waiting to be found. As long as Brian didn't touch that toy, as long as no one found her little body, she was alive. Waiting. "Take the damned thing," he growled.

Brian did. He handled it gently, turning it between his palms, staring down. There were no sparks of light, no rolling eyeballs or creepy noises. But after several long minutes, Brian said, "Marshmallow and chocolate, daisies, yellow... She's alive, Nick!" He turned luminous eyes to stare at him. "She is."

"So she's somewhere with daisies?"

"Hm? No, that's her— her trace— she's a yellow daisy girl."

He almost smiled. "Can you tell, is she hurt? Is she okay?"

"It doesn't work like that. Just..." Brian lifted his hand, his index finger swinging, pointing, left, and slightly ahead of them. "That way."

"Holy hell." Nick stared at that pointing finger, hope and fear and mistrust shivering down his spine. "Really?"

"I don't know how far. Just, that way."

"On it." He backed the car, and turned it around. As he did so, Brian's pointing swung, always west and a bit north. He couldn't trust it to be real. He didn't dare. But his heart rate picked up anyway.

He drove, and Brian pointed. He realized that Brian's eyes were closed, yet his aim stayed true, always shifting to hold his bearings no matter what road Nick took. At first Nick tried smaller roads, to stay on course, but after backtracking more than once, he shifted to the bigger routes. After an hour he was beginning to doubt again. "Are you sure this is her?"

"It's the girl who loves the rabbit." Brian's voice was strained and distant, as if he was speaking from down in a well. His arm had to be aching, but he held his aim steady.

"Okay." If this was Brian's craziness, taking them away from the real search, well, he'd drive the guy to a loony bin so fast it would leave tread marks on the road. If it wasn't, holy God, the official team would never have searched out this far.

It was almost another hour, heading northwest on 55, well out of the city, when Brian's finger suddenly swung due west, and then southwest. Brian grated, "Nick, please."

"I see you. Let me circle round." His breath came short as he made the next exit and dropped back south to 9. Now Brian was pointing almost straight ahead again.

"This road leads to New London, and some of the lakes, and Sibley State Park," he said.

"Just drive." Brian's voice was thinner than ever.

"Sure."

They passed through New London, and on toward the park. It was late, the black sky bright with stars. Only the occasional car went by the other way, high beams dipping as they approached, and then gone past them. Nick tried not to think how impossible it was for a little girl to get here on her own, or what that probably meant. *Find her. That's first.*

They passed a red pickup on the left side of the road, back window marked with a warning to tow or else. Brian's hand swung to point to it, and stayed that way. Nick pulled the car over and stopped in a shower of gravel. He swallowed. "You're sure she's alive?" He reached under the seat for his weapon.

"Yes." Brian opened his eyes and jumped out. He dashed across the narrow shoulder, tripped into the roadside ditch, and hauled himself up one-handed, the other outstretched, calling back to Nick, "There!"

Nick realized he wasn't pointing at the truck, but at the trees beyond.

"Come on." Brian staggered and lurched over the rough roadside scrub. The forest was a black, featureless mass ahead of him, but Brian didn't slow down.

Nick stowed his gun in his pocket, pulled out his stupid little LED keychain for light, and chased after Brian. He caught up and got a hand under his arm. "Let me help."

"She's there, Nick." Brian tugged him forward.

"Let's Find her, then."

It was dark under the trees, and the LED was a feeble flashlight. He'd have gone back for a better one— he had a Maglite in the trunk— but Brian was like a homing missile, and Nick wasn't sure he'd wait. Sticks and burrs and unknown things poked at their legs. Branches tangled in Nick's hair and lashed his face. Brian plunged ahead blindly, and twice Nick had to steer him aside from walking right into a tree. "Easy, easy," he heard himself murmuring. "We'll get her. Slow down so you don't knock yourself out first."

"Right." Brian leaned on him more. "When we do Find her…" He breathed heavily.

"Yeah."

"I'm gonna be wrecked. Probably pass out. You might have to come back for me."

"Okay. If I have to, I will. We'll figure it out." The mosquitoes swarmed in a cloud around his sweaty face and he batted them away, gripping Brian harder. The underbrush tried to trip him at every step. Motherfucking blackberry brambles dragged thorns right through his jeans.

Then it got easier, and he realized they'd hit a trail of some kind. The mosquitoes whined in his ears, but the trees had quit trying to flog him. He shifted his grip on Brian. "That's better. Come on, hang in there."

"And no one can know."

"Know what?" he muttered, wondering how far a little girl could have gone through this. Or someone carrying a little girl. The thought was bitter.

"About me. Finding. What I do. Promise."

"Sure."

Brian plunged to a stop so suddenly Nick almost knocked both of them over. Enough moonlight filtered to the trail to show his hand, extended, trembling like an addict in need of a fix. "Promise me! If you tell anyone, I'll end up dead."

"Fuck." Brian was right. Nick hadn't thought it through, hadn't really believed it would work. *I happened to go look for my neighbor kid a hundred miles from home and found her. Oh, and my alibi is a bunch of thugs.* He'd be in jail before he could close his mouth, and even yesterday's tracking on his cell and the surveillance might not cover him.

Brian's hand continued to shake, but his voice was loud. "They won't believe you anyhow. And I'll say it was all a lie. Bry will say you kidnapped him. Please. Nick, please."

"Fuck! I know, it's a mess." He was off radar right now, but covering for that would be tough too. "Look, Find her first. Everything else after."

Brian stayed rooted. "Promise."

You did what you had to, right? Undercover lies didn't count. "I promise."

"Oh God. Thank you." Brian half-fell against him. "That way."

It was another five minutes before they found her. Brian saw her first— a patch of white against the dark ground— and whooped joyfully. He pulled free of Nick to run and kneel beside her. Nick drew his weapon, and followed more cautiously, alert for any movement.

Keesha was flat on the ground, lying still. Nick turned in a quick circle, sweeping his inadequate light across the surrounding tangle of trees, but saw no one. He slid the gun back in his hoodie pocket, knelt, and helped Brian turn the child over, shining the light on her face. She sighed and woke, whimpering loudly.

"Hush, sweetheart. Keesha. You're all right." He flicked another glance around them, but no one pounced out of the darkness at the sound of her voice.

"Daddy?" She sat up fast and clung to him, moving well, not like anything was broken, not like she was hurt. He couldn't see clearly, but she was wailing at full volume, and her grip was strong. Her racing heart shook her little body, and he swept her into his arms.

"Hush, baby. Hush. Not Daddy but you know me. You'll be fine."

"I want Mommy! I want to go *home*!"

"And you will. I promise." He lifted her into his lap, safe against his chest, rocking her. "Are you hurt anywhere?"

"It itches!"

The mosquitoes biting him were annoying already. He could imagine them after a day spent in these woods, and hugged her face against his shoulder. "We'll get you some medicine for that soon."

"There was shouting and I wanted to go in the peaceful woods."

"The what?"

"I'm thirsty!"

"Sure. But… wait, I have a Coke here." He remembered the can he'd stuck in his other pocket and dug it out, popped the top, and extended it aside until the frothing and dripping stopped. "Just a little now."

"It makes me burp."

He held it for her to take a careful sip, and another, then held it over to Brian who was sitting on the ground beside them, breathing hard. He heard Brian chugging it, as Keesha cuddled back in against him.

She said, "That's yummy. Mom doesn't buy pop."

"There's more back at home."

"The Prices were going camping. They were gonna find a peaceful place, so I got in the truck, an' it was fun riding in back but it stopped."

"Where are the Prices?"

"No one came. No one came and no one and no one, and I got out. I walked. But I think I got lost."

"I think you did too, baby." He hugged her again. "That's all? You got in the truck?"

"I wanted to go camping too. But it's icky. There's so many bugs. I'm thirsty. It itches bad! I wanna go *ho-o-ome*!"

"We'll take you right now." Nick sat back, supporting her with his knees, and fumbled the battery into his phone. *Dumbass! What if you'd needed backup?* And then there were no freaking bars anyway. He took the battery back out fast— maybe the little blip of location would never register. He pocketed both halves, lifted Keesha, and stood.

Brian looked up at them, a bulky form in the faint moonlight, with a frost of pale hair and a smudge of white face. "I can't."

"Come on." Nick glanced around urgently. "There!" Way off through the trees, he spotted a tiny glimmer of light. Street or house or car, it was all good. "You can make it."

"Gotta sleep," Brian mumbled thickly.

Sometimes Nick wished he was six-foot-four with major muscles, instead of just five-nine and wiry. He looped the keyring on one finger, which made the light dangle almost uselessly. Shit, he needed four hands along with the muscles. He reached down and hauled under Brian's armpit. "Get up. I don't want to lose you out here where I can't find you."

Brian laughed like a steam kettle boiling over, wheezing, breathless. "Because I'm the Finder."

"Yeah, you are. Up you get. Arm over my shoulders. Keesha, you hang on."

They staggered down the trail toward that distant light. Brian stumbled about a hundred yards before he became a dead weight. Nick had to let him slide to the ground. Keesha hung around his neck, tight as a little monkey. Brian was a huddled immovable mass, clearly out of strength, and passing out. *Shit, shit, shit!*

Brian said to leave him behind and get the girl out safe. Right? She had to come first.

He knelt awkwardly with Keesha clutched against him, and checked to be sure Brian was breathing, and not choking. In the LED glow, he just looked asleep. Nick glanced at the pitch-black woods around them. This was practically the suburbs, not a wilderness, even if the park was a good size. It wasn't as if wild animals would eat Brian before Nick could come back for him. Other than the mosquitoes.

Nick hefted the child in his arms. "I'll be back," he said, although Brian made no sign he'd heard. Then he started jogging down the trail. He hugged Keesha in one arm, so he could aim the light at the ground. Her breath came in little whimpers, jolting with each stride. The trail became wider and smoother, and fairly soon opened out into a farm lane. To the right, the welcoming light turned out to be a flood lamp, mounted on the corner of a wooden barn. Nick hurried toward the dark house beside it, but at the bottom of the steps, he paused.

It was a well-kept house, the paint fresh and white, with a tub of flowers blooming at the foot of the stairs. There was a kid's bike leaning against the porch rail, and a big yellow ball half-hidden under a bush. People lived here, with children.

Keesha wriggled harder in his arms, and he set her down. She started rubbing her face, where her eyes were puffy and swollen almost shut with bug bites. He grabbed her wrists and whispered, "Don't scratch."

"It itches!"

"I know." He glanced around. He should march up those steps, pound on that door and call for help. And then… if they believed him, he and Brian would still be questioned. They'd have to be. The story was too unlikely to accept, and two men who found a kidnapped child a hundred miles from home, men who knew that child, would be more than suspect. If he was the cop hearing that story, he'd toss himself in jail, probably with a bunch of bruises.

And if Brian was asleep and they couldn't wake him, they'd put him in a hospital. When he woke up, he'd be Bry. Nick had no doubt of that; he'd seen how Bry came out when it wasn't safe to be Brian. But once he did that, once he acted like his IQ was about two, they'd be fucked. Even if Bry didn't cry kidnapping, they wouldn't let him just walk away. Then it was even money on Damon trying to break him out before they hurt him or Marston trying to shut him up before he spilled anything… No.

He clicked off the keychain and deliberately moved to put the floodlight to his back, keeping his face in shadow. "Keesha, honey, you know who I am?"

She looked up at him, her hands going back to rub her eyes, and said doubtfully, "Are you Nick?"

"Your guardian angel," he said, hardening his heart. "Say that."

"Guardy angel," she said obediently. "You sound like Nick."

"Angels can be like anyone. You're safe, so I'm just your guardian angel." He had little hope it would work, but if she seemed confused and was unhurt and he had an alibi… maybe he could come out of this without a disaster.

"Gramma has a guardy angel."

"So do you. And you're safe now. Your, um, guardy angel helped you walk down that path to this nice house."

"House? I want my mommy!"

"Yes. Soon. You go up on that porch and you ring the bell. Just like trick or treat. Remember?"

"I'm not a baby. I trick or treated lots of times." She leaned against his leg. "I'm tired."

"I'll help you go up and then you can ring the bell. Tell them your guardy angel said they'd find your mommy."

"Will they? Find Mommy?"

"Yes. Absolutely for sure. Go on now."

"Ring the bell."

"Yes."

"I'm tired." She leaned harder.

"Should I carry you up the steps?"

"I'm a big girl. Ring the bell."

He bent and kissed her head. "Go. Three steps up and ring the bell."

"Bye, guardy angel." She hesitated. "Will you watch me?"

"I'll be here till they open the door," he promised.

She rubbed her eyes again, and then walked carefully up the three steps, holding the iron railing. He faded quickly back into the shadows as she hunted around, spotted the doorbell, and rang it. For a moment nothing happened, then a light went on upstairs. He had to smile as Keesha didn't wait but pushed the bell again, and a third time, hard. He'd bet she got candy at all the houses on Halloween.

A moment later the door opened. A man stood silhouetted in the doorway, dressed in a long, belted bathrobe. Keesha looked up at him and said, "Can you find my mommy?"

"Oh!" The man took a step toward her, reaching down. "Are you okay, honey? Are you lost?"

"Camping sucks! I want my mommy."

Nick's snort was covered by the man shouting back into the house, "Nancy! Come down here quick! Honey, come in. What's your name?" The man put a hand on Keesha's shoulder, guiding her inside. "Are you all right?" Nick heard him call again, "Nancy? Hurry!" before the door closed behind them.

Nick backed away, as silently as he could, and turned for the trail. It wasn't where he expected to find it, and he hunted up and down the edge of the woods, cursing under his breath, unwilling to turn on even his feeble flashlight until he was out of plain sight. Then he spotted the opening in the trees. As fast as he could, he ran back down the path toward Brian.

It seemed no time at all before he spotted the pale mass of Brian's limp body. Nick dropped to one knee to check his pulse, which was slow and even, and ran the little LED beam over him. Brian seemed to sleep peacefully in the wan light. A bug ran across Brian's closed eyelid, and Nick shuddered and brushed it away, but Brian didn't stir. Nick slapped his face sharply, which was satisfying but did nothing to wake him up.

Shit! He shook Brian, feeling his limp weight. "Come on, you motherfucker. We won! She's safe. Don't screw it up now!" Brian sagged back to the ground when he let go, his neck at an awkward angle, still unconscious. Nick slid a hand under Brian's head to ease him flatter and cushion him from the dirt.

He'd either have to leave Brian alone here, or stay with him for however long it took him to wake up, or carry him out. Really, there was no choice— as soon as Keesha told her story, cops would be coming up the trail to check it out. Slogging through the woods carrying Brian like a pack mule was the only option.

Nick hauled him up into a fireman's carry, fumbling with the damned keychain. The little stuffed toy fell from Brian's lax fingers and he bent, groaning, to retrieve it too, and stuff it into his hoodie pocket alongside the gun. Symbolic of how his crazy night was going. Or maybe his life— a gun, a rabbit, and a passed-out secret hero. He adjusted Brian's weight better, and headed down the trail.

He'd once lugged fellow police cadets through an obstacle course without a problem, but Brian was heavy, the ground was dark and rough, and every tree in the damned forest wanted a piece of them. The trail was anything but straight. Unseen roots tripped him; Brian's weight made him stagger. Holding his light clutched awkwardly against Brian's arm made for a piss-poor illumination, at best.

He had to stop and rest every few minutes. One bit of midnight forest looked like any other. Without knowing where they'd entered the woods, he wasn't about to head off the path randomly. All he could do was keep going. He trudged along the widest trail he could see, in the opposite direction from the farm, and hoped for the best. They had to hit a road or parking area at some point. He'd figure it out.

In the far distance, he heard the wail of an approaching siren. He hoped it was headed for the farm, to gather Keesha up into safety and her family's arms.

You left a child with a stranger. The accusing voice in his head made him queasy, but he shook it off. He'd done his best. She'd be fine. He'd had to choose.

And you chose Brian.

She'd be fine.

A while later he heard another siren, a bit louder. The third one was clearer yet, telling him they were nearing the road. The trees ahead and to the left flickered, offering a glimpse of flashing lights as a vehicle swept on past. He calculated his angle, turned toward the road, and plunged off the trail into the woods.

It was even harder walking there, the underbrush winding around his legs, and twice he almost brained himself on an unseen branch. He sucked in air through his open mouth until he choked on a flying bug. His tongue felt like cotton. His back was killing him. Despite the pleasantly cool night, he was soaked with sweat under the hoodie. By the time he reached the edge of the trees and eased Brian down in the dark cover there, all he could do was collapse beside him, panting. Brian's pulse seemed fine, but the guy slept on, oblivious. All he could do was hope it was simply exhaustion.

His shoulders ached like fire. Man, he needed to work on his fitness! Driving trucks around all day was making him flabby. When his heart stopped pounding so hard, he bent over Brian and shook him. "Come on! Wake up." Why he thought that would work, when half an hour of bouncing around draped across his shoulder hadn't, he had no clue, but his heart still sank when Brian just flopped limply under his hand.

The moon had risen higher, and the pavement stretched empty in either direction. He settled Brian more comfortably on the grass under a tall dead tree, picked a direction at random, and began walking along the road, the stifling hood up to screen his face, just in case. A couple of cars passed him, but no one stopped. Less than ten minutes later, he rounded the bend and saw the welcome shapes of the truck and his car, on opposite shoulders. Suddenly he had the energy to sprint to his car, unlock it, stow the gun, and reverse in a three-point turn. The squeal of his tires reminded him to keep it more damned casual. *Almost done, almost home free.* He drove slowly back, scanning the roadside.

He jumped as two more black-and-whites suddenly raced past in the other direction. As far as he could tell, they didn't pay him any attention. That might change soon, if they began scouring the area for a potential kidnapper. *Where the fuck did I leave Brian?* His pulse pounded with the need to be gone.

About half a mile down the road, he saw a flash of pale shirt in the weeds beyond the ditch, and pulled over. If he could get Brian into the car without being seen, maybe they'd actually get away with this insane, amazing stunt. *One last effort.* He left the dark-colored, anonymous hoodie on for just a few more moments, as he got out to fetch him..

Ten minutes later, he cruised into New London, the Corolla's AC cranked up to blow across his soaked T-shirt, with Brian slumped in the tipped-back seat beside him. He parked on a side street, stuck the battery back in his cell, and found that it had a decent signal. Even so, he hesitated, before touching the dialer.

"Yeah?" William Carter's voice was even raspier than before.

"Hey, it's Nick, just checking in. Sorry, no luck yet—"

"Nick? They found her!" There was a world of relief in that rough voice. "Somewhere God knows where out there, but they found her and she's okay. Cops called us! Sue's gone out in a cop car to get to her, and I'm here with Tyrone. We're just so grateful, you know?"

"Oh, that's great," Nick said. He didn't have to fake the wave of relief. "Man, I'm so glad she's okay."

"Yeah. Oh, yeah. Praise God!"

"I'll let you go. You'll have a lot of happy people calling tonight."

"Thanks, Nick. For coming out here to try to help, I mean."

"Anytime. Good night."

"Real, real good."

The symbol went dark, and he looked down at the phone, dizzy with a mix of euphoria and disbelief. They'd done it! He turned to the silent man sleeping beside him. "You did it." Brian didn't move. "I don't know how, and it's freaky as *shit*, but you did it."

He took a couple of slow breaths, and blew them out between pursed lips. Okay. Now the next part. Go big or go home. He did a quick check for what was playing at the Anoka AMC. The fucking hard part was going to be to explain Brian's condition without linking it back to Keesha. He ran through a story, revised it, changed his mind. Beside him, Brian slept on. *Fucker. The least he could do is help with this.* But of course he'd done his part. It was up to Nick to keep them safe.

He looked at Brian's scraped arms, and the bug bites on his face. He had a second's impulse to take the guy home and watch over him until he woke up. But Damon would kill them both, probably, and besides, Nick wasn't sure what Brian needed. So… a story that wasn't too screwed up. *Good thing I'm an excellent liar.* He dialed Damon.

"Nick. Where the fuck are you?"

"Down in Anoka. Listen, we need help."

"What?" Damon demanded.

"Brian passed out. Like, he's sleeping, but I can't wake him up. Should I take him to a hospital or call 911 or what?"

"Oh! No, wait. Tell me what happened."

"He won't fucking wake up!"

"But he's not hurt, not bleeding or anything?"

"He's just out cold."

"What was he doing before that?"

"Acting fucking weird. Your brother is really, *really* strange, you know?" Nick patted Brian's scratched, bare arm in apology, although he gave no sign of hearing anything.

"How? Doing what?"

"We were just coming out of the theater after catching a movie. He suddenly said something about finding someone? Then he started turning in circles and pointing, like, for nothing. It was totally pointless."

"Then what?" Damon's voice was tense.

"Then he ran off. I mean, he was nuts tonight! He ran right out the door, down the road, and off into the trees. It was fucking dark out there. Took me twenty minutes to catch him. He kept fighting me and we both almost fell in the river. Fucking trees, fucking bugs. When I muscled him back into the car he flipped out, got really mad and said I shouldn't stop him. I insisted on driving him home, and now he's passed out. Are you sure I shouldn't call 911?"

"No! I mean it! Don't. He has narcolepsy, where he suddenly falls asleep."

"Narcolepsy?"

"Yeah. It happens when he's excited sometimes. Just like you said. He'll sleep like a log for, like, twenty-four hours and wake up just fine."

"You're sure?"

"Positive. You can check his wallet. He has a medical ID card."

"Well, fuck. No one thought they might tell me about that?"

"None of your business."

"Well, it was when he passed out on me. Crap. Okay, but what do I do now?"

"Is he in your car?"

"Yeah, crashed out on the seat."

"Bring him home, then." Damon sounded tired, but not suspicious. "He really is just sleeping. Just drive him back here. I'll deal."

"Okay. But if the cops stop me for having an unconscious guy in the car, I'm telling them this was your idea."

"Don't fucking get stopped, you hear me, Nick? Bring him home."

"Roger. Got it." Nick hung up and gave Brian one more careful look. "Okay, my friend, time to go face the Damon. We'll find out if I put that one past him." Brian slept on, oblivious. Nick kind of wished he could do the same. Joy and confusion and worry, and a hefty dose of old-fashioned fear, mixed inside him until his stomach churned. He had to take a few slow, deliberate breaths before he pulled away from the curb and headed for the Marston estate.

Chapter 18

Brian could make out voices, wavery and indistinct like he was hearing them underwater.

Nick's voice. "Are you sure he doesn't need a doctor? It's been, like, a whole day."

Damon's voice. "Nah. First time it happened I ran him to the ER, but they didn't find a damned thing wrong. He'll wake up eventually."

"It's freaky, what he did. Like, acting all weird and then passing out like that."

"He's got a fucking condition, right? None of your damned business."

"Well, he did it in my fucking car."

Brian tried to sort through his fuzzy memories, because that didn't sound right. He remembered driving with Nick, yeah. Driving, pointing, following a trace of marshmallow-yellow sweetness. He remembered woods, dark and thick, with trees that tripped him, and Nick cursing. Had he done something wrong? His stomach twisted in knots as he realized he might have told Nick about his talent. Damon would kill Nick to keep it a secret. He wanted to speak up, to warn Nick not to say too much, but he felt fuzzy-headed and weighted down. He gagged and heard himself make a rough sound.

"Hey," Damon said. "Told you he'd wake up." A strong hand shook Brian's shoulder. "Come on, Bry. Rise and shine."

Brian tried, blinking with lids so gummy they peeled open a bit at a time. There was Damon, bending over him like always. Brian worked his mouth against sweet stickiness. Damon had taken to rubbing Karo syrup in his mouth while he was out, and it might do something for his blood sugar, but it made his mouth taste like the floor of a movie theater. "Wa'er?"

The straw came between his lips, and he sucked and swallowed. He swished a bit around his mouth, before drinking it down. The next sip tasted better. "Thanks."

"You moron."

He almost laughed. How often had he woken up to that? "Yeah."

"Here, sit up?" Damon hauled on his shoulders and he braced an arm and pushed himself upright. "Gonna fall over if I let go?"

"Nope."

"*Don't* tell us what the hell you were doing, right?" There was heavy warning in Damon's voice, and Brian realized that was good. That was *excellent*. If Damon didn't want Nick to find out about Finding, that meant he hadn't found out that Nick already found out. *Or something like that.* Brian laughed creakily, and it was tough to stop. Damon punched his shoulder with a warning tap. "Quit it, goofball."

From somewhere behind him, Nick said, "If he's awake, do you still want me to hang out and watch him?"

Damon stepped back a pace, and Brian saw Nick standing in the doorway, looking just like always. When his eyes found Brian's, there was no disgust, no fear. Curiosity? Brian couldn't tell, but he clearly hadn't run off screaming. A flutter of hope caught Brian's throat. He whispered, "Hi, Nok Nick."

Damon turned to Nick. "Yes, dammit. Stay. He needs food and fluids and I have to go *now*!" He turned back to Brian. "You're a royal pain in the ass, you know?"

"Sorry?"

Damon said to Nick, "Go get a wet washcloth from the bathroom."

"Now? Um, sure."

The moment Nick was out of sight Damon bent in close to Brian's ear. "Remember your Finding's a secret. Nick can't know. Don't say *anything*."

"Yes, Damon."

"Who the hell were you tracking anyway?"

Brian's brain was fuzzy, but he remembered there was something important he didn't want to tell Damon. He picked a name, hoping it might bother Damon a little. "Stan?" he mumbled. "I couldn't Find him anywhere. He's missing."

Damon stared at him. "Stan's dead. You know that. I'm sure you do."

Brian made his sticky eyes open wide. "I forgot."

They heard Nick come back in. Damon straightened up fast. "Never mind, Bry. Keep your mouth shut, right?" He took the cloth from Nick and dropped it into Brian's lap. "Clean up, eat, drink, behave yourself. I'll be back in a couple of days."

Brian swiped the washcloth across his mouth, wishing he was more awake. For now he'd just be Bry, until he remembered better. "Are you going away? I don't want you to go."

"Gotta drive cross-country for Mr. Marston."

Nick said, "Maybe I could make the run for you instead?"

"Marston would have my balls if he even knew I mentioned it to you. Not a word, or I'll rip your tongue out through your ear, you hear me?"

"Fuck you. I'm doing you a favor on my day off." Nick thumped Damon's chest roughly with a flat hand.

Damon grabbed his wrist and twisted, until Nick was on his knees. "Not. One. Word."

Nick said, "Let go or I'll hamstring you." He whipped a little knife from behind his back with his free hand.

Bry yelped, "Don't hurt! Nick, Damon, don't hurt!" He scrambled to say something more intelligent, but Damon let go, shoving Nick and stepping away with the movement.

"Fuck, can't take a joke? And since when do you carry a knife, No-Knife Nick?"

Nick stood, rubbing his knee. "Since some motherfucker came after me with a machete."

Damon threw back his head and laughed. "I like you. Gotta run, though. Brian, you're awake? Gonna live?"

His heart was hammering, but he smiled. "Sure, Damon."

Damon glanced from him to Nick and back. "Fuck it. Try to act human, Bry, all right? And mouth shut! No blabbing about you-know-what."

"I won't blab."

"I told Nick about your narcolepsy. That's all he needs, got it? When I get back, you and me are gonna have words."

"Okay."

"Fuck!" Damon turned and hurried out. Brian could hear him taking the stairs two at a time, then the door slammed.

Brian counted to ten to be sure he wasn't coming back, then said, "What was that?"

Nick shrugged. "He has to make some kind of secret trip for Marston, and didn't want to leave you unconscious. He said I was a better wet nurse than Booker or Roy or one of the guards. Or your sister?"

"Oh."

"Doesn't Lori help you out?"

"She's not good with vomiting people. Especially now." Mom had sometimes been sick, when she was jonesing. If Lori was the one cleaning up, it was a real mess. Damon said it would be worse now she was pregnant.

"Are you going to puke?"

He sure hoped not. "Sometimes I do. Damon puts a bucket ready." He didn't have to look to know it would be there, beside the bed.

"Does Damon do this often? Sudden cross-country drives?"

"No. Sometimes." Brian rubbed his aching head. "I need to—" In front of Nick he changed that to, "Bathroom?"

"You need a hand?"

"Maybe." He felt shaky, and it wasn't any better when he tried to stand. Nick came and wrapped an arm around him, helping him walk. He was aware of his own stale smell, sweat and piss and an overload of morning breath, and Nick's touch on the bare skin of his shoulders. He tried to look away, make himself small and not breathe on Nick, concentrating on putting one foot in front of the other.

"Here you go." Nick opened the bathroom door. "You need help in there?"

"No!" He leaned in and grabbed the sink with both hands. "I'm fine."

"Well, leave the door unlocked, and yell if you change your mind."

"I'm not allowed to lock doors." When Nick's eyebrows rose, Brian realized how odd that sounded. Like he was a child, which probably was what Damon thought, but he quickly added, "In case I pass out." It sounded less dumb that way.

He nudged the door shut with his heel and stared in the mirror. *Wonderful.* He looked just as bad as he smelled. Pasty colored, hair in knots, with a dozen mosquito bites and a scrape across his forehead, no doubt from one of the trees. He wondered how Nick had explained it to Damon.

His eyes were red, pupils constricted. Suddenly he remembered— dark woods, bugs, out of breath, Finding, and then there was the girl. A little girl, looking up at Nick, saying *"I want to go home!"* and Nick's voice, *"And you will."* He'd saved a girl!

Brian's knees gave out, and he had barely the strength in his arms to turn his body so he landed sitting on the john and not flat on the floor. *He'd saved a girl.*

He'd broken Damon's rules, exposed himself to Nick, and done the thing he'd always wanted to and never dared. He remembered all Damon's warnings and threats. How if the Feds ever found out what he could do they'd send him out every two days to Find some terrorist until he collapsed and died. Or how parents of missing kids would mob him, threaten him, to make him Find their child. Damon said the world would eat him alive if they knew.

But for once— for one breathless, glorious, shining moment— he could say a little girl was home safe because of him.

He closed his eyes, feeling salt sting his sore eyelids. He'd saved a girl Nick liked. Maybe that would save him from hell somehow despite all the wrong he'd done, but if it didn't, he'd remember those little arms around Nick's neck and try not to be sorry. He *wasn't* sorry, no matter how it turned out. Sobs shook him, and he hugged himself to hold it in, teeth clenched for silence.

Gradually, his gratitude and fear gave way to the awareness that he really, *really* had to pee. He was able to stand up long enough to get the lid raised and his shorts shoved down, and he groaned with relief. After that, he turned on the shower and sat in the tub, letting the water run over him. He opened his mouth to the spray, so it rinsed his lips and dripped down his chin. The steam rose, taking the chill from his bones, and he bent his head and let the water just run and run. The tank was huge; it never got cold.

When he stopped feeling so parched and cold, he reached for the soap and washed, using it on his hair too, rather than trying to stand and get the shampoo. He rinsed, scrubbing with his fingers, the soap itching across his sensitive forehead. Then he rinsed some more. His whole body itched and ached, but the water was good, the shower was wonderful, clean and warm, flushing the remains of craziness off his skin, raining sweet mercy down upon him… *Hmm. Are we a bit spacey?* He turned the shower off and just sat in the slippery, wet tub, listening to the silence.

As the room cooled, he shivered. He should get up. He should eat. He shivered harder. That was Nick outside the door, not Damon. He'd rather pass out than call Nick to help haul his naked ass out of the bathtub. His knee beat a soft tattoo against the porcelain side in time to his shudders, and he wrapped his arms around his stomach.

Nick's voice came from beyond the door. "Are you okay?"

He tried to say a casual yeah, but it came out, "Ye-e-e-a-ah."

The door opened a crack, and Nick stuck his head in. "I'm calling bullshit."

"I'm. I'll. Uh-h-h-h."

Nick came inside, looked around, and yanked the biggest towel off the bar. "You look like—"

"Don't say it!" Annoyance gave him the strength to struggle to his feet, although he didn't refuse the help when Nick wrapped him in the terrycloth and supported him stepping over the edge of the tub. "Why does everyone say I look like *shit*?"

Nick rubbed his back through the towel. "I'm polite. I was going to say *crap*."

"Sure you were." Brian staggered, and Nick kicked the lid of the toilet back down and lowered him. "Couldn't they say, um, 'You look like you just got second place at the science fair?' Something with class?"

"Should I recognize that?"

Brian felt his face heat. "*Spiderman*."

"Okay. But I have to say, you look like you got *last* place at a science fair. Hell, you look like they slammed the door on your face."

"That's your fault." He patted at the sore spot on his forehead. "You hit me with trees."

Nick said slowly, "We should talk about that."

"Not now!" He didn't want to know yet how weird Nick thought he was, after that little demo. "My head's killing me and I need to eat."

"Okay." Nick glanced around. "Do you have sweatpants or something? I guarantee you don't want to wear the shorts you were in."

"In my drawer." He started to get up. "I can do it."

"Sit." Nick put a hand on his shoulder. He grabbed a paper cup from the holder, put some water in it. "Drink that. I'll be right back."

Brian sat obediently, sipping the water. It felt odd having Nick taking care of him, different from Damon and somehow more personal. He wasn't sure he liked it.

Nick hustled back in with a cookie in one hand and black sweatpants in the other, and handed Brian the cookie. "Eat." He knelt at Brian's feet, pooling the fleece pants on the damp floor.

"I can do both." Brian reached down with one hand and tugged the pants over his knees one leg at a time. He took a big bite of cookie and rolled his eyes at the explosion of sugary-chocolaty goodness in his mouth. Oh, man, he needed that. For a second he could forget all the trouble about to come, in the simple pleasure of sugar. Although, drugs would also be good. He stood, tugging his pants higher, and stuffed the rest of the cookie in his mouth. "Neef paifm," he mumbled, reaching for the medicine cabinet. There were several vials in a row there... with labels he couldn't read. Damon always did this part.

Well, he could recognize the ibuprofen, and they wouldn't make him as spacey as the good stuff. He grabbed the bottle and took four with the rest of his little cup of water. It had to be his imagination, but his headache already felt better. Or maybe that was the sugar.

Nick said, "There's more food and drink in your room. Come on."

For a moment he thought about saying no. He could kick Nick out, and lock the door for once, and stay in here forever. But he wasn't sure Nick would go away, and he wanted, *needed*, the food. "Okay."

Nick hovered as he walked out of the bathroom, but didn't touch him as he made his way to the armchair with the side tray, and sat. Someone, probably Damon, had put out a thick sweatshirt, which he pulled on gratefully despite the summer weather. The tray was loaded with bottled pop and wrapped sandwiches and Pringles. *Ah, Pringles.* Perfect fatty, salty food product. He popped the tube open and stuffed his face, eating the first salty-good giant mouthfuls messily. *Hah, see, I'm a slobby pig person.*

Nick just leaned against the wall, though, looking unimpressed, so eventually Brian slowed down to nonchoking speed. When the mountain of food was inside him, and only a few wrappers littered the tray, he pressed his hand to his stomach. That fast gorging might have been a mistake. Damon usually made him take it slower.

It was embarrassing— he was realizing how much he depended on Damon for basic stuff that he should do for himself. How hard was it to eat half the food and set the rest aside? Why had he never thought to mark his pills with colors or something so he'd know which was what? He'd thought he was hiding the adult Brian inside, but maybe he didn't actually have a real adult.

Nick said, "Done eating?"

"Um, yeah."

"Gonna puke?"

"Don't say that." He pressed his fist in harder and lay back in the chair.

"So." Nick moved a couple feet down the wall so he could still look Brian in the face. "We need to talk."

"Right." He wanted to go first. "What did you tell Damon?"

"Well, I didn't tell him you found Keesha. What I really want to talk about—"

"After." Brian cut in. "After I find out if Damon is going to end up killing one of us. And I mean that. Exactly what did you say?"

"I told him we went to a movie in Anoka. *Spiderman 2* is playing there again, so you know how it goes. I said when we were coming out you suddenly started muttering about finding and dowsing, and dashed off pointing. Squinting your eyes, running off into the woods and bumping into trees. Getting bit by mosquitoes, and not making any sense. When you slowed down enough for me to get hold of you, I made you go back to the car. And then you passed out in the seat. And I called him. I didn't want to say anything that would make him think about a little girl found in a park."

"That's not bad." It was halfway to freaking brilliant, really. "You're a good storyteller. What if, when I woke up, he'd asked me where we went?"

"I figured you'd be smart enough to say it was all fuzzy and you didn't remember, so you wouldn't contradict whatever lies I'd told."

Brian blinked. *I figured you'd be smart enough.* The words echoed in his mind. Maybe in his heart. His eyes watered and he rubbed at them with the hem of his sweatshirt. "Okay. That works. We were at the movies. I can say I'm fuzzy about the details."

"Are you?"

"Kind of. Um. No." It was pretty clear by now. Sitting outside the little trailer where the girl lived, holding the stuffed bunny, the trace of marshmallow and daisies pulling him along. "I remember."

"Good. So what the *hell* was that?" Nick braced his hands on the arm of the chair and leaned toward Brian's face. His hazel eyes looked gray and stormy. "*What did you do?*"

"I Found the girl."

"I know that. Jesus! Everyone's talking about a miracle and how she was led out of the forest by an angel."

"I never said anything like that," Brian grumbled.

"Right. I did. And it worked. But what you did? That was…"

When Nick didn't finish the thought, Brian offered, "Freakish? Unnatural? Unreal? A lie? A trick?"

"Don't start with me. Obviously it worked. So it's not a lie. But, um, freakish, yeah, I'll go with that."

Brian slumped deeper in his chair and closed his eyes against Nick's intense stare. "I'm a freak. What can I say?"

"You're not a freak. Okay, you have this freakish ability but, hell, maybe not freakish. Different. Useful."

"Mm."

"Seriously. Brian? Brian?"

He snapped his eyes open. "*What?*"

"If you have that… if you can do that? Why don't you use it for better things? Keesha. Do you have any *idea* how wonderful that was, finding her safe? Do you know how many kids go missing every year, every day even? Kids who never get found. You could help and you don't. Why? Don't you *care*?"

KAJE HARPER

"Go away!" He grabbed the chair and pushed to his feet, forcing Nick to step back. "Get out and take your smug, stupid, ignorant face with you." It would have been the perfect line if his voice hadn't shaken at the end.

"I'm just saying."

Brian turned his back. He wanted to argue or explain, but if he said one more word he would cry. He was *not* going to cry in front of Nick. He gritted his teeth and hunched his back and waited for the sound of the door.

There was nothing but the noise of his own rapid, shaky breaths. He wanted to turn and look at Nick, and couldn't. His vision got sparkly and he put a hand on the arm of the chair, bending over a cramp in his side.

"You should sit down." Nick's voice was low and flat.

"You should fuck off." He never said that word. Bry never, ever did. But Brian could use any words he had today. His side ached painfully and his breath caught.

"Dammit, Brian, you look like someone kicked you. Sit down before you fall down."

He crawled onto the chair instead. He was a big guy, but the chair was deep and he was able to huddle on his knees and smoosh his face against the velour upholstery of the back. He rubbed his cheek on it, feeling the rasp of his jaw against the softness, smelling a faint hint of Damon's aftershave deep in the plush.

A touch on his shoulder made him hunch forward. Nick's hand just rested there, though, warm against his back. Then Nick began to rub in slow, small circles. Brian gave up the fight and cried into the fabric of his favorite chair.

Some time later, when the chair was wet against his face and his nose was stuffy enough to make it hard to breathe, he eased down to silent shudders. Nick had stopped rubbing a while ago, but hadn't lifted his hand from Brian's shoulder. It felt *way* too good to be touched— too much for him to bear it— he shrugged irritably, roughly, until Nick let go of him.

Brian sniffed and rubbed at his nose. He straightened up to get more air, but didn't turn. A clean tissue landed near his hand and he wanted to curse again, but his nose was running and he needed the stupid thing. He grabbed it. He wasn't going to say thanks, though.

Nick said, "Can we start over?"

"Start what?" His voice was sticky.

240

"Fuck if I know. The conversation? The day? The thing where I say thank you so damned much for Finding that little girl?" Brian was surprised to hear a catch in Nick's voice too.

He flinched. "You were right, though. Hundreds more lost kids out there. I haven't Found any of them."

"I bet you have reasons." Nick came and sat on the floor beside the chair where Brian could see him if he wanted to look. "If I bothered to ask. Right?"

Brian shrugged a shoulder.

Nick nodded slowly. "So. This obviously isn't the first time you've done that trick. Hell, that day you met me at the house and you had low blood sugar— was that from Finding someone?"

"Yeah. Veronica. Mr. Marston's niece."

"You said… for a bet?"

"Uh huh."

"How does it work?"

He wasn't sure how to explain. "You saw it. For a long time we thought it was just Mom I could Find. That would've been better." It had been a cool quirk, back then. Something he could do that helped out when Damon needed to get hold of Mom. Something weird, but small and pretty useless, especially the way he collapsed afterward.

Nick's voice was gentle. "How'd you find out different?"

"Lori went out with this guy, and didn't come home. It got past midnight, and Damon was really worried, so I Found her, too. She was drunk and passed out."

"How old was she then? How old were you?"

"Fifteen."

"Damn. Was your mom still alive?"

"Yeah. Pretty much checked out, though. Damon took care of us."

"I'm sorry."

Brian looked away. "He did a good job."

"Then you found out you could do it with strangers?"

"Kind of. I left school as soon as I could. They weren't doing me any good." He remembered Damon encouraging him to celebrate his birthday by telling the school where they could shove it. "Damon convinced Mr. Marston to give me a real job, in the warehouse. Then..." He stopped because that was all the easy stuff, and the rest was where he became a bad guy. He really didn't want Nick to know about it.

He didn't want to talk about how he worked with two guys the most, Terry and Fred, and how Fred stole some stuff and ran away. Then Damon had said, "It would be cool if you could Find Fred, like you did Mom." And Brian had realized that he'd worked with him long enough, knew him well enough, to feel a trace of him. Grabbing Fred's work gloves had made that trace more solid, enough for him to follow to its hidden end before he passed out. Fred's trace was gone when he woke. Brian didn't understand why, until he heard Terry talk about a funeral. He was just as happy never to know how Fred died.

"We kind of worked it out, that I didn't have to know the person, just hold something of theirs. And Damon told Mr. Marston what I could do. He offered us the choice. I could Find people just for him, when he wanted, and let him try out some occult stuff with me too, and we'd all get paid well. Or he would—" He closed his eyes. He didn't want to think about the threats, the things Mr. Marston said he could do, selling Lori to a pimp, killing Damon. He didn't want to remember what the man Lori was to marry looked like, with the mask off and greed in his eyes. "He wanted me as his secret pet psychic. There was no way to say no."

"You could have gone to the cops."

"Not by then. Not with what Damon had done. Mr. Marston said he had cops working for him anyway, and he'd give them evidence. Damon would go to prison, for sure, if he even let him live that long." Even then, he'd known that you didn't cross Mr. Marston.

Nick asked in a strangely intense tone, "He didn't say what kind of cops he owns? Like detectives or street guys?"

"He wouldn't tell me that stuff."

"No. 'Course not." Nick made a visible effort to speak gently. "So how does your Finding work for Mr. Marston?"

Bitterness thickened his voice. "Sometimes it's someone he wants to scare, to spook them with how he has the power. He does that a lot. He loves having people think they can't ever get away from him. Sometimes I think a Find is to impress someone else powerful, like with Veronica. Sometimes it's... more. Punishment." Death.

"And you can't say no?"

"Could you? I try." He lowered his voice to a whisper. "Sometimes I say I can't do it. The trace is too faint to follow. But I can't say that a lot. He'd get suspicious."

"And he won't let you ever use that ability for a good thing? For a child?"

"Damon says no. Damon says he doesn't want anyone to know *how* we Find them or they might kill me or steal me. That's why he spreads those rumors about werewolves and stuff. I mean, I'm obviously not a werewolf. Right?" He managed a shaky laugh.

"I don't know." Nick clearly tried to match his humor. "Lurking unseen in the shadows?" He sobered. "No, I know that's not really funny. Okay. I see his point. But there has to be a way. Anonymous tips, even. Kind of like what we did with Keesha. Out of sight."

"Damon says—" He took a slow breath. "It sounds like all I do is repeat what Damon says, but I tried asking him, as much as I could without, you know, acting too weird."

"Too smart? Does he even know that Bry isn't all you are?"

"Maybe? Not really? I don't want him to know that I'm so, um, broken in half. Or that I understand what he does sometimes."

Nick softened his voice to a whisper. "Like what?"

Brian blinked hard. "Like, when I was nine and he was fifteen— the first time Mom was gone for two days, and there was no food in the house— I know he snatched some woman's purse. Or when I was ten and he was sixteen, and we were short of rent, and he went out and made us money, and he came back dirty and walking funny and had a long shower. At the time, I figured he just worked hard for the cash. Now? I don't want him to know what I think now. He broke into places for money, too." He was sure Damon had moved on to cutting people and robbing people and killing people. But he wouldn't say that to Nick.

"He took care of you when you were a kid?"

"Yeah. By the time Lori and I were ten he did more than Mom."

"Then I guess I'm glad you had him."

"We needed him. Still need him. When I Find, I collapse afterward. A couple of times I had to have a fluid IV. Damon learned how to do that." He remembered the bitter twist to Damon's mouth when Brian asked how he'd managed. *"Hang around an addict long enough, and you learn about veins."* He spoke faster, harder. "I need a safe place and food afterward, and-and-and I can't just run out on my own and Find a kid and wander back like nothing happened. I need Damon, and he says no."

"You need *someone*. It wouldn't have to be Damon."

"Would you want to cart my unconscious ass around and wash me and clean up puke? 'Cause sometimes I puke. Or pee. It's not pretty." He flushed, but he wanted Nick to understand, and to leave him alone. "Damon understands."

"I carted you on my back through the woods," Nick said. "No puke, but that wouldn't scare me. I'm a, um, adult. I can handle a little mess."

"Damon's my brother. What we do works. Has worked."

Nick rose higher on his knees, to meet Brian's eyes. "Tell me you wouldn't rather be Finding Keesha than some guy Mr. Marston wants to scare."

Or kill. "Of course I would! You think it's that simple? I'm his prize. He's obsessed with his magic stuff, and he doesn't share."

Nick tilted his head. "Does he have other magic stuff? Stuff that actually works?"

"I'm his best thing." He shrugged. "Don't know about the rest, really. He keeps it all secret."

Nick hesitated, then said, "It seems odd that he'd show you off to Mr. Granton and Veronica."

"He was weird about Mr. Granton." He remembered Damon's theory about the murder. "Really weird. Like, he didn't like him but he wanted him to be impressed."

"Did you guys ever figure out who shot him?"

"No."

They both grunted, identical sounds. A little of the tension in Brian's body unwound. He'd forgotten that he and Nick shared some of the big bad stuff too.

Nick said, "So you were planning to just, what, do this forever? Hide who you really are and help a possessive, psychotic, criminal bastard control his people?"

"That's kind of nasty coming from someone who helped hide a murder, ya think?" So much for feeling like they shared something.

Nick winced visibly. "Okay. But still, don't you want, I don't know, more than this?"

He wrapped his arms around his middle, hugging himself. "I had plans. I thought maybe once we were twenty-one, Lori and I could get away and start over, maybe with Damon too. But they both like it here."

Nick looked around. "It's a real high-class prison."

"One year, we all lived in one room, over a garage. It wasn't really an apartment, but then Mom wasn't really paying rent. There was no bathroom. We had to walk across the yard to the house to pee, which sucked in the winter. And there were a dozen other people in the house, and the bathroom reeked."

"How old were you?"

"Twelve. Lori hated that bathroom. She'd rather pee in a bucket than go there. Now she has her own master bath with marble tiles, a giant shower with three jets, and heated towel rails, and she doesn't even have to share it with her husband. She has a maid to clean it every day. Is it a surprise she likes that?"

"No."

"So her and me and Damon are all set up perfect here, right? That's what she says."

"But what if something happened to Damon?"

The pain sound must have escaped Brian's lips, because Nick reached out quickly to touch his arm. "I'm not saying it will, but what if he got arrested or had a crash or something? Could you stand to stay here with Mr. Marston then?"

"Would I have a choice? He still has Lori, and the baby." He dropped his gaze, because the baby was more of a thing right now, an idea. Not a person. Not family. He wasn't sure he'd stay for the baby, except for the fact that no baby should belong to Mr. Marston without help. "Even if Lori wanted to go too, Marston would hunt us down however long it took."

"You think he cares that much?"

"Not like love. But no one steals what's his. I remember this one time a maid stole a pair of cuff links and pawned them. He wanted her dead. I told him I couldn't Find her, and he flipped." Marston had snarled his furious demands through clenched teeth, not caring that it had been just some little tiny bit, out of all the stuff he owned. Brian had squished his eyes shut and held the woman's sweater, pretending to try but not even opening his Finder sense at all. He didn't want her trace in his head. He didn't want to feel it if she died.

"Could you leave without Lori? Are you that close?"

"She's still my sister. We're family. We're all we have."

"You'd go on working for Marston for her sake?"

"You work for him too." He'd somehow forgotten that. He had a momentary flash of fear that Nick was trying to trap him, except they'd both already revealed too much to make that likely. Who knew what Nick's angle was? "Anyway, I can't read a stupid street sign. How far would I get without someone smarter to help me?"

"You might find other help."

Brian pushed up out of the chair. His head hurt, and his stomach, and this conversation was making his chest hurt too. His life went a lot smoother if he didn't think about it too hard. "I have a headache really bad. I need to lie down." He staggered over to the bed and fell facedown. Hopefully that would be enough hint that he didn't want to talk anymore.

Nick said, "Do you need anything? Water? More food?"

"Put a pop on the bedside table, but I just need sleep." He didn't say please. He could be rude and just ignore Nick until he took his soft words and painful questions somewhere else.

Except he heard Nick put the pop down and then sit in the other chair, instead of heading out, not talking, but not leaving either. Nick just sat there, and his quiet breathing made the room feel safer. It was almost like when Damon took care of him, except different. Not worse, though. He fell asleep wondering if it was okay to let Nick sit there like he belonged, like he was family too.

Chapter 19

It was late in the day before Brian woke up, ate, and grumpily insisted he was fine. His open mood during that first conversation had disappeared into sullen single words. Nick wished he could stay and do something about that, but he had other duties he really needed to take care of despite all this mess. Brian was not, could not be, his main concern. At least he was awake and coherent when Nick left him.

Nick drove far enough to be sure he wasn't followed, then pulled over in an open area and walked away from his car in case it'd been bugged while he was playing nurse. He took out his phone. "Olson?"

"Yeah. We got your texts."

"And?" He'd taken an unwatched moment to let his boss know that Damon Kerr was headed out on a vital run of some kind.

"So far we haven't lost him. He's headed southeast, out of state. We're using a bunch of cars to hand off the tail, lots of manpower and coordination. Better hope this pans out."

"It has to be big. Kerr wouldn't let me do the drive, even when he thought his brother was out cold, and they've had me driving to the secret warehouse and the estate for weeks. This is something bigger."

"He took a sports car. No cargo space." She sighed audibly. "With our luck, it'll just be some expensive wine Marston wants for his anniversary."

"Better not be." He hoped to hell Damon's run was related to the drugs.

"Right. Where are you now?"

"Heading back to my place. How're they doing in Jersey and San Diego?" Waiting to move on Marston was wearing on his nerves. Takano swore they were getting closer. There'd been a brief but intense argument last meeting about going with the warrant they could get, versus waiting for pie-in-the-sky results to come, but Takano was running the show and apparently liked pie.

"Coming together, according to Takano. Not that he actually tells me the details."

Nick grunted in acknowledgement.

"Keep in touch and keep your shirt on. We'll text if plans change."

"I know." They had a series of text codes, disguised as *"Win a Caribbean vacation"* and *"Sorry wrong number dog picture"* to tell him if he needed to cut and run, or to call in for new information.

He drove back to his little apartment. It was hotter than ever in there, as summer rolled along. He opened the windows as wide as they would go. The smell of burnt cooking wafted in from somewhere, and a group of teens down the street were having an argument. He'd lived in worse, but he could understand Lori Kerr's willingness to ignore just about anything for the sake of her husband's money. Brian's description of their childhood had been pretty bleak.

His cupboards were nearly bare, but he was strung taut, his skin prickling with a feeling of electricity in the air like an approaching thunderstorm. He wasn't hungry. He had a sense that things were coming to a head, a weird premonition familiar from those simple operations he'd done for the Narcotics division. There'd come a moment in the longer ops, right before things broke open, when the air shifted, and adrenaline spiked. Even though he was just standing alone in his own stupid little kitchen, this felt like those times.

In the end, he snacked on cereal from the box, while watching a streamed movie he would never remember one scene of. It gradually got darker outside. Olson didn't call. Brian didn't call. Just another night except that he couldn't settle down, and the air was dry enough for sparks to snap from his fingers to the light switch. He told himself there really was bad weather coming. It was just like him to get all revved up on an actual low pressure wave.

Around ten, he went out to the Torchhouse. Roy and Booker and some of the guys were there, although of course there was no sign of Damon, or Brian. Nick let himself have just one beer, because his head felt light already, but somehow it took him to that place where he could do no wrong. He beat Booker at darts, twice. He beat Roy at pool, although that was getting easier as Roy hit the booze faster and faster. Then he beat a local guy, and then the guy's friend. By the time he won his seventh game in a row, this time by running the table, the guy he was playing muttered something about cheating.

He threw back his head and laughed. "How? Tell me how I was cheating right in front of all you dog-suckers. You moron, I'm the best. You're just too stupid to count your own balls."

The punch that clipped his ear felt great too. It was permission and vindication, and he waded in, hitting the guy one-two-three. Gut first to double him over, ribs to distract him, bearded chin to finish the job. Then the guy's two buddies jumped him and he was busy for a while. Through the red haze and the swing of his hands, the grunts and elbow strikes and body blows, he lost himself in the rhythm of the fight.

He woke back into his own skin when the cool evening air hit his face. He realized the guy wrestling him through the back door to the alley was Booker, and he pulled his punch.

"Christ, Nick!" Booker grabbed his wrist in one large hand, and Nick let him, panting through what felt like a manic grin.

Nick whooped, sucked in air, and managed to wipe the smile off. "Sorry."

"Yeah, you're fucking scary when you get going sometimes."

"Why'd you pull me out?" Nick ran a tongue over his front teeth, which felt sore but not loose. His lip was going to swell. Someone had clocked him a good one.

"The bartender was about to call the cops if we didn't break it up. I'm sick of having to bail out whichever idiot gets sucked into your fight and doesn't get out soon enough."

"Sorry," Nick repeated. He wasn't though. The fight had cleared the gnawing tension, and he felt loose and easy. And sore, especially his hands, but that went with the territory.

"Go home. Turn up sober to work in the morning."

Nick wasn't sure Booker had the authority to say that in Damon's place, but he began to feel his busted lip and grazed knuckles for real, and he wasn't going to start another fight. "Yes, boss." He hesitated, but it felt okay to say, "Where's Damon, anyway? Shouldn't he be the one busting my chops?"

"He's not here," Booker said forbiddingly. "I am. Go away."

Nick shrugged and turned for his car. The looming thunderstorm broke as he was driving. The rain sluiced down, thick enough to make it hard to see beyond the hood of the car. He slowed to a crawl, grinning as a lash of wind and water caught the Corolla hard enough to rock it. Out of nothing in particular, he wondered if Brian was safe in bed sleeping, or if he was awake.

Was Brian one of the guys who hated thunderstorms, or would he glory in the wild weather like Nick did? He imagined Brian out in the rain, blond hair slicked dark and dripping, laughing with his face upturned to the deluge. God, that would be a sight.

He pulled over completely and got out his phone. A text couldn't hurt. *~Are you keeping dry?*

He realized how dumb it was to text someone who couldn't read, but a moment later his phone chimed. *~Watching the lightning. You?*

~Was driving in it. Pulled over. You can text?

~Speech function Day one set it

~Day one?

~Day man

A different chime came in and he clicked over to see the code *~Download our new app for faster shopping.* That meant he should call in ASAP.

He cursed. *~Hey Brian, it's letting up. I'd better drive.*

~Okay see you.

At least Brian seemed to have lightened up from his sullen silence. Nick headed for Walmart. It was open 24/7, and he could dash in through the rain and find a private bug-free aisle to call the mother ship. "Yeah, it's Nick."

"Hey." Takano sounded cheerful. "Clear?"

"I'm fine. In Walmart."

"We wanted to update you. Damon Kerr's still driving southeast. He passed through Chicago without stopping and is headed toward Ohio."

"No stops?"

"Gas and food. Nothing more than fifteen minutes. We're getting very interested in where he's headed."

"Me too."

"Have you heard anyone mention someplace in Ohio, Kentucky, Virginia? Maybe even Maryland or Delaware?"

"Not ringing bells."

"Well, he's in a hurry to get somewhere."

"Don't fucking lose him."

"You do your job, I'll do mine. Speaking of which, where the hell is your audio from the last two days?"

"Ah. Well, the recorder got broken." He winced. He'd held off transmitting anything since seeing Keesha's picture on that Amber alert. He'd lied to himself about just delaying it, but the more time went by, the more he'd known he wasn't going to blow Brian's secret. At least, not yet.

"How in the fucking hell did you manage that?"

"I was in the bar two nights ago, and I got body slammed into the corner of a table. I didn't realize till the next night that it wrecked the recorder."

"Without wrecking your dick?"

"Just lucky I guess."

"And you didn't think to mention it?"

"I got busy."

"Well those things cost money. And this is a piss-poor time for you to stop gathering evidence. You think you can get away and swing by the department? You can drop off the broken one. Maybe we can still get something out of the chip. I'll leave a new one with Olson. Don't fuckin' break it, all right?"

"Yeah." He'd have to make sure the old one really was toast. "I'll try to get in tomorrow morning."

"You do that. Keep in touch."

"Roger Wilco, boss."

"And don't be a smartass. Or I'll dock the cost from your pay."

Nick pocketed his phone, trying not to think too hard about what he'd just done. But driving home in the thinning rain didn't take enough of his attention to avoid it.

He'd lied to a superior officer. Okay, Takano wasn't technically in his chain of command, but that was a cop out. He'd lied, and now he was about to destroy however many dollars of department equipment to protect the secret of a man who was at least an accessory after the fact to murder. At worst, guilty of conspiracy to commit murder. Most likely more than one murder.

On paper, or in a court of law, he was betraying his oaths. Thinking about Brian, about the fear and the pain and the weirdness and the way Bry would appear, confused and alone, when Brian was threatened? That made the picture much less simple.

He thought Damon was probably right— if word of what Brian could do got out, he'd be one hell of a hot commodity. Who he ended up with might come down to who had the biggest guns or was willing to grab him first and make him disappear. And then Brian would be fucked. Saying a trace was too faint to follow might get him out of a run for paranormal-obsessed Marston, with Damon playing backup, but it wasn't likely to work with some Russian mobster. Or the CIA. He'd be forced to try harder, with whatever kind of force it took.

Keeping Brian's secret, for now, wasn't really about hiding a crime. It was life-and-death.

And yet, letting Marston use Bry to track someone who'd ripped off a dealer was obscene— life-and-death failure of another sort.

Nick swallowed against the dryness in his throat. He didn't know what the hell the "right thing to do" was. All he knew was that if the DEA got that recording, it would change Brian's life forever. He wasn't ready to have that happen, not yet.

Brian was a good man. Under all the layers, all the weirdness, was the guy who'd told Nick his own life-and-death secret in order to help a little girl he'd never met. Was he home worried sick right now, wondering what Nick would do? Was he afraid Nick would run off and sell him to some rival of Marston's? That's what Nick Green, small-time crook, might be expected to do.

He pulled over again, to text to Brian. He wrote, ~*Secret's safe with me.* Then realized it might look odd if Damon checked Brian's phone. How could he say it ambiguously, but so Brian would understand? After some thought, he sent, ~*I won't tell anyone how flaky you are.* He hoped Brian wouldn't take that wrong.

A moment later the phone chimed. ~*I know I trust you.*

He felt a strange flash of worry to hear that. Brian didn't guard himself enough. When had Nick Green ever proven he was worth trusting?

Maybe when I left a little girl on a strange doorstep, rather than let anyone know about Brian's talent?

He pulled out onto the road again, trying not to think about that. He'd had nightmares about it afterward, waking up sweating and crying out, over and over. In a dozen dreams, that door had opened in front of Keesha's innocent face, and *something* had guided her into the dark depths of the house, and closed the door behind them. Monsters, men he'd arrested. Once, it had been the actual homeowner, but as he turned away to usher Keesha inside, Nick, hiding in the dark yard, had seen a rope in his hand, and a knife. He'd given up on sleep after that and lain awake listening to the news, reassuring himself with the stories of *"Seven-year-old found safe in State Park."*

Abruptly, he changed lanes. He needed time off. He needed to know something good had already come out of his whole muddled attempt at walking the fine line. He took a winding route to the parking ramp where his own car was stored, and switched over, texting Olson, *~Heading to my place for the night again. Back on at 9 am tomorrow.*

~Got it.

He stuffed his phone in his pocket, leaving it on in case Brian called, but it didn't weigh heavily on him. Shedding Nick Green and becoming Nick Rugo, even for a night, was like taking a lead weight off his shoulders. He hummed as he drove.

He'd go home. There was a can of stew in the trailer cupboard that would heat just fine and wouldn't bust his sore lip too badly. Across the street, Keesha's family should still be celebrating her safe return. He'd drop by, give Keesha a hug and feel her truly solid and alive in his arms. He might even get the chance to return the little bunny, and maybe have a word or a hug with Tyrone. He'd remind himself what really counted in this life.

The trailer park was quiet by the time he pulled in. The Carters' place was dark, although their car was parked there. He didn't see any reporters around. He took it as a good sign, the kids likely asleep with a school day tomorrow, everything going back to normal.

He opened his door and went in. The bed called to him, but he was an unsettled mix of exhausted and buzzed. He got out his personal phone and dropped onto the couch.

Charlie's voice was thick and sleepy on the other end. "What? Nick? Everything okay?"

"Yeah, sorry." He almost hung up, but hearing Charlie warmed something cold and needy inside him. "I just thought I'd touch base, while I have the chance."

"Well, it's good to hear from you, even if it is the middle of the night. How's the case? How are you?"

"All right." He couldn't avoid a sigh. "A bit complicated. Staying undercover like this, the lines blur a bit."

"Like… having to do illegal stuff to fit in?"

"Mm. More like getting, um, friendly with people I might end up arresting. It's complicated. There's always good people who get mixed up in shit they don't understand. There's the law, and there's justice, you know." God, he hoped he could keep Brian out of the mess when the case closed. More now than ever. Because a guy like that could do so much good in the world. *Not because I'm attached or anything.* Just fairness. Although if Brian tracked men down for Marston, did that make him an accessory to murder? Could he really just let that slide?

He'd been silent too long, because Charlie said, "How friendly? You're not going to do something stupid like let someone go?"

"Jesus!" His anger boiled over. "I'm a cop! Of course I'm not going to let anyone guilty go! Anyone really guilty." The word "really" let the air out of his righteous anger. Because yeah, he was thinking about it.

Charlie said cautiously, "You're a great friend, Nick. When you care about someone, you're there for them a thousand percent. I'd hate to see you do that for the wrong person."

Nick rolled onto his side and kicked off his shoes roughly. One of them thwacked against the TV, luckily not hard enough to do damage. "I don't want to talk about it."

"You started it."

"You asked."

"Because… never mind. You want to hear about my life?"

"Yeah, I really do." Something simple. Something that's just Nick Rugo's. He'd come here trying to get away from Nick Green, but Brian seemed to pop into his head no matter where his thoughts went. "Tell me what kind of lame shit you're into these days."

"I met a girl."

"You meet dozens." Then Charlie's tone registered. "Like, a special girl?"

"I think so…"

Nick rolled over to his back and listened to Charlie talk about her; how pretty she was and how his mom wanted to meet her; about trying to scrape up money for a fancy date and how it was hard to get together around her nursing schedule. Ordinary problems. Normal life. No drugs, no guns, no weird psychic… weirdness. No looming choices that felt like they might rip your guts out.

When Charlie ran dry, there was a quiet pause. They both breathed softly over the phone. Nick suddenly missed Charlie with an ache that hurt deep inside. There'd been times they'd get together and not do much of anything, just hang out, and Nick would know Charlie liked him just for him, not for anything he had or did, but just as someone to be with. "Wish you were here," he admitted.

"Are you sure you don't want to talk about whatever?"

"Yeah. It's just the case. Drugs and dead kids." And a missing kid brought home because Brian was willing to risk everything to do it. Exhaustion swept over him. He couldn't think about this any more. "I'll be fine. It's good to hear your voice, though."

"You too. While you're taking care of everyone else, remember to take care of yourself too."

"Always do. G'night." After all, for fifteen years, he'd taken care of himself just fine. He rolled enough to set the phone on the table. He really should charge it. And his work phone. And… he fell asleep, without even making it off the couch.

He woke to the early light coming in the sheer curtains above the kitchen sink. His phone was trying to dig a hole in his ass cheek, and he pulled it out. Almost eight already. Dammit.

He rushed through a shower and ate the stew for breakfast, standing at the window. At eight twenty he saw both kids come out of the Carters' trailer with Sue shepherding them nervously. The school bus stop was a few trailers down, and a couple of kids were already waiting. Nick didn't see any news guys, but one of the older kids took a cell phone pic of Keesha. Her mother glared at the boy, who just shrugged and said something Nick couldn't hear.

He set his bowl down and hurried out of the house. Sue looked up in alarm as he approached, then relaxed. "Nick! Good to see you."

"Not half as good as it is to see the three of you doing all right." He grunted as Keesha ran to him and slammed her head into his stomach in a tight hug. "Hey, sweetheart, I heard you had an adventure."

She looked up at him, her face still dotted with little scrapes and healing mosquito bites. "I went camping and it sucked!"

Her mother groaned. "I don't know where she heard that, but it's all over the news. They laugh like it's cute, and now she'll never stop saying it."

"Could be worse." The local kids all seemed pretty free with the four-letter words when he heard them playing outside. "Hey, Keesha, how are you?"

"I itch on my arms and this shirt is too hot." She plucked at the thin cotton of her long-sleeve blouse.

"I know, Keesh," Sue said, "but it keeps you from scratching."

Her little-girl eyes widened in dramatic pathos. "I'm too itchy for school, Mommy."

"School will keep your mind off it. Look, there's Shawnie coming. Go see her."

Keesha happily hurried to meet her approaching friend, and the children hugged each other before joining hands and heading back. Sue said softly, "I want to keep her locked in her room for, like, a year. But you can't, can you?"

"No. She looks okay?"

"She is. Mostly. I was so scared." Sue's voice broke. "I was scared they'd never find her, and then when they did, I was worse scared what might've happened to her. But all she did was hitch a damned ride in the Prices' truck and get lost in the woods. *Thank God* that was all she did."

"I heard some couple found her," Nick said, fishing for details. The news story had been full of the guardian angel line, but he hadn't heard his name.

"She wandered out of the woods to their house. My baby." Sue dabbed at her eyes. "She was lost for a whole day in the damned forest. The cops think she fell asleep in the truck bed and when the Prices' truck broke down, they got out and hitched a ride to the nearest town without knowing she was left behind in the back."

"Wow. Scary."

"You telling me? When I think my baby slept all night in the back of a pickup on the side of the road? She could've wandered out on the street and got hit, or someone could've stole the truck."

"Yeah."

"She says she woke up and wanted to find someone, and there was a peaceful park. So she just started walking."

"She's a city kid. She didn't know it could be that big."

"Yeah. She went and lost herself. Damned kid." Her mother turned a sob into a throat clearing. "She says she was rescued by an angel, and I believe it."

"Whatever works."

"Amen!"

Tyrone had been standing listening, and he said, "She told me you were the angel, Nick. I'm glad you didn't get dead or something. Don't angels have to be dead people?"

Nick had no clue. "Well, it obviously wasn't me, right?"

"Yeah. She's nuts. The whole thing was nuts."

"Good to have her home, though, right?"

"I guess." The shine in Tyrone's eyes belied the carefully indifferent words.

Sue said, "It turned out okay in the end. You know, when I said on the news about how William doesn't have a job no more, and we were fighting about money? Some guy who was looking for a press operator came and offered Will a job. It's kind of far. But I'd move anywhere to have him working again."

"That *is* good news."

"Yeah. All's well that ends well, I say." Sue frowned at Tyrone. "But I don't want *you* going off on some half-assed scheme hoping it'll end well too."

"Hey, Mom, I wasn't the one that thought I could sneak out and go camping. That was all Miss Airhead there. I was asleep."

"Well, see you don't. And look after your sister."

The school bus was approaching. Tyrone pointed to one of the windows. "Me and Carlos will watch out for her."

Sue pressed a hand to her shaking lips and swallowed. "Keesha?"

"Yeah, Mom?"

"You remember, now. If anyone bothers you about anything, you tell the teacher. Don't matter if it's a grown-up or another kid, you tell her, all right?"

"Sure."

"Come give me a hug."

Keesha ran over and hugged her mother around the waist. Sue clutched her fiercely, and as the bus door opened, Nick wondered if she'd be able to let go. But she sniffed, laughed, and gave Keesha a little pat. "Go on now. Do good at school. I'll be right here waiting when you come home."

Keesha ran back to walk beside her little friend, and they climbed into the bus. Sue held it together, waving as the bus pulled out, and then crumpled with her face in her hands. Nick managed to catch her before she fell, and pulled her into a hug.

"Hey. It's just school, right? Everyone will watch out for her."

"I know." She sobbed and sighed and then managed to get herself upright. "It's just, watching her disappear. Oh my God."

"It must have been so hard— when she was missing."

"I just about died." Sue's face flushed. "I know we're not great neighbors, and we get loud sometimes, but that we made our kid run away— that was like getting punched in the face."

Nick made a noncommittal sound.

"The doctor said it would be best if she rested for the weekend and went to school like normal today. It's *hard* watching my baby get on that bus. That makes me a good mom, though. Right?"

"I guess."

"I know the kids come to see you sometimes. I appreciate having a cop next door like that, watching them."

"It's all the booze," he said. "It scares them. That and the fighting."

For a second Sue's expression became less friendly, but then she nodded slowly. "Yeah. Gonna try to do better. A miracle gave us our baby back, and we're gonna try, day by day."

Brian gave you Keesha back. And he'd never get any thanks for it, but it was still an amazing gift, and maybe the best thing Nick had ever been part of. "Sounds good."

"Well, I should go clear the breakfast away."

"Oh, wait. Here." Nick reached into his pocket and pulled out the squished stuffed bunny. "Keesha left that near my place."

Sue took it, and suddenly pressed it to her face. She hurried back toward her trailer, her shoulders hunched. Nick thought she was crying, and wondered if he should do something more to help, but a woman in tears was scarier than a drunk biker. Whatever Sue's pain, Keesha was safe, and that meant she'd get over it. He watched until she was inside, then went back to his own place. He had perhaps ten more minutes to decompress, before it'd be time to head out, swing by his DEA contact for a new voice recorder, and return to Nick Green's life.

Chapter 20

Nick was in the small warehouse at four p.m., waiting for the dock guys to unload his truck, when his phone rang. *~Number unknown*

He answered cautiously. "Green."

"This is Marston. Something's come up. Get over here to the estate. Twenty minutes."

"But… I'm still unloading."

"Have someone take over."

"Yes, sir."

He headed for where Roy was inspecting a shipment, clipboard in hand, but before he reached him Roy's phone rang. Nick hovered just in range to hear Roy's side of the conversation, which sounded just about the same as his. He waited until Roy hung up, then hurried over. "Marston wants me at the estate."

"Me, too," Roy said, waving to a guy inside the warehouse. "Hey, Connors, take over. Count these, and then make sure the right number of cases came in on Green's truck. If I don't call by four-thirty you can all knock off half an hour early."

"Yes, sir."

Roy turned to Nick. "Give me a ride, will you? Mine's about out of gas."

Nick wanted to say no. He'd planned to call Olson and see if she knew what was up, but Roy was already heading out toward Nick's car, and it would look odd if he didn't follow. He did pause long enough to click the general *"Something's up"* text, sent it on its way, erased it, then hurried to catch up with Roy.

"You know what this is about?" he asked as he navigated the city streets toward the freeway.

"Not a clue. He sounded pissed, though."

"Does he do that a lot? Call out of the blue?"

"Never."

At the light they glanced at each other. Nick's stomach tightened. Roy began whistling tunelessly though his teeth. After a couple minutes, Nick said, "If you don't quit that, you won't live to see Mr. Marston."

"Screw you."

At least Roy stopped whistling, although the finger-tapping wasn't a big improvement. Nick wanted to ask more questions, but Nick Green was a mouth-shut kind of guy, so he just drove. The estate seemed farther than he remembered. Traffic was heavy. Roy took to cursing all the idiots on the road around them, which was only slightly better than the tapping.

They pulled up to the gates a few minutes late. Nick keyed in the outer gate and stared into the camera. The voice on the intercom was, surprisingly, Marston's own. "Get out and open the doors. Open everything up."

"Sure." He and Roy slid out of the car, leaving the doors ajar, and he popped the trunk.

The remote camera boom swung around, inspecting, peering into the trunk, before the speaker finally crackled. "Right. Drive on through. Come straight to the front."

Nick glanced at Roy, and was met by a blank stare. He drove on slowly, up the winding lane and around to the house. Booker's Jeep was already parked out front. Nick hesitated, then swung past and parked ahead of it, with a clear shot at the drive heading out. Just in case.

They caught up to Booker in the hallway, heading to Marston's office. Booker looked back and forth between them. "What's up? Where's Damon?"

"If you don't know then how the hell would we?" Roy said acidly.

"Something's weird." Booker bent, took a small pistol out of an ankle holster, and tucked it into the back of his belt, under his T-shirt. "Did Marston buzz you guys in himself?"

"Yeah," Roy breathed.

They all looked at each other, then Booker shrugged. "Only one way to find out." He led them down the hall toward Marston's office. Roy followed, and Nick brought up the rear, hanging back. His pulse hammered in his throat and his breath came short.

The office door stood ajar. Booker and Roy went inside. Nick thought really hard about turning and running, but that could go bad in a dozen ways. He wasn't armed with anything but his knife, while Booker had his gun, and the estate guards had far more. He hovered on the threshold, but in the end he followed Roy inside.

Marston stood behind his desk, a gun holstered at his hip, his expression dark and angry. There were three chairs placed in front of the desk in a row. He waved them to sit down. They all hesitated, looking at each other. Marston said, "Get your asses in those seats, gentlemen."

After a moment Booker eased into the chair on the end, and Roy and Nick followed suit. Marston paced to the window and back. "We have a problem."

Booker licked his lips nervously. "What?"

"We have a leak. Someone's been feeding the cops my personal information. Stuff from the private warehouse and more."

"Oh. Fuck."

Marston took a step toward Booker. "Is that all you have to say? You pick out the men who work at the warehouse, you and Damon. So what happened? Where did you mess up?"

"Do you know who it is, sir?"

Nick's mouth went dry as cotton, waiting for the answer. He wished he dared to reach for his cell phone and hit the alarm.

Marston glared at the three of them equally. "I have my suspicions."

"Tell me, and I'll get it out of them. We'll take care of it, me and Damon. You know you can count on us."

"I thought I could."

"I swear."

Roy nodded vigorously. "Me too. Yeah. Whatever you need."

Marston said, "What about you, Nick? Are you with me too?"

What would Nick Green say? What does he know? "Sure. Yessir."

"Right." Marston took three quick steps to a side door. "Stay put. I'm going to get the info, and we'll work out who betrayed me. Don't move."

Marston's door clicked shut. The silence in the office was heavy, as Roy and Booker stared at each other. Booker frowned heavily, crossing his arms. "Roy, tell me you didn't get boozed up at the wrong time."

"No way!"

Nick shifted uneasily in his seat, easing forward, sliding his hand casually toward his pocket.

Suddenly, Brian screamed "Nick!" from the hallway.

He leaped to his feet, and bolted through the doorway, looking around frantically. Brian appeared at his side, grabbing his wrist, yanking him sideways violently.

"What the hell?" He let Brian jerk him down the hallway.

"I don't know!" Brian's face was white as he forced Nick into a run. The next moment there was a deafening blast of sound from inside the study. Nick's reflexes turned his stumble into a dive, tackling Brian with him across the marble floor.

The mansion shook. Plaster shards and bits of wallboard showered around them. Nick shook his head to clear it, struggling to his feet. Brian got up with him, still hanging on to his wrist. The office behind them was a gaping hole, the air thick with dust.

Brian coughed, gasping, "What? Oh God! Booker?"

"Bomb!" Nick tried to get hold of his phone, but Brian had a death grip on his right arm. He twisted to look back. Nothing moved in the twisted wreck of the room, but Marston hadn't been in there— "Come on!" He yanked Brian behind him, away from the scene. Marston could be anywhere. That blast had to have been meant to get all three of them. "Run!" Brian hung back a moment, staring over his shoulder, then let Nick pull him forward.

They burst into the foyer and almost crashed into Lori who'd reached the bottom of the stairs with two suitcases in hand. "What the hell was that? Vern said to bring these—"

"Never mind!" Brian grabbed her wrist too, making her drop one of the bags. "Run!"

A shot from the hallway splintered the front doorframe, and Nick jerked their little chain to a halt. "Side door." He hauled Brian left.

Lori tried to put on the brakes. "Brian? Where's Damon? Who's shooting?"

"Marston," Nick grunted.

"He won't shoot me."

Nick yanked them both forward. "Wanna bet? He just killed Booker."

She didn't fight Brian's grip as they dashed toward the kitchen. The back door that let out into the patio was familiar. They ran past the spot where Henry Granton had died. "My car's out front," Nick said.

Shots from that direction brought them up short.

"*Shit!* If we find somewhere to hide, I'll call for help."

"This way." Brian tugged them toward the concrete building that housed Marston's personal collection.

"It's locked," Lori protested.

"Damon found out the secret pattern." Brian reached the side door, hit several buttons on the keypad, and swung it open. "He'll think we can't get in here. Damon made me practice, in case I needed to get in, or out. We can hide here."

They slipped in past him, and he pulled the door shut again. Low lights came up as they moved out of the doorway. The room had a bare tile floor and paneled walls. Long tables held a variety of objects, each with a file folder beside it. The walls were hung with masks and daggers and other less-familiar objects. The air smelled of herbs and ashes.

Lori dropped her suitcase. "What the hell is going on? Is Damon back yet? Bry, where's you guys' stuff?"

Nick fumbled out his phone, hit the emergency button and then held the phone to his ear as he speed dialed Takano.

Brian said, "I haven't seen Damon. Mr. Marston says someone's a snitch. The cops know bad stuff. We all have to get away."

"So why are we running from *Vern*? He's the one who *told* me to grab the emergency bags to make a run. Jesus, you're an idiot!"

"He killed Booker and Roy. He wants to shoot Nick."

Lori flinched. "Maybe Booker was the snitch."

Nick wished he was armed. He couldn't carry inside the warehouse, but he should have grabbed his piece from under the car seat, even if Roy had seen him do it. The call wasn't going through. He looked at his phone. "No bars. Fuck!"

Both Lori and Brian stared at him.

"What?"

"Who are you calling?" Lori asked.

"911," Nick said quickly. "I'd rather deal with the cops than a maniac who kills people with bombs!"

"You can't! Damon's coming home any minute." Brian tried to grab his phone, but Nick stepped sideways.

"I'm not letting Marston shoot me. Or you."

Lori swung her suitcase at him. He ducked away, but she clipped his elbow hard enough for him to lose his grip on the phone. It flew across the aisle, hit the wall with a crack, and slid under a table.

"You're *a cop*!" Lori stared at him, her chest heaving with her furious breaths. "You son of a *bitch*!"

"Nick?" Brian's eyes went wide.

He wanted to go get his phone, but there were lots of weapons around the room, and he didn't trust Lori not to come at him with a sword if he took his eyes off her. He held his hands out empty and eased a step sideways, playing innocent. "Hey! I just want to get the fuck out of here! Marston's a batshit-crazy murderer. He killed Booker and Roy." He felt a second of regret for them. Maybe they weren't actually dead. There were worse guys out there.

"Fuck you!" Lori's glare could have set him on fire. "It's a tough world."

Brian said slowly, almost wonderingly, "She's right. You *are* a cop!"

Nick wanted to deny it, but the certainty in Brian's eyes made him shrug instead. "Marston deals drugs. He's an evil son of a bitch." He glanced at Lori. "Teenagers ODed for the cash that buys your clothes."

Lori lowered her eyes. "I don't care."

"Drugs?" Brian turned to her. "Lori? Damon said he steals stuff."

"That too," Nick said. "But he also manufactures and sells drugs, designer shit, and sometimes the kids don't just get high. Sometimes it kills them."

"And isn't that a shame?" Marston said from behind them.

They turned together. Marston stood at the end of the aisle. Nick flicked a glance at the gun. H&K 9 mil semi, likely a fifteen-shot magazine; three shots he'd counted, so still lots of rounds left. *Shit!*

"Hands in the air," Marston said. "Oh, not you, Lori, my dear. But you stay there. Really, Brian, you brought him *here*? Too dumb to remember that every door's on the control panel?"

Slowly Nick raised his hands, trying to look confused. "What's up?"

Marston's grin was sharklike. "What did you say? I make drugs? Well, someone's told the pigs far too much about what I do. Who could that be?"

"I don't know," Nick blustered. "Might've been Roy."

"Might have. Wasn't. It's a sure thing he won't talk now." Marston came two steps closer, staring in his face. "Nick Green. What's your real name? I should've known you were too good to be true. Too helpful." He raised his voice. "Hey, Brian, what did you tell him? Did you talk about the people Damon kills? Did you tell him how much Lori loves stolen jewelry? I bet you can't wait for him to put your family in jail."

"No." Brian's voice was thick. "No!"

Lori said, "Vern? I grabbed the bags, like you said. Except I dropped yours in the hall." She hefted hers.

"Good girl. I got it." He looked at her, then at Brian, head tilted like a bird of prey about to strike. "Now come here, Lori. You're going to do one more thing for me. You'll shoot this cop. And Brian, you'll watch her do it. Then we won't hear any more about who's a criminal and a killer, right?"

"Vern?" Lori's voice wobbled.

"Come here. Don't get between my gun and the cop. Come on."

"No!" Damon's shout from behind Marston made him jerk and look back. For a second his gun moved off Nick, but it was too close to Lori. Nick gritted his teeth and didn't move. Marston stepped to the side, covering Nick but looking both ways.

Damon came down the aisle, his own gun out and steady in one hand, the other hand locked around the arm of Veronica Granton. Her eyes blazed, but she didn't fight him.

"Hey, boss," Damon said, as if it was just another day. "I caught this bitch stealing the Rolls."

"I told her to take it and go," Marston said. "Time to cut our losses and get out."

"Well, I have a problem with letting her loose," Damon said. "She tried to kill Lori and the baby."

"I did not!" She jerked back, then yelped and went to her knees as he yanked her arm up behind her.

"Yeah. Right. I never heard you and your precious father planning to get rid of the male heirs to the barony, and blame it on me. Never saw him snooping around the kitchen, asking which things Lori liked best, what was Vern's favorite, did the cook always serve the meal."

"He wasn't!"

"Never heard you discussing easy poisons to get in the US. What did you decide on? Rat bait? Yew leaves? You'd done your research."

"No!" She flashed a look up at Marston. "He's crazy!"

Marston looked down at her. "I wondered," he said. "I did wonder why you and Henry showed up."

She glanced around wildly. "You're all crazy."

Marston turned toward Damon. "You killed Henry?"

"Yes, boss. I wasn't going to, but he pulled the gun."

"I see." Marston frowned. "He was a greedy son of a bitch. But worth more than your trailer-trash family. You and that freak brother of yours have cost me everything I own. I'm on the run with just one suitcase." His gun swung from Nick to point at Brian, then at Lori's pregnant belly.

For the first time, a flash of unease showed through Damon's facade. "What are you doing? That's your baby."

"Actually, it's not."

"*What*?" Lori yelped. "The hell it's not. I *never* cheated. Not once."

"Artificial insemination." Marston met her eyes and curled his lip. "That's not my baby, it's an experiment. You think I married you for your looks? You think that stuff I did with you in bed was my kink? Hah. That's your brother's kid. I married you for your family tree, and I shoved his magic Finder spunk up in you until it took. I wonder if it'll come out psychic or with two heads."

"I didn't!" Brian's voice went shrill and panicked. "I *never*!"

Marston said, "You think I sent you whores for your pleasure? Condoms, dummy."

Damon said sharply, "Marston?"

"What?" As Marston looked around again, the muzzle of his gun shifted just a few inches, moving off Lori. Damon's shot took him neatly between the eyes.

Marston dropped like a rock. The H&K clattered to the floor without firing. Nick dove for it, but Damon got it first. For a second they sprawled there, almost nose to nose. Damon's lips pulled back in a snarl, and the gun settled in his left hand like it lived there. Nick stopped short, flat on his stomach.

The moment Damon let her go, Veronica scrambled to her feet and turned to run. Lori leaped forward and caught the back of her shirt, dragging her backward. "Not so fast, bitch!"

Veronica shrieked, struggling.

Damon raised a hand and snapped off a shot away from them, into a padded dummy on the table. The sound echoed through the room and they all froze. Slowly, a weapon in each hand, Damon got to his feet. On the floor in front of him, Marston lay still, his blood slowly pooling on the tiles under his head. If he wasn't dead yet, he soon would be.

Nick breathed fast and hard, trying to keep it silent, gathering his feet under him. Damon gestured with a gun at him. "Stay put. No sudden moves."

Brian gasped, "No!" and pressed a fist to his mouth. Nick couldn't spare attention for him right now. He kept his eyes on Damon, on the weapons in his hands.

"Look," he said, in his best calm-the-civilians voice. "No one's a threat here anymore. Let's just take it easy."

"He shot Vern! Just shot him!" Veronica's voice shook.

"Shut up unless you want the same," Damon said.

Nick kept his focus on the guy with the guns. "You don't want to do that, Damon. Think about it. Killing Marston was self-defense. Or defense of your sister and her baby, anyway. He was crazy. He murdered Booker. Was about to shoot a pregnant woman in the belly." Whether or not that was true, he wasn't sure. It might have been just a threat. But he'd give Damon the benefit of the doubt.

"I know that." Damon's calm was unruffled.

"But now, anything else, any*one* else, there won't be a defense. If you hurt Veronica, or anybody here, you'll go to prison for it."

Damon said, "It's a bit late to worry about that."

"No, it's not." Nick managed a little shift in his balance, getting a bit farther off the floor. Not like it would help much, with all the firepower in Damon's hands. Words were his only weapon now. "You haven't committed a crime in front of witnesses. Not yet."

"Please listen to him," Brian said.

Damon's voice gentled. "Bry, we'll be okay. I promise. Leave it to me."

"I don't want you to hurt anybody."

"I know." Damon sighed. "But I'm in a box now. Only one way out."

"You can get out of here if you hurry," Nick said. "Leave the rest of us here and go. Marston has a dozen cars, money, I bet he grabbed the best stuff to take with him. You can just vanish."

"Really, cop? You'd let me walk?"

"I can't stop you." Nick spread his hands appeasingly, shifting onto one knee. "So far, all I saw was a justifiable homicide. You're not going to make the most-wanted list for this."

"He killed Daddy too!"

Nick glared at Veronica, willing her to shut up, but even seeing Marston shot hadn't made enough impression on her.

268

She pointed at Damon. "He confessed it himself. He's a murderer." She turned to him. "You are! You bastard! Daddy was a peer of the realm. Scotland Yard and Interpol and... and the FBI will be after you."

Damon said to Nick, sounding regretful, "You see? I can't stop here."

"Wait!" Nick's mind raced for the right thing to say. He pointed at his cell phone on the floor. "You don't have time. Get out now. I called 911 before I dropped my phone. The cops'll be here any minute."

"This building's a dead zone. For Marston's precious experiments. Soundproof. No reception."

Nick's mouth went dry. "I called before we came inside."

"I don't think so." Damon looked at Veronica. "You had no idea, you and your daddy, what kind of league you were getting into. You two fucking cowards with your conspiracy and your poison." He smiled at her sharp gasp. "You'd love to see Lori and me dead, wouldn't you?"

"You're going to jail," Veronica retorted. "Her too. You'll both rot in prison when I'm done telling them—" The shot from Damon's silenced .22 was softer than Marston's H&K, barely louder than a cap pistol. Veronica gasped and staggered. "What? *God*." She fell to her knees.

"No one threatens my sister," Damon said, watching her collapse, her hand clutching her chest. "Or me."

Nick surged to his feet, frantically planning a next move, even though he was screwed. Damon wouldn't shoot Lori or Brian, but they were placed wrong to be cover. There was nowhere else to hide. He eyed where Lori was standing anyway. If he leaped—

"Don't try it," Damon snapped. The guns swung his way.

Nick watched it coming. Time slowed, each heartbeat taking an hour, a lifetime, moving unstoppably to the moment when Damon would squeeze the trigger and add him to the body count. He could see the cords of Damon's forearm rise under the skin as he raised his hand, holding the .22. The opening of the muzzle went from oval to round, pointing right at him. He tried to dodge, but his muscles were caught in molasses— slow, he was going to be too slow.

Then something slammed into him and he heard the gun go off. He hit the floor, still breathing, frantically trying to figure out what hurt, with a weight on top of him.

Damon yelled, "Bry! Get the fuck off him."

"No! No! Won't!"

"He's a cop!"

"I know!"

Nick wasn't too noble to hunch under Brian's body, hiding his vital bits. He was certain that Damon wouldn't shoot his brother, but that was all he knew.

"Damon, the cops are coming!" Brian's weight spread over him, and Brian's hand pushed Nick's head farther under. "Just go, okay?"

"What?"

"Go! Run! He won't stop you. You have to get away."

"He's a witness!"

Nick mumbled against the floor. "Hidden recorder got everything. You won't find it. Killing me won't help."

"Fuck!"

Bry clutched him tighter. "Don't kill him! Promise you won't! Promise!"

Damon said, "Okay, Bry, I promise. Get off him."

And that was where a lifetime of trust went both ways, as Nick realized that Brian was doing what Damon told him to. Brian rolled away, Nick tried to scramble with him, and the kick from Damon's steel-cap boot caught him in the head. It didn't even hurt. It was a shock, a jolt arcing through him, and the world went black.

****

Brian cried out, the sound ripping from his throat as Nick crumpled. "No!" *Damon, I trusted you!*

"He's not dead, which makes me an idiot. Come on!" Damon grabbed for his arm.

He dodged, trying to catch his breath through a chest clamped tight around his thudding heart. "He's hurt. Hurt bad. I can't!"

"We need to be *gone*." Damon wiped one of the guns on his shirt as he spoke, placing it in Marston's limp fingers. "He might not have phoned out of this building, but cops'll be here eventually. Marston set off a damned bomb! D'you *want* to end up in prison?"

Brian dropped to his knees beside Nick, wishing he knew if the lack of pulse under his fumbling fingers was just because he didn't know how to find it. *Why had he never learned that?* "Nick?" He opened his Finder eye and the vivid amber-and-steel trace was still there, still alive.

Lori said, "Bry. Move your fuckin' ass. They'll take care of him when they get here. We gotta take care of us. Now!"

He looked up at Damon, who'd put the other gun in Veronica's dead hand and was eyeing the bodies like they were a math problem to solve. Damon was the one who really counted, in the end. "I can't. Killing. Stealing. No more."

Lori snapped, "Grab him and let's move, D!"

Damon turned and stared into Brian's face. "It was all for you. Everything I ever did! Don't waste it!"

God, that cut deep. All Brian could do was shake his head, and plaster himself to Nick. "No more. No bad stuff." They could make him go, but if they dragged him along they'd be slowed down. He didn't want any of this. No more. His body shook with tremors from head to toe.

Damon grabbed his wrist and pulled, but he clung to Nick. With a frustrated growl, Damon let go and gave him a hard look. "Better be worth it, little bro." He bent close, and Brian wondered for a moment if he'd get a hug. Damon never did hugs, but maybe this time, since Brian was screwing them up forever, he would.

Damon whispered near his ear, "They'll trust you more if you're beat up." And he punched Brian, a quick one-two that snapped his head back and filled his mouth with blood. Then Damon whirled, grabbed Lori's bag in one hand and her arm in the other and tugged her down the aisle toward the door. Lori glanced at Brian once over her shoulder, her eyes wide and mouth tight with pain. Then the door swung and they were gone out into the sunshine.

Brian blinked hard, his left eye flaring with pain. His lip stung, his jaw ached, and his heart hurt so bad he was surprised it still beat. *Lori. Damon!* He scrabbled his feet against the floor, trying to get up, uncoordinated in shock and pain. Nick moved and groaned beside him.

Brian managed to kneel and reach for him, tentatively touching his shoulder. "Are you okay?"

Nick groaned again. In the distance through the open door, Brian heard sirens, more than one. He shivered. "They're coming. You'll be okay."

Nick opened one reddened eye and looked at Brian, his bruised mouth working like he was trying to talk. One shaking hand reached down to the zip of his jeans. "Help."

Brian bent closer. "What? How?" If Nick had to pee, no one was going to worry if he did it in his pants right now.

"Smash." Nick fumbled toward Brian's hand, and Brian let him take his fingers in a painful grip. Nick pulled their hands down to his groin, in an odd mimic of sex, until he pressed Brian's against a thick, hard lump of fabric in the zip. "Step. Smash."

"What?" Brian felt the outline of a little box inside the fabric.

"Recorded Damon." Nick coughed and licked his lip. "Shit. Hurts."

"Oh?" Brian touched the lump again. The sirens were getting nearer. Suddenly it clicked. Nick had said they were being recorded. And now he was offering a way out. *Why?* No time to ask why. Brian fumbled Nick's zip open enough to lay the flap aside on the hard floor, raised his foot and stamped. His soft sneaker was thin enough to feel the little box. *Was that enough? Did it work?*

A loud crash sound came from somewhere not too far away. In panic, Brian lunged up, grabbed for the nearest object on a table, and used the end of a heavy iron cross to pound that box, hitting it twice, drawing a yelp of pain from Nick. He thought he heard the thing crack. He looked up, and met Nick's one open eye.

For just a moment, he hefted the cross in his hand, fighting the temptation to hit Nick with it. *Who was this man, to make him want to stay and let Damon go?* He could hit Nick and run, try to catch up. Or at least run and hide and hope to Find Damon later. He might not even have to hit Nick, who was slumping, his good eye closing. Nick looked awful.

Brian dropped the cross and reached for Nick's face. "Don't go! Stay with me?"

"Not going. Head hurts like fuck."

"I'm sorry." He smoothed Nick's hair and pulled his zip back up.

Nick patted randomly at his arm. "Not y'r fault."

More sirens, as cars peeled in close somewhere out front, and there was thumping at the side door of the building. "Should I let them in?"

"Nah. Stay here. Stay down. Do wha' they say. Fuck."

"Will they tell me to fuck?" he whispered. The joke was the only thing he had left.

Nick's mouth curved in a quick one-sided smile. "Not likely. Stay close now."

"Can I be Bry?" He wasn't sure he could face this as Brian. The thumps were getting louder and more rhythmic.

"Sure. Hide. Be Bry. I'll find you."

The door slammed open, letting in bright sunlight. Two men in dark clothes and helmets, faces shielded blank and shiny, charged inside, guns ready, splitting apart and yelling, "Police. Freeze! No one move! Hands where we can see them!" Two more ran in the front door.

From the floor, Nick called weakly, "Officer Rugo, MPD Narcotics, hold your fire!"

"Hands up! Get your hands up!" They were still yelling and Bry's head hurt and his face hurt.

Bry sat tall and put his hands way, way in the air. Like in school answering a question, but both hands. "Don't hurt him. Don't hurt me. No, no. Stop!"

He could tell Nick was talking, even patting his leg, but he couldn't feel it or hear it. The air roared and fluttered in his ears with a dozen voices, yelling, speaking. He squinched his eyes shut and held his hands way up and waited for it to stop. "Don't hurt, don't hurt, don't hurt, don't hurt, don't hurt." If he said it enough, it might be true.

More footsteps, excited voices coming close. "*Check her out*" and "*This one's gone*" and "*Gun here!*" He stayed still, hiding behind closed eyelids.

Someone handled him, all over. *All over.* He froze like a scared rabbit and let them. After a bit, it got quieter. He eased one eye open. There were two men in uniform kneeling beside them, one looking at Nick's head, the other talking on his phone. Another man bent over Veronica's... where Veronica was. Behind them, a standing man was still pointing a gun at them. Bry quickly shut his eye again. "Don't shoot!" It came squeaky from his throat, and he coughed.

Nick said hoarsely, "It's okay, Brian. It's over. You're safe, all right?"

"Safe?"

"Yeah. It's okay." There was a rustling. Nick added, "You with the weapon, could you at least back off a few feet? You're freaking him out."

Someone said, "Olson confirms this is her guy."

"Told you." Nick coughed and then moaned.

Bry had to open his eyes to look. That sounded bad. "Nick? Does your head hurt?"

"Shit, yeah." Nick was lying flat, but his eyes were fixed on Bry. "I bet yours does too." With deliberate, flat, clear words he asked, "Did *Marston* hit you?"

"I don't know," Bry said. He didn't want to lie, and he didn't want to tell the truth. "It hurts."

One of the cops said, "Rugo, what happened?"

Nick rubbed his head. "It's fuzzy. Marston was shooting at us, and we ran in here. He came after us. I... damn, it's fuzzy. More shots?"

"And who's this guy?"

Nick said, "Brian Kerr. He's, um, different. Go easy with him, okay? He gets confused."

There was some bustling and stomping and more people appeared. Bry's arms were starting to ache. He said, "Hands down? Can I? It hurts."

"Wait," one of the men said. "Rugo, we'll get you clear first."

"No, it's okay." Nick's voice was thick-sounding but firm. "He's my CI. He's cool."

Bry repeated, "He's cool." Repeating was always a good way to not say the wrong thing.

"Your CI? He's weird."

Nick muttered, "He's special needs, you bastr'd. Go easy."

"Special needs," Bry repeated, because it sounded good. "Special. Need Nick. Need Damon. Need movies. Need dinner." Some part of him didn't even want to think about food, and he swallowed hard. "No. No dinner."

"Shush, Bry." Nick's hand on his knee tightened.

"You always call me Brian." Nick did. It was one of the things he liked about Nick. But maybe now wasn't the time for that. "You can say Bry, though."

"Shush."

Someone called over to them, "EMTs are here. Are they clear to come in?"

"All clear," the cop with the phone yelled back.

Nick said quietly, "An ambulance is here, Bry. You can put your hands down now." The cop grunted but didn't say no, so Brian lowered his arms.

His hands tingled a bit, and he rubbed them together. "Feels weird. My eye hurts, Nok Nick."

"I know. We'll go ride in the ambulance, okay?"

"Together?"

"Yeah. I promise."

The cop without the phone said, "Rugo, should I cuff him?"

"No!" Nick turned to stare at him, then moaned and held his head. "Fuck. Ouch. He's fine. Let him be."

"Your call." The guy sounded reluctant.

"Hell yeah, my case, my witness, my call."

"We got two dead bodies down here. Two more in the house. You can't blame me for being careful."

"Who's dead?" Bry asked, although he could remember. He thought he could remember. "Not Lori? Not the baby that isn't born yet? Not Damon?"

Nick said, "You don't remember?"

Bry pulled out a phrase he thought he'd be using a lot. "It's fuzzy. Fuzzy, fuzzy like a bunny. Fuzzy, fuzzy."

"Bry?"

"Yes, Nok Nick?" Because if he was Bry, then Nick could be Nok Nick.

"You're making my head hurt. Hush up."

"Sorry, Nok Nick."

The ambulance guys insisted on putting Nick on a stretcher, and after he tried to sit up and say no— but only made some groaning noises instead— he let them. Bry could stand up, so he did stand up, and they just took his arm to help him walk behind. They went the other way, not past the bodies on the floor, and Bry was glad. He looked around but saw no sign of Damon or Lori. There were a ton of different cars there, some police cars and some other cars and the ambulance with the lights still going round. Lots of people were walking around too.

They put Nick's stretcher into the back of the ambulance, and then they closed one of the doors.

They were going to take Nick away without him! He flailed his arms, catching one of the ambulance guys on the hip and making him grunt. "No! Nick! Special needs Nick." Those were the magic words, right?

The guy holding his arm gripped him harder. "Don't worry. We're getting in, too. He's just locking the gurney in place. Come on." He pulled Bry toward the open-door side, and Bry gladly climbed in.

"Nok Nick. I'm here."

"Yeah." Nick's eyes were closed, but the not-swollen side of his mouth curved up. "Don't push it. Sit where they say. Do what they say."

"Okay."

The ambulance ride took a while. Brian closed down, closed his eyes and pretended he wasn't there, and listened. The EMTs called the hospital to let them know they were bringing in two white males in their twenties with head trauma. They mostly talked about Nick, and they were told to start an IV and things. Bry kept his eyes shut so he wouldn't see a needle in Nick's veins.

He didn't want to, but he couldn't help thinking about Damon and Lori. He wondered where they were, what they were doing. Had they taken one of Mr. Marston's cars? Some of them were worth a lot of money, and Damon would know where to sell them. Were they still driving along on leather seats, or had they already changed to some plain, ordinary turdmobile, like Lori called the things poor people drove? Damon was smart. He'd keep Lori and the baby safe.

That moment when Damon had looked at him, before he hit him, kept coming up like the taste of sickness in his throat. *"I did it for you."* Like Brian didn't *know* that? Like he wasn't aware that Damon was smart and strong, and could have been anything if he hadn't had two kids to take care of when he was just a kid himself. Brian knew that. He did. He'd never criticized what Damon did to make sure they all survived. But there'd been this chance— this one hard, shining chance— for Brian to stop.

And he'd taken it.

"Do you want to go to prison?"

He shook, and clenched his hands together to steady them. He didn't, absolutely. He'd watched *Prison Break*, and that first season when they were in the jail had freaked him out. Hitting and fighting, and cutting off toes. Rough men, bad men, preying on smaller men. Brian might be six-two and not a lightweight, but he knew where he would end up in a prison. On the bottom.

But he'd watched Damon shoot two people, and something inside him had frozen hard as ice. He needed to not be part of that. Even if it meant prison.

Still the shaking got worse and harder, until his knees knocked around, thumping things in the ambulance, and he couldn't keep his hands still, and then he couldn't breathe. He heard the paramedics talking excitedly about seizure and panic attack, and then they gave him a shot of something into his arm. The shaking died away and everything got soft, like the edges were sanded off. As they slowed in city traffic, and began making turns, he decided Bry was the man for the job again. He'd think about Damon, and prison, much, much later.

The ambulance stopped and he was guided off. The guy holding his arm had hard, strong fingers, but that was okay because he helped Bry get where they were going. They went into a hospital, and then the man pulled Bry one way, and the man with Nick steered him the other way. Bry thought about panicking again, but the soft edges made it not happen. He whimpered, "Nick?"

Nick rolled his eye. He couldn't roll his head because they had a collar around his neck, but he looked at Bry with his good eye and said, "Be cool. Be quiet. Don't be scared. I'll be back, Bry."

Don't be scared. Like he had a choice. But he nodded. They rolled Nick off down a corridor.

Bry was taken to a little curtained room, and they had him lie on the bed. They took his blood pressure and asked a lot of questions he didn't listen to. Nick had said to be quiet, and it was easier to do that if he didn't talk at all. When he talked, sometimes it was hard to stop. After a bit, a woman with nice eyes bent over to look into his face. She asked a couple more things. Then she said, "Brian? Are you in there?"

"Bry," he said, because this was definitely Bry time.

"Bry." She had a nice voice too. "Is there someone I can call to come and be with you? Someone you'd like to talk to?"

"Nick?" he said immediately, hope rising. "Nok Nick?"

A man's voice from the corner of the little space said, "He means Officer Rugo."

"Ah. I'm sorry, Bry. I think the officer's having an X-ray right now."

"Oh. That's good. His head hurt."

"Yes, it did. Is there someone else?"

Damon. Lori. His eyes filled, stinging the right one badly. "Not anymore."

"A friend? A teacher?"

"Is Nick going to be all right? Really all right?"

"I hope so," she said quietly. "He's fine right now. Anyone else, though?"

"No." Brian said it, and made himself believe it, deep inside. He smashed down all the dumb hope of *maybe Damon will come back*, and locked it away. If Damon came back he'd be in danger. *Run, Damon, run.* "Nobody." He closed his stinging eyes and didn't listen to anyone else after that. When they got tired of him not having any answers, they drew a bunch of his blood out and gave him a pill, then put him in a clean bed in a little room and let him sleep. Bry could sleep anywhere, anytime. Even if Mom was sick. Even if she was dead. Even if Damon was gone. Bry could sleep. But Brian missed his brother and Nick with a sharpness that needled though his brain and left him gasping. Sleep was a long time coming as Brian drifted in and out of his own mind.

Chapter 21

Nick cursed at the nurse who was adjusting his fluid line. "Look, I just want to see him. I don't need all this shit. I'm fine. I have the mother of all headaches, but I'm fine."

"The doctor will be the judge of that. Just lie still."

"Fuck this!" He pushed up on one arm.

From the doorway, Olson said, "Listen to the nice nurse. Don't make me cuff you."

Nick growled, but subsided on his pillows. "What the fuck went wrong?"

She came in, followed by Takano, who looked guilty. He said, "One of my guys was coordinating the raids between the lab in West Virginia, the warehouses, and the estate. We had to bring more people on board. He gave too many details to the wrong guy."

"My fault too," Olson said. "Turns out Marston had two guys in the department, one uniform and one in Narcotics, plus one of the county sheriff's deputies."

Nick grunted in pain. Nothing like finding out someone who was supposed to be working with you was really selling you out. "They told Marston we were on to him?"

"Yeah."

"Who?"

"In Narcotics, the detective he owned told him there was an undercover officer deep in his operation. We traced the bastard back from Marston's phone. He's been arrested."

"Idiot."

"Yeah. Although I guess he wasn't expecting Marston to get shot. We got a bunch of good stuff off the phone and the thumb drive in Marston's bag. He was expecting to get away clean."

There was a little rise at the end of that sentence that felt like a trap. Nick closed his eyes and rubbed them, fingers well away from the throbbing spot on his temple. His whole face hurt. "It's all hazy. Marston's dead? Or wounded?"

"Dead," Takano said. "Ten feet from where we found you."

"Did I shoot 'im?"

"Probably not. We're waiting on the ballistics to know for sure which gun did what. You don't remember?"

"I'd've shot him if I had to," Nick said, skirting the truth. Although when he tried to remember exactly what happened, his head did explode in pain. *Jesus*, it felt like someone had taken a hammer to his whole body. Starting with his head. "Who hit me? Where's the damn nurse? Does a guy have to be dyin' to get meds?" That hurt too, and he whispered, "No shouting."

"You're the one shouting," Olson said, sounding amused, although she lowered her voice. "I'm glad you're almost making sense, though. You took one hell of a hit. Nothing you can tell us about that?"

"Nope." That was the truth. He remembered being on the floor, Brian over him shouting "*No!*" But it was all hazy enough that he might have dreamed it.

Olson went to the closet in his room and pulled out the bag of Nick's personal belongings and clothes. "Well, at least we'll have the—" She stopped short, hand in the bag. "Nick? Is there a reason why the recorder crunches when I touch it?"

Nick winced. "I don' remember. I got bounced round a bit?"

Takano said, "You're damned tough on the pricey hardware."

"Sue me. The bruise're no fun either. M'head feels like a Vikings' game ball."

Olson said, "Are you up to a statement? Without the recorder, we need to fill in the holes."

"Fuck. C'n it wait?" Moving his jaw hurt too, although he remembered a bar fight last night. Or was that the night before? "Was I in a fight? Wha' day is it?"

"Monday," Olson said. "Yeah, it can wait. The big players are either dead or gone."

Nick kept his eyes closed. "Which ones are which?"

"We found Booker, Roy, Marston and, of all people, Veronica Granton, all dead from an explosion plus at least two different weapons. Damon Kerr, Lori Marston, Marston's head of security, and the chemical engineer at the drug lab are all missing. So's the top guy in Marston's West Coast facility."

"Damn."

"We got the lab, though," Takano said. "Written and physical evidence, supplies, a dozen lower minions. We got that douchebag ex-FBI PI of his, too. It was a good op. We got a lot of the drug, stopped production, got some scumbags off the street. I'm not going to cry over Marston ending up dead. Saves the cost of the trial. I just wish we'd found the bitch who was cooking the drugs. And Damon Kerr."

"No sign of him?"

"Not one."

Nick said carefully, "What happens to Brian Kerr?" He knew he was on thin ice. Even without the most recent recordings, these two knew there was more to Brian than met the eye. They also knew Nick had a stake in Brian's safety. "Last I remember, he was throwing himself over the top of me shouting at Marston. I think. It's hazy."

"He's here," Olson said. "He got hit in the face by someone, and he had to be sedated in the ambulance. We have him in a single room down the hall, with an officer watching him."

"He's not under arrest, though. Right?"

"Not yet."

"He didn't do anything!"

"I thought you couldn't remember."

Nick bit his lip and grunted in pain. He was a freaking idiot and it hurt to talk. "Up till then."

"Arresting him might bring his brother out of hiding. Damon Kerr's protective of Brian."

"You can't!"

"Why not?"

"He's—" Nick searched for the right words. It would be easier if he had the use of more than a tiny corner of his aching brain. "He's fragile. You can't put him in a cell. He'll, I don't know, go crazy. Crazier."

"So Damon might have a strong reason to come back for him."

"No. I mean, yeah, he might, but you can't."

"It's not like we'd put him in gen pop."

"Jesus, no." Nick couldn't even think about Brian in the general prison population, with murderers and rapists. "He's young, soft, blond, weird, and gay. They'd rape his ass and eat him alive! Ouch." His head was splitting, he was sure. Brains about to drip all over the floor.

Olson took a step closer and put a hand on his shoulder. "Look, I know you like the guy. We won't hurt him, right? But he might be useful. And he lived on Marston's dime for years. He's not some innocent kid."

"He *is* innocent."

"The nurse will be back in a minute. Just don't worry, right? We'll get your statement later."

He heard their footsteps go out of the room. He wanted more than anything to wait until the nurse brought him some good drugs. More than anything, except making sure Brian knew he wasn't alone. Nick's recall might be totally messed up, but he was sure Damon Kerr had been in that building somehow, and obviously left without taking Brian with him. That would've ripped Brian's heart out.

This wasn't Nick's first hospital stay, so he knew how to clip off his IV, fumbling only a little with the plastic slide. He pulled the needle out of his hand. It bled a bit, but pressing over it would make it stop soon. One hand gripping the other, he eased around in the bed until he could get his feet over the side. The floor was cool under his bare soles. *Step one.*

Sitting straight was step two. Standing was three. Making it to his feet was enough of a triumph that he awarded himself an additional step four for not passing out. He was wearing one of the dumb hospital gowns, and he wrapped it tighter around himself. He was naked under it, his junk swinging in the wind, and he wished he could dress but he had limited time before someone ordered him back to bed. Or until he fell over, whichever came first. Cautiously, he opened the door and stepped into the hallway, keeping a hand on the wall.

He spotted the room with the bored cop in front of it four doors down. Fortunately he also recognized the cop. "Hey, Gordie."

"Rugo? What the hell did you do to your face?"

He touched his cheek. "Boot, I think. Maybe fists? Fuck if I remember."

"Ouch."

"Yeah. Listen, I need to talk to Kerr in there for a minute."

"You can't possibly be working."

"It's my case. I just need a minute."

"They said no visitors…" Gordie let his voice trail off uncertainly.

"I just want to thank him, before I go pass out again. If it wasn't for Kerr, that boot would've probably been a bullet in my head."

"Well, I guess, for a minute. Leave the door open."

"Of course." Nick stepped past him, before he could change his mind.

Brian lay propped up on the bed staring blankly out the window. He wasn't cuffed to the rail, which Nick took as a good sign. His left cheek and lip were swollen and bruised, and his eyes looked dull in the fading light from the window.

"Hey? Brian?"

For a moment there was bright eagerness in Brian's eyes as he turned, but then he went blank again. "Hi, Nok Nick. You look okay. Are you okay?"

Nick came and sat on the edge of the bed, his back to the door. He lowered his voice as much as he could. "I'm fine. Mild concussion. They're going to MRI my head again in a couple hours but so far there's no real damage showing up. Thanks to you."

"That's good." Brian's voice was barely a breath, but it was Brian, not Bry. "You scared me."

"Scared me too, a bit. And I don't remember anything much from being in that building. It's all a blur." He said that with a bit of emphasis.

"I get confused," Brian said, his voice thick. "I don't know."

"Mm." Nick pressed his knuckles to his forehead. He wished he was sharper right now, to say what he needed to. "Apparently Damon's missing. He must've run, and taken Lori. I'm surprised he didn't take you."

Brian whispered, "I wouldn't go with him. I wanted to stay there, with you."

"You...?" *God, that was too much trust.* "Oh. That's cool, but... I think it'll turn out okay for you. I hope I can convince them not to charge you with anything. But Brian, you don't really know me at all. I'm not who you think."

"I didn't do it just for you. Damon takes what he needs, what he wants, no matter who's in the way, and he'll go on like that. Lori's okay with it. I wanted to stop."

"Ah."

"I miss him, though. And I'm scared what might happen." Brian's pale eyes were mirror-shiny, the left one half-hidden by a puffy, purpling lid. "Really scared."

Nick reached out gently to touch that bruised cheek. "Who hit you?" He couldn't remember that at all, and seeing someone punch Brian should have been seared into his memory. "If it was a cop, if they were rough with you, I'll have them charged, I swear."

Brian raised a hand, and laid it over Nick's, pressing his fingers in tight even though it must have hurt him. "Not a cop. I don't remember."

Truth? Lie? Nick couldn't tell. His anger vibrated in his chest with nowhere to go. He wrapped his fingers around Brian's, moving them away from his bruised face. "If anyone gives you a hard time, if they start acting like you're a criminal, you tell them you want a phone call and call me." He realized his cover phone was no doubt locked up in evidence, and Brian likely couldn't remember the number anyway. "Make them give you my real phone number. Nick Rugo. Officer Nick Rugo, all right? I'll help."

"Okay." Brian's voice was thin.

"And if they catch up to Damon or Lori, I'll tell you. I made sure they know she's pregnant, too, and to be careful." His vision darkened a bit, but he didn't want to let go of Brian's hand.

Brian swallowed loudly. "Do you remember about the baby? What he said?"

"What who said?" Nick's head pounded harder. He blinked, trying to clear the flashes of red and wisps of dark that were veiling Brian's face. "Was it important?"

"Never mind. You look awful, Nick." Brian let go of him.

"Thanks." He licked his lips, tasting blood and sweat, and shivered under the hospital gown.

"You should lie down. I'm glad you're safe. I don't want you to get sick now."

He wanted to stay and talk. He wanted to check Brian over for other damage than what showed on his face. But it was already doubtful whether he'd make it back to his own bed without falling over. "You're right. But I needed to know you're okay."

"I'll be fine."

The cop in the doorway cleared his throat. "Rugo? You about done?"

Brian's voice changed and got loud, became Bry. "It was scary, Nok Nick. Can I go home now?"

Nick took the hint and struggled to his feet. "Not yet. But you do what they tell you, and you will soon."

"Okay. You'll come see me? Lots?"

"Sure. I'll be around."

"Bye, Nok Nick."

"Bye, Bry."

He made it back to his room on his own steam, although it was a close thing. The nurse came by to restart his IV and scold him in a voice that went right through his eyeballs. After a while he was wheeled down for another scan. And then they finally gave him something that took the edge off his headache enough to let him sleep. He really, really hoped he'd wake up sharper in the morning, for Brian's sake as well as his own.

****

285

Brian looked around the plain, little room he was now living in, although there was no part of it he hadn't stared at sixty thousand times already in the last three days. It was tiny, bland, dirty beige, and stuffy. The bed he was stretched out on had one pillow, one thick blanket, and four bolts attaching it to the floor. Add a closet with no door, shelves rather than hangers, and a lightweight plastic chair that looked like it might come apart if anyone sat on it, and that was everything. The lighting was fluorescent, behind ceiling panels with embedded mesh.

People probably tried to commit suicide in here out of simple boredom. He'd been here less than a week and he was already half-seriously thinking about how sharp an edge broken plastic might have.

The door opened. The woman who walked in, smiling warmly, was someone new. At this point, unless she was a serial killer, she was a welcome distraction. Heck, considering Damon, maybe welcome even if she was a serial killer.

"Bry? I'm Doctor Murphy."

She wasn't wearing a white coat or scrubs, so he figured she was another head-shrinker type doctor. With a sigh he hoped she couldn't interpret, he let Bry emerge. "I don't want a shot."

"I'm not that kind of doctor. I'm a psychiatrist. Do you know what that is?"

"Shrink?"

She laughed quietly. "Sure. I just want to talk to you."

He waved to the chair, and recited, "Take a seat, ladies and germs."

She pulled the chair over and sat gracefully. Her mouse-brown hair had strands of silver in it, glinting under the harsh light, and a few wrinkles in her face made her look about fifty. Her dark eyes were shrewd, and he tugged Bry closer around himself.

He decided to go on the attack. "This room is ugly."

"Yes, I guess it is."

"Ugly, ugly! I want to go out. I want to go home."

"I'm not surprised, but we have to talk first."

"I talked. I talked to the doctor and the other doctor and the nurse and the cop and the detective and Nick and the other cop and the ambulance guy and the doctor and the other guy with the bad breath and the one with the key. I talked."

She blinked at him, and he kept his face carefully blank, eyebrows raised slightly.

"Yes, I guess you did. But now you need to talk to me."

"I want to walk in the woods. I want to go to the Torchhouse and have a beer. I want to swim. Not talk."

"Do you like beer, Bry?"

Figured she'd latch onto that. "I hate beer. I hate the Torchhouse."

"Then why ask to go?"

"Damon is there. Usually he's there. Is it Friday?"

"No, it's Wednesday."

"Then never mind. He's not there."

"Bry, what would make you feel safe right now?"

Going back in time? Maybe sitting in that damned bar, watching Nick beat Booker at darts while Damon insults them both. That would never happen again. Damon was gone. Booker was dead. Nick was someone else. He blinked hard. "I want to go home."

"You know we can't do that right now. Bad things happened at the house you lived in."

Bad things? No kidding. "Then where can I go?"

"For a little while, you'll stay here."

"Here is icky."

"You could come out of your room. There's a TV in the common room. There are puzzles and books."

"I don't read books."

"Well, you could watch a show."

He was almost choked by the sudden impulse to say "Most TV shows are so dumb, the average middle schooler could write something more original." He didn't though. "TV is stupid."

"You use that word a lot. Is it a bad word, Bry?"

"What? Stupid? It's just a word." He shifted around on the thin mattress.

"Have people called you that?"

"Well, you know, only when they're being polite." He took a little satisfaction in the way she laughed and tried to hide it.

"It's not very polite."

"It's politer than moron, or retard, or loony, or crazy guy, or dummy or—" She tried to head off his litany, but he was on a roll and there was a certain bitter satisfaction to it. "—or crack-head or idiot or thick or nuts or..." Eventually he was repeating himself, but he figured Bry wouldn't have kept track and let himself cycle through again. He didn't add *schizo* though. No point in giving her ideas.

When he finally subsided, she looked at him with sympathetic eyes. "You've been insulted a lot."

Well yeah, but that was the point. That was success for Bry. "Sticks and stones can break my bones but words can never hurt me." Mom used to say that to him, back when. He'd thought it was pretty dumb even then, especially since the words often came with the sticks and stones. Whoever wrote it must have been a blond baseball player with a cheerleader girlfriend. He tilted his head and looked hopeful, like he wanted a pat on the head for that stupid phrase.

"Words are important, Bry," the doctor said. "Of course words can hurt, and words can heal. That's what I do, every day for twenty years. Healing with words."

He closed his eyes against a sudden prickle of tears. He had no clue why that would hit him, down inside. Words had never been his friend, though. "I'd rather have a Band-Aid."

"You're an interesting guy, Brian."

He flinched. Interesting wasn't good. It got you noticed.

"You remember in the hospital, when you were left in the playroom there?"

288

They'd given him art paper and pencils and crayons. He'd figured they were tired of interrogating Bry by then and were hoping he might write or draw something useful. He'd spent the time playing with the toys, though. "They had GI Joes, but they have no boy parts. They need dicks." Sex was a good distraction. He was done pretending to be straight now. One less burning torch to juggle.

"They also had puzzles. You remember? Things that came apart and went back together?"

"Loops and strings and silly things?"

"Yes. And you know what? You solved them all in record time. Some of them were very difficult toys, and you did better than I can."

He felt the blood rush out of his head, leaving him dizzy. He'd been so careful... He went for a singsong voice. "Strings are good, strings are fun, that's the way the game is won."

Dr. Murphy gave him a long steady look. "I've also heard some recordings that Officer Rugo made. Of a man who was very bright, and scared, and in hiding. Recordings of Brian."

He did pass out then, or almost. He came to awareness bent forward over his knees, with Dr. Murphy supporting his head and murmuring, "It's all right. You're not in trouble. You're safe. Breathe for me now. In... out... in... out."

After a minute he moved over enough to get away from her hand. He pulled in a careful, long slow breath. "So. What now? Am I under arrest?"

"I'm not a cop. Am I talking to Brian now? Can Bry go away for a bit and let me talk to Brian?"

He realized she really was treating him like two separate people in one head. He let it ride for the moment. Maybe it would save him to be crazy. *Maybe I am crazy.* "Sure. What do you want to say?"

"Are you Brian?"

"You have my chart. Can't you read either?"

She blinked, perhaps at the change in his tone. "Can you?"

"Not a word." He knew bitterness twisted his lips. "Not because I didn't try. The letters float."

"You mean you can't see them right?"

"I mean I have dyslexia so bad it made my teachers give up and send me to the coloring table."

"You know what dyslexia is?"

He was suddenly taken by the urge to come out. To let Brian into the light in all his crazy, but not stupid, differentness. Why not? Nick had betrayed him, recording him, flaying him open for people like this woman. Damon had left him. He was on his own, with just his wits to protect him, and those wits better not be Bry's. "It's something wrong with my brain, sure. Letters and numbers and orders go all wonky. That's dyslexia. Knowing and fixing are two different things."

"It's not something wrong so much as something different."

He laughed. "Right. You try saying that when you get on the sixteen bus instead of the sixty-one bus and end up halfway across town."

"I can imagine that would be very frustrating."

"Is that your professional soothing voice? I was nine. I wasn't frustrated, I was scared to death." He bit his lip. That was the disadvantage of taking the filters off. Other stuff could get through.

"What did you do?"

"I crossed the street to the same-looking stop on the other side, put my last dollar into the box on that bus, and prayed I was heading back where I came from."

"You didn't try to tell someone you were lost? Call your mom?"

He snorted. He didn't think they'd had a phone connected, and things changed so often he never could remember a number anyway. Or the latest address. *Get off at this stop in front of the Brown's Chicken; go half a block, turn in at the building with the cracked steps...* "It worked out okay. Damon was mad I got home late."

"Was Damon mad a lot?"

"Yeah. But at least he cared, right?"

"Damon took care of you?"

"All my life."

"Do you know where he is now?"

"No. I hope he's safe. I hope he and Lori are eating steak and laughing."

"You don't think he's worried about you?"

Brian shook his head. He'd had his chance, and bet on Nick. Given that he hadn't seen Nick since that one time in the hospital, he'd obviously bet wrong.

Dr. Murphy said, "I'm sure he is worried. He took care of you for twenty-one years. I bet he wouldn't just stop worrying now."

"Doesn't matter. The cops are after him, and he's smart. He's gone and he'll stay gone."

"And what will you do?"

Brian closed his eyes, suddenly tired. "I guess that's up to you and the cops. I guess I might go to prison." He was terrified of that, but in a strangely abstract way that didn't manage to break through the surface of everything else he was feeling. "Will I go to prison?"

"Have you done something illegal?"

"Probably." He wasn't dumb enough to actually confess. "I lived in that house. People died."

Dr. Murphy lowered her voice. "Did you kill anyone?"

Not directly. Not with my own hands. He shook his head.

"Did you hurt anyone, sell any drugs, steal?"

Bry wanted to chatter about stealing food as a kid, distraction and a bid for sympathy. He just shook his head again instead.

"Did you take drugs?"

"You guys drew like a pint of my blood in the last week. What do you think?"

"I think you tested negative for the common intoxicants, other than what the EMTs gave you, but there are uncommon ones that are expensive and difficult to test for."

"I hate drugs."

"And yet Damon and Lori helped sell them."

He snapped his eyes open angrily and sat up straight. "Leave Lori out of it. She married Marston for money, for safety and family, so we'd never be poor again. She looked the other way. That's all Lori ever did."

"Brian, I'm a doctor, even if I am affiliated with the police. Everything you say to me is confidential, private. Plus I haven't read you your rights. None of this will end up in court."

"Lori likes to live well. Damon made sure she could, without ever getting her own hands dirty. He did the same for me." *Mostly. He got your hands pretty bloodstained in the end, didn't he?*

"There are warrants out for both of them."

"Cops are dumb."

"What about Nick?"

Sudden acid burned in his gut. "Nick? He's sneaky and a lying liar and gay. That's what he is. He came on to me, you know? He tricked me." *And dumped me, and left me.* He pressed his lips tightly together against any more words.

"Are you gay, Brian?"

He nodded. That at least was easy. *Gay and just as dumb as everyone said.*

"You know, Nick's in a bit of trouble."

He kept his mouth shut with an effort. *Good, bad, what kind of trouble?*

"They think he knows more than he's saying about what happened in that bunker of Marston's. They're not sure if all his head-trauma forgetfulness is for real."

He looked down, rubbing the back of his thumbnail over the rough blanket. He didn't care anymore. He wasn't going to ask anything. Not his problem.

"And they're not sure about the way he got tangled up with you. There are some surveillance recordings missing."

"Which—?" The question escaped despite his resolve.

She shook her head. "I can't tell you. But they're worried he's covering something up."

"Nick didn't do bad stuff, except when he had to, for Mr. Marston. That's kind of why I liked him. He's a white knight."

"Would you be willing to fill in the blanks? So they can stop worrying?"

"Off the record or on?" He wasn't going out on a limb for Nick. He was just asking.

"They'd prefer on, of course. Something they can use in court."

He shook his head. "No court, not for me, not for Bry." Her frown made him sourly satisfied. *Yeah, crazy guy here.*

"Even off the record. So they can figure things out."

He shook his head again. He had no idea what Nick might have said. It seemed like he'd managed to keep Brian's Finding out of the record completely. No one had asked one thing about it so far, and Brian hugged that to him as a sign that Nick did choose him over the law, at least a little bit. Although maybe Nick just wasn't ready to be considered crazy too.

Either way, the best way to avoid contradicting each other and becoming more *interesting* was for him to refuse, and Nick to confuse. "No."

"Brian, I have to tell them you're not as simple and unaware as you seem."

"I thought you said this was all private!"

"I won't betray any specific secrets." Dr. Murphy kept her voice calm. It was beginning to really bug him.

"Brian is a secret."

"Not anymore. They've heard those recordings too."

Nick should get hit in the head again, more. "I guess."

"The sooner you cooperate with the police, the sooner you can move on."

"Move on to what?"

She finally looked uncomfortable. "Well, that remains to be seen."

"Would they cut me loose? Say, 'Here, Bry, have a dollar for the bus and get lost?' Or put me in jail? Or keep me here?"

"If you really did nothing wrong, you won't go to jail."

"Hah. Tell that to all the cons who were just in the wrong place at the wrong time."

"Nick helped them get unshakable evidence against dozens of people in three states. I don't think they'll bother to entrap you."

"So not jail? Then what? Where will I go if I cooperate?" He tried to pretend he didn't care. This was why he'd been Bry so much, all week. Not just to keep secrets, but because Bry didn't look ahead beyond the next day. Bry didn't worry about ending up living on a piece of cardboard with a begging sign he'd have to have someone else write for him and not be able to read. With his luck it would say "Throw coins to the crazy person" or offer his ass for sale. He wondered momentarily if he could do that. He'd had sex with enough pros to know there were people making a living that way, however sad they might be.

"There are halfway houses and homes."

"Institutions for crazy people."

Dr. Murphy shook her head. "I don't think you're crazy. Scared, alone, with some unique coping mechanisms. But not crazy."

I wish I was as sure. He wasn't up to any more of this. He pressed his palms over his eyes. She said some other things, but they buzzed around in his ears and didn't make it to his brain. He was lost enough to be startled by her touch on his shoulder. He dropped his hands to look at her.

"I'm going now, Brian. Is there anything I can do for you?"

"Can you ask—" He was going to say *ask them not to give me any drugs.* He'd been given three different "vitamins" again yesterday, and been hard pressed to hold them in his mouth long enough to spit them out without getting caught. It was only because they figured he was too dumb for that trick that he'd succeeded. But if he asked, and they didn't listen, they'd know he knew. They might mix them in his food or move on to shots. In the end he shook his head.

She said gently, "I'll see if Nick Rugo might be able to visit."

"I don't want to see him!" The lie was so thick it was amazing it fit out of his mouth. "I don't."

"All right."

"Are you a shrink for people in here? A counselor?" He'd fought her, and yet he'd revealed more than he had to anyone but Nick. There was an honesty about her that was reassuring.

She shook her head, though. "I work for the police and the DA's office."

"Figuring out if criminals are going to get a Not Guilty because they're insane."

"Sometimes. Plus employee counseling. And this— interviewing witnesses. Sometimes witnesses are too fragile or unsure or scared to do well on the stand. If I think their story will fall apart, I may advise the DA to plea bargain rather than take a chance on a trial."

"What about me?"

Her sigh sounded involuntary. "I think you could be a really awful witness, if you wanted to be, without ever being called into contempt."

"Huh?"

"Never mind. I'm going to advise them not to put you on the stand. Not to count on your testimony. That's a good thing for you, actually. They have a lot of hard evidence, and plea bargains will shorten this whole mess up, so you can go back to living your life."

"In an institution."

"Maybe. That's not up to me."

He had to ask, "But if it were?"

"I don't know, Brian. You're not a simple guy. One half-hour conversation isn't enough to tell me whether you could make it on your own. I do know one thing. If you were my patient, I'd be scheduling you for a lot of therapy in the near future."

"Good thing I'm not," he grumped under his breath.

"Brian? There is no shame in needing a little help. Or a lot of help. I think a bunch of people failed you when you were a child, and you deserve to change that now."

"Hey, I made it! Right? Where I grew up, half the kids were addicts or drunks or gang bangers or hookers by the time they were eighteen. Damon, Lori and I? We made it out."

He hated the sympathy in her voice as she said, "I didn't say you didn't survive, I just said you made it out wounded."

He huffed a breath and turned away.

"Even your dyslexia, Brian. There are all kinds of teaching methods, work-arounds. How much effort did your teachers really make?"

After Mrs. Harrison? Not much. He stared at the wall.

"Take the help. It would be a shame for you to spend your life being less than you can be."

He sat, trying to see abstract images in the scuffs on the paint, until he heard his door close. Then he threw himself back on the bed, staring up at the light again. Was it a hundred and forty-eight little grids of mesh long, or a hundred and forty-nine? And if he lost count more often than not, and wouldn't be able to tell the two numbers apart when he saw them written down, did it really matter?

He only managed to spit one of his meds out that night, and his sleep was deep and full of confusion.

Chapter 22

It was three days later, or maybe four, when Brian finally gave in to boredom and went to the common room. He tried messing around with a jigsaw puzzle. Puzzles were hit and miss for him, sometimes going together almost without thought, sometimes acting like a page of words, blurring and changing. He'd given up wondering why. This one was fine, and he was debating over two slightly different shades of blue, when an orderly grabbed his arm.

"Come on, Bry. Upsy daisy."

He yanked his arm free before he could control his reaction, then babbled, "Sorry. Upsy," and stood. Either Dr. Murphy hadn't told anyone here about him being Brian, or they hadn't believed her, because they still treated him like a five-year-old. Even Bry wasn't *that* slow, but he went along with it because the more he cooperated, the more they ignored him. "Are we going home?" The pang in his chest at the word caught him by surprise, and he clenched his teeth.

"Not home. You have another visitor. Let's go."

He let the orderly tow him forward, not to his own room but through the doors beyond the nursing station and out to the hallway with the little rooms. He guessed they were visiting rooms— the upholstered furniture, carpeted floor and softer lighting fit with that. He'd been in two of them already, sitting there like a lump while different cops questioned and teased and nagged and eventually threatened him. He'd kept quiet, his attention focused on the nubby red fabric of the chairs and the worn tan of the carpet, until they became the most real things in the room. He could do it again.

But this time he barely saw the room, because Nick was sitting on one of the chairs, his hands clenched in his lap. As they came in, Nick stood smoothly.

"Hey, Brian."

Brian looked at him without speaking. Six different exclamations surged up behind his locked teeth, each trying to get out, until he couldn't speak at all past the logjam of thoughts.

The orderly said, "Give us a shout when you're done," and went out, closing the door behind him.

Nick looked him over. Brian wanted to wince, and wanted to cry. Also wanted to punch Nick's lights out for being there, for seeing the way he looked now, in baggy hospital clothes with his hair three days out from his last shower. Of course, Damon had already punched Nick for him, hadn't he? "Your eye's still black."

Nick touched the side of his face. "More like green and purple now. Yours looks better."

Damon hadn't hit him as hard. He didn't point that out. There was another long, uncomfortable pause. In the end, he said tiredly, "Why are you here, Nick?"

"To talk. Just talk. Would you sit down?" He gestured at a chair.

Brian thought about being stubborn, but there was no real point. He had no power here, at all, except the right to remain silent. He sat and folded his hands, and waited.

Nick sat too, shifting around restlessly. "So. Um. I thought maybe the best thing to do was this." He pulled a small device out of his pocket and put it on the low table. "This is a recorder. I'm turning it on now." He clicked a button.

"Why?" There was a note of pain in Brian's voice that he couldn't control.

"Because." Nick looked at him steadily, although a flush climbed his neck. "By now you know I recorded our conversations, more than once, although a couple of times the device was damaged." He gave Brian a silent nod.

Against his will, Brian remembered Nick in pain, half-conscious, telling him to smash the micro-recorder that held proof of Damon's guilt. He bowed his head, not quite a nod back, but... something.

"I thought, if I said I wasn't recording, you might not believe me. So here, I am recording. That way we know exactly where we stand."

"Or sit."

"Right." There was an even longer pause. Eventually, Nick said, "How've you been?"

"The food is bad." He kept Bry's flat tones, but met Nick's gaze with his own anger. *How do you think I've been, locked in here while you're walking around out there?*

"I'm sorry to hear that."

"The bathroom stinks."

Nick cleared his throat. "That happens. Listen, Brian, I need to ask you some questions."

"People did. Lots of questions. Doctor questions and cop questions and lawyer questions and nurse questions, and did you see him shoot someone, and did you move your bowels?"

Nick winced, then their eyes met. Brian somehow couldn't keep a hint of amusement from rising, and he saw the moment when Nick caught it. His hazel eyes brightened, and his mouth curved up. "I don't need to know about your bowels."

"Good thing, 'cause this food doesn't help them."

Nick pressed his lips together briefly. "Moving on."

"Bowel movement?"

That got him a snort, and for just a second it felt so good to sit there with Nick and be silly, like this wasn't a mental hospital and Damon wasn't missing and Nick wasn't a cop. Except he was. Brian looked down at the recorder. "What do you want us to say?"

"I'll say I'm sorry. Maybe I should start with that. Brian, I had a job to do. Marston was selling drugs, bad stuff that killed some teenagers. I'd have done more than lie to you, to stop him."

"I thought…"

"Thought what?"

"That he was stealing stuff. Or scamming people. Forgery. Smuggling. But not drugs. Damon hates drugs, after our mom. He wouldn't."

Nick's tone gentled. "I can't say what Damon knew, but Marston was definitely selling illegal designer drugs."

Brian swallowed hard and dropped his eyes. Did Damon know where the money came from? Did he help? Were there junkies out there neglecting their kids, lying and stealing to chase a high they bought from Damon? Could he have changed so much, without Brian noticing? He thought he knew what Damon was, with a knife in his boot and a gun under his shirt. Why did this feel worse than murder?

"You didn't realize?"

Brian shook his head. "I still don't think he would. Damon, I mean. Mr. Marston would do anything."

"Do you know anything about the rest of it? Smuggling, you said? Stealing?"

"No. I tried not to. I didn't want to."

"What about murder? Henry Granton's murder, for instance."

"You were there, Nick!" Brian glared at him. "Anything I know, you know."

"Afterward, did Marston talk about it? Did Damon? Did they ever figure out who the shooter was?" Nick's gaze was steady.

Did that mean Nick hadn't told them Damon confessed? Or did Nick not even remember? His flat expression didn't give Brian any cues. "No one talked to me about anything, including that." *Which wasn't quite a lie.* No one had been actually talking *directly* to him in that storeroom.

"Who are Damon's friends?"

Brian let his tone get bitter. "Stan. Booker. Roy. You."

Nick lowered his voice. "Anyone still alive he might go to?"

"You know who drinks at the Torchhouse. You know as much as I do."

"Hardly. Who visited him? Was there anyone he went out of town to see?"

"He went out of town a lot. I didn't ask why." *Didn't want to know.*

"Where did he go?"

"I didn't ask that either."

"Do you have any idea where he might be now? Or where Lori is?"

Brian shook his head. "I try not to wonder. I don't want to know. Together, I hope." *Surely together. Damon's mission had always been to take care of Lori, and of him. Damon might be down to one kid now, but he'd make sure Lori was fine, and there'd be the baby later.* "I hope they stay safe forever."

"Even with what Damon's done?"

"I don't care. You have no idea!" He let himself get loud, because it was easy to let the pain be about the past, not the future. "When there was nothing but cornflakes in the cupboard, Damon found food. When the kids in school made my life hell on the playground, Damon convinced them it was a *bad* idea. When mom's trick for the night snuck into our room, Damon heard him and made him leave before he could hurt Lori or me." *With one of his knives at the guy's flabby throat that first time, asking which little kid he'd been planning to rape. Damon had been just fifteen then. They'd moved again the next day, skipping out on rent…*

"I know he took care of you."

"You have no idea. I'll never help you find him."

Their eyes met, Nick clearly also hearing the double meaning of that word.

"Won't! Never!" Bry wanted to come out, but Brian bit his lip and said carefully, "What Damon did for me buys him a lifetime pass for anything."

"Even though he was selling drugs? Even murder? Even though he left you behind?"

The drugs were the bigger gut-punch. Damon had been so vicious in his hatred of smack and meth, and the destruction they caused. But he said steadily, "Even though."

"Would you testify against someone else, if we need you to? Maybe Coop?"

Brian let his eyes go flat and blank. "I get confused."

"Prison would be worse than this place. If you say no, the DA might bring charges. You could go to jail."

He shrugged. All his life, he'd had to struggle for any kind of control over what happened to him. He had none now. He'd have none in prison. Maybe he could just go deep in Bry, where he wouldn't care.

Nick said clearly, "All right. I won't push you now. But I'll be back." When Brian opened his mouth to snap a response, Nick glared and put a finger to his lips. He bent forward, and clicked the recorder, then said in a softer tone. "It's off now."

"Sure it is."

"You don't trust me?"

He had to laugh. It was hard to stop. His chest ached.

Nick leaned closer to the recorder, and without touching it, said softly, "I, Nick Rugo, lied to my commanding officer about my actions and eyewitness testimony more than once in the course of the Marston investigation. I failed to report important evidence." He sat back, eyes on Brian.

"You'd better hope that switch isn't broken."

Nick winced. "Hell, yeah."

"It's really off?"

"Really." Nick continued in the same quiet voice. "They only let me come because you stonewalled the other two guys, and I said you might talk to me. I promised to record it."

Brian pointed at the recorder. "You're breaking your promise."

"Only halfway. Only because you matter more."

Brian's eyes stung and he looked away. The walls in here were the same puke-beige as the rest of the place, but fresher and a lot less scuffed. Had they seriously repainted that awful color more than once?

"Brian? How are you, really?"

"I don't know," he admitted, staring at the wall. "Scared, a bit. They keep trying to give me drugs, and sometimes I have to take them. I hate drugs, and that crap makes me spacey. The best shrink I've met so far was the one who worked for the cops. When I ask about leaving, they change the subject. And the food really does suck."

"I'm sorry." Nick's voice had a hoarse quality that pulled Brian's attention around.

"It could be worse." Probably would be if Nick had told everything he knew. "What about you? You got kicked pretty hard."

"I have headaches. Nothing I can't handle."

"Were they happy with you? Your bosses? Did you solve the case?"

"We got a boatload of dangerous synthetic drugs off the streets and closed down both the lab and the main distributor, so yeah, they were happy."

"You let Damon get away."

"I did? I don't remember having a chance to stop Damon." Nick started to raise his eyebrow, then winced and squinted.

Against his will, Brian leaned forward and reached out a finger to touch Nick's still-swollen face. "I'm sorry you got hurt." *I'm sorry my brother hit you.* Not that Brian had any control over what Damon did, but it felt like he'd sucked Nick into the mess. Of course, for an undercover cop, that was probably a good thing. "I'm confused," he admitted. "I don't know what's real anymore." *Were you ever my friend? Or was I just an angle you could play, to get close to Marston?*

Never ask questions you don't want to know the answers to.

Nick caught his hand, pulled it away from his face but held it, rubbing Brian's fingers with his thumb. "I bet that being in here doesn't help the confusion."

Brian tried for a smile. "The loony bin. If you're not crazy when you get here, you will be soon."

"You're not crazy, Brian."

"I'm not exactly sane either."

"Sure you are. Just, um, challenged. Stressed. Handicapped, in a way. I keep planning to check into treating dyslexia. There must be something that can be done. I've just been so fucking busy, and getting online in front of a screen makes my head want to explode."

"It's not just the dyslexia, you know." *Most sane people don't have two names who could come out and walk around in their skin.*

"Whatever. Look, they lock people in here because they can't survive on the outside without hurting themselves or other people, right?"

"I guess. Or just can't manage day to day."

"Well? You had a job."

"I mowed the lawn."

"Still, they paid Mario for that job. You could earn money. You can still do all the day-to-day life shit. And you're not about to off yourself. Right?" Nick actually waited for him to answer.

Am I? Not any time soon. Not even from the sheer boredom of the place. The idea of turning a plastic chair into a working knife wasn't really serious. "No. I don't plan to kill myself."

"You probably could use some therapy, but it doesn't sound like you're getting it here anyway."

"I guess they tried." Having the doctor decide after fifteen silent minutes that he wasn't cooperating and shove medications into him wasn't hopeful, though. Maybe if he actually tried to make it work. Maybe if the shrink didn't look so uninterested. "They might keep trying."

"Well, you can get counseling on the outside. Maybe someone better. Don't you want to get out?"

"God. Yes." He scrubbed his face with his hands. "I'm not even sure what day it is."

"Thursday. Listen, I'm going to work on it, all right? I'll find out what it'll take to spring you."

"I'd be grateful. Why would you bother, though? I bet the cops like having me safely locked up in here." He realized that he was thinking about Nick and the cops as two different things. He needed to remember they weren't.

"I'd rather have you come out the other side of this in good shape." Nick's grin was a decent effort, but his eyes stayed sober. "I've already risked a fair bit, and I'd hate to see it wasted."

"We Found Keesha." It was a good reminder for himself too. Whatever happened, he'd Found that little girl. "It can't be wasted."

"She's doing well." Nick leaned closer. "I saw her heading off to school like nothing happened."

"Brave kid."

"I hope the scare helps her folks make some changes."

"She's really all right?" He couldn't help reaching out, and Nick took his hand.

"Yeah. And so's her big brother, who felt so guilty about not stopping her. You did real good."

"*We* did." For a moment he remembered what it was like— Finding with Nick, being pulled along toward something hopeful and useful and, in the end, joyful. He squeezed Nick's fingers, and they suddenly both seemed to realize their hands were still clasped. Nick let go abruptly, and he jerked his arm back. "That was the best thing I've ever done."

Nick nodded. "And that's a whole other possible ball game, but for now… If you got out? If you could live any way you wanted, what would you do?"

Find Damon? Except he wouldn't. If he'd wanted that, he'd have gone with him in the first place. All the reasons to let Damon go were still real. Well, except for worrying about Nick. *Where would I go? What would I do?*

"I'd like a small house. Like, really little. Something I could know every inch of. But with a yard, 'cause I'd like dogs. Big dogs, like Luger and Glock, with furry coats." His throat tightened. "Do you know what happened to Luger and Glock?"

"Those were two of the guard dogs, right?"

"Yeah. They're good dogs. They're not mean, they were just doing their job. They should have a home." He hesitated, because maybe it was better not to know. But it would haunt him forever if he didn't. "Can you find out where they went?"

Nick shifted uneasily in his seat. "I'll see what I can do. So a tiny house with a yard and dogs. What else?"

A man to come home to. Work that actually means something. "A big TV screen with one wall of DVDs and one wall of audio books."

"Audio books? Really?"

"Yeah. They're cool. You don't have to read at all. It's all on the disc."

"I know, I'm just surprised. You had a bunch of movies at the pool house, but I don't remember books."

"Damon likes movies better. He let me pick them. I bought *Frozen* mostly to bug him, but it turned out to be pretty good." He suddenly remembered sitting there, as the ending credits rolled unreadably across the screen, still caught up deep in the world of the movie. Damon had whacked him on the ear with a potholder. *"You dummy, that's a kid movie. Come on, burgers are done."* But he also remembered that Damon had timed the burgers not to be ready until his movie was finished. He hadn't potholdered Brian upside the head until the last line was spoken.

A sudden rush of grief tangled his tongue and made his heart clench. He closed his teeth hard against it. He'd made his own bed, and now he'd lie in it. He had no right to feel sorry for himself. He sucked air in and held it, until his throat was dry, but not shaking. "Can I get any of my stuff, do you think? From the pool house? Personal stuff?"

Nick looked startled. "I hadn't thought about that. They'd have to let you have some of it, although everything bought with Marston's money is forfeit."

"All our money was Marston's, originally, unless Damon was doing something I don't know about."

"Well, your used clothes can't be worth much. I'll try to find that out, too."

"I really just want to get out of here," Brian said. "Naked, even."

"You walk out naked and they'll send you right back," Nick said. "Sorry. Bad joke. I swear, I'll try."

"If I have to talk to the shrinks, whatever I have to do, you'll tell me?" He'd lie and sign away his firstborn child to get out. Well, maybe not the child. That had always been a figure of speech, for a gay guy. The thought that it wasn't, that inside *Lori*... He dizzily forced his mind away from that thought. Later for that. Much, much later. How had his life become this crazy? Maybe he was crazy.

He reached out with an unsteady hand and touched Nick's shoulder, just to have something solid under his fingers. "You think they'll let me leave?"

"I'll figure out something." Nick's phone beeped and he cursed. "I have a meeting. I have to go."

Brian sat back and folded his arms. "Wow. You allowed, what? Twenty minutes for me to spill my guts? Way to make me feel important."

"I allowed an hour." An interesting flush rose in splotchy color on Nick's neck and cheeks. "I, um."

"You, 'um'?"

"I sat in the car for a bit. And walked the grounds. It's not that ugly here."

"Outside the buildings. Beyond the locked door."

"Well, yeah, I guess."

"So why were you out there prancing through the lilacs?"

"I don't prance. Jesus." Nick rubbed a hand across his hair, leaving it standing on end. "I was thinking. Planning. I was worried you might be mad and refuse to see me."

"I didn't think I had a choice."

"If you'd had a choice, would you have said no?"

He shrugged. "It's pretty boring here."

"I'm sorry. I know I owe you a lot."

"You owe me *nothing*." Not for sex, not for staying when he was hurt, not for anything.

"I did out you as gay and as Brian, to the department and the DEA."

Well, maybe for that. Funny how he kept forgetting Nick had recorded their private conversations and played them to a bunch of cops. Perhaps his brain didn't want to remember.

Nick stood, moving out of reach. "Seriously, Brian, hang in there, okay? Don't get too weird, and don't get lost to where they think you can't function. *Normal*, okay? *Boring. Ordinary.*"

"I'll try."

"Do you have anyone else, anywhere? A friend? An aunt? Anyone who might be willing to stand up and say they'll help keep an eye on you when you get out?"

"No. No one."

Nick hesitated, then gave him something that was half wave, half salute, with a safe five feet of space between them. He turned, opened the door, and left. Brian got up and followed him out, but he was quickly intercepted by an orderly.

"Now, now, Bry." The man took his arm. "You know you can't go that way."

Brian stood still, feet rooted to the floor, fighting the impulse to break the man's grip and run after Nick. Good sense won eventually, and he let himself be steered back toward the inner doors. *Be boring. Ordinary.* Neither Bry nor Brian came off quite that way, but maybe he could go for something in between. "So what do you think dinner will be?" he asked the orderly casually. "Food or building materials? That toast last night could've been used for bathroom tiles."

The startled look the man gave him, as he muscled them back through the inner door and made sure it locked behind them, didn't suggest that Brian was any good at being ordinary.

Chapter 23

Nick glanced around the table at the men and women who'd been putting the Marston case together. Takano had the suspects and charges and evidence laid out in a pretty chart on his laptop. Nick stared at the screen, trying to pay attention. Most of the suspects were in the process of agreeing to plea bargains, since the physical and recorded evidence was so strong. A few minor players were still pleading not guilty by reason of being too dumb to know what was going on. Most of them would be convicted easily enough.

Takano wrapped up his presentation. "Luckily, Marston was a solo player. He recruited the drug designer, arranged the pipelines for the raw materials through his import business, and set up the lab himself. With Marston dead, and the chemical engineer finally in custody, we don't expect anyone to try to sabotage our cases."

"What about Damon Kerr?" Olson asked. "Any chance he'll show up to make trouble?"

"I wish he would," Takano said. "It might be the only way we'll find him."

Olson said, "We did contact Scotland Yard. With Granton and his daughter both dead, that baby of Lori Marston's is the heir to a boatload of money when the old guy snuffs it. If the Kerrs make a move to claim it, the Brits will be ready."

One of Takano's DEA guys chimed in, "The younger brother's our best lever, obviously. Question is, how do we make Damon come after him?"

Olson said, "We can charge Brian Kerr with being an accessory after the fact for the Granton murder. We have the recordings to show he was present. The only way he'd avoid a conviction would be with an insanity plea, and that's no luxury hotel. Damon might try to save him."

"Bad idea," Nick said quickly. "If Damon thinks his brother's in real danger, he'll come in hot and hard. You don't want Damon shooting up a mental hospital to get Brian out of there."

"We'd have to move him to a secure facility," Takano mused. "Maybe St. Peter."

"Damon's not dumb enough to attack a secure facility head on," Nick said, trying to hide his worry. The thought of Brian in an institution for the criminally insane turned his gut to ice water. "He'd wait, maybe attack along the route or at the courthouse, when Brian's scheduled to appear. Damon's a planner, he thinks outside the box, and when it comes to his brother and sister, he's ruthless. I'd almost bet on innocent people getting hurt. I could imagine him using a bomb or another shooter as a diversion."

"I think we could handle him."

"You want to bet lives on it when we don't have to?"

"Okay, smart boy, do you have a better idea?" Olson asked.

"Let Brian out of the institution and do long-term surveillance. Put him in an apartment or halfway house or whatever, and monitor him. I'd bet Damon will make contact one day, and it won't be with guns blazing, the way it will if Brian's in bad trouble."

Takano made a face. "You know how much that kind of monitoring would cost? It might be years before Damon shows up, if ever. And who knows what crimes he'll commit in the meantime?"

Nick took a breath. "Look, Brian Kerr isn't going to manage well on his own, right? He's going to get into a mess out there, and his brother'll know that. Damon took care of him for twenty years. I'd bet my badge he'll be keeping an eye out, watching for Brian."

"It doesn't seem like much leverage. Waiting for Brian to happen to need a rescue."

"I'm guessing it'll be months, not years, before Damon makes contact. Seriously, you give Brian a minimum wage job, with no reading skills and his scatterbrained approach? He's not going to keep above water long."

"So you're suggesting we take a guy the hospital docs say has—" Olson consulted a paper in front of him. "—Dissociative Personality Disorder, severe dyslexia, and mild intellectual disabilities, and cut him loose? And hope Damon shows up to help?"

"How is that worse than sticking him in prison to become some con's bitch, in case Damon might try to help?"

"In prison, he's not going to hurt any civilians."

"*Brian* won't?" Nick forced a laugh to cover his anger. "He wouldn't hurt a fly."

"His brother's a psycho. It could run in the family."

Nick turned to Gomez, who'd been in charge of the Torchhouse surveillance. "You saw the action in the Torch through dozens of fights. Did you *ever* see Brian Kerr so much as raise a fist?"

Gomez shook his head. "He hid in a corner or under the table until it cooled down."

Nick turned back to Olson and Takano. "I gave Bry good reasons to haul off and slug me, and he never came close to trying. He's harmless."

Olson said, "There's still the cost of a long-term surveillance. We can tap his phone, wire his room, but we'd have to assign someone to listen to the recordings, and watch him when he goes out, track his movements. And how long would we keep it up? A month? Six? A year? Two? I like the idea of charging him as an accessory. I bet it'll bring Damon running."

Nick was trying to muster a better argument when Takano said slowly, "Or we could make Rugo do it."

"Do what?" Nick stared at him.

"Extend your undercover assignment. Keep surveillance on Brian Kerr."

"For months? Years?" Nick swallowed hard. He wanted Brian out, yes, but not like that. Not with Nick forced to lurk in the background, hiding, watching for Damon, while Brian lived his life.

"Close surveillance," Takano said. "Let him rent a room from you, and watch from right close by."

"I *what*?" Nick said, in the same moment as Olson muttered, "You're crazy."

"No, hear me out." Takano looked right at Nick. "Despite everything, he trusts you. He talked to you when he wouldn't say a word to anyone else. We'll tell him that the docs will only release him if someone takes responsibility, and the halfway houses are wait-listed."

"Which is true enough," Olson put in. "The docs say if we don't charge him, they'll eventually have to dump him out to the street. No assisted-living-facility beds available."

Takano continued, "So you tell him you're willing to sign on as his support person, and they let him out."

"I can't." That was even worse than spying on Brian from the rose bushes. Spying on him from the inside? "I doubt he'd go for it."

"Given a choice between prison, St. Peter, and your trailer? I know what I'd pick. I doubt Brian Kerr is any different."

"He'd think I'm coming on to him, like, for sex," Nick said painfully. "It'd be a mess."

Olson had begun nodding, though. "It could work. I trust you not to cross the line. He could use a friend. You be that friend, and keep your eyes open."

Desperately, Nick pointed out, "If I'm there, Damon Kerr won't have a reason to come back. He'll assume I'm taking care of Brian for him."

Takano grinned. "No, it's perfect. After a couple, maybe three weeks, you can have a fight with Brian. Toss him out on his ass. And who's he gonna call?"

"Damon," Olson agreed. "And we'll be set up and waiting. That's not bad. We can control the timing, and odds are Damon will come in with stealth instead of force."

"Brian doesn't deserve to be used as a pawn like this!"

"Rugo." Olson's frown was heavy. "I know you like the guy, but remember he could just as easily be put away for accessory to murder. Look at it this way— you're actually doing him a favor. Hanging out at your place is better than any of his alternatives."

"We can't use my real place!" Nick realized he was losing this battle. He'd gone from refusing to negotiating terms. But still, he didn't want Brian in his real home, laughing in his kitchen, dozing peacefully on his couch, like he'd imagined once or twice. He couldn't live with that dream all twisted, bugged, spied on. "There's no room in my fucking trailer."

"All right. We'll find you a rental. It's not like he doesn't know you're a cop, though. No worries about maintaining a cover."

His headache flared and he rubbed his forehead. "Maybe I can say I moved, found a bigger place, wouldn't mind a roommate. Shit."

She smacked his arm. "There you go. You'll do great. You have excellent undercover instincts. And this'll be easy. You don't need to do anything except keep a watch out for Damon Kerr. You're on light duty for a month anyway. It'll be like a holiday."

A holiday where he destroyed whatever fragile trust Brian might still have in him. He had no illusions. If he betrayed Brian by using him to trap Damon, Brian's anger would be nuclear. There'd be no coming back from that. And yet, if he said no, he wouldn't put it past these two to try the same thing with someone else, someone who would use Brian without caring one bit if he got hurt. Or worse yet, they'd go back to the original plan that put Brian in with violent convicts.

Damon Kerr killed people. Damon Kerr was happy to sell drugs to pay for his sister's fancy clothes. Nick had to remember that.

He was a cop, and Damon was a guy he could be proud to put behind bars. If Brian could somehow be launched into a safe life first, no matter how bad he got hurt in the process, that would have to count as a win. "All right," he said. "But I get to decide when we have our fight. It has to feel natural." *It has to not happen until Brian has his feet under him, so he can survive without Damon or me.*

"Sure," Takano said easily. "We'll get the details worked out, and figure out what electronics you'll need. Do you want to find the rental place or have the department do it?"

"I will," Nick said. What had Brian asked for? A tiny house with a big yard? Nick could at least give him that. *With a side order of betrayal.* "Oh, by the way, do you know what happened to the guard dogs Marston owned?"

Francis, who was in charge of the financials end of the case, pulled up a list and ran through it. "Here we are, among forfeited assets. Four purebred Shepherds and four Belgian Tervy-somethings. It looks like one was put down as a vicious dog, six were actually moved into our K9 training program. One is listed as going up for sale when the paperwork goes through."

Nick wanted to ask which dog was put down, but the odds were Francis wouldn't know. "Okay, thanks."

"Why'd you ask?"

"Getting in good with Brian Kerr," Nick said without inflection. "He wanted to know. Now I can tell him."

"Right, moving on," Takano said, as if he hadn't just made a hot, steaming mess out of Nick's life. "That list of drug-dealing head shops that was found in Marston's files included some we didn't know about..."

Nick listened with a fraction of his attention, and tried to pretend his skull wasn't trying to split open like a melon. He'd wanted to be a cop, hadn't he? He'd picked this life. He should have no complaints if they put his talents to use.

****

Brian glared at Nick, to cover his confusion. "What the hell is that? An ultimatum? Blackmail? I know you're not inviting me home with you for the wonderful sex."

"No sex!" Nick actually put a hand up between them. "This is totally not about sex. That's off the table."

"Then what?" Brian ignored the chance to make some kind of crack about having sex on the table. He couldn't be bothered. "You tell me I have three choices, and they turn out to be prison, the loony bin, or going home with you? How are those choices?"

"Look, this is completely not my fault. The halfway houses are full, and the docs are convinced that you're too psycho to turn loose without a keeper. What happened? I thought you were going to act ordinary."

"I did. An ordinary guy wouldn't sit still while some orderly tried to shove pills down his throat."

Nick glowered at him. "They did what?"

"They put me on more meds. I hate meds. I don't need them. But then this orderly caught me spitting them out, and he tried to make me eat them, and I kind of kneed him in the balls. And it went downhill from there." He shuddered. There'd been no way to win, from the moment the fat bastard caught him palming the pills, but he'd had to try.

"You couldn't just take it and not fuss?"

"Fuss? My mom had a Cesarean when Lori and I were born, and when it didn't heal right they put her on pain meds. Then she got depressed, and they put her on antidepressants. She had some kind of reaction to that, and they put her on other meds to counteract them, and she lost her job and her health coverage. But she figured out that smack made her feel even better than the prescription stuff."

"You were a baby. How do you know all that?"

"Damon said so." Brian backed up a step. "So you tell me— should I just let them stuff whatever pills they want down my throat? Or should I fight it until they give me a shot? Because *Just Say No* doesn't cut it around here." He dashed the back of his hand across his eyes. He was so tired. Tired of fighting and tired of being scared and tired of pretending he was sane and happy and whatever it was they wanted him to be. Especially since he'd clearly failed that little test. "Yeah, I want out. Whatever you need to make that happen, you get. Including blow jobs."

314

"Shit!" Nick whirled and punched the wall. Brian took a sour satisfaction in seeing the shiny surface dented, out here in visitor-land. Nick shook out his fingers. "Ouch. Dammit, Brian, I'm trying to be a good guy here."

"Are there good guys?"

"I like to think so. I like thinking you're one of them. You don't belong in here, Brian."

"Tell them that."

"I *have*! Jesus. And they won't mind getting rid of you, either, but they won't let you out unless someone signs up to be your support system. If you can find someone else, be my guest. If you know where Lori is and she wants to come back and act like she's saner than you, go for it."

"And have her arrested on sight. Right."

"Well, you sure as hell better not call Damon."

Brian dropped into a chair and lifted his feet to the seat, wrapping his arms around his legs. He was so tired. He laid his head on his knees. "Okay. Whatever. You show it to me, I'll sign it. Not like I can read it anyway."

"Screw this. I'm leaving. Are you at least saying yes to sharing my place for a while?"

"I don't get why you want to. I really am crazy, Nick. Although not crazy enough to say no."

"I'm your friend, you oblivious bastard." Nick lowered his voice. "You know, it doesn't have to be forever. A month, maybe two and we can stage a big bad-roommate fight. Then I can move out and there you are on your own. No matter what they say now, if you're doing okay, paying your bills and not frothing at the mouth, they're not going to drag you back here."

"Oh. That might work." He didn't want to admit it, but even though he hated not having the choice, being on his own was a scary idea. Maybe by then it wouldn't be. Maybe in a month he'd borrow some of Nick's self-assurance. "I probably should say thank you."

"Say it in a month. When you might mean it."

He sighed. "Now what?"

"Now we get the details arranged, and then we spring you out of here."

"Can't happen too soon." He let Bry out, just for a moment, just because it was easier. "The food stinks and the rooms stink and the macaroni-gluing stinks and they put boring stuff on the TV."

Nick looked startled. "You do macaroni-gluing?"

"Well, no. But it would stink if I did." He felt a little satisfaction at seeing a hint of amusement in Nick's eyes.

"Take care. Don't make too many waves. I'll be back for you. Promise."

He realized that he did believe that. "See you soon, Nick."

****

Soon turned out to be not so soon. Brian kicked the canvas bag at his feet, not because he had anything against it, but because he couldn't hold still. He wanted out of this place in the worst way, and Nick was late. He'd tried to work up plans to let Nick spring him and then run away, but hadn't gotten far. His planning brain was drowned in a fluffy mush of whatever meds they had him on. Prozac and something else he couldn't remember. It left him floating, without really caring, in a cotton and cardboard world.

Except right now he cared about *getting out of here*. The impatience was almost welcome, the strongest and clearest thing he'd felt in days.

Finally, there was Nick, coming in the doors. His wind-ruffled dark hair and his bright hazel eyes made Brian feel like a rush of fresh air had come in with him. Nick strode rather than shuffled. His T-shirt clung to his strong chest, rather than draping him in shapeless folds. Brian finally believed this might be over.

Nick smiled at the nurse at the desk. "Sorry. Traffic was a bitch. Any papers we need to sign?"

"Just this." She stood and held out a clipboard. "Both of you need to sign out, that he has his belongings, and that he is accepting the discharge. *Here* and *here*."

Nick took the form from her, scrawled on it, then held it for Brian, his finger in front of a blank line. "Your turn."

For a second Brian tried to read it, as if somehow all this might have kick-started his brain. It hadn't, of course. Random letters jumped out at him, dancing in their usual infuriating way. He took the pen, set it where Nick's finger indicated, and scrawled the loopy thing he used as his signature.

Nick passed the form back to the nurse. "Done. We're outta here." He bent and grabbed Brian's bag before Brian could stop him. "Come on, man. Before they stop us." He jogged toward the door.

Brian hurried to catch up. They paused to let the nurse code them out the door, then it closed behind them, and he was halfway out. Nick jogged to the next door, pushed the buzzer. It opened too.

Free. His heart beat fast and his breath caught for no reason as he followed at Nick's elbow, down another corridor, one flight of stairs, through a lobby, and out into the sunshine. One more flight of stairs, and the parking lot lay beyond. He stopped, grabbed the railing, and sagged onto the bottom step, his knees shaking too much to carry his weight.

Nick walked on a couple of steps, noticed, and turned back. "Are you okay?"

"Yeah." It was easier sitting down. His breath wasn't as short and the sparkles in his vision were going away. "Give me a sec."

"We don't have to get your stuff now, we can just go straight home," Nick said, hefting the canvas bag up and down like he couldn't stand still. "You can get some rest."

"I've been resting for weeks. It's just the meds, I think. They make me woozy." He wasn't sure if that was an excuse or the truth, but it worked either way.

"What are you on?"

"Not sure. There are two scripts in that bag." He had no intention of filling them.

"Maybe you should just take it easy. The mansion will wait."

"No!" he said sharply. This was the start of the rest of his life, and he wanted to shed the old one in a fast, hard, Band-Aid-ripping pull. "I want to get my things."

"Well, okay." Nick came back and held a hand down to him. "But if you're going to fall over or something, warn a guy first, right?"

"You'll be the second to know," Brian agreed, taking Nick's hand and hauling himself upright.

They were silent on the drive. Brian stared out the window, trying to decide if he recognized this stand of trees, or that corner gas station. At last, familiarity took over. He knew where he was, knew the turns to get to the drive, could count the heartbeats it would take to get home. Except it wasn't home anymore.

He was surprised at the pang of loss he felt, unexpected real emotion that made it through the Prozac fog. If you'd asked him before, he'd have said Mr. Marston's estate was never really home. He'd always been aware that someone else owned it and ran it, that he was there because he was a useful possession, not because he belonged. He'd been Bry there, most of the time, and not let himself be anyone real except when he was alone. But they'd lived there three years, and that was the longest he'd stayed in one place that he could remember, ever. Maybe it wasn't surprising he was a little attached.

They turned in at the gates. Nick pulled a number up on his phone and punched in the code on the keypad. Of course that had changed. Of course the top corner, bottom corner, top, top, that Brian had memorized wouldn't get him in anymore. They pulled forward, and Nick showed his badge to the camera, not his eye. Brian started laughing, and couldn't seem to stop. Nick drove forward through the opening inner gate and rolled toward the house with a couple of doubtful glances toward him.

"What's so funny?"

"Just thinking of what Mr. Marston would say about his system being used to let cops in and keep crooks out." Except Mr. Marston was dead, and had no say in anything now. He'd fallen over, his head a bloody mess. And Damon had casually gone on, like it was nothing, like it didn't touch him. The memory stopped Brian's giggles.

They pulled up in front of the pool house and got out, and a guy in a security uniform came around the corner from the big house to meet them. "I have to document everything you take out," he said without introductions. He raised a little video camera.

"You can wait out here." Nick gave the guy a hard look. "Film it when we bring it out."

"Right." The man's grin was unpleasant. "Good thing the incendiaries didn't go off, huh? It'd be a pile of ashes."

Nick said, "Yep."

Brian followed him down the walk, and whispered, "Incendiaries?"

"Marston planted other bombs, besides the one in the study. They were supposed to start a fire— destroy evidence and cover his escape. Except the bomb squad disarmed them."

"Oh." Brian had a vision of the whole mansion going up in flames, all the good and the bad and the wicked, burning to the ground in gold and red and smoke-black. Would that have been such a bad thing, if he'd had to start over, with nothing from that life weighing him down? This whole process suddenly seemed like too much effort. "I don't need my stuff, really," he said. "We could just skip it."

"No way." Nick gave him a little push toward the door. "We're getting your things."

Brian let himself be propelled forward, through the door once Nick unlocked it, and into the front room. He looked around. "Um. Wow." The place looked like a herd of moose had rampaged through it. Everything that could be on the floor was. The couch was overturned, the fabric underneath the seat cut open. All Damon's books were scattered across the rug; the DVDs were in a haphazard stack under the window, half the cases open.

"Sorry." Nick sighed. "The guys aren't neat when they search."

"It's a mess." He turned in a small circle, wondering where to start. Really, why bother? What did he need anyway?

"Let's go to your room first," Nick suggested. "Some clean underwear might be good."

Oh. Yeah. He led the way up the stairs, turned right, walked down the hall. Automatic pilot brought him to his door, which stood open. The mess in his room was nearly as bad. "What now?"

Nick came up close behind him and laid a hand on his shoulder. "Look, why don't I pack your clothes. There's no reason to pick through. I'll just grab everything. You look at the other stuff. Are those CDs?"

Brian glanced over. "Yeah. I have a player somewhere." CDs had covers he could recognize. They'd been in a wooden rack beside the bed. He walked over there stiffly, and bent to pick one up. The disc matched the open case and he shut it, stuck it back in the rack, did the same with the next one, searched for the disc for the next empty jewel box.

"Good idea," Nick said in a voice that seemed deliberately soothing. "Fill the rack and we'll just bring it with. I'll grab the stuff from your closet."

Brian sat on the floor, beside the discs. What had they been looking for inside the cases? Porn? Computer discs? Why bother opening every one? It didn't matter though. This was a task his fuzzy brain could do, matching cover picture to disc picture, snapping them in place, closing, filling the rack. He didn't look up, just listened to Nick moving around the room, the click of hangers, the creak of a drawer.

Nick said, "You have a duffel bag here. I'll fill that, okay?"

Brian shrugged, and kept looking through the loose discs for the one to match the one with the jet plane on it. He'd never been on a plane. Maybe one day he'd fly away like that. He found the CD, snapped it into place. The hinge of the case had a crack, but it still closed. He put it into the rack. The next few just needed to be closed and racked.

"I'll take this down to the car and be right back, okay?" Nick told him.

He shrugged again. But when he'd heard Nick's footsteps on the stairs, he got up and went down the hall to Damon's room. He raised his hand to knock, because he never went in there without permission, but stopped with his knuckles an inch from the door. *How dumb is that? Damon's never going to be in there again.* He reached down and turned the handle instead.

Somehow he'd expected this room to be untouched, neat as ever, as if Damon's power would have kept it safe and unviolated. Of course, it hadn't. If anything, the search had been more thorough here. The covers of the bed were stripped away, the mattress overturned. Damon's clothes were pulled out and tossed around. His shoes lay jumbled, the insoles pulled out of a couple of them, like disemboweled corpses.

He didn't know he'd moved until Nick squatted beside him and reached over gently to take the damaged shoe out of his hands. "Are you okay?"

"He liked nice shoes." His fingers clung stiffly to the shiny leather, refusing to unclamp. "Once, he saved up and bought some fancy sneakers, and this group of boys beat him up and stole them." He didn't add the rest of the story. Damon had known who did it. He'd got the one who'd kept the shoes alone somewhere, and pulled a knife on him. He'd taken the shoes back and cut every stitch of clothing off the boy, and a bit of skin here and there too, leaving him naked and bleeding on the street. Brian had heard the kids in the neighborhood whispering about it.

After that, they didn't mess with Damon. The older boys wanted to jump him into their gang, but Damon was a lone wolf, always. Anyway, they'd moved again, not long after. "He loved buying shoes." He should be glad his awful, criminal brother was long gone, but he just felt empty.

"He's not dead." Nick managed to uncurl Brian's fingers and set the shoe aside, but didn't let go of his hand. "Damon's a survivor. He'll be okay."

Brian nodded. He could tell there were tears on his cheeks, and yet the emotion was so distant it was like it was happening to someone else. The shaking and the short breaths were somewhere outside of him, and when Nick sat next to him with a deep sigh and pulled him into a hug, he didn't really feel that either. It was cold where he was, and warm arms couldn't reach him there. He appreciated the effort, though. He put his cheek against Nick's shoulder and waited for his stupid body to stop whatever it was doing.

Eventually, it did. He let Nick haul him up to his feet, and left Damon's room without looking back. He didn't take much of his own stuff after that. Nick had grabbed his clothes. It wasn't like he'd had that much. He hated shopping. He collected the CDs and the player, a few pictures of him and Lori and Damon, crowded into a photo booth at some mall before Marston ever happened, a box of colored pencils, a couple of cassette tapes.

Nick looked curiously at the tapes as Brian set them on the pile to take. "*Little House on the Prairie*? *Where the Red Fern Grows*?"

Brian shrugged. One of his teachers, way back when, had set him up in the corner of the special ed room with a tape deck and books on tape. He'd been the only kid in the room with the patience to sit there and listen, and not make trouble, which had been all that teacher asked of him. The books had been the weirdest mix of things, maybe rejects from the school library, but those two had been the first stories to make him see what he was missing by not being able to read. When Mom had gotten evicted again and he'd changed schools, he'd stolen them, and kept them ever since. Just like Damon— stealing what he wanted most. He picked them up again and tossed them into the corner, hearing one of them crack.

"Hey!" Nick touched his arm lightly. "I wasn't making fun of them, you know."

"They were pretty old anyway. They'd probably break if I tried to play them. I'm starting over."

"Okay." Nick looked down at the meager heap of things on the floor. "That's really all you want?"

"Yeah."

"How about the movies downstairs."

He flinched. He wanted them, yeah, *Butch Cassidy*, and *Crouching Tiger, Hidden Dragon*, and *Chicken Run*, and the *Pirates* movies. But he didn't want to spend more time in this house. "Don't care."

Nick lifted the rack of CDs. "Here, take this." Brian held out his hands, and Nick passed it over, then laid the smaller items on top. "You take that down, I'll find a bag and grab some of the movies. It'd be a shame to waste them, and we need something to do for fun."

"Okay."

"Careful on the steps."

Nick stayed at his elbow and opened the front door for him, then ducked back inside. The sun outside was bright, and Brian blinked for a moment, disoriented. *What was I doing?* Oh, yeah, loading things in Nick's car. The back door was open, the duffel bag on the seat. Brian stuck his armful of stuff in there too, then jumped and hit his head on the frame with a thud when a gruff voice behind him said, "I need to film those."

He'd forgotten the security guard. He backed out of the car, rubbing his scalp.

As the man leaned in, running the camera over the stuff, Brian said, "What happens to all the other stuff now? The house and everything?"

"I don't know. I'm just here to make sure no one steals it." The man pulled back out and stood, huffing as if leaning over had made him out of breath. He was heavy and red-faced and middle-aged. If not for the gun holstered at his hip, Brian thought he'd be pretty useless protection. The man swiped his arm over his forehead and said, "I guess they'll auction it off. Proceeds of crime, you know. They seize them."

"Oh." Did he care? Brian decided he didn't. He just wanted to leave and never look back. He got into the passenger seat and closed his eyes, ignoring the sounds as Nick came and went, packing more things into the car, having some kind of discussion with the security guy.

He must've fallen into some kind of trance, because he jumped when Nick got in beside him and started the engine. The first puff of air from the vents was hot and nasty, but the AC quickly cut in. Brian realized he was sweaty and grimy, and his head hurt.

"You okay?" Nick asked quietly. "Anything else important we should look for?"

Did Marston have files on his Finding talent that he should try to get? Stuff in the lab building that should be in safe hands? He decided he didn't care about that either. "Can we just go?"

"Sure. Should we run by a pharmacy for your meds on the way?"

"Nah, I have enough for a few days," he lied. Well, it wasn't a lie because if he wasn't planning to take any, then zero was enough. "I just want to go home." *Meaningless word, "home."* Especially for a place he'd never been. He kept his eyes closed and didn't look back as they swung around the curve of the driveway, passed the gates, and turned out onto the road for… somewhere. *Anywhere but here.*

This was the start of his new life. He'd have to make the best of it. He had long, long practice doing that.

Chapter 24

Nick glanced over at the passenger seat as he turned down the dead-end road that led to the rental house. Brian had been really quiet since that breakdown in Damon's room. Quiet was probably better than shaking and crying, but the blankness of his expression worried Nick.

"So here we are," he said, turning into the driveway. He heard the false brightness in his own voice and winced.

Brian glanced around for the first time in half an hour. "Is this your house?"

"No. It's a rental. Um, remember we talked about faking a roommate fight later on?" He was supposed to keep that plan a secret, but he wasn't going to just ditch Brian, like everyone else in the guy's life had. "I can move back to my own place, and here you'll be, all set up."

"Oh." Brian looked at the little house like he wasn't even seeing it. "I guess that makes sense. How can you afford it though? Two places?"

There wasn't a good way to say the department was covering it. "It's just for a couple of months. Then you'll take over the rent here, right?" Nick turned off the car and reached for his door.

"I guess." Brian didn't move. "If I find a job. If I can figure out how, in a month or two. Maybe I should have stayed in the loony bin instead, and waited for some halfway house."

Nick heard the bitter undertone, and reached over to punch his shoulder lightly. "Hey, think positive. I'm not going to pretend-dump you until you're ready for it." When Brian's set expression didn't soften, he added, "And who knows. Maybe we'll be such great roommates that I'll sell my trailer instead, and stay here."

That did finally make Brian turn to him. Unfortunately he looked more pissed than pleased. "Don't lie to make me feel better."

"What was a lie? I don't know how this will work. I haven't lived with anyone since I turned eighteen and aged out of the system."

"What system?"

"Foster care. Family placements." He'd been lucky with a May birthday. His last place had let him hang around the extra month until he graduated high school. He'd couch surfed for a couple of months after, until he found a job and a tiny basement room to rent. "I've been on my own since then, so who knows? Maybe I'll like having someone here to clean and cook and take out the trash and do the laundry."

He was pleased that Brian's expression eased at the teasing in his voice. "Or you might end up dead of food poisoning."

"What? You can't cook? Wait, put that seat belt back on. I'm returning you."

"Actually, I can make grilled cheese. With Velveeta. Does that count?"

"You're hired. Come on." He swung out of the car and opened the back, grabbing a couple of bags without looking at Brian. Turning away, he headed up the porch steps. A minute later, he heard Brian come up behind him. He unlocked the door. "So you said you like small, which is good because this place ain't big."

He took Brian's stuff through and set it at the bottom of the stairs. "Kitchen, bath, living room, one bedroom down here. I dibs that one. One bedroom upstairs with a slanted roof. You get that one."

"Wait, I'm taller than you are."

"But I had the concussion. No head trauma allowed."

"I forgot." Brian reached out and touched Nick's shoulder, and he turned back. Brian's fingers rose to brush his cheekbone, then fell away. "You still have some green and yellow there."

"It's almost gone." He stepped back and picked up a bag. "Come on up."

The upstairs room was a conversion, the space under the slanted roof insulated and drywalled. The ceiling in the middle was eight feet high; it just didn't stay that way around the edges. He'd brought a box spring and mattress up, but put them on the floor. With the slant roof it was safer— less chance of sitting up and knocking yourself out. There was a beanbag chair, and an open bookshelf. At one end, a dormer window looked out on the back yard. At the other, a corner was curtained off to make a closet of sorts.

Nick set the bag down and looked around. "It's not much, I know. We should've liberated more of your stuff from Marston's. A TV at least. A stereo."

Brian kicked his duffel bag over to where the roof dipped down, and shook his head. "I don't care. I don't want anything he paid for. I definitely don't want the cops saying I stole it."

Nick managed not to remind Brian that he *was* the cops.

Brian walked over to the dormer and leaned on the frame, looking out. Nick stepped up behind him. "That's another thing that's better than the trailer," he said softly. "You wanted a yard. It's not big, but there's your yard, fenced and all. No dog, but maybe someday."

"Did you ever find out what happened to Mr. Marston's dogs?"

"Yeah." He decided to skip over the one that was put down. "Most of them got taken into a training program. I think one's still waiting to be sold. They were all purebreds. I'm sure they'll find good homes."

"That's good." Brian turned toward him, and suddenly they were just inches apart. "Thanks for checking."

"No problem." Their eyes met and held. At this distance he could tell that Brian's pupils were tiny, his lids heavy. Something dark passed over Brian's face, and his lips parted.

It didn't quite look like arousal, but Brian leaned in and kissed the side of his jaw.

Nick said, "Wait!"

"What?" Brian licked down Nick's neck, then slid to his knees, tugging Nick's waistband with one hand. "Can I? Right now?"

"Oh! No, wait." Nick couldn't help getting hard at the sight of Brian in front of him, but he *could* help doing anything about it. He was very glad they hadn't decided to wire the house for sound. He grabbed for Brian's groping fingers on his inseam. "I meant it. No sex. Not happening."

Brian looked up without letting go. "I want to. I want to feel like an adult."

"Blowing someone doesn't make you an adult. Take it from someone who did it at thirteen."

"Who *what?*"

He hadn't meant to say that. "Never mind. It was no big. Just me trying to show how grown-up I was." *Trying to make someone want me enough not to send me away.* He wondered if that wasn't what was happening here. "It didn't work."

"I like making you feel good." Brian bit his lip and slid his hand closer to Nick's zipper. "I want to feel something too, something real."

"I could suck you," Nick suggested unsteadily, before he remembered his resolve. "No, wait, bad idea too."

"Let me." Brian popped Nick's button open.

"Damn." Nick bent and pulled Brian upward. For a minute he resisted, his whole weight in Nick's hands, then he gave in and stood.

"Sorry. Now you'll think I'm a whore." Brian looked at the floor, his face and neck flushed red. "Trying to pay for my room with a blow job."

Nick held him, his hands still bunching Brian's shirt under his arms because he thought if he let go Brian might run. "We both know that's not what it was. And for what it's worth, I haven't forgotten you have a great mouth. I just think we have the weirdest relationship ever" —*and you don't even know the half of how weird it is*— "and sex right now won't make it simpler."

"It'd feel good."

"So would a hug. And no guilt afterward."

Brian flashed a look up, his eyes meeting Nick's for a moment. Nick thought there was an equal chance whether he would break free or laugh or punch him. Instead he sagged toward Nick, and Nick stepped in close, sliding his hands up Brian's back. At first it was just him holding Brian, but after a moment Brian's arms came around him too. Nick said softly, "You know, I've had a lot more blow jobs in my life than I have hugs."

"That's sad." Brian tightened his arms. "Really?"

"Well, since my mom died anyway. Yeah." He'd meant this as a distraction for Brian, but to his surprise it was making him a little blurry-eyed. How strange. He squeezed back hard for a minute, then eased out of the hug and stepped back. "So. You still have more stuff in the car. Why don't we bring it in and then order out for pizza?"

"Okay." Brian's smile almost looked genuine. "Next best thing to sex, right?"

"You betcha," Nick agreed.

Pizza didn't take long to arrive. Luckily they both liked sausage and mushrooms, so that was okay. Nick joked that a conflict over pizza toppings had broken up many a couple, only realizing what he'd said after Brian flushed and looked away. Nick bit his lip, but correcting himself would only make this odd limbo they were in worse. Instead, he paid for the pizza and passed the box to Brian.

The house was very sparsely furnished. Seeing his old stuff in this new space, through Brian's eyes, made Nick realize how little he actually owned despite three years in a full-time job. The kitchen table had a wobble, the chair cushions were worn, and the couch had a definite sag in the middle. His glassware was a mix of garage sale castoffs.

"Maybe we can get better stuff soon," he said, as Brian went through into the living room and sat carefully on the end of the couch, laying the pizza box on the water-stained coffee table.

Brian glanced up at him. "I've lived with far worse. And I don't have any money to chip in. Do I have money? I don't even know." He rubbed his face. "Damon took care of all that. I should have tried harder to figure it out."

"Hard to do that when you were being Bry," Nick pointed out, setting down their pop and sitting on the other end of the couch.

"I guess."

Nick picked up the remote, and flipped through channels. He found a movie of some sort, people in helicopters swooping across the desert. He didn't recognize it, but you didn't have to know the plot to watch things blow up. He took some pizza and settled in to snarf it down.

Brian stared toward the TV, but the blank look on his face suggested he wasn't seeing the hot guys in flight suits. In the middle of a chase scene, he suddenly said, "I need a job."

"Yeah, I suppose."

"That's part of being an adult, right? Earning your way."

"No huge rush," Nick told him. "Rent is paid, you don't eat that much."

It was meant to be funny, but Brian's jaw tightened, although he didn't look away from the screen. "I don't want to be like your kid or your pet, or something. I want to be equal."

"Okay, I get that."

"Problem is, all I'm good for is labor. Lifting boxes, mowing grass, shoveling ditches. Lots of guys are looking for that kind of job. Most of them can read and write."

"Lots of them are flaky or unreliable or lazy, though. I'd hire you."

"I'm crazy. I have no job references that aren't from my drug-dealing dead brother-in-law. Well, I collected shopping carts for a supermarket once. They liked to hire special-needs workers. We came cheap and didn't complain."

"Ouch."

Brian set down his pizza and scrubbed at his face with his hands. When he turned to Nick, his lip trembled. "I'm going to be an awful grown-up."

"You need practice. And a bit of help." There was a smear of pizza sauce on Brian's cheek. Nick reached out and swiped it off with his thumb. "We didn't charge Mario's garden service with anything illegal. He can be a reference."

"He knows me as Bry."

"Oh. Right. Still, he can tick off some of the boxes. *Works hard. Reliable.*"

"Maybe." Brian straightened his slumping shoulders. "I'll find something. I swear. And I actually can cook."

"More than finding plates to put a pizza on? More than Velveeta?"

Brian didn't smile back. "Yeah. We took turns when I was a kid. I can make stretch loaf from scratch."

Nick decided he wanted to know. "Stretch loaf?"

"Meatloaf, but when you only have a little bit of ground beef. You mix in bread and canned beans or peas and an egg and plenty of ketchup. It's not bad."

"I think we can spring for real ground beef, if you cook it. I never learned how. None of my foster moms could be bothered to teach me. I'm good with a microwave."

"What happened to your family?" Brian quickly added, "You don't have to say."

"No big mystery. Dad died when I was five, Mom when I was seven. There was no one around who wanted us."

"Us?"

He hadn't meant to say that. He added casually, "I have a sister, Ariana. She doesn't live around here." *I don't know where she lives. I don't even know if she's alive.* He had a sudden urge to ask Brian to help find her. All that weird talent— surely it could be used to Find Ariana? But after seventeen years there was no chance, no way to get something of hers for Brian to latch onto. It wouldn't work, and trying would hurt like hell. He'd made his peace with letting her go. There was no reason to open that wound again.

He stood, covering a sudden ache in his chest by bending to pick up the empty pizza box. "I'll do the nonexistent dishes. You want a beer?"

"I think I'll go to bed. It's been a weird day, and the meds make me sleepy."

"Okay. See you in the morning."

"Do you have to go to work?"

"I'm still on light duty. Anyway, most of what I have to do is sign off on reams of transcripts of my recordings. I've been doing that from home." He saw Brian look away like something bothered him, so he went for a joke. "I'll expect you to make breakfast, Kitchen Man."

"Those transcripts. Are some of them... of me?"

Oh. Fuck. "Some. When the recorder wasn't smashed." He flushed a little at that too-obvious reminder that he'd already broken rules trying to protect Brian, twice. *I tried. Does that count?*

"Can I hear them?"

"No." That sounded like a really bad idea, all the way around. Not just illegal, but he really didn't want Brian to know how much of his painful honesty had been recorded, transcribed and read by half a dozen people. "I mean, if it were ever going to be used against you in evidence, you could. But as it is, most of it will be archived and never looked at again." *Unless we arrest Damon.* He tried to keep his mixed emotions out of his face.

Brian nodded slowly and stood up. "I'm gonna clean up and go to bed." He headed toward the bathroom, then stopped and slowly turned back. "Nick? Thank you. Seriously. I mean, things are a bit of a mess, but I know you're on my side. I'm grateful." He disappeared into the bathroom.

Nick grabbed the empty pop cans with an inward wince and headed to the kitchen. *You're a cop; don't forget that.* Tricking someone to get a murderer off the street was part of his job. It didn't matter who that someone was. Anyway, there was a good chance Damon would never surface, and then Brian would never know Nick had any other motive.

****

Brian squared his shoulders and looked across the parking lot to the door of the garden center. This was his fifth job interview in a week of living with Nick, and he was losing any optimism he'd ever had. He clutched the new printouts of his resumé and the letter of reference from Mario, then forced his hand to relax as the paper crumpled. He felt so stupid sometimes. If Nick hadn't read the letter aloud to him, he'd have no clue what it said.

He imagined himself proudly setting down a piece of paper that said, *"Rich man's idiot brother-in-law got a job with me because he was related to my boss!"* Nick promised it said nothing of the sort, just a basic note that said he'd done his work right, willingly, and without any problems. But how could he tell? He had nightmares that woke him with a gut-dropping rush, where some possible employer started reading his papers and it said he tracked men to their death or was dumber than a potted plant.

He plastered on a look of cheerful willingness, or possibly nausea, and walked to the door. Opened it. Said to the woman at the cash register, "I have a job interview with Mr. Knowles?"

She waved to the back. "Out there. He's inspecting the watering system. You can meet him over by the herbs."

There were probably signs, but he thought it would be okay to ask, "Can you tell me where that is?"

"Out that door, turn right, about six rows back."

"Thank you."

He crossed the store and let himself out the back into the nursery part. It smelled pleasantly of earth and green growing things, with a hint of musky compost. The closer part was covered by a canopy, the rest open to the sky. He walked back, counting six rows, turned and took a look at the people nearby. Two were women, and one was an elderly guy, clearly checking the price on a large pot of something-or-other. That made the middle-aged guy in overalls, kneeling beside one of the gravel beds, the likely candidate.

He walked over and asked from a respectful distance, "Mr. Knowles? I'm Brian Kerr. You said I could come by to talk about a job?"

"Oh, yeah." The man squinted up at him, but didn't stand. "Hey, want to give me a hand for a second? Grab this." He pointed at a thin pipe running along the outside of the railroad tie that framed the bed.

Brian hesitated for a second. He'd prepared for a job interview and worn his best, and only, pair of dress slacks. But he wanted this job, so he stuck his papers in his back pocket, knelt, and reached for the pipe.

"Hold this piece steady. Good." Knowles reached for another bit. "I'm going to unscrew this. When I do, raise that end a foot or so, so the water drains back and not out all over the place. Got it?"

"I think so. Raise this here?" He gestured with his free hand.

"Right." Knowles worked the short section, until suddenly the pipe came apart. A little gush of dirty water escaped, soaking into the knee of Brian's slacks. He quickly lifted his end of the pipe so the flow stopped.

Knowles glanced at him. "Got it?"

"Yes, sir."

Knowles dug inside his end of the pipe with a wire, and dragged out a clump of something nasty. He shook it off onto the rock bed. "Knew there was a blockage. Damned if I know how that got in there. Okay, let's put it together."

Brian lowered his end as directed and Knowles recoupled the pipe. Then he stood and Brian did the same, aware that his slacks were now wrinkled and dirty and wet. Knowles glanced him up and down. "So, you're here about the job?"

"Yes, sir."

"Hm. Any experience working in a nursery?"

"Not quite. I did work for a landscaper. I have a letter." He wiped his fingers on his already-grubby slacks, dug Mario's brief page out of his pocket, and passed it over.

Knowles glanced at it, then stuck it in his own pocket. "Fair enough. So tell me, what do you think is your best talent? Why should I hire you?"

Brian tried to come up with something that would sound right. "I can work hard. I keep my word. I don't drink or goof off." He bit his tongue as, for some reason, Bry's words, Bry's rhythm, wanted to come out. Instead he said, "I'm pretty good at figuring out how to make something work." He'd been jury-rigging stuff for years, until Marston came into their lives.

"You look like you'd fry in the sunshine."

Brian knew he was flushing. "Yeah, a bit. But that's what hats and sunscreen are for."

"Mm. How strong are you? We're talking about moving rocks and bags of dirt, trees with big root balls. It's hard work."

"I'm stronger than I look."

Knowles pointed at a bag of gravel off to the left. "Can you bring that over here?"

Brian hoped so. He couldn't read the weight on it, but he bent his knees and used his whole arms, and was glad he had. He was able to stagger over with it and put it down again without dropping it, but he had a tough time hiding the effort it took. He dusted his hands, aware that his good shirt was now as grubby as his good pants.

"Mm." Knowles tipped his ball cap back a bit more. "So what do you think you do worst?"

Brian took a breath and said simply, "I don't read. I can't. I'm not stupid, I'm... I have dyslexia. So if you leave me a note or instructions, I'd have to find someone to read it to me." When Knowles didn't comment, one way or the other, he added, "I'm trying to work on it. I might find a new teacher." Nick had suggested he could help, but Brian already depended on Nick way too much. He'd manage another way.

Knowles gestured at Brian's clothes. "You got a bit dirty. Are you mad about that?"

"Huh? No. I'll have to do laundry tonight, though."

"But you don't mind I made you kneel in the dirt?"

Brian shrugged. "Maybe I should have been smarter about what I wore to come here." Of course he should have. Who applied for a casual labor job dressed like an office worker? He'd wanted to make a good impression, and had only managed to look dumb.

Knowles nodded. "Well, I hate to say it, but I filled the position. But I like you. If you leave your contact information with the lady at the cashier's desk, I'll keep you in mind for the next opening."

He said some other things too, but Brian didn't really hear them. Five times he'd had to tell people his painful secret. *I can't read. I'm not stupid, I just seem stupid.* Five times he'd been turned away. He'd known it would happen, but Nick's optimism had made him imagine it might not matter. Of course it did. He realized Knowles was holding out his hand, and he shook it automatically.

"Thanks for your time," he managed to say, before turning around and heading back across the nursery. Knowles had said to leave his name with the desk lady, but who was he kidding? Brian didn't want to look at anyone. He headed out the side gate instead.

The street in front of the gate had no sidewalk. Apparently this was one of those suburbs that expected everyone to drive everywhere. Brian walked along the road on the grass, not looking at the cars that went by. *Now what? Now where?*

Nick had said not to worry about money right now. Nick had said lots of things that were meant to be kind and which burned, because each one meant that he didn't see Brian as a real equal. Cooking a few meals, fixing the loose hinge on the door, or lugging a load of clothes three blocks to the laundromat didn't count for much. He'd done that kind of stuff when he was ten. An adult paid rent and bought groceries.

So what was left? He knew about ways to get cash in a tough part of town, but there wasn't one of them that he could expect a cop like Nick to turn a blind eye to. Anyway, he'd never been any good at grift, theft, or hustle. When Damon had needed a partner to do more than look dumb and innocent, he'd always picked Lori.

He could stand on a street corner begging with a cardboard sign. Except he couldn't write out a sign… He raised one hand and smacked his own cheek for that bit of self-pity. *Dumbass. Focus.*

There was always his gift, his Finder sense. Damon had talked many times about what he called *monetizing* Brian's talent. Damon had chosen Marston, but Brian remembered the other options he'd suggested.

Of them all, the one that felt the least slimy, the least like taking advantage, was the idea of Finding someone with a reward already on their head. Someone that Crime Stoppers or a watch group would pay money to Find. It wasn't like asking the family of a missing person to pay him to Find their loved one. It wasn't likely to lead to an avalanche of people begging him to do it again, especially if he could keep his method on the down low.

There was only one problem. He'd always assumed Damon would be there to handle the actual contact with the reward people, to drive where he pointed, and to catch him when he passed out. But maybe there was a way around that. If he could somehow arrange it. A taxi maybe. With orders… no, he didn't want to go to a hospital. And he couldn't pay an hour of taxi time up front. But somehow.

He didn't realize how far he'd walked until a hint of breeze made him look up to see the sun much lower in the sky. His face felt tight and hot, and the tops of his ears hurt. He touched his forehead and realized that for all his acting smart about sunscreen, he'd managed to fry himself. Lovely. Perfect. His eyes watered. He wasn't even smart enough to come in out of the sun.

He was out of the residential area into a section with small businesses. He moved into the shade under the awning of a hair salon and pulled out his phone, and turned the ringer back on. It warbled annoyingly, and the little telephone scroll symbol blinked at him. He tapped the icon for his voicemail.

"You have four new messages. First new message sent today at..." He listened through Nick asking if he was ready to be picked up yet, Nick asking if he was going to be much longer, Nick demanding that he answer his phone, Nick yelling at him that if he was dead or kidnapped or something he was going to kill him. He pressed the button for returning the call, and Nick's phone rang once, twice.

"Brian! Where the hell are you? Are you okay?"

"I'm fine. I, um."

"I went by the garden center after three fuckin' hours and they said you'd interviewed and left."

"He'd already filled the job."

"Oh." Nick's heat eased off a bit. "That's too bad. So where did you go?"

"Walking. Thinking. And no jokes."

"About what?"

"Me thinking."

"Dammit, Brian, you know I know that dumb thing is an act."

"Not always. Not really."

"Stop. Listen, tell me where you are now."

He looked around. There was a road and another road and a sign he couldn't read, and a hardware store and the salon, with signs he couldn't read either. "Hell if I know. I'll keep walking. Sometime I'll end up somewhere familiar." Or the river. Or a cool dark woods where he could sit and catch his breath.

"Screw that. Is there a shop, a house, a fucking pedestrian walking by?"

"I'm outside a hair place."

"So go inside and say, 'I'm a bit turned around. What's the intersection out there?' And tell me what they say."

"Um." He flinched. "Just like that?"

"We're gay guys. We don't have to follow the straight guy handbook. We're allowed to ask for directions."

He was surprised into a gasp and a laugh, his breath lost at that simple statement said out loud. *We're gay guys.* It shook him out of his funk enough to make him do as he was told. The girl at the salon desk told him the cross streets without much interest, and he went back out and relayed them to Nick.

Nick swore softly. "You did get a bit off course, huh?"

"I don't know." His face hurt, and now he thought about it, his feet hurt.

"Look, stay put, all right? Stay right there. You make me hunt for you and I swear I'll order anchovies on the pizza for the next month."

"You hate anchovies."

"You hate them worse. It'll be worth it."

"I'll stay put." He suddenly had no energy at all. He put his back to the brick wall of the building and leaned, tempted to slide down to sit on the pavement. He didn't want to look like a homeless guy, though.

Nick said, "Keep your phone turned on. I'll be about twenty minutes."

"I'm sorry."

"Shut up and stay put, okay?"

Brian clicked off the call and tucked the phone in his pocket. Even under the awning, the air was hot and heavy. Brian felt like his body was draped in lead. His head ached and sweat glued his shirt to his back. The hollow feel in his stomach made him wonder if he was coming down with something. Probably he'd just missed a meal.

Counting all the ways his body didn't feel right distracted him, and it took a squawk of the car horn for him to realize that Nick had pulled over at the curb in front of him.

He pushed away from the wall and got in the passenger side heavily. Nick glanced at him as he pulled back into traffic. "You look hot." Nick smiled. "And not in a good way."

Brian grimaced, pulling his shirt away from his chest. "Too much sun." The AC in the car was a sharp contrast, and he shivered violently and hugged his arms across his chest. His forearms were pink and sore too.

At least Nick didn't give him the lecture like Damon would have. He just said, "Sorry the job didn't work out. I'll get online when we get home and see what else is out there."

Brian decided now was not the time to bring up his idea, so he just said a kind of noncommittal "Hm." He really felt like crap. Which he'd brought on himself, of course, but he decided to just give in to it. He huddled in his seat and closed his eyes. He'd try to be strong again later.

When they got back to the house Nick said, "You look like you belong in bed."

Brian wished he could riff on that idea, but he felt tender to the touch all over and probably looked half-fried. Instead he said, "Could you do me a favor? On the computer?"

Nick unlocked the door and waved him inside. "Sure. What?"

"Can you see if there's still that reward offered for the guy, Fred Young? The one who shot up his girlfriend and kids." He headed into the living room and didn't realize until he eased himself down on the couch that Nick had stopped by the front door, frowning.

"Why?"

"Why do you think?"

"I'm afraid to ask." Nick set his keys into the dish on the counter and came over slowly.

"Three months ago, there was a reward of twenty thousand dollars for information leading to him being found and arrested. Damon said it was a pity Marston would never let me do stuff like that."

"Brian, that idea sucks donkey balls. You know that, right?"

"Why? It's something I can do. Probably. Unless he's dead or out of state, in which case, no harm, no foul, right? Why not try? Twenty grand is enough for me to pay my way here for months. Maybe a year."

"It's risky." Nick sat on the other end of the couch, looking at him. "Risky two ways. First because this is a murderer you're talking about. You can't just waltz up to him and slap a pair of cuffs on him."

"I know that." He tried to smile. "That would be your job."

"Thanks so much." Nick shook his head. "Even if you could Find him and he did get busted, what then? Are you really ready to be out about this talent of yours? The one thing Marston did right was keep you from being outed to all the kooks and crazies and desperate people out there who'd want a piece of you."

"Marston didn't care. He liked knowing he owned proof of the paranormal, that no one else had. He liked keeping me secret because it made him seem scarily powerful when he could Find someone anywhere, anytime."

"Sure. But it worked out for you, too."

"There are dozens of people out there who claim to be psychic," Brian argued. "Some of them have a success or two. Most people still don't believe it. I can do this, get the money, and walk away."

"Not alone, you can't. You'd need my help, and I don't think it's a good idea."

Brian sighed. "I bet I could find someone else to help me for a cut of the twenty K."

"Oh, hell, no!" Nick leaned toward him, glaring. "That had better be a threat, not a plan."

"You want it to be a threat?"

Brian jumped when Nick slammed a fist into the back of the couch, hard enough to shake it. "No! Yes! Fuck!"

"I need the money." Brian rubbed the treacherous stinging out of his eyes. "Why can't you understand?"

"I do. Hell, I know it's hard for you to feel like you're dependent. But there must be a better way. You could file for unemployment, maybe. Assistance. Something."

"Right. I should take benefit money when I don't need it, and that'll make me feel really adult."

"At least it won't make you feel like a freak."

Brian threw himself backwards into the corner of the couch. His queasy stomach was doing escape loops, and he had to talk through gritted teeth. "Is that what you think of me?"

"No! Jesus!" Nick reached for him and Brian half-rolled off the couch to avoid being touched. "Brian, you're not a freak. Not! But people are going to say it. You know they will. They'll treat you like shit and have you believing that everything you do is wrong, no matter how you use your talent. If they find out—"

"*If.*" Brian got up, his hands in fists at his side. "That's the point. I'm going to try to do this without really explaining it. Damon said the safe way to make money out of being a psychic was to make the smart people sure I was a fake. Add all kinds of mumbo jumbo, so they figure it's a fluke I ever find anything."

"That's... okay, yeah, maybe you could make it work. But who're you going to get to help you that you can trust?"

Brian opened his fists slowly and deliberately, dropping his eyes to the worn carpet. "I was kind of still hoping it would be you."

Nick was silent so long that Brian had to look up. Nick sat staring at him, his lower lip caught in his teeth, eyes hazy and uncertain. Eventually he said, "A pity you don't have Damon around, huh?"

"What?" Brian shook his head, feeling like his sore brain wasn't tracking right. "If I did, I wouldn't be doing this in the first place. I'm sure Damon had money stashed away, and he'd insist on using that instead." And right there was the trap he'd walked away from, living off Damon's crimes. "Anyhow, he's long gone."

"Do you miss him?"

Every minute. And not at all. "It's complicated." He liked who he was without Damon, a thousand times more, and yet there was a big black hole in his life. Living without Damon was like tightrope walking toward heaven, without a net.

"Could you Find Damon, if you had to?" Nick looked away as he asked, but there was an underlying intensity to his voice.

Brian wished he was sharper. His sunburn was making him shiver again, and he really wanted some Tylenol and an ice pack. Did Damon matter to Nick because Brian missed him, or because Nick remembered that kick to the head, or because he was a cop? Either way, he decided to lie. "I doubt it. He's too far away."

"Oh."

"Look, I can't do anything tonight. I'm going to bed. If you don't want to help, I'll pay someone who will. If Young's already been caught, I'm sure there's someone else with a reward on them that I can Find."

"Dammit, Brian, that's blackmail." Nick stood too. "Or extortion or something. Can you even Find on the meds you're taking? It might not work."

"I'm not taking any meds."

"The ones from the hospital, the prescriptions… that you never bothered to fill. Shit." Nick sighed. "Was that smart? Aren't you supposed to taper off drugs like that slowly?"

"Don't know. Don't care. Don't like them." Although maybe that explained why he'd felt so crappy off and on all week. He'd assumed it was the stress and all the changes, but maybe it was chemicals still messing with him.

Nick moved toward him. "How about a truce? You go lie down in bed and don't do anything rash. I'll look up Fred Young online. For all we know, he's been caught, and the reward is gone. If not, well, hell, then we can talk about it. I'm not saying there's no way at all that I'd help you. I'm just saying it would need some very careful planning, right?"

"Right."

"Can I get you anything?"

"I'll be fine. I'll take some Tylenol before I go up."

"And water. I heard somewhere that you should drink lots of water for a bad sunburn."

"Yes, Mother."

"No one likes a smartass."

"You do."

It was just a flip answer, but Nick's eyes warmed and his lips curved up. "Yeah, you know, I do. Go put some burn cream on your nasty pink skin, smartass."

Brian couldn't manage an answer, so he went into the bathroom. The mirror over the sink showed that "nasty pink" was generous. His forehead and nose were bright red, his cheeks and arms blotchy. From a lifetime of living with his pasty white skin, he knew that was going to hurt, a lot, and then peel for a week, until he looked like he was trying out for a zombie movie. All while living with the hottest guy in the state. Who might already, no matter how he'd backtracked, consider Brian a freak. *Just kill me now.*

Since he didn't have an assassin lurking in the shower to oblige him, he washed in cool water, gulped down a couple of pills, and soaked a towel to take upstairs with him. He heard Nick, busy out of sight in the kitchen, as he took his par-broiled carcass upstairs. Stretching out on the bed, he draped the wet towel over his face and waited for the pain-killer to kick in.

He lost track of time, because he jumped and the now-warm towel slid off his face when Nick said, "I brought you some water."

"Thanks." He tossed the useless towel aside and took the bottle Nick held down to him. It was too much effort to uncap it, so he reached sideways and put it down on the crate beside his bed.

Nick hovered, looking worried. "You think you'll want dinner?"

He must have missed lunch, but he wasn't even slightly hungry. He could stand to lose a few pounds anyway. "Nope, just sleep."

"You should wear a hat or some sunscreen with that sexy pale skin like you have."

"I *know* that!" he snapped, before the rest of the words registered. *Sexy?* Well, even if Nick did have weird tastes in guys, Brian wasn't going to be sexy or pale for the next week at least. He closed his eyes.

After a minute, Nick said, "I, um, hope things aren't too screwed up between us. If you need anything just yell."

"Thanks," Brian said, because he knew perfectly well who'd screwed up all day, all week, really, and it wasn't the cop in the room. "Don't worry about me."

"Hah. Now he says it," Nick grumbled, so softly that Brian wasn't entirely sure if it was meant for him or not. "'Don't worry,' like I have any choice at all." His footsteps retreated down the stairs.

Brian was left to try to sleep, with a face that felt too tight, feet that ached, and a hollow space inside he wasn't sure how to fill. Yet for once, he'd got through a day's worth of hard moments as himself, no hiding, no letting Bry act dumb to diffuse things. And if he had no job, at least he had a plan. So his life wasn't a total failure. Yet.

Chapter 25

Nick parked the car and glanced over at Brian. His skin was still pink and peeling at his hairline and the tops of his ears, and he looked tired. In the last two weeks, he'd tried doggedly to find work through a bunch more failed job applications, and one interview that left him silent and miserable. Nick's arguments had worn down as Brian had slipped further and further away. He talked less, laughed rarely, and stared off into space way too often. He hadn't quite resorted to Bry's short, repetitive phrases, but there were times when Nick thought he was using a dull, uncaring, almost-Bry front to cover how he really felt.

God, he hated seeing that. Something had to change, and they hadn't had any better ideas, so here they were. "Are you sure?" he asked one more time.

Brian didn't answer, just opened his door and got out.

All right, then, show time. Nick did the same and stepped ahead of him as they reached the door. "Let me set it up, like we planned."

"Yes, Nick."

He glanced at Brian, but the bland steadiness of his eyes didn't give any clues. *Fuck, this could go so wrong.* He strode up to the reception desk confidently. "Officer Rugo and Mr. Kerr. Mr. Emerson is expecting us."

The receptionist checked her computer. "Oh, yes. Come this way, please." She touched a button, then got up and headed down the hallway to her right. Nick followed her, with Brian at his elbow. She gestured them through an open door and turned away.

The room was an office, neither bare-bones nor lavish. The big desk at the end was wood, but not fancy, and the man seated behind it wore his shirt sleeves rolled up and no tie. He stood as they came in, showing himself to be a big guy going slightly to fat. He had a shaved head and bushy salt-and-pepper eyebrows. Nick estimated him about sixty, a man used to commanding others, from the way he stood without greeting them, eyeing them like he thought they might crap on the carpet.

Nick didn't have as much innate respect for authority figures as he probably should, for a cop. He figured that'd helped him be successful undercover though, so he wasn't too eager to change. Before Emerson could say anything, Nick strode forward, dropped sideways into one of the two straight chairs in front of the desk, and leaned casually, elbow on the back, crossing his ankles. He looked up at Emerson in what should have been an inferior position, except his unconcern kind of worked against that. He said, "Hey, you're expecting us. I'm Rugo."

Emerson glanced down at him, a flash of surprise crossing his face. He took another look at Brian who still stood by the door, then turned his attention back to Nick. "You said you're a cop?"

"MPD." Nick pulled out his badge folder and flicked it onto the desk.

Emerson picked it up and checked it, noting down the badge number, before leaning forward far enough to pass it back. He hesitated visibly, then sat and gestured at the other chair. "Have a seat, Mr. Kerr?"

"Bry," Brian said in his thick voice. Nick hid a flash of surprise. They'd talked about Brian keeping in the background as much as possible, but he hadn't meant that much. Too late to change it now.

"Do sit down, Bry." It was a good sign that Emerson's tone got less harsh and not more. "We need to discuss this."

"Okay." Brian came and sat, straight as a kid in school, feet together, hands folded in his lap, eyes down.

Emerson hesitated again, then said, "Officer Rugo, you said this was not official police business, correct?"

"Not even slightly. The badge is just for confidence and identification, you know. That we're not here to scam you." The MPD would not be amused if he claimed any kind of authority for this little exercise.

"Mm." That wasn't total agreement, but Emerson added, "Can you repeat your proposal?"

Nick had laid it out in the email that was probably up on Emerson laptop screen, but he said easily, "Sure. It's a win-win. You provide my psychic— Brian, here— with one item of Fred Young's, something he owned long enough for it to be identified with him and that has no real monetary value. If

Young is nearby, if the item is usable and the psychic gets a hit, we'll give the local cops any clues we can to help find Young."

"He's armed and dangerous, you know," Emerson said.

"Obviously. We'll call in the locals, who'll do the actual arresting. Once Young is in custody and booked, and his identity is confirmed, we'll call you. The posted reward of twenty thousand dollars will be paid to Brian Kerr by cashier's check within seventy-two hours."

"I'd rather do an electronic transfer."

Nick hid a grin as he realized Emerson was planning for success and not just failure. "No doubt, but Mr. Kerr prefers to keep his banking information private. We'll give you an address, if you prefer to courier the check."

Emerson turned to Brian. "What about you, Bry? Is this how you want it?"

"Yes."

"Is Mr. Rugo a friend?"

"He's my roommate."

It was impressive how just a shift of tone and a change in posture turned Brian, a guy who Nick was starting to think of as half genius, into slow, stolid, limited Bry. Nick wondered uncomfortably how much was deliberate acting. He'd had no luck getting Brian to agree to any kind of therapy or counseling, or even refilling his meds, despite Bry having five months of health insurance left that might pay for it. After this incredibly wrong-headed little adventure was over, he was going to give that discussion another try. Assuming they got through the next few days without any disasters.

Nick cleared his throat. "I assure you, the money will go into Mr. Kerr's own account. He will control it."

Bry said, "I'm not completely dumb. Can we do this thing now?" with just enough rush and confusion to make the first part sound like a lie.

"Um. Sure." Mr. Emerson pulled a printout from his desk drawer and passed it over to Brian, deliberately not putting it within Nick's reach. "Is this right?"

Brian took the paper and flicked it to Nick without even looking at it. "Is it right, Nick?"

Nick read it over, making sure that, as far as he could tell, it was the same simple contract he'd had a lawyer friend write and email to Emerson. "Looks like it. Mr. Emerson has signed it."

"Okay."

Nick briefly thought about reaching over and just taking one of Emerson's pens out of the desk penholder, but it didn't pay to be too much of an asshole. He gestured. "May I?"

Emerson passed him a ballpoint. "Here."

Nick laid the page on the corner of the desk, gave Brian the pen, and pointed. "Sign here."

Brian scrawled his loopy signature. Nick lifted the top copy for him to sign the second, and passed one back.

Emerson took it with a wordless grunt and slid it into the drawer. "First contract for a psychic I've ever signed. Now what?"

"You give us the item. We go off and he does his thing, and with luck, we find Young."

Emerson reached down somewhere out of sight by his feet, and brought up a ball cap. "Here, this should be old enough."

Nick reached for it, but Brian beat him to it. He took the cap in both hands and stood.

Emerson said, "Wait! Can he, um, test and make sure it'll work? I have other things, if that doesn't."

Nick looked at Brian. "Your call. Want to try it out here, or plan to come back if it flops?"

Bry licked his lips, and looked down, mashing the cap between his palms. "I should try."

"Okay. Sit down?"

"Uh-huh." Brian sat back down, pressed the cap to his forehead, and closed his eyes.

They sat in silence for a minute. Brian was still as stone. Emerson's gaze shifted between them, something cautious in his expression. Brian opened his eyes. He reached over and set the hat in front of Emerson on the desk. "It's your hat. Yours."

"What?" Nick stared at him, then glared at Emerson. "Is he right? What the hell was that?"

Emerson shifted in his chair. "A test?"

"What the fuck for?" Nick was aware his voice had risen. Of course, if he'd been Emerson, he'd have done the same, but his anger heated anyway.

Finding took a hell of a lot out of Brian. Damn it, they'd made plans for an IV if it got bad. How *dared* Emerson jerk him around just for a test?

Nick shoved his chair back. "We're going. There are other people who'll pay for us to find someone. You can stuff your reward—" He shut up when Brian reached out quickly and grabbed his wrist, clamping down hard.

Emerson said, "Well, can you blame me? I mean, *psychic*? It was a simple test—"

"Which you didn't know how hard he'd need to work to pass, right?" Nick slammed his palm on the desk. Brian's grip on his other wrist became painful, and Nick glanced at him. Brian shook his head, a tiny motion, and released his arm. Nick gritted his teeth and reined in his anger. "Okay, sorry Bry, it's your call. But if he dicks you around any more, I say we walk."

Brian said calmly to Emerson, "Do you have something good? Something real?"

A little flush rose in Emerson's face. "Yes. I have a shirt of Fred's here." He reached down again and came up with a gray fleece sweatshirt, which he held out across the desk.

Nick caught Emerson's wrist to halt the motion. "This better be the right one."

"It is." Emerson's lip curled. "As I'm sure your psychic will tell you."

Brian reached over and took the shirt. Emerson and Nick sat back in their chairs, although this time Nick knew he was breathing too fast, and the tension of a frown tightened his face. He pulled air in deliberately through his nose and tried for his cop stoneface. He didn't usually lose his temper with the public like that, not until he was out anonymously afterward, working off steam.

With Brian around, he was having trouble keeping his life organized. There was an unfamiliar mix of the personal and the professional, and it put Nick off-balance. He felt protective and angry, and keeping his cool was way, way too hard for someone who'd dealt with dirtbags every day for three years.

Brian said, "The shirt is not his. Not this man's. It's someone's. I think I can Find someone. Maybe."

Nick managed a steady flat tone. "All right then." He turned to Emerson. "If he does find the person that belongs to, and it's not Fred Young, I know the contract says you don't owe us. But you know how damned stupid you'll feel, especially after I leak the story?"

"That one is Fred's," Emerson replied, dragging his gaze away from Brian. "You think he can do it?"

"Maybe." They'd deliberately downplayed Brian's success rate, so success could look like a fluke. "You'd better hope."

Emerson gave him a glare of his own. "And don't bullshit me about going to the press. You're the one with the no-publicity clause in the contract."

"If you make him fail, there'll be nothing on our end for them to find. Just you looking like a fool."

"If he fails, it will be because this psychic stuff is crap. I still think you're covering for a friend of Fred's who doesn't want to be seen ratting him out."

Nick shrugged. "If we are, it's still a win, right? As long as we get Fred Young." It was actually a good cover, and he'd happily use it to keep Brian's talent a secret.

Emerson's curt nod held a hint of irritation. "Keep in touch. I'll expect progress reports."

"You'll hear when we're done, like the contract says." Nick stood quickly. "Come on, Bry."

They left the office, passing the receptionist at a brisk pace. She looked up curiously, but didn't speak. It was warm outside, the midmorning sun already summer-intense. Nick opened the car door and stood outside it for a moment before getting in and starting the AC. Brian took his seat without comment, the sweatshirt clutched to his chest.

Nick kept the car in park, letting the AC kick in until cool air hit their faces, scanning the parking lot for movement.

Brian reached for his bottle of energy drink in the cupholder, drained the dregs, and asked, "What are we waiting for?"

"Waiting to see if he's going to have us followed. He seems like the type."

"Oh. Anything?"

"Nothing obvious. I'll make sure we lose any tail once we start, though. Or do you want to drive around a bit first and see?"

"No." Brian's voice was strained. "Let's do it." He closed his eyes and held his hand steadied on his knee, index finger pointing left.

"Okay. Like last time? Go where you point? Will it throw you off if I detour a bit?"

"It shouldn't. It's like a compass, not a map."

"Got it." Nick pulled out of the lot and turned right, taking a quick look at Brian as he straightened out. "Do you have to close your eyes? Just curious."

"No. But it's easier."

"No problem." Nick drove steadily for a couple of miles south and west, following Brian's steady direction. He kept an eye on the rearview, and as they hit the next suburb, he decided that blue sedan had hung on his bumper too long. "Going through a parking garage," he said. "A few turns coming up."

"All right."

There was a sign for a local mall. He took a left and a right, and the same damned car hung with him, so he pulled into the indoor part of the lot, headed left, up a level and out a different exit. The sedan hadn't followed him in. Either they were innocent, or they were waiting for him to emerge. Either way, their tail seemed clear. "Done," he told Brian. "Getting back on course."

"Was someone actually following us?"

"Maybe. But 'was' is the right word, because they're not back there now."

"Okay."

Nick took another look at Brian. The tendons in his neck stood out, and his skin was paler than ever, the remaining sunburned strips showing pink on his forehead and ears. "You hanging in there?"

"I'm fine. He's out there. That way." Brian swallowed and cleared his throat, still pointing.

Nick shut up and drove.

They hit city streets, traffic-filled and potholed. The car bounced, and Nick had to slow down. He kept his eyes peeled for bikes and pedestrians, watching Brian in fast sideways glances. They stopped at a light, then another, and another. Brian still pointed ahead and slightly left. Nick swung over one block, then straightened out again on a smaller street. "Can you tell if we're close?"

"Maybe? Yeah, not too far."

Another six blocks and then Brian's hand suddenly tracked right and back. Nick pulled over. Brian's head was cranked over his shoulder, his eyes still closed.

"We passed him?"

"Yes." It was a thread of sound between Brian's pale lips.

"Okay. I'm going round the block. Keep pointing."

"M'kay."

A few turns let Nick figure out that Young was somewhere near a row of small stores, with apartments above them, and taller tenements behind. It was a crappy neighborhood, but probably not too dangerous. At least not in daylight. He found a space along the curb on the far side of the block and pulled over. "Problem."

"Hm?"

"Still too many possible locations to call it in. We'll have to get out."

"Okay."

"You have to open your eyes."

"Oh. Yeah." Brian sat up straighter and blinked blearily at him.

Nick leaned closer. "You with me? Can you walk a bit? Because if you're going to crash, I'd rather tell Emerson to stuff his fee."

That made Brian frown, looking sharper and less dazed. "I can do it. Where are we?"

"Richfield. At least, I think so. Which kind of sucks because they have their own PD and I'm not one of them. Still, cops are cops. We should be all right." He got out his phone, and pulled up a number for the RPD, ready for one-touch dialing. "All right. Which way?"

They both got out. Brian looked around, blinking hard as if the sun was too bright, but then gestured. "There."

Nick moved in close beside him, but didn't touch him as they walked down the sidewalk.

It was kind of like a life-and-death game of *Hotter-Colder*. Or maybe *Dowsing for Douchebags* as they walked along, passed the spot, turned back. Brian kept both hands close to his chest, clutching the sweatshirt, moving only his finger. Forward, to the side, back.

On the third pass, Nick was pretty sure Brian was indicating a small hardware store with a couple of apartments above it. Brian had begun swaying like a drunk on his last legs. Nick stepped up against him and put a hand under his elbow, as he raised his phone and dialed Richfield.

It took a few minutes and the invoking of his shield number to get through to someone who would actually listen. Brian got heavier, and Nick shifted his leg to brace Brian's hip. "Look it up," he told the next cop on the other end of the line. "Fred Young. Forty-one years old, six-one, a hundred and ninety, brown on brown, wanted for the murder of one of his kids and attempted murder of two others and his girlfriend in Minneapolis. I have an informant who tells me he's currently at this address." Nick rattled it off again. "He's listed as A&D, so you'll want a tactical unit standing by. And you'd better move fast, because he could be gone at any moment."

He listened to the guy on the other end snap out a couple of orders, then come back to him with more questions. Brian was shaking, fine tremors that traveled the length of his body. He slumped farther sideways. Nick said into the phone, "Gotta go. I'll call again if my informant has news." He hung up, silenced the ringer, and stuck the phone in his pocket.

Brian blinked at him. "Are they coming?"

"Yeah. I think so. You want to sit down?"

"Not yet. I'll fall asleep. I want to be sure they get him."

"You've done your bit." Nick thought *pass out* was more likely than *fall asleep*. "Come on. The car's back here."

"No. Wait."

"I'm sure they'll get him."

"I'm not." Brian cocked his head as if listening. There were sirens in the distance, coming closer.

Nick cursed under his breath. Surely they weren't dumb enough to come in hot, trying to arrest a fugitive. It had to be a badly timed coincidence.

Brian said, "He's moving."

"Fuck."

"That way." Brian pointed to their right. "Come on." He broke out of Nick's hold and hurried off.

Nick swore and jogged up to him. "Look, you can't get too close, right? Not your job."

"Call them. Tell them he's moving."

Nick caught his arm to slow him down. "I will, but—"

"He shot kids, Nick. He killed a little kid. We can stop him."

Dammit! Nick shifted his grip to support. "All right, but we're not getting in close, you hear me? You're a civilian."

"Do you have your gun?"

"Yeah, but this isn't my city. Just keep pointing." He managed to get the phone redialed and to his ear. "Hey. On Fred Young. Listen up." He didn't wait for a response. "The asshole is running, headed west from the named location, probably along the alley." He figured he'd see the guy if he was on the sidewalk, but Brian was pointing parallel, so presumably a back alley. "On foot, I think." From the angle of Brian's hand, they weren't losing any ground, like they would if Young was moving fast in a car.

There was some kind of response on the phone, but Brian stumbled; Nick focused on catching him and hauling him upright, and he missed it. He stuffed the phone in his pocket, the line still open. If this got bad, he wanted a hand free for his gun. He tugged Brian slower and sideways, ducking behind him until he could change arms for support, freeing up his right hand. A few people on the sidewalk stared at them, but so far no one got in the way. A marked patrol car pulled over to the curb up ahead, lights on but siren silent. At least they got that part right. The cop driving it jumped out, glancing in their direction.

There was a screech of brakes from their right, and then as Nick slowed his pace, Brian's hand suddenly swung forward. A big man burst out of the gap between two buildings ahead of them, looking back over his shoulder. The cop beside the patrol car hesitated, looking from Nick to Brian, unaware of the man behind him. How many six-foot-one guys would be running in the summer heat around here?

Nick saw Young reaching for his hip, saw the kid in uniform, who had to be a rookie, still staring at Brian instead. Nick dropped, dragging Brian down to the pavement with him, and yelled, pointing, "Gun! Young!"

The rookie's attention snapped around. He was fast enough to draw before Young could get his gun clear of his pocket. "Freeze! Police! Freeze!" Young hesitated, hand at his side. Suddenly there were more cops, yelling, guns out. Nick stayed down, covering Brian with his body, cheek against his hair. Every muscle tensed to stone, waiting for someone to pull a trigger.

Then Young raised his hands. "Don' shoot! Don' shoot!" His voice was slurred, his gestures sloppy. *Drunk as hell.* The cops closed in on him, guns out, voices loud.

Nick closed his eyes for a second in relief. He murmured, "Hey, Brian, they got him. You're good. You're done."

Brian didn't reply, but Nick could feel the steady rise and fall of his breathing. A voice from behind Nick said, "Hands where I can see them. Don't move."

Nick froze again. All he needed was for some adrenaline-charged suburban cop to shoot him by mistake. He said clearly, "I'm Nick Rugo, Minneapolis

PD. I have a badge in my right hip pocket and a gun in a shoulder holster, left."

"Don't move."

"Not moving."

Someone stepped in closer, fingers reaching into his back pocket, digging around roughly. *So not the time to make a crack about groping me.* He held still while they dug out his badge folder, then reached around to pat him down and ease the gun out of his holster.

The voice said, "Get off that guy. Move real slow."

Without shifting an inch, Nick said, "Did you get the other guy? The fugitive? I'm not moving till you say yes."

"He's down and cuffed. Move."

Slowly Nick eased sideways. Brian lay sprawled on the sidewalk, his face pale as milk. Another cop hurried over. "Is he hurt? Shot?"

"No. Just fainted, I think." Nick reached for Brian's shoulder.

"Don't touch him." A hand grabbed Nick's arm and hauled him back. "Get an ambulance here."

"Fuck." Nick glanced around at the ever-growing crowd. "Look, he's a friend. He…" He remembered Brian's fallback explanation. "He has narcolepsy. When things get stressful, he passes out. There's a card in his wallet."

They found the wallet and the card, but Brian still ended up in an ambulance when the paramedics couldn't wake him. Nick ended up— where else— at the Richfield cop shop.

They'd had a plan for this. A third choice plan, because the first choice had been to get Young into police custody without ever being seen in person, which would have let Nick keep Brian an "unnamed informant." Second choice would have been getting Brian the hell out of Dodge after they were IDed. This was a distant third. It involved, well, not lying to cops, but a lot of misdirection. Okay, maybe some lying.

Yes, Nick said, he'd been told by an unnamed informant where to find Young. No, he couldn't reveal the guy's name. The guy was scared. Yes, he brought a friend along in the car, but he'd never meant for Brian to get out of the damned car in the first place. No, Brian was not a cop or a criminal or undercover or anything. He was a damned stupid idiot who thought he was invincible and was curious about Young.

Nick managed to say that with enough heat that the RPD cops kind of believed him.

Yes, he'd waited to tell the RPD what he was doing because he didn't completely trust his informant to be right. Yeah, he should have made the call anyway. Yeah, he should have known the address was out of the Minneapolis city limits. Yeah, he was an idiot.

He fell into cop mode where nothing made him mad, nothing shook him. He could do this all day. Short answers with not much content. No, he couldn't name his informant. No, he hadn't expected Young would run. Yes, a perimeter would have been smart. Hindsight was 20/20. No. Yes. No.

He really, really wanted to know how Brian was doing, but when he asked, they gave him just about as much information back. He didn't want to seem too worried. Narcolepsy. Routine. He swallowed his anxiety and leaned back in his chair, feet spread, hands easy on his thighs. Next round.

Eventually, the interrogation room door opened but it wasn't another RPD guy. Olson stood there, looking at him with a twisted expression. "Rugo. You couldn't wait to do this until you were off my books?"

"What, boss?"

"Whatever you did. We just heard our last defendant is copping a plea. The case is done. You're going back to active patrol next week, dammit, under someone else. But no, you couldn't wait."

"Hey, an informant told me where to find a murdering son of a bitch. I was supposed to wait?"

"You were supposed to hand it over to the local PD."

"That's what I did, boss. Once it was verified."

She sighed. "Well, RPD says you're free to go. I'll even give you a lift. Where to?"

Nick shoved his chair back and stood, the sudden drop of adrenaline making his knees shake momentarily. He covered it by pushing the chair back into position, leaning on the back as he lined it up square. He straightened, worked his shoulders out. "Am I getting my phone back? And my gun?"

"Since you didn't fire it, or even pull it...?" Olson paused for confirmation. Nick shook his head. "Then I imagine so. Come on."

He did, although it involved a form and a wait and a rise in blood pressure. Maybe that was a good thing. At least he didn't feel limp anymore. He took a moment, standing in the hallway while Olson was talking to one of the brass, to call Emerson. Voice mail. He left a message. "Young is in custody in Richfield. Contact me when the payment is ready."

He shoved his phone in his pocket as Olson turned to wave him over. "Yo, Rugo. Time to go."

In the car, heading back to where he'd left his own parked, he leaned back and closed his eyes. He should have known that wouldn't stop her though. "Why was Brian Kerr with you?"

"I give him a ride lots of times. I didn't want to take the time to drive him home first?"

"Are you asking me?"

It felt less like lying that way. He sighed. "No, ma'am. I should have kept him out of it."

"Yeah, you should. Are you going to tell me who your informant is?"

"No, ma'am."

Olson huffed a breath. "Rugo, you're one hell of an undercover cop, but it amazes me that your commanding officer hasn't lost his nut, dealing with you in uniform."

He decided to be offended by that. "I'm a good patrolman."

"That's a miracle of some kind." She thought for a while. "How's Operation Lure Damon Kerr going?"

Nick shrugged. "So far I don't think he's contacted Brian."

"You don't think?"

"I'm almost certain. I'm pretty sure he'd tell me. He considers us friends." That had a bitter taste on his tongue. Although Brian was much smarter than Olson realized. Maybe smart enough to know Nick would be between a rock and a hard place if Damon ever came around. Maybe smart enough to never tell him if Damon called. Nick realized unhappily that he kind of hoped that was true. *Some cop.*

On the other hand, Brian had just helped pull a very dangerous man off the street. Young had apparently made specific threats against his ex and family again when they hauled him in— Nick's interrogators had asked if his informant ever mentioned Young's new murderous plans. Working with Brian had defused a guy who was a powder keg, ready to do more damage to innocents.

Damon's a knife in the dark.

He silenced his nagging subconscious with the thought that maybe he and Brian could do this again. Maybe they could get enough bad guys behind bars to make Nick feel less like shit about hoping Damon stayed safely gone.

He'd been quiet too long, because Olson pulled up at a stoplight and gave him a dubious look. "Are you telling me everything I need to know?"

"I hope so," Nick said honestly.

"How close are you and Kerr?"

"I'm not fucking him." Although not because he didn't want to. Over the last three weeks, he'd caught himself a dozen times reaching out to touch Brian's arm, his hand, his face; he'd gotten half-hard more than once, at some glimpse of Brian's body in an unguarded moment. Worse yet, he was learning just how much fun it was to have him around, working in the garden, laughing at a movie, or cooking his surprisingly edible meals in their kitchen. Nick would have said he was the last person to want to be domestic, but he'd started liking it somewhere along the way.

It wasn't forever, of course. He'd promised to stage that fight and give the guy his independence. But before then, he wanted to get Brian into a good headspace. Maybe find a therapist. Or a teacher. There had to be a way for a guy that smart to get past his dyslexia. Maybe now Brian would relax about the cost, with twenty grand in his hands, and be willing to pursue it.

He realized Olson had said something. "Huh?"

"Never mind." She stopped, double-parked beside Nick's car. "Say hi to him when you see him. But Nick?"

"Yeah?"

"I know you tap-danced around stuff about Brian Kerr, in your reports. I let it slide because I didn't think it would've helped us bust more scumbags, and your cases were solid. If I find out later I was wrong, I'm going to come after you, got it? You'd better remember you're a cop. Remember what really counts."

Nick nodded and got out. As he stood beside his car, watching Olson drive away, he wondered what he'd do if it ever came to that. If he had to choose between Brian and upholding the law... He had the uncomfortable feeling he'd already made that call.

Chapter 26

Brian blinked his sticky eyes and squinted. The light above him was harsh and unfamiliar, but the feelings weren't. He was thirsty and starving, and yet nauseous at the same time. He clearly had used the gift that kept on giving. He tried to lick his lips, with a tongue that felt as sticky as his eyes, and slurred out, "Damon?"

"Not here," a quiet voice said off to his left.

Quiet. But not usually quiet. *Nick*. The name floated to the top of his cotton-fuzzy brain, and a lot of other things followed. He lay still and let it come together. Marston was dead. Damon was gone. Lori was pregnant with... with... he decided there were things that didn't need to be remembered right now. Nick. Nick was good to remember. He squeezed his eyes tight, then opened them wide. There was Nick, only slightly hazy, looking tired.

"Hey. Nick. Good. Hi." He cleared his raspy throat and tried to remember to be Brian. Bry was easier at first, when his thoughts tried to escape his dizzy head, but he remembered he didn't want to be Bry around Nick. Not if he could help it. "How long was I out?"

Nick glanced at his watch. "Thirty-two hours, you lazy bastard."

Something nudged his lips, and he realized it was a sliver of ice. He opened eagerly for it. The melting chill on his tongue was almost orgasmic. "Wow. That's good. Water?"

"Not till the doctor okays it."

"I'm fine." He blinked harder and looked around. He was in the hospital? Oh, yeah, that would explain the lights and the odd smells. He cleared his throat and tried to sound bright and normal. "Can we go now?"

Nick laughed, which made him look a bit less worn out. "Not yet."

"But I'm really okay. This is what happens. I sleep like a log and when I wake up I'm hungry and thirsty and—" He realized the one thing that was different this time. "—usually I have to pee. They didn't, um, put a tube in?"

Nick's smile tilted wickedly. "In your dick?" He waited a couple of beats, then said, "No, but I think you're wearing a diaper."

"Ew." Brian shuddered. Not something you wanted the hot guy you roomed with to say, ever.

"Better than a catheter."

"I guess." He coughed drily.

"More ice?"

"Please." After five or six chips he felt a lot more human. Enough to find the control for his bed and start pushing buttons. One did nothing but make a grinding noise, but the next brought the head of the bed up. That was better. Not that he minded looking up at Nick, but he'd been trying so hard for them to be equals, and this wasn't helping. He cranked himself almost upright. "So, did I Find…" He drew a blank on the name. His brain never tracked right when he first woke, but it used not to matter much. Now it really did.

"Fred Young? Yeah. You don't remember?"

"It comes back better after I get some water and something to eat." It was as good an excuse as any, and might even be true.

"I'll see what I can do, but you freaked the doctors out a bit. They couldn't figure out why you wouldn't wake up, because everything checked out normal down to the MRI scan. And the CT."

"They ran tests?"

"Hell, yeah. You're probably anemic from all the blood they drew."

"But they didn't find anything?"

"Not that they shared with me."

Brian nodded slowly. "I'm surprised they let you be here."

"I claimed to have your medical power of attorney. Which we should really make true ASAP. Since they talked to the, um, loony bin, they knew I signed off on your release plan there, so they bought it. Plus being a cop was a bonus. They didn't ask to see the paperwork."

"Oh, good." He closed his eyes for a moment. "So they let you in, but they think I'm some kind of nut case."

"Maybe. Does it matter? As long as you're healing up and they let you out?"

Brian looked over at Nick, who really did seem unconcerned. "I guess. There's nothing to heal, though. It's more like I just ran a marathon. Damon used to give me a gallon of water and a power bar when I woke up, and then I'd be at Marston's table for dinner just like always."

"You go from a coma to table manners that fast?"

"Bry has lousy table manners."

Nick laughed. "Wow. Well, that's good. That's better than I thought. It was kind of scary when you wouldn't wake up and wouldn't wake up."

"I was out for two days once," he said, wishing there were more ice chips coming. Although his thirst wasn't as bad as usual, probably because he had an IV stuck in his arm. He was starving though, the nausea turning to a hollow need for food. "Damon actually hugged me when I woke up. Only time I ever remember." It had been early on, before they had a handle on what he could do.

"I'd hug you too, if you didn't have all the tubes and wires." Nick gestured at the beeping display by the bedside, with wires leading back underneath the sheet. "Well, and if Frau Linkmeyer out there wasn't heading this way."

Brian rolled his head to see a tall, thin nurse with gray hair coming toward the windowed wall of his room. She pushed aside the curtain and hurried in. "What are you doing sitting up?"

"Sitting up," he said with a wide smile. "I like sitting up."

"Well, you should wait for the doctor to get here. I just let him know you're awake a minute ago."

"I'm awake. Can I go home now?"

"We'll see." She shouldered past Nick to come and stand over him, checking the IV in his arm and the readouts on the machine behind him.

"I'm hungry," he added, because it was true and simple. "I want a cheeseburger. Two cheeseburgers. Maybe three."

"You can tell the doctor when he gets here." She patted his shoulder. "Now lie still and don't worry."

"I'm not worried. I'm hungry."

He'd hoped for a smile, but she frowned instead. "All you need to do is lie still for a bit. Just wait." She glanced at Nick. "You can step out until the doctor has a chance to do a full exam on Brian."

"No exams. I flunk exams." Brian cleared his throat— that was probably a bit much. "I want to go out and eat with Nick." He flipped the sheet back with his free hand and swung a leg toward the rail, except yuck, he was wearing a hospital gown and that wet diaper. He yanked the sheet back up to hide it. "I want real clothes."

Nick stepped close and put a hand on his shoulder. "I'll just keep him here until the doctor arrives, okay?"

The nurse glared at Brian. "You were in a coma. Stay quiet. You can't just walk out."

He wanted to say "Wanna bet? Watch me." But Bry wouldn't do that, and Nick's hand was heavy on his shoulder, so he looked up at Nick. "Do I have to?"

"Yeah, you do," Nick said, a hint of humor glinting in his eyes. "Doctor now. Cheeseburgers later."

"They'd better be double patties," he grumbled. "I'm really hungry." As if to make a point, his stomach rumbled loudly.

The nurse checked him over again, a deep crease between her brows, before she hurried out to go to the room across the bay.

Brian waited until she was out of earshot, then said, "Where am I?"

"Abbot Northwestern. Intensive Care."

"Wow. They did freak out."

"Coma. It's a scary word."

Something in Nick's tone made Brian reach up and cover his hand where it still rested on his shoulder. "You weren't worried, right? I told you this would happen."

"You said maybe a day. You're well past that."

"It varies. I should have carb loaded some more, maybe."

"This is just a trick to get more pizza, huh?" Nick pulled his hand free and paced the two steps to the window, looking out at the rest of the ICU.

Brian said, "Pizza would be good." His stomach rumbled again in agreement. "What else happened? Do I get the money?"

"Yeah. Emerson agreed." Nick turned and leaned on the window frame. "He wouldn't send the check though. We have to go pick it up. I think he's worried I'll steal it from you or something."

"That goes on my to-do list, right after the pizza."

The doctor appeared at that moment and shooed Nick out so he could examine Brian. Brian had meant to stay in the present and have a real adult conversation with the doctor, but the moment the man asked, "What were you doing before you passed out?" Bry emerged to say, "Walking. Talking. Falling over." And after that, Brian couldn't really go back on it. He did try to be less dumb than usual, but the doctor quickly gave up asking him complex stuff, which was the point.

He was allowed to put on underwear, and they moved him down to a regular ward because the doc said no one got discharged straight from ICU. By midafternoon, he was bored out of his mind. Hospital food, once he'd proved he wouldn't puke it back up, was awful. Plus there wasn't enough of it. Nick snuck him in a deli sandwich, and he ate that. The nurse came in as he was finishing it to find him dressed, sneakers on and ready to leave, for the third time. She sighed heavily. "Nick." They were on first-name terms by now. "Can't you convince him to stay in bed?"

"He's still in the room. I'm counting that as a win."

Brian scratched at the inside of his elbow where the Band-Aid from the IV itched. "I want to go home. Please? Soon? Pretty please?"

Nick asked the nurse, "Any chance we can get someone to discharge him? I have to leave sometime, and I think he's just going to walk out the door when I do."

She sighed. "I'll try to contact his doctor."

When she was gone, Nick looked at him, head tilted curiously but with a shadow in his eyes. "Are you doing Bry on purpose?"

He wanted to say of course he was, but he'd vowed to try to be truthful with Nick. So he said, "I think so. Bry can be a lot more annoying than I can, and he gets asked a lot fewer questions before they give up. I don't want to talk about you-know-what, and Bry can just babble and not have to lie."

"Mm. Does it bother you that you talk about yourself in the third person?"

He felt the flush, knew his face had turned red. "Better than not knowing there are two of me. Um. That didn't come out right. It's weird, okay?" *I'm weird.*

Nick sighed. "I'm just a cop. What do I know anyway? Is there something else I can do while you wait?"

"Smuggle me out?"

"I just said 'cop.' Something less illegal?"

"Bring me a burger?"

"On top of the sandwich?"

"I'm hungry again."

A new person in a white coat stuck her head in the door and said, "Brian Kerr?"

"Yes, ma'am!" He saluted, for the heck of it.

She came in, a clipboard and stethoscope in hand. "My best nurse tells me we either discharge you or we'll find you escaping down the laundry chute."

He shook his head hard. "I'd use the elevator. Hospital laundry is naaaasty."

She eyed him shrewdly, and he dipped his head to break the stare. "Okay." She glanced at Nick. "Why don't you step out for a minute and I'll do a discharge exam."

Nick said, "I'll be right here in the hall if you need me," and went out, closing the door behind him.

The doctor turned to him. "Now then, Brian, let's check you out, shall we?"

"Sure, Doctor...?" He let his voice rise in a question. It was annoying, although he usually managed to hide it, how many people would call him by his first name in that patronizing tone and not introduce themselves at all.

She tapped her name badge.

He had to grit his teeth to say, "I can't read it." He gave her Bry's big grin. "Forgot my... reading glasses." He let his tone make it an obvious lie.

"Dr. Goldstein. Here, sit up a bit, I want to listen to your heart." Once she'd listened and prodded and shined a light in his eyes, she made a couple notes on the clipboard and then set it aside. "Brian?"

"You can call me Bry." Maybe that would help keep this simple. Right now Brian was too close to the surface, and he could feel himself slipping in and out. "Yess'm? What'm?"

"Can you tell me what happened to you?"

"I fell asleep. I have the narco, and sometimes I do that."

"Just fell asleep?"

"Yes. I was running, I think. If I get really excited, sometimes it happens. I didn't get hurt. But I'm hungry."

"When you came in, you had low blood sugar, high ketones, and a few other abnormalities that almost looked like starvation."

"I'm not starving." He patted his stomach which was actually flatter after a long Find, but still more meaty than he wished. More soft and flabby than Nick's, for sure. "I eat good. But I'm hungry now."

"You live with Nick?"

"We're roommates."

"Just roommates? Nothing more?"

"He's helping me look for a job."

"Did you find one?"

"Not yet." He looked around. "Could I work here? Lots of people work here."

"You'd have to check with the hiring office. Bry, do you feel safe at home?"

"Sure. It's a nice house."

"Do you ever get scared of anything? Of Nick?"

He realized she was seeing him as Bry, a vulnerable adult who could be taken advantage of. Too late to shift gears now. All he could do was say, "Nick's good. He's really safe. But I want a dog."

"A dog?"

"Nick picked a house with a yard so I could have a dog. But I don't. Yet." He suddenly missed Luger and Glock with a pang that brought tears to his eyes. He didn't miss his old life, not really. All of Marston's wealth and his pool and the nice cars and fancy meals didn't come close to pizza on the couch with Nick, but he really missed the dogs.

"Maybe you will soon." Her voice was kind. She went and opened the door and beckoned Nick back in. "I'm going to sign off on your discharge, although I'd really rather keep you another day."

"Nope," he said. "No."

"Right. I don't want you leaving AMA. Against medical advice. But Nick? I do want you to stay with him for the next twenty-four hours. And you, Bry, eat lots of little meals, drink a lot of fluids. No alcohol, no aspirin or ibuprofen. Are you still on the Prozac?"

"Huh?" He remembered she had his records. "No drugs. Not any."

She looked at Nick. "When did he come off it?"

Nick shrugged. "He wouldn't pick up the refill. It's been at least a couple weeks."

She shook her head. "Maybe that contributed to how long he crashed. You're supposed to taper off them. Well, Bry, if you feel dizzy or confused or have blurry vision or anything else that isn't right, you tell Nick right away. Okay?" She gave Nick a meaningful look that Brian pretended he didn't see.

"Okay."

She nodded and took some papers off the clipboard. "Since I'm guessing you won't wait for the discharge nurse, you might as well take these now. And good luck, Bry." She set them on his bedside table, and gestured with her head at Nick. "Walk with me for a second?"

They left the room, the doctor talking in a low voice. Brian shoved down his annoyance at knowing they were discussing him. He'd made that call by being Bry, hadn't he? Bry didn't get full adult treatment. Bry was the easy route. He really, *really* needed to stop doing that.

He picked up the papers he'd never be able to read and shoved them in his pocket. Who was he kidding? He deserved to be treated like an idiot.

Nick said from the doorway, "Keep frowning like that, and your face'll freeze that way."

"Shut up!" he snapped back.

Nick raised his hands. "Whoa. Hospital really does make you pissy. Or is it being hungry?"

Brian took control of his temper. Nick clearly meant well. None of his mess was Nick's fault. "Maybe both. Can we find a drive-through?"

"Sure. You've been cooking way too healthy. We both could use some good grease and carb loading." Nick grinned at him, and Brian felt a hard knot in his chest dissolve. Nick was completely talking to Brian, not Bry. Whatever the doctor had said, Nick took it in stride, as part of his act, and it didn't change things. Brian realized that living with a guy who'd done undercover work was probably the best his craziness could ever hope for. Nick was way too good for him, but Brian was going to take his blessings and count himself lucky.

"I'll make salad dinner tonight to make up for it."

"The hell you will." Nick gestured him out of the room. "We'll stop and buy steak to celebrate. On your dime."

"Didn't you say I don't have the money yet?"

"Well, you will soon. In fact, I can call Emerson. We'll stop at his office between Wendy's and the grocery store, and pick up twenty thousand dollars."

Brian really liked the brightness of Nick's eyes when he said that. He felt an answering smile tug at his lips. "Sounds like a plan."

****

A few days later, Nick parked outside a suburban cop shop— a long, low brick building with half a dozen patrol cars parked outside— and looked at Brian. "You're sure about this?"

"Of course."

"It's a small house. Marston's dogs were big. You don't even know which one is left." He'd gotten a house with a yard so Brian could have a dog, sure, but he hadn't planned on one of the guard-trained Shepherd-things of

Marston's. As a cop, he'd run into enough nasty dogs to have a healthy respect for them, which translated to liking them on the other side of a strong fence. He'd been thinking a Golden Retriever, or maybe a Lab. Something friendly.

"Come on." Brian got out, and Nick had no choice but to follow. When they'd picked up the money from Emerson, the guy had asked Bry what he'd spend it on. The way he asked it made Nick think he was also worried Bry was being ripped off and might never see the money. Brian had answered in his slow-voice, "A dog, a bike, and a big TV." It turned out that although he'd said it like a child, he hadn't been kidding. They got the TV the next day, the bike yesterday, and here they were for the dog.

Brian led the way inside, and they told the cop at the desk that they were looking for Officer Craig. A few minutes later, Craig showed them down a hallway to a concrete-block kennel with half a dozen dogs. "The humane society we used for impounds closed its doors," Craig said over the barking. "This was supposed to be temporary, but it's been three months." The kennels had rusty iron bars for doors, and the floor was stained. "We hadn't had dogs here for probably twenty years. And frankly, none of us wants to be on dog-shit duty." He pointed to the end. "That's the last Marston dog. Be careful, he's not all that user-friendly. Did you bring a muzzle?"

"Do we need one?" Nick asked.

Craig shrugged. "He's not as aggressive as the Shepherd they put down, but he watches you like he's waiting for you to turn your back. I wouldn't have him loose in my car without one."

Brian said, "We don't need a muzzle." Nick glanced at him and noticed he had his eyes squeezed shut.

"Brian? You okay?"

"Just wondering who…" Brian opened his eyes and went down the row of cages. He squatted in front of the last one. "Luger." The name came out on a soft breath. "Hey, Luger, it's me. We're gonna get you out of here." He stuck his hands through the bars. Craig drew a fast breath, but it was pretty clear that the furry dog on the other side was wriggling with pleasure, licking Brian's fingers and trying to squeeze through the bars to get close to him.

Craig turned to Nick, eyebrows raised. Nick said, "He used to work on the Marston estate. The dogs knew him."

"Oh, sure. Well, I guess that works out. That's a good-looking dog. I'm glad he'll have a decent home."

Nick dragged his attention away from the little reunion. When had Brian ever looked that happy? He couldn't remember seeing that open glow in Brian's eyes. Not even when they were watching a movie together, or hiking in the park. Never that Nick could recall, and he felt a pang— that surely wasn't jealousy *of a dog*, was it? Of course not. "So what do you need from us?"

"You did all the paperwork. All we need is for him to sign off on the receipt."

Nick raised his voice. "Brian, you wanna quit mauling your dog and put a leash on him?"

Brian looked up and laughed, his eyes bright and open. "Yeah. For sure." He unwrapped the leash and collar he'd wound around his hand and opened the run gate. "Hey Luger, walkies."

"Walkies," Craig muttered, but not unpleasantly.

Brian buckled the collar around the dog's neck and stood. "Luger, heel." The dog fell in at his left side on command.

Nick followed, watching as Brian led his new dog out behind Craig. Brian chatted with the cop briefly about what the dog had been eating, and then signed without comment where he was directed. Luger leaned against his knee silently. When the paperwork was done, Brian bent to ruffle the dog's ears, then ran out the door, the dog loping beside him. Outside in the sunshine, Nick saw him actually jump in the air, fist raised.

Craig glanced at him. "I guess he likes the dog."

"I guess he does. Thanks."

Nick went out and leaned on the car. Brian ran the dog back and forth down the drive, his best speed not even making Luger break out of a trot. A marked car approached and Brian tugged Luger aside, leash held short, as it turned in to the parking area. The cop got out, gave them each a measuring glance, and headed inside.

Brian walked back, his face flushed, smiling. "Sorry for the wait. I thought he needed to move a bit, before getting in the car."

"Good idea."

"It's Luger."

"I gathered." Nick cleared his throat. "He's one of the ones you liked?"

"Yeah. Him and Glock." A momentary sadness passed over his face. "Well, I knew there was only one left. I hope Glock likes where he's at." He brought the dog right up to Nick and knelt beside Luger's furry shoulder. "Luug, this is Nick. He's a friend. Friend." He glanced up at Nick. "Hold out your hand for him."

Nick held his hand down, and the dog sniffed at it. Nick wasn't sure that the expression in its amber eyes was friendship, but it turned away like it wasn't interested. He'd settle for that. "Let's get out of here."

Back at the house, Brian turned Luger loose in the yard. The dog crisscrossed the area in an efficient pattern that seemed to cover every inch. Nick was reminded that, despite the long furry coat, this was a professionally trained guard dog. But then Luger ran three quick circles around a tree, dropped in a bare spot and rolled in the dirt. He got up, shook his coat in a cloud of dust, and swear-to-God laughed at them. The dog's jaw dropped, his tongue lolled out, and he cocked his head.

Nick was jolted off-balance by Brian's sudden fierce hug around his shoulders. He staggered, but returned it. Brian said against his neck, "I'm happy. Really happy. Oh man, Nick, thank you!"

"It was your money," Nick muttered.

Brian let go and stepped back, looking at him. "*So* not the point. It's… all this. The house, Luger, you being you, me being me without looking over my shoulder to see who's listening. I don't remember when I ever felt like this. Maybe as a little kid, with Lori, when we found a safe place to play, but not for so long I'd forgotten how it feels." He tipped his head back, laughed and turned in a circle, arms outstretched. "Wow. Just wow!"

Nick couldn't help smiling. "I'm glad."

Brian stopped and looked at him, his lips curved upward, eyes bright. "You're happy too, right? I mean, I know you could do better, but you aren't, like, in a hurry to leave, right? I told you we should split the money."

"No. That's yours." He avoided thinking about what would happen if Olson found out about it. He'd helped Brian open a new bank account, with a handy debit card. She'd be beyond pissed about that.

Nick vividly remembered his last phone call with Olson.

"I heard you're helping Kerr buy a dog. What the hell is that for? We want him to be alone when you dump him, so he really needs to find Damon."

Nick hesitated, wondering for the tenth time if Olson knew more about Brian's Finding than she let on, or whether that was just a chance turn of phrase. He scrambled for an explanation she might buy. "It gives him an anchor here. He won't leave the dog. He won't off himself, if he has the dog. And if he takes it along to find Damon, it'll make him much easier to keep track of."

"I guess. When are you going to move out?"

"Not yet. Not till I'm sure he won't just fold into a catatonic ball."

"You think that's likely?"

"I don't know. I think he should be in therapy before I do it."

"All right, but don't let worrying about Brian take your eye off the prize—arresting Damon Kerr. Remember which side you're on."

The acid guilt hurt his chest. He wondered if there was any way to be on both sides. He tried to smile at Brian. "Yeah, I'm good right now."

Brian's joy dimmed at that lukewarm statement, but he said, "And I bet you'll be better once you're back on patrol, right? Now that you're cleared to go to work?"

"Yeah. That's good too." He'd lied to the doc about his headaches, and she'd found nothing else wrong, telling him he was in the lucky fraction of people with no long-term effects from a bad head injury. He was itching to be back doing useful work that didn't make him choose sides. "You're right. Can't wait."

"I'll do better too," Brian said, stepping closer. "As a roommate. I'll try. I'll watch that cooking show, and learn some new recipes, and I'll walk Luger lots so that'll get me in better shape. I'll learn to ride the bike soon, so I can run errands for us, and, um, I can pay for stuff now. I might look for a teacher, you know, for my dyslexia—"

"You already do just fine," Nick interrupted. He liked happy, confident Brian. The worry growing in his voice was painful to hear. For once, he just went with what felt right and pulled Brian into another hug, holding him close. "I'm a crap roommate too. I'm the one who should learn some cooking, and I'll try not to kick the garbage over when the lid jams, and I promise not to throw the remote."

Brian chuckled, leaning against him. "I'll make you sign that one in blood. That's my new TV." He quieted, his arms looped around Nick's waist.

Nick felt like he should break this up, but there was something about standing here, with Brian's taller, bulkier body against him, that felt so good he didn't want to shift a muscle. "I have a temper. You don't really know."

Brian's arms tightened. "I've seen you fight, Nok Nick. I think I have an idea."

"I like to punch people. Not you, obviously, but... I get mad."

"Maybe we should get a heavy bag for the basement."

"Maybe." It wasn't the same. Nick wondered if he'd have to go back to finding a rough bar somewhere. Not the Torchhouse, obviously, but the Twin Cities area had lots of dives where a fight wasn't a novelty and there were people who deserved a smackdown.

"Luger likes you."

That gave Nick a reason to step back and glance over at the dog, which had stretched out in the sun, front paws neatly crossed, watching them. "The hell he does."

Brian nodded. "Really. He hasn't growled at you once."

"He'd better not," Nick muttered. "Do we need 'Dangerous Dog' signs on the gates?"

"Maybe. Until he figures out he's not on duty anymore."

"And a doghouse."

"He'll sleep in my room."

Nick almost said "The hell he will," but he caught the words before they left his lips. It wasn't his decision, and anyway, that might be good. Knowing Luger was stretched out on the floor of Brian's room would be a great way to stop waking in the night with the impulse to climb the stairs and see if that bed of Brian's could hold two. Sharp teeth and bare cocks did not go together. "All right."

Brian said, "It'll work out. I know it will. First time in my life, I think I'm going to be real."

Nick couldn't rain on that. "I'll help," he said. "Any way I can."

Chapter 27

Brian looked up fast, for probably the hundredth time that evening, turning around on the couch to stare toward the front door. A car on the main road rumbled on past the corner without turning in. *Damn.*

Nick was two hours late coming home from his shift. Brian's brain knew he was probably worrying for nothing. Being a cop wasn't that much more dangerous than being a tree trimmer or a construction worker. But he could picture Nick in that sexy blue uniform, standing his ground while some meth addict came at him with an axe, or running into a burning building to save a baby. If there was trouble, he was sure Nick was the kind of cop who'd run toward it, not away. There'd been nothing scary on the local news, but sometimes the reporters were late to a story.

Luger shifted against him, sensing his mood, and lifted his furry head to lick Brian's chin. Brian rubbed his ears. "Yuck. Don't suck up to me. You're probably glad he's late. You know he doesn't like you up on the couch."

Luger looked unimpressed, settling back down with his head on Brian's knee. Brian bent over the book on his lap, trying to stay focused. The simple letters swam before his eyes, and every sound from outside distracted him. He was about ready to give the book to Luger as a chew toy, except it was a library book.

He'd taken his new bike the six blocks down to the local branch. It'd taken fifteen minutes in the bathroom for him to get up his nerve, but then he'd gone to the nice old lady behind the desk and asked her how you could find out about dyslexia when you can't read. She'd given him a warm smile and admitted that there was a definite problem there. She'd pointed to the seat across from her desk and suggested he sit down and let her check into it.

The simple answer was that there was no simple answer. Apparently there were different kinds of dyslexia, and it took tests to figure out what he had. He'd always hated tests, even the ones that didn't need writing. But he was determined not to depend on Nick forever, so he asked her to find out where he could get tested. She wrote a couple of phone numbers down for him, and he'd picked out some easy readers from the children's book section, pretending it was for his kid or something, and brought them home.

It was clear that just being determined wasn't going to make this any easier than when he was six, though. The letters still flipped around, a *b* becoming a *d* when he looked away for a second. He recited the alphabet to himself again, reassuring himself that yeah, he really did know the basic letters. How hard could this be? "A c-a-t is not— *No!* ...on." Deep breath. "A cat is *on* tea— *the*..." He stopped because clearly the next word was "bed." There was the picture right there of the stupid cat curled up in the covers. But the word flipped around. He framed it with his fingers. It looked a bit like a bed, with posts on each end and puffy pillows in between. ...bed... He closed the book. If he had to memorize what every single stupid word looked like, he'd have a decent reading vocabulary by the time he was ninety. Maybe.

The sound of a car turning into the drive broke him out of his slump. He quickly shoved the book under the couch cushion and nudged Luger to the floor. Nick came in the door, his crisp light-blue shirt a bit rumpled but without blood, no soot, no smoke. Brian took a breath. "Hey. Long day?"

"Hell, yeah." Nick didn't meet Brian's eyes as he made a beeline for the fridge. He grabbed out a beer and popped the top, downing what looked like half the can in one long swallow. Then he set it aside, went into the freezer, got out a bag of frozen peas and draped it over the back of his right hand.

Brian got up and went around the counter to look closer. "Did you get hurt?"

"Nah. Hit something," Nick muttered. He grabbed the beer left-handed and drank some more.

"Something, or someone?"

"Thing. A wall, if you have to know."

"Ouch."

"Better than a person."

"I suppose." Brian wasn't sure whether to ask what happened or let it go. But they were just roommates, so maybe it wasn't his place to push. He said,

"Do you want any dinner? I made some coleslaw, and there's hot dogs, and corn in the freezer. It'd only take five minutes."

Nick looked at him, momentarily distracted. "You *made* coleslaw?"

"I went to the library and I found a cookbook in the audio books. It's a diabetic cookbook, so some of the stuff is probably pretty weird, but I was browsing through, and there was coleslaw. I got most of what it needed." He wouldn't tell Nick that his problem with doing steps in order, without forgetting or leaving anything out, meant he'd made two batches, and the first one was in the trash. "I think it came out okay."

"I'm sure." Nick shrugged. "You know, I think I want this beer and then, um, maybe I'll go out and get something fattening. Bar food."

"Sure. Where do you want to go? I'm up for anything."

Nick bit his lip, flushing oddly. "I think I just want to cruise around, maybe find a place that looks like it fries with lard, stop there. I'm not hungry right now, but maybe I will be later." He opened the freezer, stuck the peas back, and shook his hand out, looking away from Brian. "So anyhow, I'm going to shower and change and then I guess I'll head out. Um. Alone."

"Oh!" He felt so stupid. "Sure. Right."

"It's not that..." Nick took a breath and turned back. "It's not that I don't want to hang out with you and eat, it's that I want to find someplace I can work off a bit of steam. And you don't need to be around to see that."

"Like, you want to get in a fight?" He'd seen Nok Nick in action, long before Nick started doing his undercover work. It shouldn't have been a surprise that he was looking for a fight, but it was.

"Yeah. I guess." Nick's laugh held very little humor. "There's not a lot of satisfaction in hitting a wall when it can't hit back."

Suddenly daring, Brian reached out and grabbed Nick's hand. Nick didn't pull back hard enough to really count. His knuckles were reddened and swollen, and the skin was split over his middle finger. Brian let go, and said as lightly as he could, "You really want to hit something else tonight? Going for actual broken fingers?"

"Hah. Gut punches are pretty safe."

"You want to talk about what that wall did to deserve to get smacked?"

"Not really." Nick chugged the last of his beer and stepped away. "I need a shower."

While the shower was running, Brian let Luger outside, then took the dog up to his room and shut him in. Luger actually did like Nick, but his tendency to get in between Nick and Brian when their voices got loud could be a problem. Brian thought voices might get a bit loud this time. He went back down to the hallway and leaned on the wall, waiting. The shower went off. There was some muffled banging and scuffing as Nick got out. The door swung open.

Brian never got tired of looking at Nick. Usually when he was half-naked like this, with just a green towel wrapped around his hips, Brian only let himself have a quick glance. This time, he ran his gaze slowly up, from Nick's bony, hairy, strangely sexy feet, over his wiry legs, dark chest hair, angular jaw, stormy hazel-gray eyes, dark rumpled hair, and back to Nick's set mouth. That expression didn't look welcoming, but Brian had come too far to back down now.

He moved a step closer. "There's more than one way to work off steam."

"Brian, what are you doing?"

He shivered, because that was Nok Nick's voice, the one that said an ass-kicking was on its way, the one he'd crushed on and avoided for months. He took another step. "I'm just saying, I bet you haven't got laid in a month, and maybe we could get your heart rate going without breaking any more knuckles."

Nick's hand came up between them, landing on Brian's chest as he moved forward. It could have been a blow, but it wasn't. Nick's palm stayed there, hot against his shirt. "You don't want to be around me when I'm riled up."

"Maybe I do." Brian carefully set his hands on Nick's arms, curling his fingers around solid biceps. He moved slowly, as if Nick was a bomb he might set off with a sudden motion. "I've seen you drink, and yell, and fight. It was amazing. I've wanted a taste of that, up close and personal, for a long time."

Nick's other hand snaked out suddenly and grabbed Brian's hair. The sudden pull was painful but Brian didn't let himself react. Instead he smiled and parted his lips.

Nick stared into his eyes. Brian tried to put all his heat, his want and willingness, into his expression. *Yes. Please. Whatever you need. I need it too.* He leaned forward. Nick could have stopped him, but the hand in his hair just followed his motion as he found Nick's mouth with his own.

God, yes. This. He'd almost forgotten what it was like to have Nick's mouth and his taste and his lean strength up close. Brian groaned, and realized he was pressing Nick back to the wall, humping against him as they kissed. But it was so good, *so, so good*, he didn't care how desperate and clumsy he seemed. Nick must not have minded too much. He pulled his hand out from between them, let go of Brian's hair, and grabbed Brian's ass in both hands, pulling him closer. His dick against Brian's thigh was just as hard, just as trapped as Brian's own.

Brian closed his eyes and concentrated on letting Nick know with his mouth and his hands and his whole body that yeah, he wanted this— needed it. Whatever Nick was up for, bring it on. He opened gladly for Nick's tongue, and gasped when Nick nipped his lower lip, almost to the edge of pain. Nick broke the kiss and leaned back. "We shouldn't."

"Oh yeah, we should." Brian let go of Nick's arms and trapped his head between his hands instead, holding him against the wall, bending just enough to find a good angle for a kiss. He had a lot less experience than Nick did, but he intended to fix that problem. Or any other problem. He rubbed his thigh against Nick's towel-covered erection, then knelt with an awkward thump and tugged the terrycloth away, dropping the towel to the floor.

He opened his mouth, and Nick said, "No."

For a second, Brian was going to just do it anyway. What guy would keep saying no when his dick was in someone's mouth? But this wasn't a school bathroom, where the other guy would walk off while still zipping up, and never look him in the face again. This was Nick. So he didn't back off, and he didn't close his lips, but he didn't lean forward either.

Nick reached down and touched his cheek, then his lower lip. Brian turned enough to suck that fingertip into his mouth. Nick said hoarsely, "You really want to?"

"God, yes." Brian bent forward slowly, so slowly, and kissed Nick's bare hip instead. He let his hair brush against Nick's cock, accidentally on purpose. "I've always wanted to. Long before you ever knew my name. And even more now."

"It'll complicate things."

"It doesn't have to."

Nick bent and put a hand under his left armpit. Brian let himself be pulled to his feet. Nick said, "If we start fucking we aren't going to want to stop."

"That's a problem?"

"We were scheduled to have a mock fight, and I was moving out so you could be on your own."

Brian swallowed hard. "Yeah, that was your plan. But I like sharing the house with you. I'm not sure I'm cut out to be on my own, even if I can make the practical stuff work out." He blinked his suddenly stinging eyes. "Still, if you want to move out later that would probably be okay."

Nick put a hand on his chin, thumb tipping Brian's face down. "I'm already kind of addicted to your dumb jokes and your cooking, and having my laundry done. Now you're adding sex. I may never want to leave."

Would that be so bad? He went for a bright tone. "One day at a time. Isn't that what all the therapists say?" He could have cursed himself as he saw Nick's eyes dull at that reminder of how screwed up Brian was. So he quickly added, "And today I want sex." He bent and kissed Nick again, hard and needy.

When he pulled back, Nick said, "I'm going to hell, you know that, right?"

"For gay sex? I thought that was automatic."

"For messing with you."

"Who trapped who against the wall?" Brian asked.

"Yeah. That'll be my defense." Nick reached up and took his hand, folding their fingers together. "Come on. If we're doing this, I want it to be worth the fallout. My bed."

Nick's room was dark and neither of them touched the light switch. Brian wished he could see Nick, but he didn't mind the dim light from the hall letting him hide his own flaws. Funny how he could burn a gazillion calories Finding, and be right back to his usual weight a few days later. But right now, he didn't have time to care. He had a bed, and Nick Rugo, and license to explore. Better than ten years of birthday-candle wishes.

Nick said, "You should get naked. Make it fair." He slid onto the bed, a dark mysterious shape, the mattress creaking under him as he moved. Brian tugged his T-shirt off, got out of his jeans and boxers. The shorts tried to tangle his feet and he felt a flush of embarrassment, because how clumsy did you have to be to get stuck in your underwear? But when Nick added, "Come on, I need you here," all that was left was heat.

The bed dipped when he got into it. Nick's hands were already on his thighs, and he tipped sideways, fumbling with the covers. Nick pulled him in so they were on their sides, face to face. There was enough light to kiss without mashing noses. Brian wouldn't have minded slowing down, but Nick was driven, demanding, and Brian wasn't about to object. Nick rolled them to pin Brian with his weight, thrusting down against him. Brian got a grip on two handfuls of tight ass, and pulled him in closer, pushing up just as hard.

Nick kissed him with lip-bruising force, then moved down to bite his neck, his throat, his collarbone. That one was hard enough to hurt, and Brian gasped and winced.

Nick froze. "Sorry. Too rough. I'm in the wrong mood for this."

Brian drove a hand between them and grabbed Nick's cock, squeezing hard enough to make Nick grunt. "I won't break." As fast as he could manage, he pushed Nick over and wriggled down the bed until he could guide that damp cockhead to his lips. He sucked hard and fast. The angle was awkward and he shoved Nick's hip enough to get him all the way on his side again. Nick went with it, laying a hand on Brian's head but not doing more than tugging a lock of his hair. Brian really wished he could see, but it was fine like this, with that long rigid shaft gliding over his tongue, with the taste of salt-sweet precum in his mouth and Nick's speeding breaths turning to moans up there in the darkness.

Brian pushed Nick's thighs apart and pressed his face in there, rubbing his lips down against rough curls and the soft curves of Nick's balls. He kept a hand around the base of Nick's erection, pumping in short, firm tugs as he licked and nuzzled and tasted the tender skin of Nick's sac.

"God. Feels great," Nick groaned. "Mm. There."

Brian sucked a testicle into his mouth, rolling it against his tongue, slipping the thin skin over the roundness of it. The hair was just part of it all, part of the textures and tastes and shapes that were Nick's own, sliding across his lips. Brian was suddenly hit with a wave of fear, that this might be his one and only chance; this might be all there was. He pushed his face in tightly against Nick's groin, breathing through his nose. Nick rubbed his head. "Brian? Doing okay?"

He laughed against the salty warmth of Nick's skin, because "okay" was completely the wrong word. He didn't know what the right one was. If his mouth was full, he wouldn't have to think of it. He rose up on his knees and sucked Nick's cock back down, savoring the stretch and the breathlessness of taking his lips all the way to meet his hand, forcing that rigid length into the back of his throat. Each slide, each long sucking pull, fed his soul with rightness, gayness, Nick-ness. He wanted to do this forever.

Nick gasped and grunted as Brian bobbed his head. "So good, so good. Wait, wait!"

Brian froze with Nick deep in his mouth, tasting little trickles of liquid, feeling the shivers of tension in Nick's cock, and up and down the hard thigh under his hand.

Nick grabbed his arm and tugged upward. "Here. C'mere."

Reluctantly, Brian let Nick's erection slide wetly out of his mouth as Nick guided him up. He could see better now, and he lay facing Nick, sharing a pillow, their faces inches apart.

Nick leaned forward to kiss him, more gently than he expected. "You have a great mouth."

"You have a tasty dick."

Nick tipped his head back, laughing softly, his neck a glorious curve in the dim light. Brian nipped his throat, then his jaw. Nick groaned, cupped Brian's head tighter against him and bucked their hips together. Nick's cock stroked along Brian's, damp and hard. Brian reached down and wrapped his fingers around both of them. A second later Nick's free hand joined his.

"Mm." Brian humped into their fingers, the friction rough and dry, and yet almost perfect.

"Lube." Nick let go and leaned away to fumble with a drawer. "Is this what you want?"

"Sure." Brian kept his hand tight and pressed their shafts together, rubbing his thumb over the fluid at Nick's slit.

"Here. Wait." Brian heard a plastic sound, and Nick brought his hand back dripping and slick. "Like this." The grip of Nick's fingers below his was just this side of too tight, but the lube made everything slide and rub in sloppy smoothness. Brian pumped his hips in a short stroke. Heat arced through him as he drove along Nick's warm dick, thighs, pubes, skin on skin. He shuddered.

"Yeah, like that." Nick returned the stroke, gliding against him between their hands. They moved in rhythm and then out of it, thrusting in counterpoint. Brian's hand slipped off, and he fumbled, found a better angle. Nick spread his fingers, and the lube squelched and dripped along the crease of Brian's groin. He buried his face against Nick's neck and humped mindlessly. Nick dug hard fingers into Brian's ass, holding and guiding him.

Brian's breath came in harsh, needy gasps. Dimly, he could hear Nick echoing him, deep grunts in time with his own. Brian locked his teeth, arched his back, and his climax rose, unstoppable, until he came. The relief nearly made him sob as all that built-up heat surged through him and out, and out, spilling into their hands. *Yes. This. God. Yes.*

He shook, easing past the first blinding pleasure. Nick was still thrusting against him, each motion ending in a strangled moan. Brian said, "Let me." He eased his dick free and closed his hands around Nick's shaft, tugging, rubbing. This he could do. This he was a champion at. Nick seemed to like it firm, so he kept his strokes fast and hard, up over the head and down, around and down, rubbing Nick's balls with his other hand. Nick flailed randomly, grabbed Brian's hip and gasped. His cock jerked and shot in thick, wet splashes against Brian's chest and hands, and even up to his cheek and lips.

Brian laughed with the sheer joy of it. Nick's cum was on his skin and in his mouth. Nick's sounds had no words left in them, and his fingers bruised Brian's hip. Brian leaned in and mashed his cum-slick mouth against Nick's open one. Nick grabbed the back of his head and shoved his tongue deep in Brian's mouth, then pulled away and dragged in a ragged breath. "Fuck."

"Uh huh."

They stared at each other, breathless in the filtered moonlight. Brian leaned in and kissed Nick again, more slowly, more softly. Nick's lips curved under his. Brian pulled back to look at him, tugging a pillow under his head.

Nick's smile was rueful. "I'd planned something a bit more, um, *planned*, if we ever did this."

"Seize the moment," Brian said lightly, to hide the way his heart had leaped at the thought that Nick had been thinking about sex with him.

"I guess." Nick reached for the sheet, and stopped with a grimace, eyeing his fingers. "Man, we're a mess."

Brian grabbed it anyway, and pulled the light cotton over them both. "I'll do laundry tomorrow."

"It's my turn."

"Whichever." He hesitated, but he'd always wanted to spoon a guy. *Seize the moment indeed.* He pushed at Nick's shoulder and pulled his hip, hoping his intentions were clear. After a second of resistance, Nick rolled obligingly to put his ass against Brian's thighs. Brian wrapped an arm around him, setting his palm over where Nick's heart still beat hard enough he could feel it. "So good."

"Mm."

Brian wondered if Nick would fall asleep, or even better, be willing to talk. But Nick just lay there, not rigid, but clearly a long way from relaxed. Brian slid his leg down, opening up a bit more space between them. Nick sighed, and turned a few inches. His back was warm and damp against Brian's front, and there was something sticky making itself felt.

"This is kind of awkward, isn't it?" Brian muttered, letting go. Maybe spooning was one of those things that sounded better than it worked.

Nick rolled to face him again. He swiped Brian's chest with a finger. "Cleaning up might be good."

"Sorry."

"Hey, it's my mess. Well, half."

"We could shower."

"Might have to do it together. There's not much water left, I bet."

"Aw, too bad," Brian said, more lightly than he felt. He rolled and sat up, swinging his feet over the side. His shorts were down there somewhere. He squinted as Nick got out the other side and flicked on the bedside light. Nick looked good, flushed and rumpled, dark and intense.

Brian sighed. He was probably just a pale sticky mess. He turned away, scanning the clothes on the floor for his boxers.

Nick's fingers caught his chin, making him look up. "What?" Brian asked.

"Nothing. I like looking at you."

"Really?"

"Yeah. You're a hard man to resist. Obviously." Nick let go and walked around the bed to scoop something off the floor. "Here— your shorts. Shower?"

"Sure." He followed Nick toward the bathroom. Watching Nick's lean back and tight ass made him wish the walk took longer.

They both went in, jostling each other in a friendly way as Nick turned on the water. Brian peed quickly while his back was turned. Then he got in the shower first, while Nick took care of business too. He was enjoying the spray on his face when Nick pulled back the plastic curtain and stepped in behind him. Brian noticed that the fingers holding the edge of the plastic were bruised and swollen, and remembered how they'd ended up here. Nick seemed more cheerful and relaxed, and Brian didn't want to say anything to break the spell, but as they turned sideways to try to share the water, a flash of tenderness made his throat ache.

Nick always seemed so strong, so fierce when someone got out of line, so in control. But apparently that fierceness was covering something painful, and the control was an illusion. He'd seen Nick break loose before, but hadn't realized how much anger there was under the surface. He felt like he'd finally seen the real Nick Rugo tonight in the bleakness of his eyes.

Suddenly Brian felt stronger, bigger. Nick was inches shorter, pounds lighter, but Brian had always felt like the littler guy. Tonight he didn't. He slid an arm around Nick's shoulders, hugging him in under the warmth of the spray. Taking Nick's damaged hand in his, he raised it and laid one gentle kiss on the worst-bruised knuckle. Just a token to say he knew, and wasn't going to push. He stepped back more, to give Nick the better shower space, and laid his cheek against Nick's head, breathing in the scent of him that rose in the damp steam.

He could do this. He could be better. He could become someone who wouldn't just sponge off Nick, someone even a tough, smart, independent guy might lean on when he'd had a bad day. If they only got the time, and the peace, maybe life would keep on getting better for them. Brian knew he was a hopeless optimist, but he decided to believe in that with all his heart.

****

Nick let the water run down his chest, and closed his eyes. He'd forgotten about his bruised hand in the heat and electric pleasure of sex, but it ached now. Luckily, he'd punched the wall in the hallway, out of sight of the other cop and the paramedics and all. No one would know.

Except Brian. Who'd kissed it and not asked questions. Nick leaned back into Brian, surprised at how solidly supported he felt with his shoulder planted against Brian's chest. Brian reached for the soap and shared a squirt. Nick felt him slide a soapy hand up and down between them, cleaning Nick's thighs, and his own belly. Yeah, they'd gotten sticky. Right. *Feels so good.*

He'd screwed up tonight. The whole plan had been to keep this roommate fiction lightweight, so he could walk away without pain. Now, that was flushed down the half-clogged drain at his feet. He could still pretend this was a one-time thing. He could even tell himself it was just a hand job, and not real sex. But he wasn't into self-delusion. That sex had been as real as any he'd ever had, and more intimate than with the guys who'd let him fuck them. He didn't know why he and Brian felt so right together, but he wasn't going to pretend it wasn't true.

So what now?

His orgasm-buzzed brain didn't seem to be able to come up with anything better than "Do it again soon." Life used to be simple. Work hard and keep his cool, play hard and work off steam, and live alone, moving from one to the other. He wasn't sure he was the right guy for complicated.

Brian said against his hair, "Water's getting cold."

So it was. He reached down and turned it off, shivering at the rush of cool air over his wet skin. Brian hugged him for a second, bending to suck drops of water off Nick's neck and shoulder, then stepped back. His light-blue eyes looked wary. "Was that too weird? I wanted to taste the water on your skin. That's probably weird, right?"

"Oh, hell, no. Stick with me. I'll teach you about weird." He leaned in to lick the clean water off Brian's chin in return. Brian's sweet smile was his reward.

Nick pulled the curtain back and got out, grabbing Brian's towel and handing it back, before wrapping his own around him. The bathroom was quiet, other than the slow drip from the showerhead. The air was foggy with moisture, blurring the mirror to an abstract of skin tones and towel colors. He shivered again, and Brian reached over to rub his back softly through the towel.

"A bit higher. Mm." He wriggled against those fingers, turning the rub into a back-scratch. Less intimate, less tender. Stepping away the six inches he had room for, he flipped the towel over his head to dry his hair. Through the terrycloth he said, "Hell, I have to change the sheets. I should make you do it."

Brian's voice was hesitant. "Unless you did laundry today, there are no clean ones. You could, um, have my bed instead."

"Have? Or share?" He tugged the towel off, and smiled to show it was a joke, but it was too late. Brian's eyes had lit with pleasure.

"Can we?"

How could he crush that? He sighed. "Sure. But I'm a restless sleeper, and it's too early anyway. I can just camp out on the couch later."

"The couch sucks," Brian returned, a little flush rising in his cheeks. "For sleeping, I mean. We could watch a movie or something. And eat." His face fell. "Unless you still want to go out to a bar later. You don't have to wait till I fall asleep. If that's what you need, just say so."

Nick realized that he didn't have the energy to go out hunting for action, or the desire anymore, honestly. He didn't know what it was about Brian, because in the past Nick had liked his sex fast and rough, with guys who could take it and give it right back, and it'd revved him up rather than putting him to sleep. But there was something soft about Brian, something comfortable. Not that he wasn't a big, solid guy, but he had no corners or jagged edges for Nick to bounce off of.

Brian was different. Wanting Brian was a steady background heat, that sometimes flared warmer, instead of an abrupt firecracker explosion of need. Although that was a dumb analogy or simile or whatever it was. He'd taken too long to answer, because Brian's gaze had dropped and closed, like someone pulling the curtains across his eyes.

"Nah," Nick said, as casually as he could. "I think I've busted my hand up enough for one night. A movie sounds good. And maybe food?"

"Really? I should let Luger outside for a minute, and then I could make you that hot dog, or a sandwich."

"I can make my own damned sandwich," Nick pointed out. "You're not my servant."

They ended up in the kitchen, dressed in shorts, Nick stacking cold cuts and cheese and pickles on bread, while Brian dished out coleslaw. Nick noticed he put some on a second plate for himself. "D'you eat your dinner yet?"

"Not really." Brian's voice was shy, and he looked down.

"Aw, you waited for me. Why didn't you say so? What do you want on your sandwich? Or what *don't* you want?" He waved a pickle.

"I'll eat anything," Brian said, then blushed.

Nick grinned. "I like that in a guy." He leaned over and kissed him without thinking, before grabbing two more slices of bread.

Brian put the dog back up in his room with a chew-bone, away from the human food, and they settled in on the couch to eat and watch a movie chosen at random from the box Nick had packed at the pool house. Brian was as omnivorous in his movie choices as his food, and he'd confessed that most of what he owned had been grabbed off sale racks because he liked the covers. Tonight was an old Doris Day comedy, in which the best part was a dog named Vladimir. The rest was so bad it cracked them up a bunch of times, although probably not where the moviemakers had intended it to.

It was loud, fast, and dumb enough to keep him distracted. When they'd finished the sandwiches, he pulled Brian in against his bare chest, *for warmth of course*, and that was distracting too. As the credits rolled, Brian sighed. "Lori would've taken that rich guy for every dime and then smothered him with his banana cream cake, and found someone less dumb to marry."

"We've come a long way, baby," Nick muttered. The film was fifty years old, and it showed.

Brian asked, in a barely audible voice, "Do you ever wonder where Damon and Lori are?"

All the time. "Sure. Although it's probably better if I never find out." He thought that was as clear a warning as he could stand to give. *If I find your brother, I'll have to arrest him. I might even feel good about doing it.*

"Me too," Brian said. In an odd voice he added, "I never want to see that baby."

Nick pushed him over enough to see his face. "Really? I thought you liked kids." He had vague memories of Marston pointing a gun at Lori, of raised voices, Damon cold as ice. Something about the baby, threatening the baby. Damned concussion had messed with his memory more than he liked to admit. He shook his head to clear it. "Because it's Marston's baby?" Did it remind Brian of the bad choices Lori had made?

"Something like that." Brian stood in a rush. "I'll toss the paper plates. You can go on up."

Nick thought about saying he'd changed his mind and would take the couch after all, but he didn't. He was dimly aware of memories of the *fun* parts of his workday still waiting to ambush him. Maybe they wouldn't find him if he hid in Brian's bed. He climbed the stairs and opened Brian's door. A soft *woof* warned him an instant before Luger's wet nose landed on his bare stomach.

He managed to cut his yelp short. Behind him, Brian said, "What? Oh! Cut it out, Luug. Down, boy. Sorry, Nick."

"It's okay."

"I can put him downstairs tonight."

"That's not necessary. Unless he plans to share the bed with us?"

Brian's giggle sounded nervous. "I don't let him on the bed. He has his own rug."

"Yeah, right. And I'm the queen of China."

"Does China have a queen?"

"I don't know. It's a saying." Nick stepped past the obedient dog crouched on the rug, and moved toward the bed. "We're not doing anything, you know. Just sleeping. Right?"

"Right." Brian nodded firmly. He switched on the bedside lamp, and turned off the overhead. "Door open?"

"Shut," Nick said. Shut doors gave you a little extra warning when shit went down.

"Do you, um, want to pick a side?" Brian hovered near the bed. His pale hair stood up, adorably rumpled, and his eyes were wide and anxious. He gestured, a fluttery wave of his hand.

Nick raised an eyebrow at him. "Are you sure you really want to share?"

"I'm nervous. I've never slept with anyone since I was a kid, and I want you to like this. I want you to stay."

Dammit, sometimes Brian made speaking the truth seem so simple, when it really wasn't. "It's just for tonight. Until I can do laundry."

"Of course."

"You get in, and I'll join you."

Brian pulled the sheet down and climbed onto the mattress, still wearing his boxers. Nick got in beside him. Brian stretched over and shut off the lamp. The room went dark and warm, a hint of city glow filtering in around the edges of the curtains. Nick rolled on his side away from Brian, and saw a faint amber flash of the dog's eyes as it turned his way, catching the faint light. He wondered for a moment whether waking loudly from a nightmare might make Luger attack him. Well, he'd have to count on Brian to protect him. He chuckled softly.

"What?" Brian murmured at his shoulder.

"Nothing." He lay there, caught between tension and tiredness. He was never going to fall asleep like this.

Brian's hand touched his shoulder, lightly at first and then more firmly, rubbing circles. Nick felt Brian's other hand come up and do the same at the small of his back. Brian said, "You're still all tight."

"It's not your fault. I mean, the sex was good. It was excellent. I'm actually more relaxed than usual after…" He stopped. He didn't want to talk about it, but this was where Brian would start asking questions. Wanting to analyze him. He should have taken the couch.

Brian rubbed in bigger, slower arcs. His fingers were stronger than Nick would have expected, digging into his shoulder muscles, then down his arm to rub his biceps and triceps, and up again to the meat of his neck. Finally, Brian said, "Did you take any pain-killer for your hand?"

Nick had been braced for questions he didn't want to answer, to the point where it took a second for that to register. "Yeah, took some aspirin before driving home."

"Good." Brian just kept rubbing him.

Perversely, that irritated Nick. Brian was so perfectly stoic sometimes. Wasn't he curious? Didn't he want to know? "I hate domestic calls." He heard his own voice, as if at a distance. "People who're supposed to love each other beating on each other. And the minute we step in the door, we're the bad guys. Half the time, the one who was getting beat up suddenly wants us gone. You turn your back for a second to put cuffs on the husband, and the battered wife jumps you."

Brian made a soft sound that could have been a question, or just sympathy.

"You know a lot of times they won't press charges, and then when they do, the abuser will get a slap on the wrist and be back after them a week later. It's really fucked up."

Brian moved in closer behind him, fitting his thigh under Nick's and wrapping an arm across his chest.

"This time the drunk son of a bitch hit one of the kids. We're there asking the wife if she needs an ambulance, and she's lying about getting her black eye falling against the counter. Then one of the three kids, who shouldn't even be in the room, sees us getting ready to put the cuffs on the husband and comes running over, tugging at my sleeve, saying, 'Don't take him away. He didn't mean to hit Mommy. He didn't mean it.' And the douchebag gets a hand free and he backhands this little kid, hits his own kid, and yells at her to shut up."

He was shaking, remembering it. The kid had been trying to defend her waste-of-space father, and he smacked her so hard, knocked her down. She sat there on the floor, blood on her split lip, looking up at her dad as he raged at her for being a stupid bitch, for not keeping her damned mouth shut. Nothing was going to take that memory away from her. She'd never forget that you couldn't trust people, that you could try to do the right thing and get a fist in the face in return.

He felt the damp brush of Brian's lips against his neck. "What did you do?"

384

"Me? I helped cuff the douchebag and get him out to the patrol car. I called an ambulance to check out the mom and the kid." *And I punched a dent in the drywall outside their door.* "Delivered the bastard downtown and got him booked, and filled out six reams of reports."

"So, you did your job?"

"Yeah." His shaking was easing against the bulk of Brian's body. He closed his hand lightly on Brian's arm. "The job sucks."

"You arrested him, though."

"Yeah. And he hit the kid in front of two cops. Whether the wife wants it or not, he's gonna get charged. He deserves everything he'll get." There was some satisfaction to that.

"Is that why you like to punch people in bars? Because you can't punch the people you really want to?"

Was it as simple as that? Not always. "Sometimes, I guess."

There was a long silence. Nick's body finally relaxed, as if telling Brian about it had let some of the pressure off. It was a warm night for spooning together, but Brian didn't let go, and Nick wanted the heat to reach into the cold places in his heart. He pushed back more snugly, sweaty skin and all.

Brian said, "Will she be okay? The little girl?"

"Physically? Yeah."

"Mm." After an even longer pause, Brian mumbled, "Are you 'kay?"

Nick figured Brian's voice was so garbled with sleep he probably wouldn't even remember asking, let alone recall the answer. He rubbed Brian's forearm where it crossed his chest, the hairs that were near-invisible in daylight ruffling under his hand. Sure enough, Brian's breathing slowed and deepened into sleep.

Nick thought about getting up. He knew by now that Brian was a deep sleeper. He could probably ease off the bed and go downstairs without waking him. But he didn't move as the faint light from the moon moved across the bedroom floor.

How had he ended up here? He could pick out the important moments, the crack-brained choices that had led to this place, and yet he couldn't tell which one he should have undone. What had Brian said a week ago? He was happy for the first time since he was a little kid. There was a lot Nick still didn't know about Brian, but he knew for sure Brian deserved a little happiness.

If this didn't last, if everything fell apart somehow, was that worse than not having it at all?

And if it didn't? If they never heard from Damon? For a moment, Nick let himself imagine a future, hanging out together, occasionally fucking, or maybe frequently. Taking care of each other. Having someone who cared that Nick was home late, cared enough to listen to him and rub his back. Someone he could help out, a place where he mattered as a man, not just as a cop. *Plus sex*. He could feel the smile on his face, and rubbed his lips against the pillow.

There was Brian's gift too, his eerie, unlikely, but undeniable talent. So far they'd brought one little girl home, and taken a child-killer off the streets. There had to be a way to keep doing that. Something that wouldn't put Brian in danger, or in a nut house, or a coma. Nick felt a chill, and rolled over. Brian was pliable and sleepy, willing to turn around and snuggle his back against Nick's chest. Nick wrapped his arm around Brian's shoulders, pulling him close.

Maybe this was wrong. Maybe they were doomed to disaster. But just maybe, before it all came crashing down, they could keep making a dent in the unfairness of the world, one missing person at a time.

Damon had kept Brian alive and safe through some unknown number of Marston's vicious manhunts. Well, anything Damon could do for his little brother under bad conditions, Nick could do even better under good ones, for the man who was… becoming his friend.

Nick didn't let himself unpack that thought. He resolutely closed his eyes to sleep. Reciting the lyrics of favorite songs was one way to keep his thoughts occupied, and he did that now, murmuring them in near-soundless movements of his lips against Brian's hair. Eventually, somewhere between *Can't see you laughing, if I turn and walk away…* and *Oh, Danny Boy…* he lost the thread and fell asleep.

He woke up more than once, rousing halfway from sleep to a fuzzy awareness of the unfamiliar room, the man against him, and the quiet night. Twice, he leaned over blearily and met the shining eyes of the dog, opening briefly to look back at him before closing again. Luger lay dozing lightly, not on his soft mat in the corner, but on guard between them and the bedroom door. Once, Brian must have felt Nick moving restlessly, because he pulled him into a hug with a wordless murmur, holding him close. Brian's arms were strong and warm around him. Nick should have felt trapped, or smothered. Instead, he felt safer and more at home than he had in a long, long time.

****

About the Author

I get asked about my name a lot. It's not something exotic, though. "Kaje" is pronounced just like "cage" – it's an old nickname.

I was born in Montreal but I've lived for 30 years in Minnesota, where the two seasons are Snow-removal and Road-repair, where the mosquito is the state bird, and where winter can be breathtakingly beautiful. Minnesota's a kind, quiet (if sometimes chilly) place and it's home.

I've been writing far longer than I care to admit (*whispers – forty years*), mostly for my own entertainment, usually M/M romance (with added mystery, fantasy, historical, SciFi...) I also have a few Young Adult stories (some released under the pen name Kira Harp).

My husband finally convinced me that after all the years of writing for fun, I really should submit something, somewhere. My first professionally published book, *Life Lessons*, came out from MLR Press in May 2011. I have a weakness for closeted cops with honest hearts, and teachers who speak their minds, and I had fun writing four novels and three freebie short stories in that series. I was delighted and encouraged by the reception Mac and Tony received.

I now have a good-sized backlist in ebooks and print, both free and professionally published, including Amazon bestseller *The Rebuilding Year* and Rainbow Award Best Mystery-Thriller *Tracefinder: Contact*. A complete list with links can be found on my website "Books" page at https://kajeharper.wordpress.com/books/.

I'm always pleased to have readers find me online at:
Website: https://kajeharper.wordpress.com/
Facebook: https://www.facebook.com/KajeHarper
Goodreads Author page: https://www.goodreads.com/author/show/4769304.Kaje_Harper

Other Books by Kaje Harper

Self-Published/Indie:

Tracefinder: Contact (Tracefinder #1)
Tracefinder: Changes (Tracefinder #2)

Second Act

The Family We're Born With (Finding Family #1) – free novella
The Family We Make (Finding Family #2)

Rejoice, Dammit

Unfair in Love and War
(in the charity anthology *Another Place in Time*)

Not Your Grandfather's Magic
(in the charity anthology *Wish Come True*)

Don't Plan to Stay

Audiobook:

Into Deep Waters
(Narrated by Kaleo Griffith)

The Rebuilding Year
(Narrated by Gomez Pugh, coming fall 2017)

Re-releases:

The Rebuilding Year (Rebuilding Year #1)
Life, Some Assembly Required (Rebuilding Year #2)
Building Forever (Rebuilding Year #2.5)

Sole Support

Gift of the Goddess

From MLR Press:

Life Lessons (Life Lessons #1)
Breaking Cover (Life Lessons #2)
Home Work (Life Lessons #3)
Learning Curve (Life Lessons #4)

Unacceptable Risk (Hidden Wolves #1)
Unexpected Demands (Hidden Wolves #2)
Unjustified Claims (Hidden Wolves #3)
Unsafe Exposure (Hidden Wolves #4)

Storming Love: Nelson & Caleb

Full Circle

Where the Heart Is

Ghosts and Flames

Possibilities

Tumbling Dreams (in the anthology *Going For Gold*)

Free series stories:

And To All a Good Night (Life Lessons #1.5)
Getting It Right (Life Lessons #1.8)
Compensations (Life Lessons #3.5)

Unsettled Interlude (Hidden Wolves #1.15)
Unwanted Appeal (Hidden Wolves #2.5)

Can't Hurt to Believe (Into Deep Waters #1.005)

Stand-alone free novels:

Into Deep Waters

Nor Iron Bars a Cage

Chasing Death Metal Dreams

Lies and Consequences

Laser Visions

Changes Coming Down
(in the free anthology *Hunting Under Covers*)

Stand-alone free short stories:

Like the Taste of Summer

Show Me Yours

Within Reach

A full list and links can be found at:
http://www.kajeharper.wordpress.com/books/

The author acknowledges the trademark status and trademark owners of the following wordmarks mentioned in this work of fiction:

Band-Aid: Johnson & Johnson Corp.
Blue Jays: Rogers Blue Jays Baseball Partnership
BMW: Bayerische Motoren Werke, AG
Bud Light: Anheuser-Busch, LLC
Coke: Coca-Cola Company
Corolla: Toyota Motor Co., Ltd.
Crime Stoppers: Crime Stoppers USA, Inc.
Crunch Berries: Quaker Oats Company
CSI: CBS Broadcasting, Inc.
Facebook: Facebook, Inc.
GI Joe: Hasbro, Inc.
GMC: General Motors Corporation
Goodwill: Goodwill Industries International, Inc.
Happy Meal: McDonald's Corporation
Hummer: General Motors Corporation
iPad: Apple, Inc.
Jeep: Chrysler Group, LLC
Karo syrup: ACH Food Companies, Inc.
Maglite: Mag Instrument, Inc.
Marshmallow Peeps: Just Born, Inc.
Netflix: Netflix, Inc.
Nike: Nike, Inc.
Porsche: Dr. Ing H.C.F. Porsche, AG
Pringles: Pringles, LLC
Rolls: Rolls-Royce Motor Cars Limited
Sci-Fi Channel: USA Networks
Superman: DC Comics Publications, Inc.
The Muppets: Muppets Studio, LLC
Tylenol: Johnson & Johnson Corp.
Twins: Minnesota Twins MTI Partnership, LLP
Velcro: Velcro Industries B.V.
Velveeta: Kraft Foods Group Brands, LLC
Vikings: Minnesota Vikings Football Club, Inc.
Walmart: Wal-Mart Stores, Inc.
Wendy's: Oldemark, LLC